Birth of a Legend

Also by Jane Shoup

Down in the Valley
Spirit of the Valley
Will of the Valley
Knightfall
The Restoration
The Key
A Choice of Captors
Ammey McKeaf, Book 1~ The Chronicles of Azulland
Heirs to the Throne, Book 2 ~ Chronicles of Azulland
Into Shadow, Book 3 ~ The Chronicles of Azulland
Charity Cases
Santa:2020 The Final Ride
The Time Tunnel of August Kaplan
An American Baroness, Book 1~ Sons of Barons
Nearly a Marquess, Book 2 ~ Sons of Barons
London's Adonis, Book 3 ~ Sons of Barons
Christmas at Manoria, Book 4 ~ Sons of Barons

This is a work of historical fiction. The expedition and subsequent massacre of Bishop James Hannington and his party occurred, minus the addition of the Shaffer family. The events of the 1908 Olympic Games described are factual, as are the descriptions of the British-Franko Exhibition. Edgar Rice Burroughs was indeed a pencil sharpener salesman before he wrote Tarzan of the Apes for The All-Story Magazine in 1912.
I hope he would approve and enjoy this story.

'How futile is man's poor, weak imagination by comparison with Nature's incredible genius.'
— Edgar Rice Burroughs

Chapter One

Far beneath a mackerel sky of whitish cloud and bright blue beyond, two young women walked back toward a house through softly blowing, knee-high grass with tennis rackets in hand.

Patience Caldwell, the fair-headed one, normally had an ivory complexion, although now it was blotchy and pink from the exertion of the game. "Your man needs to mow," she remarked.

"Where's the adventure in that?" Arianna Day teased, brushing back the strands of her copper-colored hair that had come loose. "Then you could actually see what we were walking through. Snakes and such."

Patience squealed at the thought and began hacking the grass in front of her with her racket.

Arianna laughed. "Yes, that should do it! You've put them on alert."

Patience broke into a mad dash for the cut part of the lawn. Once she reached it, she turned back with a scowl. "You are so mean! You know how I loathe the things. In fact, it's the only reason you said it. Admit it!"

Arianna jerked to a halt and looked down in horror.

"What's wrong?" Patience demanded suspiciously.

"S-something *has* me," Arianna cried. She went lopsided and then fell dramatically.

"So amusing," Patience retorted, folding her arms. "First you frighten me with talk of poisonous snakes, and then you mock me."

Arianna popped back up. "I never said poisonous."

"Oh, honestly, Ari! Patience turned and started toward the house. "I don't know why I bother."

Arianna bounded to her feet and ran to catch up, grabbing her friend's arm. "Because you're my dearest friend in all the world and you love me beyond all good sense."

"That's an excellent way to put it. The beyond all good sense part, I mean."

A rap at a window above made both girls look up to where Arianna's uncle gestured for her. Ari waved back.

"Did you speak to him about going home yet?" Patience asked in a confidential tone.

"This is my home, not bloody Charleston. And, no, I have not brought the subject back up because he thinks I should go. For a *visit*, he says." She huffed. "I have no desire to visit my father or brother ever again. Do you know we haven't exchanged a letter in nearly three years? This last letter of his was out of the blue ... after three years."

"It is a terribly long way to go for a visit," Patience commiserated.

"I can tell you this much with full assurance," Arianna said in a perfect British accent. After more than ten years in England, she could fool even the most discriminating ear. "He is not to be trusted. The nerve of the man saying it's time I return home. Home!"

They walked in the back door and Patience followed Ari into the parlor where she spied a covered pitcher of iced lemonade and two glasses. "Wonderful! I'm parched."

Arianna poured and handed her a glass and then poured one for herself and drank half of it before plopping down on the settee. "How much of a sin is it to wish your own father would go jump in a lake?"

"You should go see your uncle. I have to go, anyway. I have a fitting this afternoon for my new gown."

"I thought you had all your gowns for the season."

"This one will be for the Harvest Ball. Mamma finally consented to one with Empire styling," she added gleefully.

"That is exciting," Ari said comically.

"Scoff all you like. I *love* the new styles. And I love the Harvest Ball, because it's ours, you know? Northampton's own."

"I know. I love it too."

"Oh, Ari," Patience pouted. "I don't want you to go to America. You just got back from India."

Ari barked a laugh. "We got back six months ago."

"My guess is that your father's learned of all the traveling to wild places and—"

"He hasn't cared a whit in all these years, but suddenly what I do and where I go is disturbing to him?" She shook her head. "No. I am *not* going back to Charleston. I've made up my mind."

"What? Just now?"

"That's right. It's my life and I'm not going. I, too, want to enjoy the full season."

Patience cocked her head with a pained expression on her face. "You'll have to come up with a better excuse than that. It won't fool anyone who knows you."

"Well, my father doesn't know me."

"He's your father," she said gently. "I don't believe you've changed that much in all the time you've been here."

"Of course, I have. People change and I'm older."

Patience frowned worriedly. "That's true. Twenty-three. Do you never worry about being considered too old?"

"For what?" Ari asked with a fluttering of her eyes.

"You know what."

"Oh, you know I'll probably marry Marshall and have two or three sons, who look exactly like their father."

Patience giggled. "I think you should. He's handsome and rich and very proper."

"Yes, yes. I can see it now," Ari said drolly. "We'll attend all the right functions, and I'll wear the latest fashions. We'll have scores of servants. Will I even know all their names, do you think?"

The smile on Patience's face had vanished. "You don't have that sort of feeling for him, do you?"

Ari shrugged. "Your mother would say that was of no importance."

"Yes, she would. That's precisely what she says."

"I don't have that sort of feeling toward him," Ari admitted. "But I suppose I see the sense of it."

Patience frowned thoughtfully. "I think the concept of marrying with one's head rather than one's heart is more English than American, really. You would be miserable stuck with someone you don't love."

"Are you saying you wouldn't?"

"I am," Patience replied earnestly. "I expect it."

It was a terrible thought. "You do not!"

"I do," Patience replied apologetically with a shrug. "I already know my parents will have to approve if not select. Besides, I think I may not be capable of those sorts of feelings. You know, where your knees go weak and your heart pounds out of your chest at the sight of a man. I never feel that. I've never felt anything close to it."

"Neither have I."

Patience sipped her drink. "I think some of us might fall in love, but some of us will not. You will, or you should, and I think Nan will. At least, I hope she will. She has such a soft heart. But I won't," she continued with a resigned shrug. "Delia won't. It's a matter of," she considered, "I don't know. Passion? Is that the right word?"

"You have the best heart in the world! I cannot imagine why it wouldn't happen for you."

Patience smiled sweetly. "It won't. One just knows some things, and I know that. But it's fine. Really. It doesn't bother me."

"It bothers me!"

"If you are not going to America, you'll need the modiste to start on more gowns straight away. The season is upon us, for Goodness sake. Why, you'll need at least—" She broke off when Mrs. Herbin, the housekeeper, appeared at the door.

"Your uncle is asking for you, dear," Herbin said to Arianna.

Patience set her glass down and rose. "I must go. We could play again tomorrow if the rain holds off, but at my house. The entire lawn is mowed."

"No sense of adventure," Ari teased, also rising.

"Shall I invite Delia and Nan?" Patience asked as they walked to the door.

"Yes, do. That'll be fun."

Patience left, and Ari continued upstairs knowing it was time she broached the subject of Charleston. *About Charleston,* she'd begin. *You know, Uncle Sully, it's my life.*

This place, Somersly Manor, was her home. Built more than seventy years ago as a hunting lodge for a wealthy tycoon, it was comfortable with spacious rooms and large windows. It had a smoking room, a trophy room, and an enormous billiards room. In short, it was a bachelor's paradise, which made sense given that her uncle, famed photographer, Sullivan Vinson, was a bachelor. A bachelor, used to great freedom, who had taken in a niece and cared for her well and lovingly – something her father had not been capable of after the death of her mother.

She stopped in the open door of his study and watched her uncle biting on the stem of his pipe, completely absorbed in a letter. As always, the room smelled of tobacco and leather. She experienced a surge of emotion. She loved him. She didn't want to leave him. Of course, she had other reasons for not wanting to go back to Charleston, reasons she'd kept from him since her one and only other visit home three years ago. She cleared her throat as she stepped into the room.

He looked at her and smiled. "I received the most remarkable correspondence several days ago."

"From whom?" she asked as she sat across from him.

He set his pipe aside. "North."

Charles North was a renowned zoologist and a close friend. "What's he up to?"

"He is in Central Africa, part of an expedition to find some new breed of gorilla."

"A new breed of gorilla?"

He nodded. "Apparently, some German fellow discovered unusual gorilla skulls a few years ago."

"Unusual in what way?"

"I don't recall, but the British Museum got their hands on them and determined they were the skulls of an unknown breed. So, the Royal Society got involved and off a group went in search of the beasts with North leading the way."

"Have they had any luck?"

"Not in locating the new breed," he said haltingly.

She cocked her head, intrigued by the gleam in his eye. "Then what?" She took a seat.

"They arrived and set up a base camp. This is in middle of the jungle."

She nodded.

"They began observing. Gorillas move around all the time. They don't stay in one place. But North's group was able to observe several bands."

"But no new breed."

"No. Nothing but plain old mountain gorillas."

"What's the excitement then? You can hardly contain yourself."

"That's because they encountered something amazing. Beyond amazing, really. There is a *man* who occasionally lives among one of the bands. Interacts with them. North says he seems more animal than human, but he's definitely a man."

She blinked. "A man who lives amongst gorillas?"

He nodded, "A *white* man. Although, North said it was a band of great apes. I believe they are different from gorillas."

"Uncle Sully! North is pulling your leg."

Sullivan shook his head.

"But—"

Sullivan held up his hand. "Hear me out."

"But it's impossible!"

"No. It may be illogical and unlikely and incredible, but it's not impossible."

She considered him for a moment. "Go on."

"North saw the man with his very own eyes. He queried local tribes, and it turns out that they know of the man. They've known of him for years. They call him different things. Names that translate to wild, white man. Or lost one. *Matokeo ya utafutaji kwa*, apparently means *the untamed one*."

Ari's expression changed from wry amusement to one of confusion.

"There are many languages and even more dialects in Africa so I'm certain the translation is flawed, but the accounts were consistent. The man is believed to be in his late twenties, based on sightings throughout the years. It is believed he's lived in the jungle for most his life."

She shook her head. "But … how? How could he have survived? Moreover, why would a *white* man be there for almost the whole of his life?"

"That's what North asked me to dig into. Which I have done." He smiled. "I think I may have found the answer. I believe I have."

"I can hardly wait to hear!"

"Twenty-three years ago, a bishop by the name of James Hannington traveled to Africa with a group of men, fellow missionaries, porters, and a few surveyors. They hoped to find a new and better route into Uganda and possibly set up missions on the way."

She nodded.

"Things went fine at first. Until King Mwanga gave orders to stop them."

"Stop them," she repeated.

He nodded. "They were set upon, thrown into a filthy rat and vermin infested hut, and held for a week until they were executed one by one."

A cold shiver ran up her spine. "How terrible!"

He nodded soberly. "Yes. Incomprehensible, really. Wanting to be thorough, I dug up the list of men who'd been traveling with Hannington and discovered that two of the men's wives went along. One of them, Mary Fuller, wife of Joshua Fuller, became ill and stayed behind in Freetown. The other, a lady named Catherine Shaffer, went further. It's not known how much further, but presumably, all the way, eventually meeting her death with the others."

Goosebumps rippled on Ari's arms. It was so dreadful. "What else? What was your big find?"

"That the six-year-old son of Tom and Catherine Shaffer accompanied his parents to Africa."

She exhaled in a rush of breath. "They brought a child?"

"Yes. I only found it mentioned in one place, but yes."

"Oh, Uncle Sully. You are suggesting that child survived and lives today amongst *gorillas*? Or apes or whatever they are."

"Yes. The man is he right age, in about the right location. It fits with what the locals believe. Not only has he been sighted on numerous occasions, but the locals sometimes leave him gifts of food and clothing, and they have done for years. Some of them believe he has strange powers. That he can talk to animals. That he can fly."

Her eyes grew round. "You're going, aren't you?"

"Of course, I'm going! To be the first to photograph the poor creature if they manage to capture him? I simply must go."

"I want to go too!"

He looked regretful. "Arianna—"

"I'm not going back to Charleston, no matter what."

"I thought we decided a visit was for the best," he said gently.

"Everyone decided except for me. And it's *my* life."

"It is your life, dearest, but your father will be most displeased."

"I don't care. I am sorry if that makes me sound hard and unfeeling, but it's true."

"Don't be silly. There is nothing hard or unfeeling about you. I'm not sure your father will understand, however. His letter was rather insistent."

Arianna raised her chin and held his gaze stubbornly.

He shrugged slightly. "What will you tell him?"

"The truth. He knows that my life is here. He agreed to the arrangement a long time ago when it suited him, and now he only wants me back when he wants something from me."

Sully drew back. "What do you mean? What does he want from you?"

She felt her face grow warm. "I don't know. He probably wants me to marry someone."

"Ari," he objected. "What in the world makes you think such a thing? I thought we were talking about a brief visit."

"That's what we thought last time. Remember? I arrived and he was all charm until he managed to confiscate my ticket home."

He sighed. "Because he thought it best for you."

Arianna prickled with resentment because that was not what her father had thought at all. It was what had worked best for him once it was made known that Jason Barton wanted to marry her. Being connected to the wealthy, powerful Barton family was all that had been important to him. Not her. It had never been her.

"Is there anything you're not telling me that you ought?"

She hated lying to him, and she suspected it showed all over her face. "No," she replied anyway.

He pursed his lips.

"So, when do we leave for Africa?"

"It is a long, difficult journey to a hot and dangerous place."

She nodded. "I realize that. So was Bombay and Cairo and—"

He smirked. "Is this argument supposed to wear me down?"

"It's not an argument. It's fact. When have we ever cared about long, difficult journeys to hot, dangerous places? We're *adventurers*. Oh, please! I want to go."

"Arianna, there is a time for a young woman to give up wild adventures in exchange for something calmer and more … well, domestic."

She crossed her arms. "And yet you did not raise me to be a governess."

He tossed back his head in laughter. "I suppose I didn't. Alright then, we'll go as soon as I can make arrangements. It will be soon. A day or so."

She squealed and rushed around the desk to kiss his cheek. "Thank you!"

"Go write to your father."

"I will. I'll do it right now."

"And perhaps you should see that Derringer fellow? *Hmm*? Let him know?"

"Yes, of course, I'll tell him." She started from the room tingling with excitement but turned back at the door. "What was the boy's name?"

"Sebastian."

"Sebastian," she repeated softly. "Can you imagine the life he's had, if the story is true?"

"Not really, no. I'm fervently hoping Emerson will consent to go along. I've written and explained the situation."

She nodded. Not only was John Emerson one of the best anthropologists in the field, but he was also one of the kindest people she'd ever known.

Sully picked up his pipe again. "The question in my mind," he mused, "Is can a wild man be brought back into civilization successfully?"

"I wonder if he realizes he's a man, or does he think he is one of the apes?"

"Well, we are distant cousins, you know," Sully said as he struck a match.

Arianna grinned as she went to her room to see to the necessary correspondences. She wrote notes to Patience and to Marshall and sent them out with Mr. Murrow, their man, as Patience frequently put it. Mr. Murrow was well into his seventies and beyond all good use, but he was part of the family and would live 'in service' at Somersly for the rest of his days.

The letter to her father was a more challenging task. He was an awkward figure in her life and always had been. Early in her life, he'd pursued commerce diligently. When her mother, his second wife, died after a brief illness, he'd been at a loss as to what to do with her. Raymond, her elder brother, or more accurately, her half-brother, worked alongside him so, at almost seventeen years of age, he posed no complications. She, however, needed more attention than her father could provide. She also needed the guidance of a lady, he'd insisted.

When he declared that she would go live with his sister, she'd felt dread. Then, Sully had shown up like a godsend. When he offered guardianship, her father had leapt at the idea, especially when Sully established that he would share custody with his elder brother and sister- in-law, Lord and Lady Vinson of Muirhead Hall in Oxford. The arrangement not only provided her the influence of a lady but a family of nobility. Lord and Lady Vinson also had a home in London where Arianna would enjoy each season and eventually have her own coming out.

Ari rose and meandered to the window. To the east, the pond shimmered brilliantly. To the west were the gardens and a tennis court. Some of the grass was tall, but she even loved that. It waved in the breeze, changing colors. It was a sea of greens and yellows, and above that, the simple majesty of Queen Anne's lace seemed to float, nodding in approval. Arianna treasured the view. She treasured her home, her uncle, her friends, and her life.

She didn't actually dislike her father, but nor could she claim to love him. And after the last trip home, she certainly didn't trust him. She would have gladly made time for him here, but he didn't care enough about seeing her to embark on such a journey. It was ridiculous that it still bothered her as much as it did, but it couldn't be helped, or she would have already done it.

Maybe it was a wicked thing, but she did wish he would jump in a lake. Not to drown, of course, but just to get good and wet and muddy — and be occupied drying off instead of bothering her.

Chapter Two

M rs. Herbin sighed in disgust at the haphazard piles of clothing spread out upon the bed. They weren't even folded well, and after she'd ironed them. "Look at this mess," she scolded. "Why don't you let me do it?"

"Because you always overpack."

"I do not. Oh, perhaps on occasion I have, but I won't this time."

Ari donned a sad expression. "You always say that, but then you always do. Beautifully, I will admit. Far more beautifully than I am capable of. But the problem is I will have to spend just as much time unpacking all the unnecessary things and repacking the necessary ones as it would have taken to pack in the first place."

"It's not right, a lady doing her own packing."

"It's sensible," Ari cajoled.

Mrs. Herbin folded her arms stubbornly. "You are getting to the age, Arianna, where you should consider being less sensible and more … correct."

Ari struggled to contain the burst of laughter that wanted to escape. "Is that so?"

The housekeeper eyed the items Ari was bringing. "Where is your nightgown and robe?"

"I'm not bringing them." The horrified look on Mrs. Herbin's face was too much and Arianna gave into her merriment. "I'll sleep in that," she explained gesturing to a chemise. "It's light and doesn't take up much room. Where we're going is very warm and you must understand how far our trunks are going to be lugged."

"Oh, I know how far! Halfway around the world, where no young lady belongs."

"I will have a tent to myself—"

"A tent," Mrs. Herbin scoffed.

"No one will see me at night. It's not as if I'll be having cozy chats by the campfire wearing my nightclothes."

Mrs. Herbin clucked her tongue. "We can discuss this later. I came to tell you that Mr. Derringer is here."

Ari huffed. "Why didn't you say so?"

"I just did, didn't I?"

Ari started from the room.

"He's in the library," Mrs. Herbin said over her shoulder.

"After you," Ari said from the door.

Mrs. Herbin turned to her with a scowl.

"Come on," Ari coaxed. "I know you. You'll have three trunks neatly packed and ready to go by the time I get back, two of which I will not need."

Mrs. Herbin resentfully vacated the room. "It is better to have it and not need it then need it and not have it," she cautioned.

"Why does that have a familiar ring to it?" Ari mused. "Could it be I've heard it a hundred times before?"

"Apparently, it's not gotten through your head yet."

Ari planted a kiss on the housekeeper's soft cheek and walked on. She reached the staircase and sailed down the stairs, mentally bracing herself for seeing Marshall. He could not have gotten her note yet and he was not going to like that she was going to Africa, but it was her life. How many opportunities like this would come her way?

Marshall's back was to her as she entered the library, but he turned when he heard her footsteps.

"Hello," she greeted.

"Hello," he returned cheerfully.

She suddenly dreaded the impending conversation. He was handsome, even though his lips were a bit on the full side. As a spoiled only son, he had an almost regal air which frequently rubbed her the wrong way. Their courtship, if it could be called that, had been disturbingly informal from his perspective while entirely too formal from hers. It had also probably gone on long enough. Still, to sever the tie altogether—

"Are you well?" he asked.

"I am. And you?"

"Fit as a fiddle. I've been mulling something over. I think, perhaps, the same thing you were hoping to discuss with me."

The statement puzzled her. "Oh? What's that?"

"Going to Charleston together."

The words stymied her. Why would he have thought she would want him along? "I decided not to go," she said haltingly.

His expression darkened. "I thought it was definite."

"No. It was a … probable. A possible. My father requested it, but I really do not want to, nor do I see a reason to go."

He considered her. "What if there was a reason?"

She felt a curious panic mounting. "But there's not. Besides, something else has come up."

He looked aggravated. "What?"

It was ridiculous how uneasy she felt about saying it. "Africa."

"You *must* be joking," he exclaimed. "Really, Arianna, this is madness!"

"It's not madness at all. It is a unique situation and a once in a lifetime adventure."

"Aren't they all?"

"You don't understand. I mean, yes, they are, but this one is different."

"So, tell me!"

She crossed her arms, disturbed by his indignation and his proprietary stance. She didn't need his permission. She really didn't even need his understanding. Nevertheless, she would explain the situation calmly like the rational, intelligent person she was. "A man has been spotted in the jungle living amongst gorillas. Or rather apes."

He scoffed. "That is preposterous."

"I agree that it seems preposterous, but it is true. It's possible he was abandoned when he was only a small child and has somehow survived against all odds."

"Absurdity. It's sheer absurdity."

"Charles North is there and has seen him," she rejoined. "The expedition is backed by the Royal Society and The British Museum. It is not absurdity."

He shook his head, at a loss for what to say. "Even so, I don't see how *you* belong there."

"It's not that I belong there. It's that because of Uncle Sully, I have the opportunity. It will be the adventure of a lifetime!"

"Haven't I heard that before?" he asked irritably. "How long would you be gone?"

His phrasing did not go unnoticed. How long *would* you be gone instead of how long *will* you be gone? Because he thought she could be talked out of it. She uncrossed her arms and tried to relax her stance. "I don't know. Three months perhaps. There are so many variables."

"You'll miss the entire season," he complained. "Which you don't care about at all, do you?"

She hesitated. "Not particularly. No."

His eyes narrowed. "Do you ever want to settle down?"

Her throat tightened. "Of course. One day."

"Marry? Have children?"

She nearly crossed her arms again but stopped herself. "Yes. I do. Of course."

"I feel I've been very patient with you."

Her breath caught as a prickly anger took hold.

"But I am growing impatient," he continued. "Don't you want to know why I'd decided to go to Charleston with you?"

Again, his phrasing, his assumption, grated on her nerves but he was steering the conversation, determined to get his way. "I'm sorry you feel impatient," she said levelly. "Naturally, you should analyze precisely what that means and deal with it accordingly. As for myself, I made the decision not to go back to Charleston because I do not wish to. I made the decision to accompany my uncle to Africa, however preposterous it may seem to you, because I do wish to. It's that simple. I will not change my mind, nor will I plead for your understanding of the matter. If this is some sort of impasse, then so be it."

"I didn't say it was an impasse," he snapped. "But you have made your position quite clear. Have I?"

"You're impatient," Ari replied coolly. "You made that perfectly clear."

"I want to marry you, Arianna, but I will not wait forever."

The declaration stunned her. He'd never before stated he wanted to marry her, and he had certainly never proposed. She'd suspected it. She'd even joked about it with Patience, but to hear it spoken was unexpectedly affecting.

"I hope this trip to Africa gets your days of wild adventuring out of your system. If not," he paused and sighed. "Well, then, I'm afraid we have reached our impasse."

She struggled for something to say but could think of nothing.

"Would it make a difference if I said I wanted you to stay?"

She hesitated but then shook her head. "I'm sorry if it hurts your feelings, but I want to go. It feels important."

"I see. Well." He lifted her chin with his forefinger. "Then go get it out of your system or be ready to tell me goodbye once and for all." His gaze raked her face and then he leaned in and kissed her lightly. "Safe journey." Still miffed, he turned and left.

Ari bit on her bottom lip. Was she making a mistake? Just because she wasn't swooning over him didn't mean marrying him wasn't the right decision.

~~~

The following day, Ari's friends played croquet without her. Dark-haired Delia took careful aim and swung, knocking her ball through the wicket. "Where is the world traveler off to now?" she asked in a bored tone.

"Guess," Patience said with her eyes twinkling.

"Italy," Nan called with enthusiasm.

Patience grinned and shook her head.

Delia turned to face them, the handle of her mallet resting on her shoulder. "China. To etch her name upon the Great Wall," she said sardonically.

Patience shook her head again.

"Africa," Nan guessed.

Patience burst into a wide smile and nodded, whereas Nan and Delia both froze in shock.

"You're teasing," Delia accused.

16

"I'm not."

"Africa?" Nan squeaked. "Aren't there cannibals there?"

"She has lost her mind," Delia remarked. "And if she's not careful, she'll lose Marshall."

The smile on Patience's face dimmed.

"My turn," Nan said sweetly. She walked over and swung her mallet.

"Arianna will miss the season," Delia commented.

"Marshall knows, of course," Patience replied.

"He can't like it though," Delia mused.

Patience felt a twinge of concern at the satisfaction on Delia's face. Delia was beautiful. Why couldn't she just be happy? As girls, Ari had once suggested that the four of them have codenames. Delia's should be Beauty. Of course. Nan's Sweetness. "What about me?" Patience asked.

"Patience would be perfect for you if it weren't already your name. Maybe Faithfulness. Or Love."

"That is so sweet. And yours?"

Ari mulled for a moment. "Spirit?"

"Yes! But I do not think we should share the idea with Delia. She's quite aware of her beauty. Too aware, I think."

"Oh, no. You're wrong," Ari rejoined, affecting stupidity. "She's not aware of it at all. After all, she's always asking everyone how she looks. Obviously, the poor thing has no idea. She must not even own a mirror."

Now, as Delia took aim at her ball, Patience wondered why she did not settle on one of the many gentlemen who had set their caps for her. Was it that she had secret designs on Marshall? Was she in love with him? Or did she simply want him because he'd chosen Ari? Was she that competitive and petty? There was no question as to her beauty, and yet she was not more pleasing to the eye than Arianna. Ari was exceptionally pretty; she just never fixated on it and because she was so witty and amusing, they tended to forget it.

"I would have rather played tennis today," Nan commented.

"I don't know why," Delia replied lightly. "You're no better at tennis than you are at this."

Patience sighed aloud and rolled her eyes at Nan, who merely smiled back. She really was Sweetness.

~~~

Four thousand miles away, the wild man silently investigated the campsite of the strangers, having watched most of them go off to the places they slept. He curiously studied the objects they'd left behind. A cup filled with something. He picked it up and smelled it. He wrinkled his nose in distaste but tasted it anyway. He cringed and spat it out.

An eight-inch knife was driven into the ground near the campfire. He squatted, pulled it out and studied it. In the light of the dying campfire, he turned it in his hand, studying the blade. He ran his finger along the sharp edge, slicing it open. He sucked in a breath and stuck his finger in his mouth to stop the bleeding. With a flick of his wrist, he drove the knife back into the ground.

On a table, a platter with a few hunks of cooked meat remained. He sniffed at it and tasted it. It was strange, chewy, but not bad. On second thought, he spit it out. At the sound of snoring, he looked in the direction of tents. The strangers did not belong here, but they were fascinating. Some were light skinned, some dark. They communicated easily. He didn't comprehend their sounds, but they understood one another. Their bursts of loud laughter had startled him at first. It still baffled him. He sensed one of the men on guard duty returning, and so he faded back into shadow and made his way back into the jungle.

Chapter Three

Arianna looked up sharply from her packing, having been startled by Mrs. Herbin's sudden appearance, not to mention the lady's alarm. "They're waiting on you," the housekeeper cried.

Before Ari could ask who, she realized she was naked. She was standing in the middle of her room, packing her trunk completely naked. Blushing wildly, she reached for her robe.

"I told you that you'd need it," Mrs. Herbin scolded. "Now hurry."

"But I'm not dressed!"

"You must go to them at once."

"Who? Why am—" But Mrs. Herbin wasn't there any longer and Arianna was moving down the hall toward her uncle's study listening to vaguely familiar voices.

She was inside the office.

Her uncle stood behind his desk looking hurt and betrayed. She turned an accusing eye to the cause of his distress and gasped to see her father standing next to Jason Barton.

"She is my wife," Jason declared, pointing at her.

"But you're dead," she stammered, struggling to come to terms with the fact he was there and very much alive. "I thought you were dead!"

"Why do you think I told you to come home?" her father demanded.

Ari jerked awake with the words still ringing in her ears. She sat, breathing shakily. She threw back the covers and got up, anxious to be free of the nightmare. She bundled herself in a long wrap. Mrs. Herbin had wisely, if sneakily, packed several of them.

She felt claustrophobic in the ship's small cabin, so she crept out to the deck. It was early, before sunrise, and the deck of the *Maracruz*, the six-masted schooner transporting them to Africa, was empty. They'd had smooth sailing these last three and a half weeks. It would not be long until they reached their port destination near Cameroon.

She walked to the railing breathing the salty air deeply. She gripped the railing and stared out at the rolling whitecaps on the black ocean. Jason was dead. The fair-haired man had been her husband for all of five weeks before he'd contracted a deadly fever that had ravaged Charleston with a vengeance. Jason was dead and gone. That period of her life was dead and gone.

She remembered the burial vividly. The heat had been sweltering, and Jason's mother, hysterical with grief, had fainted. The other mourners had covertly glowered at her as if she were somehow to blame, which was ludicrous for so many reasons. Of course, those reasons were none of their business. She would never explain to any of them, or to anyone at all, what a miserable few months she'd endured since making the colossal mistake of marrying into the Barton family.

Apparently, Jason had seen her and fallen into such deep infatuation that he'd offered enough money to satisfy her father's debts on the day of their nuptials. Naturally, when her father came to her, pleading his case, she'd found the suggestion abhorrent. But like a fool, she'd eventually relented. It was a mistake she had grown to detest herself for.

Why had she cared about pleasing her father, a man who had never truly cared about her? He'd claimed that they would finally be a family, but then he'd gone right back to his life and promptly forgotten about her. And why not? He had his money. His debts had been satisfied, and she had never been important to him. Nor had Jason truly fallen in love with her.

She shuddered, thinking of the intimacy between them. What a repulsive thing performing one's wifely duty was. The memory of his fumbling hands and his hair in her face made her feel queasy. The act had been painful, and afterwards she'd felt bruised and tainted and desperately lonely. To think she would have to fulfill that same role as Marshall's wife—

20

Was her aversion to making love, although she resented the implication *love* could be made by such a distasteful act, part of the reason she was less than eager to marry Marshall? It was, she realized. It was not her only reservation, but it loomed large.

She felt such shame about the ill-fated marriage. She was grateful her uncle did not know of it. Disappointing him would have been crushing. Knowing that she had surrendered her judgment would have been bitterly disappointing to him. Unfortunately, the flip side of the coin was that not telling him felt like a lie when she never lied to him. Sometimes she sensed he knew the truth, but they had never spoken of it.

As the sky began to lighten, she made her way back into her cabin, hopeful that she could sleep again.

~~~

Five of the men in camp were playing poker as one of them, Reece, finished a story. "Shot right between the eyes, it was." He said tapping the space between his own eyes.

The others guffawed.

"My ass," Wellesley declared.

"What about it?" Reese said. "Besides that it's smelly and hairy."

Charles North had been cleaning his rifle, but he'd stopped to listen. "Hey, Reece. Anyone ever tell you that you get a certain look when you talk shite?"

Reece smirked. "Yeah? What look is that?"

"Shut up and deal," Wellesley said.

"Yeah," I'll deal," Reece said. "I'll deal you the bone hammer," he said brandishing his fist.

The others laughed.

Reece, who never took himself too seriously, grinned as he assumed a fighting stance. "What? Think I can't take you all?"

~~~

The wild man watched them as he did most every evening. His arms looked like theirs. His hands. His mostly hairless skin. They walked and moved differently than he did, though. He had tried to mimic it – standing upright, shoulders back. It was strange. His balance felt off.

One of his companions joined him, which irritated the man. He gestured for him to leave and then pushed him. His companion shoved back, knocking him over. The man grunted and then looked back to see if the others had noticed. They hadn't. The man made a gesture and sound to his companion. It was as quiet as he could make it while being a warning. *Go. This is mine. Go.*

His companion grunted unhappily but left.

~~~

"I'm turning in," North said as he started toward his tent.

The others barely noticed.

A sharpshooter named Bolton slammed down his winning hand and laughed while the others groaned. "What did I say?" he crowed.

~~~

The man startled at the outburst, but the words had struck an inner chord of remembrance. "Whaasay," he mouthed, very little sound escaping. He'd heard it before. He knew those sounds. Didn't he?

Enough.

He'd seen and felt enough. He slunk back in the jungle to rejoin his band where he belonged.

~~~

Clad in a blue, nearly off-the-shoulder gown, Delia sipped punch as she looked around.

"Henry Morehead is here, I see," her mother said under her breath. "And that Printess fellow."

"Jack," Delia said.

"I have made a few discreet inquiries about him."

Delia gave her a black look.

"It's time, you know. You have quite enough suitors. You just need to give one of them that special nudge. A man's ego is so fragile."

"Really, Mamma. You should save such basic advice for Wynonna."

"Your sister is hopeless in that regard. She does not have the benefit of your beauty, but nor does she have your ambition."

Delia was about to retort when her gaze fell upon Marshall standing across the way. As usual, he was totally in his element, occasionally being cutting and clever; she could tell by his expression and the reaction of the others. Why he had set his sights on Arianna, she would never understand.

"Nan looks as well as I've seen her," Mrs. Bradford commented.

Delia followed her mother's gaze. Nan was dancing with Thaddeus Mansfield. Dressed in a gown of pale coral, she did look attractive, although it was last year's gown. "I don't think she acquired a single new gown this season."

Mrs. Bradford sniffed. "A shame. I wonder if young Mr. Mansfield realizes the state of their finances. She cannot have much of a dowry."

"She has none at all, but he does know. I mentioned it last spring."

Her mother looked at her sharply.

"She's my friend, you know," Delia explained. "I couldn't bear to see her hurt if he cared about that sort of thing."

"They *all* care about that sort of thing, whatever they say."

Delia looked back at Mr. Mansfield. "It does not appear so."

"Mr. Derringer comes this way," Mrs. Bradford remarked discreetly.

Delia did not outwardly react, although her pulse began to race. "You need another glass of punch."

With an amused quirk of her lips, Mrs. Bradford and walked away.

"Miss Bradford," Marshall said a moment later.

Delia turned to face him. "Mr. Derringer."

"You look lovely this evening. That color is most becoming on you. In fact, Fred Casely was just remarking that very thing."

"How nice to hear," she replied stiffly. "I was just thinking what a shame it is that Arianna is not here. I wonder what she's doing right now."

"Hopefully getting this traveling nonsense out of her system."

He looked bitter about it, which provided a thrilling surge of optimism. "Do you really think she will? I have my doubts." His expression hardened enough that she felt a warning tingle up her spine.

"There will be a point in time when her adventures are a thing of the past, and it is not far away. Mark my words."

Delia smiled sweetly, affecting nonchalance. "I do hope so. In those places she goes, anything could happen."

"If I may be so bold, what are your thoughts on Casely?"

It took a moment to reel in her disappointment. "He is nice enough, I'm sure."

Marshall grimaced. "That sounds like the kiss of death. Whatever shall I tell him? He'll be positively laid out if I tell him that."

"Why don't you tell him the subject did not come up," she suggested tightly.

"Because I told him I would bring it up," he replied smugly.

"Then pass on what I said. I don't care."

"I fear I may have ruffled your feathers, Miss Bradford," he said, clearly enjoying himself at her expense. "I do apologize."

"You did no such thing, Mr. Derringer."

"If you will excuse me, I should rejoin my party."

She nodded once in response, seething, but damned if she'd show it.

Chapter Four

B y the time their guide led them into camp, Ari had begun to doubt if they would ever find it. North had provided coordinates, but the phrase *in the middle of nowhere* had taken on new meaning.

They had been on many challenging treks, but this had been the most difficult. It was hot, humid, and the terrain was rough going. The landscape was astonishingly beautiful and exotic, emerald green trees and waterfalls that shot from a thousand feet above, but her focus was on each step she took.

Besides the hired guide, two other natives lugged their belongings through dense brush, narrow trails, and steep mountain paths. Never once had they complained. At the outset of the journey, they'd offered to carry her in a rickshaw. She had firmly declined. She had ridden in a rickshaw in India, but so had Sully. It was common and expected. But here? Now? After pleading to come along? She was determined to keep up. Still, when they arrived at North's camp, she could have cried with relief.

"Here he is," North cried exuberantly. "Arianna," he greeted warmly, but with surprise when he saw her. "I didn't know you were coming."

"I learned what you were doing and ... well, I grabbed hold of Uncle Sully and would not let go. I just *had* to come along."

"You know I understand," North replied. He and Sully shook hands. "Sit and rest, all of you," he said.

Food and drinks were provided, and Sully and Arianna were introduced to the eleven men encamped. Six white men, including Charles, and five of African descent. Two were scientists, one was a cook, and the rest were trackers and hunters. They were a pleasant, boisterous lot.

"Miss Arianna," a brash Brit by the name of Blake said after a meal of simple stew. "You want a tour of camp? I can do it from right here."

"By all means, tour away."

"Tents," he said pointing to where they were pitched. "Dining hall," he said, gesturing around them. "Shitter," he said, pointing to the crudely constructed outhouse in the distance.

She looked and nodded at each thing, remaining utterly expressionless.

"Sorry," he said quickly. "I meant to say …uh, powder room."

She looked distressed. "Oh, dear. I forgot my powder."

The men broke into rowdy laughter.

"Perhaps I could borrow some?" she said to Blake, who pointed at her with a smirk and a nod.

"Have you found him yet?" Sully asked North.

North shook his head. "Haven't seen hide nor hair since that one time."

Ari leaned forward. "What was it like? How far away were you?"

"Three, maybe four furlongs," Charles North replied. "It was through my binoculars. I was settled in, hidden in the brush, watching the great apes. Then I saw him. For a second, I didn't know what I was looking at. He was crouched like some of the others." North shook his head. "Then he seemed to sense me. He stood up staring right at me."

Ariana was enraptured.

"He came toward me. I put down the binoculars and stood, watching, my heart thundering in my chest, but I didn't see him again. It's as though he disappeared. But the sight of him … it's etched in my mind. I'll never forget it."

"What did he look like?"

"He's a white man. He's not pale, of course, but he's Caucasian. Dark hair. Facial hair. More than that, I couldn't say. It happened quickly. And then I went in search of answers."

Sully nodded. "I have more. A possible explanation."

"What is it?"

The others were just as interested. After Sully told them about Hannington's ill-fated party and the possibility of who the boy was, they were all silent.

"Did you hear from Emerson?" North asked. "Is he coming?"

"I wrote to him and explained, but we left before I heard back. I'll be surprised if he doesn't show. The opportunity is too irresistible. Assuming the man can be found."

"I hope so. On both counts."

~~~

Arianna and Sully were each provided a tent with a canvas cot, chair, and a table. There was a chamber pot, and a bowl and jug. She was shown the path to a swiftly running creek. The accommodations would have horrified her friends, but it was a great improvement over the past eleven days without such luxury.

By now, her friends would all be in the city attending balls and functions most nights and sleeping until noon most mornings. No one could have paid them to be here, but never, ever would she have traded this for that. She intended to absorb everything she saw and heard and felt. There would not be another experience like this one.

The views were unlike anything Ari had seen, and worth every mile they'd come. The air felt different. The trees were different. The sounds of birds and chirping monkeys, trumpeting elephants, and things she could not identify, were constant. The atmosphere filled her senses. She had never imagined such wildly colorful birds as they saw. Majestic wildlife roamed in a place that seemed untouched by the passage of time. Lions, zebras, antelope, and rhinoceros.

Guns were kept at the ready, but rarely used. Daily treks ended by early evening because of a need for natural light, and because of the apes' habit of sleeping after their final meal.

Sully was having a wonderful time. Like North, this was his element, and it would show in his photographs. Sometimes, as she watched him across the campfire, laughing and smoking a cigar, she wondered how much she'd held him back over the years. How many more of these excursions might he have enjoyed except for her?

Many of the men had grand adventures to tell, and they were entertaining if not always believable. The nightly ritual was enjoyable until it veered toward the bawdy, at which time Arianna took her leave with humor and good grace. She bathed at the creek, wrote her impressions in a journal, and went to sleep.

"So why is a pretty and so very nice girl like you unmarried?" one of the African scouts asked her on their eighth night in camp.

"It's not for lack of gentlemen trying," Sully spoke up. "I can tell you that. As a matter of fact, she's due to give a certain answer to a gentleman when we return."

Her eyes widened in surprise since she hadn't been aware he knew.

"Derringer?" North asked Sully.

Sully gave her a questioning look, wondering if he'd said too much.

"Yes," Ari admitted.

Charles North pursed his lips. He was a distinctive looking man in his late forties. "Will he allow you to think for yourself?"

Arianna smiled. "As if that could be helped."

Charles shrugged. "He's not the sort to like it."

She drew breath to reply, but the sound of drums started from the closest village. She peered into the dark jungle. They'd heard drumming before, but this rhythm seemed different. As it progressed, the tempo and volume increased. "What does it mean?" she asked North.

"Danger, I think," he replied thoughtfully. "It's a warning of sorts. I wish Emerson were here. He'd know."

"Do they mind us being here?" she asked.

He shook his head. "No. They know we're here to study the wildlife, not conquer it. We kill no more than what we need to live. We made them aware of our presence and offered gifts."

Ari was glad to hear it.

~~~

The wild man they sought watched them from a safe vantage point. He watched them all, but especially her. He studied her body and her movements. The sight of her made his blood stir. The sound of her voice captivated him. Her mannerisms. Her shape. She was here for him. To be his mate. She would be his.

Twice, he had crept into her sleeping place and watched her in the darkness. He'd leaned close enough to feel her warm breath on his cheek. Her scent caused an aching hunger he'd never known before.

When the drums from the village began, he listened. The cadence meant a stranger was coming. He turned his attention back to the group as she looked toward him. Did she realize he was there? Was she silently beckoning to him knowing he would protect her?

~~~

Ari stifled a yawn and rose. "Goodnight, gentlemen."

"Aww," they objected in such unison that there was a bout of laughter.

She smiled but kept walking.

"She's a good girl, is she not?" the African scout asked Sullivan.

Sully blew out a ring of smoke and then nodded. "She's the apple of my eye."

~~~

The man watched her as she stood and said something. Those around the campfire made a sound and then laughed. He felt a wrenching separateness. She started toward the place where she slept, and he watched knowing that she would stop his loneliness.

Chapter Five

A ri moaned in her sleep. She was experiencing yet another erotic dream in which the untamed man hovered over her, not touching, but so close she could feel the heat from his body. He sniffed her, wanting her so badly he almost couldn't restrain himself. It felt so real, so physical, that her body responded.

This is where the dreams had always ended before, but this time she felt the cover being pulled away. Drowsy desire turned into confusion, and then she knew utter panic as she was grabbed. God in heaven! It was really happening!

She was tossed over his shoulder. She cried out as he went through the flap, but it sounded curiously small in the vast space. She drew breath and screamed, and he broke into a flat run.

She kicked and pounded on his back. How could he possibly see where he was going? It was pitch dark. She screamed again and tried wriggling free. Panicked, she twisted and rose up only to hit the side of her head against a stout limb, knocking her back down again with a bolt of pain.

A rifle shot rang out, but the man didn't falter. She couldn't breathe, couldn't get free of him, and his hand was on her *bare buttocks* because she'd worn her chemise to sleep in. Heavenly God! What was she doing here? She'd been asked to stay home, but what had she done but exactly what she wanted to do? Foolish, headstrong girl that she was!

Not only that, but all those nights, all those sensual dreams hadn't been dreams. He'd actually been in her tent, and she hadn't told a soul. She felt a trickle of warm blood down her forehead. "Stop, please," she cried.

The man began walking, but she screamed again, and he ran.

"Help me! Help!" She tried to lift up again, but it did no good. He wasn't stopping. He wasn't even slowing. She whimpered.

When he finally stopped, she tensed knowing he would finally set her down, but instead he readjusted her on his shoulder and began climbing a tree. She went rigid with fear as they went higher and higher. The moonlight made brief, fickle appearances, which added to the nightmarishness. If he slipped and fell, they would both die here and now.

She was set down on a crude platform. Her knees buckled, and she crouched and clutched at the structure beneath her, tree limbs strung together with vines and softened with foliage. She was too frightened to do anything but stare at the man's bare legs. He was unclothed except for a loincloth. His body was lean but well-muscled.

He squatted before her. It was the first time she'd seen his face, not that she could tell much in the patchy moonlight. As North said, he had long dark hair and a good deal of facial hair. He frowned at the blood on her forehead, wiping it away and gingerly feeling her head to determine how hard she'd cracked it.

"Please—" she uttered in a shaky voice.

He squinted and studied her.

She shook her head. "You can't simply—" she stammered.

He took hold of her shoulders and forced her to sit and then to lay back. Panicked, she turned onto her side facing away from him, and curled up in a fetal position. He settled behind her and wrapped a powerful arm around her. His arm rested on her waist while his hand clutched her wrists. Deeply shaken, she listened to his breathing and realized he was barely winded. Her heart was pounding, and her entire body shook. "C-can you understand me?" she asked breathlessly.

He grunted and gave her a squeeze.

"That hurts!"

He gave a louder grunt and tighter squeeze. Because he didn't want her to speak.

Fine.

She wouldn't speak. They'd stopped and he wasn't forcing himself on her. He probably didn't even know what he wanted with her. The others were coming for her, so she would lay still, listen for their approach, and then yell with all her might.

How far behind were they? Would she see their torchlights first or hear their calls? She was so tense; she couldn't breathe properly. The weight of his arm wasn't helping. She tried to edge away from him, but he wouldn't allow it. She would never be able to sleep. Never.

And then she awoke with a start. It was early morning.

Oh, no.

What if she'd missed the rescue party? What if she'd slept through it? No, she wouldn't have. Couldn't have. She looked out at the lush canopy of trees. The rising sun filtered through with blinding flashes of gold.

She didn't feel or sense the man behind her, so she slowly rolled onto her back and confirmed he was gone. She sat up, freshly mortified that she was all but naked. She would be rescued like this. She put a hand to the sore spot on her head where she'd hit her head and tenderly felt the raised bump, but then she lowered it again, having noticed a great ape watching her from another tree.

She gulped for air. She got to her hands and knees and crept toward the side of the platform. Not only did the height she found herself at make her dizzy, but there were more great apes on the ground. They were massive beasts. Her stomach clutched in terror and goosebumps rose all over her skin.

Her eye caught on movement below, and she saw the man returning. He looked up and their gazes linked. She was stunned by his physical perfection as he walked through the apes, unfazed by them. He scaled the tree effortlessly with bananas over his shoulder and a mango tucked under his chin. She scooted back, wishing she could cover herself. The best she could do was to cross her hands over her chest and sit with her legs curled beside her.

He made it to the platform. He squatted and placed the fruit before her. His eyes were fringed by long dark lashes, and they were blue. When she didn't make a move, he gestured she was to eat, and then split the mango open and handed the part without the seed to her.

She took it. "Thank you."

He frowned with concentration as he watched her.

Was communication possible? Could she find a way to reason with him? She began to eat the sweet, juicy mango, but his staring was disconcerting. She focused her attention on the apes. They were stirring and scratching. It would be nothing for the beasts to kill her, to kill them both. They didn't because he was one of them somehow. She hadn't doubted Charles North's word, and yet it was so astonishing. She looked back at the man and found him still studying her. Not watching or even staring – but *studying*. "I'm Arianna," she stated clearly.

He gave no response.

She patted her chest. "Ari." His gaze dropped to her chest which was not what she'd intended. She gestured to him. "Sebastian?" Their gaze met again, and his eyes narrowed. "I think that's your name. Sebastian."

He looked aggravated. He gestured that she should eat. Then he looked below to the apes as they began leaving, although they seemed in no hurry.

~~~

It was time for him to leave the band. In many ways, they'd been distancing themselves from one another since the tribe of men had come. It was time, but his heart felt wrenched as his companions moved on. They often left first, and he followed, but he would not this time. He knew it and they knew it. He saw the sorrow in the eyes of the younger ones and in the old female who'd cared for him as a child. He lifted his chin and looked to the tops of the trees to quell the ache in his chest.

His new mate watched him warily. She made sounds, but he had no idea of her meaning. Her eyes were beseeching, her posture one of self-protection, and so he gestured she was now his, and he would protect her. Provide for her. She said something more slowly and he watched her mouth. It caused a stirring in his loins. She made sounds again and used gestures. This time, he got the gist and did not like it. She was indicating he should take her back.

He stood, pointed to the ground below and gestured for her to come.

Her eyes widened with fear, and she shook her head. "I can't," she uttered.

He felt a chill because he'd understood. He turned his back to her and pointed at it, then watched as she stood. Shakily.

She reached out one hand, touching his back, and then crept forward, pressing herself to him, clutching tightly. He bent, reached behind to cup her buttocks to hoist her up, and then he wrapped her legs around his middle. He felt her body quaking with fear.

~~~

"Oh, do we have to?" she asked breathily, burning with shame that her chemise had risen up. Her private parts were *touching* him. But the humiliation was merely a momentary distraction because the view as he moved to the edge of the platform was so terrifying. He propelled them over the platform and down the side of the tree, and a muted squeal of terror escaped her before she squeezed her eyes shut. She felt the movement of his body and knew when he'd reached the ground.

She opened her eyes, and then managed to release her death grip on him. Her legs felt weak as her feet touched earth, but he gave her little time to recover before he grabbed hold of her hand and led her onward. Her mind raced. If the information that Sully had uncovered was true, Sebastian had been six when he'd been abandoned to the wild. That would mean he had language skills and comprehension buried in his mind. If only she could rekindle the memory.

He finally stopped beside a creek and pointed to the ground. "I have to," she began and then gestured to a cluster of trees. She should not have to say it.

He gave a simultaneous grunt and jerk of his hand.

She started off tentatively, hoping he'd understood. She looked behind and saw he was watching her but not following. She found a secluded spot, did what she needed to do, and stood again, feeling a fresh wave of humiliation over her lack of dress. What if she stood here and started screaming at the top of her lungs? Would the others hear her? Would it lead them to her faster? Obviously, he would get to her first, even if she ran as fast as she could. How angry would he be? He had not hurt her; in fact, he seemed protective, so screaming wasn't worth the risk. Either he would retaliate, or he'd retreat further into the jungle, or she'd run into something even more dangerous than him.

What she needed to do was to delay, to give the others a chance to find them. She took as much time as she dared before returning to him. He was watching her carefully. Had he expected her to run? She tensed as he came closer. He tugged at her chemise and made a gesture for her to remove it. She huffed and took a step back shaking her head and blushing hotly. "Are you mad? No!"

Frowning with determination, he gestured again.

She stiffened with fear and mortification. "I will not. No!"

Out of patience, he pulled it off despite her best efforts to keep it on. She hadn't been able to stop him nor was she able to grab it back from him. She crossed her arms in front of herself and squatted, trembling with panic and frustration. He squatted in front of her, close enough that their knees touched, and studied her with a curious frown.

"Don't do this," she pleaded. "Sebastian." She shook her head. "No!"

His gaze was searching. Then he pointed to the ground.

"No, I will not! I wish to talk. You must remember words."

"No," he said crossly.

Her breath caught from the shock of hearing him speak. "And the opposite of no is yes," she stammered, speaking rapidly. "Remember?"

He grabbed her so suddenly she lost her balance. A moment later, she was on her back and he was on top of her. He held her hands to the sides of her head and leaned close, sniffing her skin and studying her breasts with fascination.

She squirmed furiously. "Get off me!" He licked one of her hardened nipples, and tremors pulsed through her body. "I will scream," she warned, but she merely gasped as he sucked the nipple deeply into his mouth. She drew breath to scream but didn't.

Because it wouldn't matter. No rescuers were near, or she would have heard them. "You … you can't—"

Except he was. He was sucking and then studying, fascinated and utterly unselfconscious. His male hardness pressed against her. He let go of her hands and mounded her breasts together. Immediately, her hands flew to his shoulders, resisting him, pushing and then slapping. Undeterred, he moved down her body, lips close to her fevered surface.

"No," she cried. She grabbed at his arms and pulled, but he shrugged her off. He grazed the skin of her stomach with his lips and licked a protruding rib bone. She tried to twist and to pull free to no avail. "I said no! Stop!"

He lowered himself even more and forced her legs apart. Panicked, she alternately slapped and hit, crying out with each blow. She grabbed a handful of his hair and yanked. This irritated him enough that he shifted around and pinned her hands down with his calves. She could only gasp with shock at the sight of his bare backside and fully engorged manhood mere inches from her face. For a moment, she was too stunned to move or utter a sound. Good God! *That* was what it looked like?

Powerful arms held her legs apart while an eager finger touched tentatively between her legs. Mortified, she drew breath to scream, but she didn't. He blew gently on her enflamed vagina and then stroked it. She gasped as a finger moved inside her. Her whole body burned and thrashed as he stroked the length of her valley, and then dipped his fingers inside her again. Never in her life had she felt or even imagined anything like it. *The sensations.* "Please," she whispered.

Her stomach muscles were tight, and her skin was hot. When he lowered his mouth to her and tasted, she cried out. Her jaw jutted and she panted as he explored with his tongue and finger. This was wrong. This was so very, very wrong. It was horribly sinful. A wave was building in her unlike anything she'd ever felt. It was frightening, bigger than she was. Her breath came in ragged gulps as the wave broke free, and she cried out, her body jerking spasmodically. For a moment she thought she might be ill; the physicality was so overwhelming.

He climbed off and stretched out beside her, watching her closely. She squeezed her eyes shut and rolled onto her side, away from him, burning with shame, but when he fondled her buttock, she instantly rolled onto her back and came up on an elbow with great alarm. "You can't just take something because you want it! You can't just … *have* me."

Frowning quizzically, he reached out and stroked her face with the backs of his fingers. It was so tender, so surprisingly, intoxicatingly tender that tears sprang to her eyes. *What in the world?* He didn't want to hurt her—he simply wanted her. His beautiful, blue-eyed gaze was searching, but there was vulnerability there too. She could see it, sense it. Despite his physical strength, there was such need in him. He didn't understand how wrong this was. He'd been surrounded by animals for more than twenty years.

He made a sound as he touched her chest before making a fist and hitting his breast.

She blinked.

He repeated it. He made the sound as he touched her chest, and then hitting his own breast.

She swallowed. He was declaring that she belonged to him. It made her feel all sorts of strange. It was so primal.

He maneuvered her onto her side, facing away from him. She felt his erection press against her. She lacked the strength to stop him. That's the only reason she wasn't fighting, she reasoned. It's not as if she *wanted* him. Her fingertips dug at the ground as he slowly pushed inside her. She stared at the fluttering leaves on the trees. Was this the lost Garden of Eden? A low guttural sound escaped her as he moved. With an unselfconscious grunt, he shoved his full length inside her, and she cried out.

This was nothing like her experience with Jason. Nothing. She didn't know what this was. He stroked her arm, and then began to move again. His thrusts were shallow at first but then grew deeper and more forceful. When she realized she was moving with him, she felt an instant of piercing shame, but she blocked it out. She couldn't stop him and so she rocked into him in search of something she could not have named. An implosion seemed to come from the centermost part of her. She cried out and felt her muscles clamp around his shaft. He cried out. Moments later, he collapsed beside her.

Thank God she was facing away from him. How would she ever look at him again? How would she look at anyone? As her breathing slowed, she knew she would never feel normal again. If anyone learned what happened, she'd be ruined. She would be utterly ruined.

No! When she was rescued, which she surely would be, she would deny that anything bad had happened. She would swear that he had not touched her. What he really had done, and how she had felt during it, would remain a secret. It wasn't as if he could claim differently.

He stroked her back, which was slick with sweat. He ran a hand over the curves. He pushed her hair away from the back of her neck and blew on it to cool her. When he got up and walked off, she felt too drained to move. She was sore but not hurt. Not really.

He was back. He knelt and offered her a wide leaf, cupped and filled with water. She sat and drank. When he went back to the creek, she watched the way he walked and moved. The muscles in her legs were jumping, but all her other muscles felt limp. She felt *changed.* It was bewildering how changed she felt.

This time, when Sebastian returned with the filled leaf in hand, he bent to tend to the tender flesh between her legs, making her gasp. She grabbed his arm. He looked at her curiously. "No," she pleaded. "Please, sit." She patted the ground. "Please."

He studied her mouth and then looked into her eyes. He hesitated and then sat.

She twisted around and reached for her chemise, which was turned inside out. She righted it and put it back on. He seemed ready to listen to her, but, *Oh, Lord God.* How to begin? She needed a moment and so she got up and walked to the creek to wash. She washed her hands and face and the back of her neck. She glanced back at him. Naturally, he was watching her. She lifted her chemise as she waded in.

She took her time returning to him. Her skin was still damp, the chemise clinging as she knelt a few feet away from him.

"Man," she said, gesturing to him. "Woman," she said, gesturing to herself. "Yes," she said, nodding her head and smiling slightly. "No," she said, shaking her head and frowning.

"No," he repeated softly.

She tingled with excitement. "Arianna," she said, gesturing to herself. "Ari," she said slower. "Sebastian," she said, gesturing to him.

He shook his head. "No."

She gestured to herself again. "Ari."

"Ari," he repeated with great concentration.

She huffed a laugh and tears sprang to her eyes. She nodded. "That's right. You remember, don't you? You remember words?"

He looked away suddenly agitated. He rose, took hold of her hands, and pulled her up.

She yanked away. "You must try to remember." He took hold of her hand again and started to lead her away, but she resisted. He turned back, curious. "We have to be able to communicate."

He frowned stubbornly and started them moving again.

"I won't stop talking, you know. I'll just keep on and on. You are Sebastian. Remember? You were six when you came here with your parents."

Again, he turned back, but this time his frown was different and directed several yards away. She looked too, but didn't see anything, and yet he was so tense that she inched closer to him, half expecting an animal to suddenly charge. He positioned himself in front of her, and then something was flying at them. Several things, like large insects. One hit him, and he gasped and jerked back.

Darts.

Natives burst from the jungle armed with blow-darts. Ari caught a glimpse of a familiar white face and realized they were there for her. She drew breath to cry out for them to stop, not to hurt him, but she was hit in the shoulder and stumbled backwards, stunned by the pain. She fell and watched helplessly as Sebastian was repeatedly hit. "Stop," she whispered. She tried to hold up a hand, but it was so heavy. She was so heavy. She collapsed and stared up at the sky knowing that her rescuers had killed her. They'd killed them both.

Chapter Six

A rianna forced her eyes open, but her vision wavered so greatly that she couldn't grasp where she was. *Ah!* She was staring at the canvas wall of her tent. The flap of the tent was open, and she heard the murmuring of deep voices from beyond, although she couldn't make out anything being said.

As events came back to her, she experienced a flood of dread and remorse. The men that attacked them had been there to rescue her. They hadn't understood that Sebastian meant no harm. A rush of embarrassment and shame came next, remembering her state of undress. She struggled to sit, but quickly lay back down again, nauseous, and lightheaded.

"Ari," Sully exclaimed as he rushed in. He sat on the chair beside her, hovering close. He felt her head and reached for her wrist to take her pulse.

"What happened to him?" she asked hoarsely.

"He's alive. Unconscious but alive. Did he hurt you, my love?"

She shook her head slowly. "No."

He heaved a sigh and pressed a kiss to her forehead. "Sleep. You'll feel better in a day or so, and we'll leave then."

"No, please, I don't—" She needed to say more, to express herself, but the sick fatigue was too much.

~~~

Across camp, John Emerson hovered over Sebastian's prone body trying to get a pulse. It was faint. "What was the toxin in those darts? Do we know?"

"As best I can make out, it was acokanthera and oleander. It wasn't supposed to be lethal."

"Well, I'm sorry to say it may have been. Acokanthera is a cardiac glycoside."

North gave him an impatient look. "And for those of us less informed than yourself?"

"It affects the muscles of the heart."

"Killing him was not our intention, but we had to get Arianna back, didn't we?"

"Yes, of course," Emerson relented. "How is she?"

"Still unconscious."

"No," Sullivan said, as he entered the tent. "She woke briefly."

"That's a relief," North said. "Perhaps he'll wake, too."

"He took more blows than she did," Emerson stated. "And his pulse is weaker than hers was."

"What did she say?" North asked Sully.

"That he didn't harm her," Sully said.

"Thank God," North exclaimed. "Although, I'm not terribly surprised. He sensed us before we closed in, and he stepped in front of her. He tried to shield her."

Sullivan sat heavily in one of the chairs, bone weary. "I should never have brought her."

"I know that girl," North said. "She'll be fine. And have a grand story to tell."

"I doubt you could have kept her home anyway," Emerson added.

"We must convey to the others the necessity of confidentiality," Sully said. "Word of her being taken cannot get out."

"Confidentiality is part of their contracts," North assured him. "I'll reaffirm it though. Knowing these men, it won't be a problem. It certainly won't be initially because they still have pay due them. After that, can I see them blabbing after a night in the pub?"

Sully sighed. "I'll see her back home and settled. If she marries Derringer—"

"Yes," North said. "It'll be done."

Sully looked over at the man they had come so far to see. "It is a remarkable thing," he said. "Seeing him. He's not what I expected somehow."

"About that," Emerson said as he sat in the other chair. "Assuming he wakes, naturally we will try to convey what's happened. But he should be allowed to choose what will be. He should be allowed the choice of returning to England or to the jungle and the life he's known these many years."

North drew back. "Allow him to go back? To very possibly be lost forever?"

"Once he understands the choices, yes."

"I agree," Sullivan spoke up. "The man has been given no real choices in his life. He should be given this one."

"What if he doesn't understand?" North challenged. "Do we not do him a terrible disservice to let him return to the wild?"

"It's wild to us," Emerson said. "But it's what he knows."

North frowned. "You should know that the primary patron of this expedition, Lord Bluford, has pledged full financial support for him. Sebastian will be taken care of. Offered a home."

Emerson considered. "Offered a home where?"

"Assuming he can be made civilized enough, he'll be the permanent guest of Lord Bluford. I believe he spends half the year in London and half somewhere in Sussex. Iverson House?"

"I've met the man," Sully said. "He's sharp and well-intentioned, although getting up in years now."

North nodded. "Nearly seventy but spry enough and sharp as a tack."

"It's a lot to comprehend, isn't it?" Sullivan mused as he peered down at the unconscious man.

"My point precisely," North agreed. "You say he's to be given a choice, but how can he be when he doesn't even remember what civilization is?"

"I see your point, of course," Emerson replied. "But I stand by my opinion. I'll do my best to get through to him, but the choice should be his." He paused. "If he chooses to return with us, it will take time before we can leave here. He'll need to be prepared."

"True."

"We are all in agreement about no publicity for the time being, correct?" Emerson asked.

"Absolutely," North replied. "Long term, it'll be up to the Royal Society and the Museum, but mum's the word for now."

Sully looked to Emerson. "Any thoughts on how you might reach him?"

"Not yet. I just hope he survives."

"I would like to stay long enough to see him recovered and to take photographs," Sully said as he stood. "But then we'll go." Sebastian was so still he did not even appear to be breathing. "When all is said and done, you have to wonder, was it a good thing we came or not?"

"That is the question," Emerson agreed.

Chapter Seven

S ebastian was dazed and horribly weak. Where was he? It took great effort to sit. He'd seen this tent, or one like it. He was in the camp of the men.

Ari. Where was Ari?

He got to his feet, but everything veered. When he recovered his equilibrium, he picked up a stout club left by the door and stumbled outside.

Men yelled, jumped to their feet, and reached for their guns. He sought a path of escape. Two of them started toward him, and he crouched, ready to spring. One of the men yelled something and waved the others back. Placating. He clutched the club tighter.

~~~

Ari hurried from her tent, having heard the commotion, and ran toward the confrontation. The men of camp had guns and knives drawn and looked poised for violence. "No, please," she cried, sticking her hand in the air as she came forward.

It had taken two days for Sebastian to come around. It had taken her that same amount of time to feel normal again. At least, from the effects at the toxin. She rounded the tent they'd had him in and stopped abruptly as she came face to face with Sebastian who was holding a club. For a split second, he looked stunned to see her, but then he moved like a shot, grabbing hold of her and jerking her to him. Tension escalated, and the others closed in. "It's fine," she called to them. "He won't hurt me!"

She looked into Sebastian's eyes, silently pleading for him to be reasonable. "You're safe," she assured him. "These are my friends. They will not hurt you." He was pallid and sweaty, and she felt him shaking. Effects of the toxin.

Emerson was suddenly there. "Oh, dear," he said.

"It's fine," Arianna said soothingly. "Everything is fine. Sebastian, this is John Emerson. He came a long way to meet you. To help you. I have known him for many years. He's a good man and a friend."

Sebastian moaned and swayed. He dropped the club.

Ari wrapped her arms around him. "Come," she said, easing him back into the tent. He allowed it, or he was too ill to stop it. Once he'd sat on the cot, she knelt beside him. "Lay down," she urged.

He did, and she placed her hand atop his chest. He covered it with both of his hands before his eyes rolled back in his head, and he slipped back into unconsciousness. Emerson was there, pulling a chair up.

Ari looked at him beseechingly. "We cannot let them hurt him."

"We won't. I'll stay here myself from now on."

"They don't understand," she said brokenly. "He means no harm."

"They meant no harm either. He is a fearsome creature."

"He is a *man,*" she retorted. "Not a creature."

"I know he is."

She flushed, feeling badly that she'd snapped at him.

"But he's a man who's lived in the wild for more than two decades," he said. "Naturally, the others are wary. As they should be."

Sully burst into the tent. "Are you alright?" he asked Ari.

"I'm fine," she assured him.

"I see he wasted no time in latching onto you again," he declared angrily.

"He woke for a few minutes," she replied steadily. "For a terrifying few minutes when he didn't understand where he was or what was happening."

Sully took off his hat and shook his head. "I was hoping to get a photograph of him once he'd recovered, but I'm afraid we cannot wait. Not given his obsession with you."

She drew a sharp breath to speak, but he held up his hand to stop her.

"I won't risk him getting his hands on you again. We leave in the morning."

He won't take me again," she pleaded. "Not with all these men standing guard."

"Did he not just grab you? In front of all of them?"

"To *protect* me, as he tried to do in the jungle before we were shot. As you can see, I am right here. No harm done."

"*This* time. No! I cannot risk it, Arianna. I will not! We leave in the morning and that is final."

"I saw him, Sullivan," Emerson said cautiously. "He won't hurt her."

"Perhaps in his mind he wants only to protect and care for her," Sully returned. "But he took her away once and, given half a chance, he'd do it again. I'm standing firm on this." He looked at Arianna. "Be ready in the morning."

She nodded in acceptance. She owed him that.

"In the meantime, I will not have you alone with him," Sully added. "Not for a single minute."

"I'll be right here," Emerson said. "You have my word."

Sully left, punching his hat.

Ari looked back at Sebastian with tears in her eyes. His hands still covered hers, and under it she could feel his heart beating. "I've spoiled everything," she said flatly.

Emerson shook his head. "I doubt we would have ever seen him in the flesh if not for you."

She felt the tug of warring emotions. "I've never seen Uncle Sully so angry."

"Not angry so much as worried. Men are not reasonable when it comes to their loved ones, nor should anyone expect us to be."

A tear rolled down her face and she wiped it away and then looked at Emerson. "Will you let me know how he fares?"

"I will," he promised.

Arianna brushed Sebastian's hair back with her free hand. "He's handsome, isn't he? Under all that hair."

"He has very fine features. I'm more concerned about the state of his mind, of course. My biggest fear is that I won't be able to get through to him in time. He's sure to be frightened, and if he doesn't understand everything that's happened and what's being offered, he may run, and we'll never get this opportunity again. If we try to hold him, restrain him, he'll panic. He'll either be hurt or hurt someone else, which won't make communication any easier."

"I know you are the right person for this. I wish I could stay and help," she said wistfully.

"I know you do but, in Sullivan's place, I'd make the same decision."

"I've ruined this experience for him. If not for me, he'd stay."

"If not for you, we would not have seen him."

If that was true, and if Sebastian died, it was because of her. How would she live with that?

"Now," John said, "since we may not get another chance to talk before you leave, what about this Derringer fellow?"

"I don't believe he'd make it a day in the jungle," Ari said lightly, preferring to avoid the topic.

"I don't imagine most of us would." He paused. "Is Derringer the one for you, do you think?"

There was such concern in Emerson's face. "He'd like to be." She sighed tiredly. "How do you ever know if it's the right decision? How did you know?"

He leaned back in his chair with a wry smile. "Mercy me. It was so long ago now."

She extracted her hand from Sebastian's, and rose to her feet, saying, "I would wager that you recall it quite clearly."

"So I do," he admitted.

She moved to the free chair next to Sebastian's bed and sat.

"I saw her from across the room at an art show," Emerson began. "She was the loveliest thing. There was something unusual and so graceful about her, about the way she used her hands when she spoke. She's deaf, you know."

Ari nodded.

"I don't know if I can explain it, but her affliction made me love her all the more. More ferociously, more immediately. She'd known adversity and met it with great dignity and courage. I admired that. I wanted to protect her from any further hurt."

The affection on his face was sweet to see.

"She is the stronger and wiser of us. Anytime I'm met with rudeness or adversity, it's her that helps me rise to the challenge of handling it with aplomb. She always says the more mean-spirited someone is, the kinder we should be in return. They're the ones shamed, even if they don't realize it."

Ari smiled. "I admire the philosophy, although it's not an easy one to live up to."

"She has a sort of inner peace because she's accepted herself for all that she is and is not. I don't think many of us can say that. But back to your question. I believe that when you find yourself with the right person, they fill your heart and soul enough that you know you would never feel complete or truly happy without them. There is a certainty in it."

Arianna felt tears rush to her eyes and she looked away from him, embarrassed. What in the world was she getting emotional about? Sebastian stirred, and she leaned forward, breath held, but he slept on.

"There's something else to consider," Emerson added. "Who you are when you're with that person."

This struck a chord with her. "You're right. Do you feel comfortable in saying what's on your mind or does it seem there's no point?"

"Exactly."

"Do you feel appreciated for who you are, for the *totality* of who you are, or only valued for some small facet of that?"

He nodded. "And it *is* our totality, including weaknesses and peculiarities that make us who we are. How very dull it would be if we were all without flaws."

"I would very much like to meet your wife. Jane, isn't it?"

"Yes. And you will meet her. We'll arrange it when we get back. She doesn't like to travel. In fact, she doesn't much like to leave Larkhall Rise, the street we live on. But she will if it's important to me."

"If she'd rather not, I could come there."

He grinned. "One way or the other, we'll see the thing done."

~~~

It was nearly dusk, and she was packing, when she heard a man clearing his throat outside her tent. She looked up and saw Wellesley standing there.

"He's up again," he said. "Taking a bit of food."

Ari dropped the items in hand and came quickly. Sebastian had been helped to the courtyard where he sat at a table, looking dazed and terribly pale. Sully was taking his photograph, but whether Sebastian was aware of it or not, she couldn't tell. The moment he saw her, his expression changed, and he struggled to stand, but she shook her head as she rushed forward. "Don't get up."

"Here," Emerson said, offering her a chair.

"Thank you," she said. She sat next to Sebastian. Before him was a bowl of fruit.

"He's had water and a bit of bread already," Emerson said. "I think he understands he is safe and among friends."

Sebastian only had eyes for her. "Eat," she coaxed, gesturing the same way he had done to her.

He glanced at the others and then reluctantly turned his attention to the food and ate using his fingers. His hands were shaking.

"He's so pale," she said quietly.

"His body is still fighting the toxins," Emerson replied. "But he should be over the worst. His pulse is stronger." He gave her a wan smile. "You were pale, too."

"Have you tried to communicate with him yet?"

"I've spoken," John replied. "I'm not sure how much he's understood."

Arianna realized Sully was still taking pictures. She started to ask if she was in the way, but Sebastian swayed, and she reached for him as he slumped into her arms.

"I believe he's reached his limit for today," Emerson said. "Help me get him back to his bed?" he asked the men. A couple of them stepped forward, picked Sebastian up and carried him back into the tent. Sebastian was weak but still conscious, and he watched Ari as she led the way. He was eased onto his cot. She pulled up a chair and sat next to him.

"It's progress," Emerson said.

Ari nodded, but all she could think was that she might never see him again. Sully was determined that they would leave first thing in the morning, and there was no chance he would change his mind. She leaned forward and brushed Sebastian's hair back, soothing him enough so that he would sleep. He struggled to stay awake and to maintain eye contact with her, but he could not hold out.

Chapter Eight

S ebastian slowly sat up the next morning and looked at the older man sleeping on another cot, the one who'd tried to speak to him before. There was a cup of water on the table that he drank down. He stood but battled a wave of dizziness and nausea. Once it passed, he stepped outside to relieve himself and to find Ari.

He had only taken a few steps outside when he saw that her tent was gone. Panicked, he looked around as other men took notice of him. They were on edge and already reaching for their weapons.

~~~

"Emerson! You dead or what?"

Emerson woke and sat, rubbing his face. "No," he called. "I'm fine. Relax!"

Sebastian looked at him as he emerged from the tent, undoubtedly looking disheveled. "Put your weapons down please," he ordered calmly.

Reluctantly the men relaxed their stances, but their guns stayed poised at their sides.

"You look upset," he said to Sebastian. "Is it that Ari is gone?"

Sebastian's eyes narrowed.

"I want to help you, Sebastian. I believe I can help you if you let me. My name is John Emerson, in case you don't remember from when we spoke yesterday. You had poison in your system. That's why you were feeling so ill. *Are* feeling so ill," he corrected himself.

"Everything alright here?" North called as he came closer.

Sebastian looked at North, quickly assessing that he was unarmed and seemed to pose no immediate threat.

"Sebastian, this is Charles North," Emerson said.

"What makes you think he can understand you?" one of the others asked.

"We all want to help you," North stated, speaking to Sebastian. "To offer you another sort of life."

Sebastian looked at the other men suspiciously. He took a sideways step. No one made a move for him. He took another few steps.

"He's going to bolt," someone warned under his breath.

"John, are you sure?" North asked worriedly.

"We'll be here," Emerson said to Sebastian. "I will be right here. I can teach you, work with you, bring you back home to England. If you choose it, Sebastian. Only if you choose."

~~~

The meaning of the words seeped through Sebastian's consciousness, but that only fueled his panic. He ran. He ran through the vine-tangled jungle, hardly seeing what was in front of him. There were blinding hues of green, branches that scratched, vines that caught at him. They were of no notice. He was desperately trying to outrun the words and images exploding in his mind faster than he could process them.

A ship's railing in hand – salty wind in his face.

A sideways glance from his mother.

Her gloved hand reaching for him.

Snow. Impossibly soft, cold snow blowing in his face.

A church. He'd craned his neck to see the spire.

An older man patting his cheek. "You're a fine boy," he'd said.

The natives they'd seen upon arrival, shocking in their state of undress. Women's breasts. Their strange lip plates.

Brick houses.

Fences.

Sidewalks.

The sharp smell of horse dung.

An omnibus.

Sebastian scrambled up the tree to his sleeping place where he dropped to his knees and covered his head with his hands. Squeezing his eyes shut didn't help. He still saw the man with large hands and a handlebar mustache. *"You're a fine boy,"* he'd said. *"Never forget that."*

A train—with a red car in the back. The noise and the smoke.

Boots. His boots with thick, black ties, scuffed at the toe.

He didn't want this. He didn't want this roaring in his head, this feeling of overwhelming panic. He rose into a crouched position and then leapt from the platform with all his strength. He clutched a vine, which stretched and snapped, but not before he'd caught another, swinging wildly.

In a matter of seconds, he was back on the ground and running.

A plate of bangers and mash.

A wooden chair in the corner of room.

Dog—a stray dog with sad eyes. He'd wanted it for his own.

A lady smiling fondly at him. "She'd follow you anywhere," she said.

Tea In a china cup.

A coat. With a fur collar.

A pistol. Shiny, black muzzle.

He slowed and then stopped running, doubling over as he caught his breath. His panic was ebbing. These were memories from his long-ago past; they could not hurt him. "Word," he said slowly, drawing it out. He could still see Ari's face and hear her voice.

"You remember, don't you? You remember words?"

He ran his hands through his hair and squatted trying to make sense of the dull pain in his chest. All he knew is that he had to find her.

Chapter Nine

Distant thunder rumbled as Sebastian walked back into camp a day later. John Emerson reined in his almost giddy relief as he looked up from his game of solitaire. "I was hoping you'd return," he said as calmly as he could. He gestured to the chair next to him. "Sit, please."

Sebastian hesitated a moment and then moved closer and sat, eyeing him warily.

"I was passing time playing a game. I'll teach you sometime if you'd like."

"Yes," Sebastian said.

Emerson blinked in surprise. He'd sensed that Sebastian had some understanding of what was said, but he had not spoken until now. "Do you remember your numbers?"

Sebastian made no reply.

"Most of these cards have a number. You see?" Emerson held up a nine of spades. "This is a nine," he said, pointing to the numeral. "And there are nine of these. This is a six," he said, picking up a six of diamonds. "And you see there are six diamonds. One, two, three, four, five, six. You see?"

Sebastian's gaze flicked from the card to Emerson.

"I understand you were only six when you were left alone."

"Eight," Sebastian said. "I was eight."

Emerson considered him thoughtfully. "You speak well."

Sebastian shook his head. "No."

"Oh, but you do. I hoped that you understood me earlier, and I thought you might have, given your reactions, but I am delighted to hear you speak."

"Ari."

"Arianna has returned home. She will be on a ship soon." Sebastian was watching him intently. "You came here on a ship many years ago. From England. Do you remember?"

Sebastian's face tightened. "Why you not go?"

"I was waiting for you. I would very much like to work with you, Sebastian."

Sebastian glowered at him. "I want Ari." His blue eyes were blazing.

Emerson took a moment to respond. "Arianna wanted to stay and help." Sebastian seemed to be absorbing the words. "But she has gone home with her uncle. If you choose to return to England with me, and when you're ready, we can ask if she's willing to see you again."

"I am ready."

Emerson smiled. "Yes, I can see that. I think she may want to see you too, but we will have to ask when the time is right. Do you remember my name?"

"John."

"That's right. John Emerson. And your name?"

An invisible veil seemed to fall over Sebastian's eyes.

"I believe it's Sebastian?"

"No."

"It's not Sebastian?"

The younger man looked away, his brow furrowed.

"But it *was* your name when you were a child, wasn't it? Do you remember that?" Sebastian looked back at him but did not reply. His expression had closed off. Defiance or defensiveness? It really didn't matter why the wall had come up. "I think I may understand. You had to become someone else in order to survive. Is that right?"

Again, there was no response.

Clearly, very early on, language had ceased to be important to him, but it was still in his mind. It could be extracted; but he had to be willing. "Shall I call you something else?"

"I want Ari!"

"I understand that, but she has gone home," he said patiently.

"Then we go," Sebastian stated, hitting the table in frustration.

"You should say, 'Then we should go,' or 'I would like to go.'"

"We go!"

There was a good amount of stubbornness that would have to be worked through. "I am not opposed to that, but it is a long trip. A long voyage. Do you remember that from when you were a child?"

Sebastian hesitated. "Yes."

"Do you remember your parents?"

Sebastian scowled.

Obviously, it was a sensitive subject. "So, what shall we call you?" he asked, changing the subject. "It can be anything you like. How about ... Joseph? Or Charles?"

Sebastian gave a curt shake of the head.

"It's rather exciting to claim a new name for a new phase of your life. What about James? Or Michael?"

Another shake of the head. "No."

"George?"

"No."

"Henry? Harrison? Sam?"

"Zan," Sebastian said abruptly.

"Zan?" Emerson repeated, exaggerating the consonants.

Sebastian nodded once.

Emerson nodded. "Alright, Zan it is. I rather like it. It suits you. It's short and to the point. Like your answers," he added with a sly smile.

The cook came strolling across camp but stopped abruptly when he saw Sebastian. "He returns."

"He has," Emerson replied pleasantly.

"Will he stay?"

"Let's assume so. Please make something meatless for supper."

The cook grunted and moved on.

John Emerson chuckled. "You see there, Zan? Some sounds, like the grunt," he paused and grunted to demonstrate, "are universal. Used by all languages." Zan didn't smile, but his expression lightened. It was a minute change, but Emerson felt encouraged by it. He gathered the cards and set them aside. "So, let's begin, shall we? We will be in this together, and we will find our way. Alright?"

"Ari."

Emerson stifled a sigh. "Perhaps Arianna waits at the end of the rainbow like a pot of gold. I cannot promise that, of course, but we shall see. I don't want you to expect too much of her but, by then, I hope you'll understand."

Zan frowned.

"It is vital that you are not afraid of speaking, even incorrectly, because the more you speak the better you'll get."

Zan's chin jutted. "Not fraid."

"You should say 'I am not afraid.'"

"I am not afraid," Zan repeated fiercely.

"I believe you. And so, we begin. Tell me, what is this?" he asked, holding up his hand and pointing to it.

"Hand."

"Yes. That's right. And since it's part of my body, you should say, 'your hand.' If you hold up your own hand, you say, 'This is my hand.' And this?" he asked, pointing to his face with both hands. "What is this?"

"Head."

"Yes. And the front of it, here?"

"Your face."

"Good! And this?" He held up a foot.

"Your foot."

"Wonderful. This?" he gestured to his elbow.

Zan thought a moment. "Arm."

"Yes, it is an arm, and this is the elbow."

"El-bow."

"That's right. It's all there in your mind, Zan. And now that you've begun, it will come easier and easier. You'll dream in words. They'll come back to you when you're not even trying to think of them. Let's try something else," he suggested as he rose. "We'll take a walk, and I'll point things out, and you'll name them."

Zan stood.

"And sometimes I'll say a word and you name the opposite of it," Emerson continued. "Do you know that word? Opposite?"

"Yes, no," Zan said.

"Exactly like that! Or what if I say 'stay?'"

Zan hesitated. "Go."

"Wonderful!" They started off, walking at a leisurely pace. "Big."

Zan thought about it.

"It's fine if you don't get the right answer," Emerson coaxed. "But try."

"Small?"

"Yes! Very good."

~~~

Reece, having been observing the exchange, sauntered over to the cook. "Crazy," he commented with a shake of his head.

"Sane," the cook quipped, rather liking the game.

The Englishman scoffed. "It'll never happen. Emerson may be good and all at what he does, but he won't civilize him."

"Oh, I think he will. On the surface, at least. *Matokeo ya utafutaji kwa* wants the girl."

Reece scoffed. "Who wouldn't? But not even a wild man can be that stupid."

~~~

"Will you be comfortable here?" Emerson asked late in the evening as Zan looked the tent over.

Zan nodded.

"How would you feel about us cutting your hair and shaving your face tomorrow? So, there would be no hair here," he stroked his own face.

Zan nodded.

"That would be fine?"

"Yes."

Emerson suspected Zan remembered a great deal more language than he was enunciating yet, but that was fine. In part, it was emotional pacing. "Are you tired of speaking?"

"Yes!"

Emerson chuckled. "Then I bid you a good night." He left the tent and walked over to the men sitting around the campfire. They would all be leaving soon. "Baker, I wonder if I can ask you a favor."

"You can ask," Baker said lightly.

"Zan needs clothing, and you're the only one close to his size. May we borrow something or purchase it?"

"I've not got a thing worth purchasing, but I can come up with a shirt and pair of trousers for him. I don't have a spare pair of shoes."

"Thank you. We'll buy what he needs when we get into town. I do appreciate it."

"You really think you're going to get him on a ship headed to England? You don't think he'll bolt on you again?"

"I don't think he will," Emerson replied thoughtfully. "He's doing extraordinarily well and he's anxious to go."

"Anxious to get his hands on Miss Day again," Baker smirked.

"He does want to see her again, of course, but that will be her decision. He may not understand that now, but he will before we reach the English shore."

Baker shrugged, unconvinced.

"Besides he hasn't seen another woman … as an adult male. Perhaps when he does, the desire to see Arianna will lessen."

"Did you see him when he looked at her?" the cook asked.

"I did," Emerson admitted. He looked sideways at the tent. "Yes, I did," he murmured.

Chapter Ten

Z an stepped out of his tent the next morning into an early, gray mist. There would be no going back to the life he'd known here. He only needed to return to his sleeping place for one thing. The camp was still and quiet as he left.

~~~

Ari stood on the deck of the ship, her arms crossed in front of herself, the loose strands of her hair whipping in the wind. There was no land in sight, in more ways than one. There was such vast hollowness inside her. They were headed back home to the life she'd left behind, but it felt like she was aboard a prison ship headed to a desolate frontier. Given the choice, she would have turned the ship around.

It was maddening not to know what had happened with Sebastian. Had she only brought him only pain and suffering? Plus, she'd ruined a great adventure for Sully.

She experienced a cramp that made her breath catch. For a few days, she had feared the possibility of being with child, but that fear was eliminated. However, in its place was a bottomless melancholy. Was it the monthly curse affecting her so or something far more significant?

~~~

Emerson did not hold back an enormous sigh of relief when Zan walked back into camp. Zan appeared calm, as if he'd simply gone for a walk, and perhaps he had. A walk and a swim, judging by his wet hair. "Good morning."

"Good morning," Zan repeated carefully.

Emerson noticed the object Zan held, a rock of some sort. "Have you eaten this morning?"

"Yes."

"Shall we get started then? I thought we might start with the haircut and shave, and I have some different clothing I hoped you might try. It will all be an adjustment, of course, but I can't help wondering if a physical change might not help with the emotional side of things."

Zan observed him carefully as he spoke and then nodded when Emerson paused.

"If you'd like to put that in your tent," he said, gesturing to the object in his hand.

Zan did it and returned in a matter of seconds.

"Here you go. Sit here."

Zan sat, his posture erect.

Emerson had a comb and a pair of scissors handy. "No second thoughts?"

"No."

"Alright, then." He began to cut.

"I went back for my rock."

"I saw that. A lucky rock, is it?"

"Lucky," Zan said, as if testing out the word. He sighed. "I do not know if it is lucky."

"When did you find it?"

"My mother gave to me." His words were halting.

"Ah! Then you've had it a long time. It does have special meaning then. Did you mother always have the rock or—"

"No."

Having cut the bulk of Zan's hair, Emerson began to work the tangles from Zan's hair as gently as he could.

"The priest," Zan said.

"The priest?"

"He knew they were coming for us. He gave it to her, to hide."

So, Sebastian did have some memory of the event. He hadn't blocked it out. "That must have been so frightening."

"Yes."

"Did you understand what was happening?"

"Yes."

"Can you tell me? Is it something you can talk about?"

Zan was silent.

"I imagine your mother wanted you to hide as well."

"Yes."

"What did she look like?"

Zan was quiet for a few minutes. "I don't know. She had dark hair."

"I imagine she was quite beautiful. Can you recall her voice?"

"No."

"I wonder if you resembled her or your father."

"I looked like her. I think I looked like her."

Zan's body was tense. Time for a lighter subject. "What color is your rock?"

"Yellow."

"And what color is the sky?"

"Blue."

"And snow?"

"Snow," Zan mused.

"Do you remember snow?"

"It is white."

"White and cold and lovely to see falling. I imagine it will be quite a thrill when you see it again."

"Snow," Zan said again.

Chapter Eleven

June 15, 1908
Somersly Manor,
Northampton

Sullivan looked up from the correspondence at the sound of a knock, and then glanced down to make sure the newly developed photographs were all put away. "Yes?"

Arianna opened the door, which pulled a welcome draft from the window. "Dinner is ready."

"I'll be down in a bit."

She started to shut the door.

"Ari?"

She opened it back up. "Yes?"

"Have you let Patience know you're back?"

"I sent a note. They're all in the city, you know."

"Of course. I wonder how the season is going."

"Like every year, I imagine." Ari started to shut the door again.

"And that Derringer fellow?"

Ari opened the door back up, this time with a smirk. "Why do you always call him that?"

"Don't know really."

"I plan to send word to him tomorrow," she said haltingly. "Or the next day," she added with a shrug of one shoulder. "Now, is there anything else?" she asked slowly. "Or do you want to wait until the door is nearly shut to say?"

"No, that's all."

She smiled and started to close the door.

"Except—"

She opened the door back up to see a big teasing grin on his face. "Mrs. Herbin will not be amused by your antics if the meal gets cold."

"Quite right you are. Two minutes."

She closed the door quickly and he chuckled, but his pleasure did not last long. The dark circles beneath Ari's eyes were evidence of her poor sleep these last weeks. She was withdrawn but would not share her reason why. Obviously, it was the experience in Africa, but she'd seemed fine directly afterwards. In fact, she'd wanted to stay and make sure of Sebastian's health. They had been home for days, and she'd done little but rest. She ought to have gone off to the city to join the festivities. She had enjoyed it in the past.

He reached for a flat leather envelope, opened it and withdrew the stack of photographs from within. The top one was of Arianna and Sebastian sitting. A table was in front of them, Emerson was slightly behind. Ari's expression was arresting. There was such tenderness. On Sebastian's face as well. If a casual observer had seen it, they would have guessed the two of them were close friends. Perhaps even in love. Sully slipped the photographs back into the folder and put it away. Ari didn't need to see them.

Chapter Twelve

As Zan sat across from Emerson in the ship's cabin, ready to work, it once again occurred to the older man what an impressive figure he cut. After the hack job he'd originally done on Zan's hair, it had been cut fashionably. His cleanshaven face revealed excellent bone structure, and his gaze had a directness that was compelling. His blue eyes were beautiful, fringed with long lashes.

It was a shame Zan wasn't less handsome because his appearance garnered so much attention. It was an appreciative, sometimes awe-struck sort of attention, and Zan both clearly saw and felt it, but no matter what Emerson said, explaining it to be a compliment, Zan believed it to be proof of being marked. Different. Wrong, somehow.

At first, Zan had moved, stood, and walked differently, influenced by great apes. He had also stared too fixedly at others. However, he had worked to correct it all. To blend. To emulate.

"Did you get very far with *Treasure Island*?" Emerson asked. It was one of the books he'd purchased before they'd sailed.

"I finished chapter one."

"Did any of the vocabulary give you pause?"

Zan thought about it. "Diabolical?" he said, pronouncing it brokenly.

Emerson nodded. "It means devil-like. In the next book you'll read, *The Strange Case of Dr. Jekyll and Mr. Hyde,* which is by the same author, a diabolical personality comes to life. Were there any other words you didn't know?"

"Some, but I could—" he frowned as he puzzled over how to phrase his thought.

"You could determine what was meant?"

"Yes."

"Most of us do that on a frequent basis. Today, I thought we would work on expounding your sentences and practicing some basic social interactions."

"Expounding?"

"It means to draw out. To elaborate. For example, I could say to my wife, 'You look well.' Or I could expound upon it and say, 'You look lovely in that gown. The color suits you.'"

"More words," Zan commented. "More words is better."

"That sentence should be, 'More words *are* better.' Remember? When the subject is plural? The girl is playing. The boys are also playing. But no, it's not always true that more words are better. Sometimes the opposite is true. But words are our primary means of communication. They're certainly not our only means, but it's important to communicate well with words. Expounding on your thoughts is one of the things that you are least comfortable with, and so we need to practice it. I'd like to see you begin to enjoy speaking. Enjoy the sound of your voice. Feel satisfaction from getting your viewpoint through to another. I know it's work right now, but it is becoming less so each day. It's coming more naturally."

"What is social interactions?"

"What *are* social interactions? Well, when you meet someone, either someone you know or a stranger, you exchange greetings. You may have a conversation. Arianna, for example."

Zan's attention grew keener.

"Let's say we attend a function—"

"A function?"

"A dinner party. A ball. A lecture or gathering."

Zan nodded. "A function."

"Yes. So, we go to this function, and you see Arianna or anyone that you'd previously met. You might bow slightly and say, 'Hello, how nice to see you again. I hope you're well.' If it's a close acquaintance, a lady, you might kiss the back of their hand."

Zan waited for more.

"If you have not met someone before, you say, 'How do you do?'"

"How do you do," Zan repeated. "That's all?"

"That's all. And they answer in the same way, perhaps a different inflection. 'How do you do?' Or they may say, 'Very well, thank you. How do you do?'"

Zan rose and took a few steps away, suddenly filled with nervous energy.

"What is it?" Emerson asked.

"What will people think of me?" He paused before adding. "They'll know."

"Know what?" Zan didn't reply. "Know that you've had tragedy in your life? Nearly all of us have tragedy in our lives. It touches us or a child or a sibling or a well-loved friend." He paused. "Or perhaps you meant they'll know you were *matokeo ya utafutaji kwa*. Is that it?"

Zan nodded.

"No," Emerson said firmly. "They will not. Not unless they are told. People may sense you are different, but those differences will be far more positive than negative."

"They will think I am an animal."

"No, they will not, because you are not. No more so than any of us."

"I think I am."

"I know that you're not. Now shall we get down to work?"

"I'd rather walk and hear your stories."

"I believe you've heard quite enough of my stories."

"I like them. I like hearing about your family."

"I imagine you could tell me about them by now." He smiled and shrugged. "Why don't you?"

"Your wife is Jane. She cannot hear."

"Expound upon that, if you please."

Zan thought about it. "She had sickness when she was young and lost her hearing."

"That's right."

"But you have a great love."

Emerson was taken aback. "I didn't say that but … yes, we do."

Zan sat again. "You had four children, but a son died when he was young."

"Yes. It broke our hearts. We felt we would never get over it."

Zan nodded solemnly. "Your other son is Wyatt. He is married to Vivian, who is now your daughter-in-the-law."

Emerson nodded. "Daughter-in-law."

"Daughter-in-law. They have a son called Johnnie."

"You have an outstanding memory, Zan. You really do."

"Since you showed me a photograph, I picture them in my mind."

"Do you remember how old Johnnie is?"

"Ten."

Emerson nodded.

"Your first daughter is Virginia. You call her Ginny. Her husband died."

Emerson nodded again. "It was a dreadful accident. His carriage overturned, and he sustained a head injury. Poor man lingered for weeks."

"Ginny lives in your home," Zan continued when Emerson's sentence trailed off. "Her son, your grandson, Luke, is twelve."

Emerson smiled. "And such a good boy. He's fair, like his mother, and hers. There's a gentleness about him. I can see him growing up to be a physician or a clergyman. Whatever he does, he will do it well."

"You love him very much," Zan noted.

"I love them all, of course! But I *like* him so very well. And he's at home with us, so I've taken on more of a parental role with him, I suppose you could say. All my other grandchildren have their parents, so our roles are different."

"Your youngest daughter is Alice, and she married Donald Kramer."

Emerson chuckled in astonishment at his memory. "And their children?"

"Sally and Beth."

"I wish I had a tenth of your capacity for memory."

"I like thinking about them. About a normal life."

Emerson took a moment to respond. "I know that a normal life, your own normal life, is difficult to conceive right now, but it won't always be. Chances are you'll eventually marry and be happy and have a child or maybe several children."

"I would love them," Zan stated.

"And you will make a wonderful husband and father. Now, why don't we talk about politics?"

Zan made a face.

"I know," Emerson commiserated. "But you should know the basics."

"I would rather be tested on table manners again."

Emerson guffawed. "That is saying something, isn't it?"

~~~

Patience knocked as she entered Arianna's room, smiling broadly. "Hello, sleepyhead! Why are you still in bed at nearly eleven o'clock?"

Ari pulled herself up and leaned against the headboard. She'd been trying to make herself get up for more than an hour, but she kept drifting back off. "Still tired from the journey, I suppose."

Patience sat on the bed and embraced Arianna, talking all the while. "I've missed you. So much has happened since you've been gone, but you go first. Tell me everything." Only when she pulled back did she see the haunted expression on Arianna's face. Her smile vanished. "What is it?"

"Nothing. I missed you too. That's all."

"Are you ill?"

"No, I'm perfectly fine."

Patience felt her forehead. "No fever."

"No, of course not. I said I was—"

"What's happened?"

Ari drew breath to deny that anything had happened, but she couldn't form the words. Instead, tears filled her eyes.

"Oh, Ari." Patience took hold of her hands. "It's something terrible, isn't it?" Ari glanced at the open door, and Patience popped up and shut it before returning to her. "Tell me everything. From the beginning, when you left."

Ari took a deep breath and exhaled. "There is nothing exciting about that. The voyage was uneventful. When we arrived, a guide led us to the camp. The trek was difficult, but I managed it."

"Was it very deep in the jungle?"

"Yes. Very."

"What about the men in camp?"

"They were very nice and respectful. Between my uncle and Charles North, whom I've known since I was a child, no one would have dared disrespect me, but they wouldn't have anyway." She paused. "I can't begin to tell you how beautiful it was. Hot, exotic, colorful … beautiful."

Patience nodded.

Ari bit her lip. "You didn't tell anyone the reason we went, did you?"

"No! You said not to."

Ari nodded.

"Did they find him? Did they capture him?"

Arianna hesitated and then nodded slowly. "But not before he captured me," she said just above a whisper.

Patience's eyes grew wide. "What? No! Did he hurt you?"

Arianna shook her head.

"Oh, Ari, he did, didn't he? How long did he have you?"

Arianna swallowed again, but the lump in her throat remained. "It was a matter of hours," she said thickly. "It was late when he took me. It was overnight and into the next morning."

"Oh, dear God!" She grasped Ari's hands. "You must have been terrified!" She shook her head as she searched Arianna's face. "Was he wild? Was he a beast? Tell me what happened."

Ari swiped at her eyes, took another deep breath, and allowed the truth to spill out. The words came haltingly at first but then faster and faster, and the more she spoke of it, the better she felt.

When she finished, Patience took a moment before speaking. "You must never tell anyone else that," she cautioned in a low voice.

"I know."

"You would be ruined. It was not your fault, but people would find a way to blame you."

Arianna knew it was true. She had flouted convention, went traipsing off halfway around the world, put herself in harm's way, and then wanted to cry foul. That's what they would say. She cringed thinking of the cautionary tale she would become. Besides that, she would end up an outcast. How lonely it would be if she were cast from society and not allowed back in. She would be a pariah. Her friends would all be a part of something she'd be forever banned from. And how long would they remain close when she was no longer a part of their social world?

Patience got up and paced, her hands clutched in front of her, then she turned back to face Arianna, her eyes alight. "This is what happened." She paused, wanting to phrase it perfectly. "You arrived at the African camp after a long, grueling journey and learned the wild man had been captured. So you are back home, safe and sound, although fatigued from the trip and disappointed that you went such a long way only to be … robbed of the adventure you'd hoped to have."

Ari was warmed by Patience's fervor. She nodded.

Patience walked back over and sat beside Ari. "I would say to deny the existence of the man altogether, except word of it will get out. Oh, Lord! The others on the expedition—"

"They have all sworn to confidentiality."

"But there will be publicity about the man, won't there? How could there not be?"

"I assume so. I believe the museum means to capitalize on the venture at some point in time."

Patience nodded. "So, you tell a select few and ask them to keep quiet about it. The way you really would do if—"

Ari nodded.

"Where is the man now?" Patience asked.

"That's just the thing. I don't know. When we left, everyone was still there. It had been decided that they would not force him to leave the jungle if he did not wish to."

Patience blinked. "Wish to," she murmured.

Ari nodded. "He's been offered support by a wealthy patron of the museum if he chooses to return to the city, but I just don't know. What if Emerson couldn't get through to him? What if Sebastian didn't understand? What if he panicked and left?"

"Sebastian?"

"That's his name. When he was just a child, he went on a missionary trip with his parents who were killed there."

"How terrible!"

"I know. To be abandoned like that."

Patience's pity altered to mystification. "You don't hate him, do you?"

"Of course not! All he's ever done is what he needed to do to survive. He had no intention of hurting me. Ever. Just the opposite. How could I hate him?"

"But … what happened—"

"Yes. What happened," Arianna repeated, looking off.

"Arianna?"

Arianna looked back at her. It was so tempting to tell her about what had happened in Charleston three years ago, about Jason, about how terrible the intimacy had been. Otherwise, how else could she understand what was now so clear to her, that intimacy could be powerful and good. Intoxicating, really. She'd only had the one encounter, and it had changed her entirely.

"What he did, was it not … terrible?" Patience asked haltingly.

Arianna shook her head.

"I suppose that's good to know," Patience said with a wan smile. She placed a warm hand on her arm. "I cannot tell you what to confide in Marshall, but—"

"I do not love Marshall," Ari blurted. "I cannot marry him because I do not love him. Sometimes I do not even like him."

"But, Ari, you're upset. It almost seems as if you're in mourning."

Ari blinked, surprised at the notion and how accurate the description felt.

"Don't make any big decisions you may regret later. Take some time."

Arianna nodded slowly.

"I have to tell you something," Patience said regretfully. "I fear, and I don't know exactly why I fear this. It's just a feeling."

"What is it?"

"I suspect that Delia may have feelings for Marshall."

"I know that," Arianna replied with a quick shake of her head. "Good gracious, she's not even discreet about it. I've known it for ages."

Patience blinked. "Well, I haven't!"

"That's because you believe the best of everyone."

"I do not! Sometimes I think perfectly awful things."

"Like what?"

"Well, I don't know. Oh, I do know! At a party last Saturday, I saw Lars Neely and thought how terrible it would be to have a red-headed husband." She shuddered. "And to have red-headed children?"

Ari laughed, it was so absurd and wonderful.

There was a knock at the door before Mrs. Herbin opened it. "You are coming down to luncheon?" she asked Arianna worriedly.

"Yes," Arianna replied. She looked at Patience. "You will stay?"

"If it's alright," Patience replied, looking to Mrs. Herbin.

"When was it never alright?" Mrs. Herbin asked. "Half an hour then, girls," she added before closing the door.

"Do you think she'll always call us girls?" Patience asked with a cockeyed smile.

"I do. We'll be forty, she'll be seventy, and we'll still be girls." Patience giggled, and Arianna smiled in earnest. She drew her knees up and hugged them, feeling more like herself than she had in weeks. "I'm so glad you're here. I needed to see you."

"No more than I needed to see you. When you're gone, it's as if part of me is missing. What will we ever do if one of us has to move away when we get married?"

"Refuse to go," Ari declared.

"Why don't you get up and get dressed, and after lunch we'll practice telling people about your trip. And once we have that down pat, to where you are perfectly believable, you … you will tell me all about it, won't you?"

"About what?"

Patience gave her a look and blushed scarlet. "*It. You know. What a man does.*"

"Oh. *It.*" Ari nodded. "Yes, I'll tell you."

"I don't know where else I'd learn anything of value," Patience said just over a whisper.

"So what's the news?" Arianna asked as they made their way downstairs. She'd put on a day dress and pulled her hair into a simple twist. Having shared her secret with the only person in the world that she could share it with, she felt lighter. "Tell me all about the balls."

"Do you remember Charlotte Biggs?"

Ari nodded.

"She got intoxicated at her coming out, fell down, and broke her front teeth."

Ari cringed. "Oh!"

"I know. Her poor mother was mortified, and I haven't seen Charlotte since. I don't know what they're going to do about her broken teeth. What can you do?"

"I don't know."

"And Nan—"

Ari stopped abruptly. "What about her?"

Patience smiled. "She's in love."

Ari gasped. "With whom?"

"Thad Mansfield."

Ari beamed a smile. "He's adored her for ages. So, she finally got over her shyness?"

Patience nodded, and they walked again, arm in arm. "She's the youngest of us, you know," Patience said in a clandestine tone.

Ari rolled her eyes. "You're twenty and so is she."

"Yes, but my birthday is in January and hers is in September. She's months younger than me."

Ari rolled her eyes in amused exasperation, but at least it was a familiar and comfortable subject.

~~~

"Turn," the seamstress said.

Wynonna turned slightly to allow the hemming to continue.

"You *cannot* be serious," Delia said from the doorway. "That fabric has a sheen to it. Good Lord, your hips stick out like a tabletop. I could put a cup and saucer on them."

Wynonna glared at her sister. "Go away!"

"It's just that you have no taste," Delia said sweetly. "You either choose colors that make your skin look like putty, or you choose designs like that, that make you stand out for all the wrong reasons. It's no good for me if you're a laughingstock, you know."

"Get out," Wynonna screamed.

"Oh, what is it now?" Mrs. Bradford called from down the corridor.

"Don't ask me," Delia said. "Ask the unattractive one."

"Oh, Delia," Mrs. Bradford snapped.

But that was all. Wynonna swallowed hard, hoping something else would follow, some fitting admonishment, but it didn't. It never did.

"What is it, Wynonna?" her mother asked in an impatient tone from the doorway. "What are you bellowing about now?"

"About your hateful daughter coming in here and spewing her poison as usual. Tell her to stay away from me!"

"This petty bickering is beyond wearing," Mrs. Bradford stated coldly.

"Being in this family is wearing," Wynonna exclaimed. "Having only mean-spirited harpies around me is wearing. I don't suppose you've ever seen the world from my viewpoint, have you, Mother?"

"Oh, Wynonna. You make me wish I'd had a son."

Wynonna's jaw went lax, and her eyes filled with tears, which slipped down her face the instant her mother had walked on. "Stop," she said in a strained voice. "Just stop."

The seamstress pulled away and looked up at her dispassionately.

"Is she right? Do my hips look like a tabletop?"

"You have broad hips," the seamstress stated with a shrug. "I can't help that."

"We're done," Wynonna said, stepping down from the stool.

"But—"

Wynonna kept her eyes straight ahead as she left the room. Her chest ached from holding in the rage and misery that wanted release. She *hated* her mother and sister. They were evil! They were more hateful and spiteful and meaner than anyone in the entire world. Why had she been stuck with them? It was so hideously unfair.

She made it to her room, slammed the door, and pulled the gown off, getting stuck and scratched with pins as she did. Crying bitterly, she threw the gown in a corner and began to unfasten the corset. Maybe she was ugly and too heavy, square-shaped was what Delia always called her, but she had feelings!

She went to the full-length mirror and made herself stare at the tall, lumpy creature she was. Her face was too broad, her nose too long, and no one would ever love her. Crossing her hands over herself, she raked her sharply pointed fingernails down her arms as hard as she could, cutting into the skin's surface until the lines of blood appeared.

She threw herself across her blood-spotted bedspread, sobbing. Only the thought of killing herself gave any comfort, but she would not give in to that state of mind yet. She had to suffer enough to go through with it.

Chapter Thirteen

A rianna paced nervously in the foyer as she waited for Marshall to arrive. Like Patience, he'd taken the train from the city as soon as he received her note. She turned at the sound of a throat being cleared and saw Murrow standing there, one bushy, white eyebrow lifted in an absurd attempt to look stern. Perhaps if he were not such a cherubic looking oldster, it might have worked. "Good morning," she said.

"Should you be waiting by the front door, Miss Arianna?"

"Seems as good a placed as any," she replied lightly.

"Why don't you wait for Mr. Derringer out in the garden? There's a pleasant breeze."

"You're right."

He nodded. "I'll send him through when he arrives."

The moment she stepped out the backdoor, she felt a lifting of her spirit. She'd spent entirely too much time pining. As she walked to the garden, she inhaled the scented air with appreciation. It was the smell of home. She rounded the thick hedgerow and passed the bench where they would sit when Marshall arrived. What exactly she was going to tell him, she did not know, and she had thought about it for days. "You will play it by ear," she said under her breath.

It was possible that another lady had snagged his interest during the many parties and events he'd attended. What a relief that would be. She picked a sprig of freesia. She smelled it and then stuck it behind her ear.

She loved this rambling old garden. When she arrived as a girl, a swing had been installed in the old oak for her, and she'd spent countless hours there lost in her own world. Sully frequently said he didn't know who had benefited from it more – her because she enjoyed it so or him because he'd derived such gratification from her simple pleasure. He claimed when she was happily swinging, everything felt right with the world. She was tempted to swing now, but Marshall would find it absurd and childish.

And Sebastian?

She sucked in a breath and experienced a daydream of him standing behind and swinging her. He would not find it absurd. She imagined the feel of his hands on her back.

"Arianna," Marshall called on approach.

Ari jumped and then turned to face him with a flush of guilt.

He reached her and pulled her close and kissed her. "Let me look at you. In one piece, I see."

It did not appear that he had met and fallen in love with someone else. "I am."

He pulled the flower from her hair with a puzzled look and flicked it aside. "And back sooner than you'd thought. I'm so pleased."

She nodded, unsure of what to say.

"The finest balls are still to come," he said happily. "You should leave for your aunt and uncle's tomorrow."

She realized she had stiffened, and she made an effort to relax. She wished he would take a step or two back and give her a little space. "Shall we sit?" she asked, gesturing to the bench.

"Yes. Tell me all about your trip. Did they find the wild man?" he asked flippantly.

Damnation! If only she hadn't told him! "They did."

He stopped, stunned by the words. "Really?"

"Yes."

"Seriously? They caught him and brought him back?"

"He has not been brought back," she replied haltingly. "He may be. I don't know." She was flustered and blushing. She felt the heat in her face. "The entire expedition is being kept confidential for the time being."

Marshall sat. "I'm shocked! Not that I didn't believe the story, but it is farfetched. How did they catch him?"

"First, you must promise you will not say anything to anyone about this," she said somberly.

He smiled as if amused, but then he saw she was serious. "Fine. I pledge, on my honor, that I will not say anything about this top-secret mission that you are about to share with me. Until such time as it is made public, I assume?"

She nodded. "Yes."

"Shall I take out my pocketknife and cut my hand? Make it a blood oath?"

"That's hardly necessary. I will take your word."

"Thank you so much," he replied sardonically.

She walked over and sat next to him to buy a moment. "They found him using local villagers, some of whom used blow darts to subdue him."

"Good Lord! How barbaric. Were you with the group that got him?"

She swallowed. "No."

"Did you see him at all?"

"I did," she managed to get out.

"What did he look like?"

She shook her head. "He had long, dark hair. Facial hair. He was tall and strong."

"I wonder what they'll do with him. Put him on display in the zoo?"

She rose, huffing in disgust. "He's not an animal! John Emerson is working with him."

"Working with him to do what?"

"To teach him, of course. To remind him of language and customs."

"If the man has run wild for the better part of his life, it's a lost cause. He must be more animal than man by now. If he's violent, he ought to be put down. Put out of his misery."

She struggled to maintain her composure. Marshall was completely ignorant and hateful, and he did not even realize it. "I cannot believe you just said that."

"Well, darling, it's true. Sad, but true. You did have new gowns made for the season, didn't you?"

She shook her head in disbelief, but on second thought, she didn't want to pursue the subject with him. His position would only make her more disgusted. "Yes."

"Let's leave in the morning, shall we?"

Good Lord. I really and truly do not like him.

"Ari?"

She crossed her arms tightly. "I can leave in the morning."

He stood. "Capital! We'll have a wonderful time." He stepped up to her. "You are happy to be back?"

"Of course," she replied weakly.

He took hold of one of her hands. "We'll stay in the city for the rest the season and see some of the Olympic Games. There are all sorts of interesting foreigners about. You'll need a dozen new gowns, at least."

It suddenly felt as if she were outside her body, watching the two of them. How meaningless it all was. How perfect looking on the surface and yet how empty. Was she really doing this? Was she really going to be attending one party after another for the next month? It had been great fun for a season or two, but she'd outgrown it.

"Arianna, about what we discussed before you left. Is your gallivanting at an end?"

"I have no plans to travel anywhere else for the time being," she hedged. "Other than the city, of course."

"Good." He kissed her hand and then reached into his pocket, extracting a small velvet box. The muscles in her stomach tightened as he opened the box. Inside was a ring of rose gold with a large diamond surrounded with a circle of rubies. He removed it and put the box back into his pocket. Smiling, highly pleased with himself, he slipped the ring onto her finger. "I used another of your rings, and had it sized already," he said. "What do you think?"

She tried to speak, but words failed her.

"It was my grandmother's. The diamond is six carats, I believe, and there are fourteen rubies surrounding it. It's wonderful on you. I knew it would be." He kissed her hand again.

She was speechless. He had just put an engagement ring on her finger but had not asked the question. In a way, it was a reprieve. If he did not ask, she would not have to answer.

"Let's go show your uncle," he urged, taking hold of her elbow.

She balked. "I believe he's out."

"Ah. Well. You'll show him later then and I'll see him in the morning. I'll come for you about eight. Be ready, all right? Because the train leaves at half past nine."

She nodded again. Like a mute.

He led the way back toward the house prattling on about the news of the season, and she walked along beside him feeling completely numb. At the front door, he took hold of her hands again. "Are you happy?" he asked, as if there could only be one answer and he already knew it.

"Honestly, I'm … stunned."

"Good. I hate when things are too expected." He leaned in to kiss her lips. Pulling back, he said, "We'll be the toast of the town."

Not a single word of response came to her.

He smiled toothily. "I believe I really did stun you."

"You did," she said breathily.

"Go have a lie down, have Mrs. Herbin see to your packing, and I'll see you in the morning." Smiling happily, he kissed her on the cheek again and left. Shutting the door behind him, she turned and leaned on it, feeling sick to her stomach.

"Ari?" Sully said.

She looked up the stairs and saw him peering down at her.

"Was that Derringer?"

She nodded.

"Why do you look like that? Did you have words?"

She shook her head and held up her hand for him to see.

"Oh my," he exclaimed. He quickly came down the stairs and took hold of her hand. "So, he asked you."

"No," she said in a small voice.

He looked into her face, puzzled.

"He didn't ask, he assumed. And then he put this *thing* on my hand."

He looked back down at the ring. "Worth a king's ransom."

She suddenly felt like crying. "Do you think I should marry him?"

Sully looked pained. "I think he thinks you're going to marry him."

"But do you think I should?"

He hesitated a moment. "It seems to me that the only reason to marry someone is that you can't imagine *not* marrying them. Personally, I never felt the compulsion."

"You didn't mention love."

"Can you imagine not marrying the man?"

"Of course, I can. But I can imagine being married to him, as well. I'm not certain what that means."

"Well, what does being married to him look like?"

"Like putting up with his family," she said wryly.

He gave her a look. "You don't really dislike them, do you?"

"Susan is fairly horrible. Vapid and vain and shallow. And his mother believes he walks on water."

"What do you think your life would be like with him?"

She frowned as she thought of it.

"On the other hand, what if you did not marry him? What would you be doing a year from now?"

She shrugged. "I don't know. Perhaps you and I would be off on a dig in the Mohave Desert or sailing to Japan. I don't know."

He grinned. "You'll make the right decision. I know you will."

She made a face. "I'd rather you just tell me what to do."

"When have I ever told you what to do?"

"Not very long ago," she said lightly. "In a jungle in Africa."

"Except for that." He glanced at the ring again and blew out a breath.

"If you don't object, we'll be going to the city tomorrow. I'll probably be there a month."

"You should go. Go and have fun. Tell my brother and sister-in-law I'll see them soon."

She threw her arms around him. "I love you."

He patted her back. "And I you, my dearest."

She pulled back and glanced down at the ring on her hand with a soft sigh. "I'm going to go swing."

"Then everything is still alright in the world."

Arianna stretched out in bed that night as a breeze carrying the scent of rain wafted over her. The swinging had done her good. She'd kicked off her shoes and swung high and hard, loving the freedom and exhilaration of it. Whatever her decision would be regarding Marshall, she was going to stop harboring thoughts of Sebastian. She felt for him, but she would not be the one to rescue him. That was Emerson's job, and Lord Bluford's responsibility by his own choosing. She had asked for a report from Emerson, and she would be glad to receive it, but then she would think no more of it.

Would Sebastian return to the city? "Stop it," she whispered. With a heavy sigh, she closed her eyes and tried to sleep.

Chapter Fourteen

Arianna followed Susan Derringer, her least favorite of Marshall's three sisters, from the train, accepting Marshall's hand as she stepped onto the platform at Euston station. As usual, it was smoky, noisy, and bustling with activity.

"Excellent," Marshall said as he spied someone. "Jakes is here."

Indeed, the footman was headed toward them. Arianna was relieved because it meant no delay in getting away from the station and ultimately from Marshall and Susan and the insipid conversation of the past two hours. "There are two trunks," Marshall said to Jakes with a flick of his hand.

The gesture so grated on Arianna's nerves that she began walking away to conceal the expression on her face. She'd been conspicuously quiet on the journey, although they hadn't seemed to notice. In her experience, the only person who chatted more ceaselessly and meaninglessly than Susan was their mother. So that was one thing to be grateful for, that Beatrix Derringer had not been there.

Arianna liked the other members of the Derringer family. Louise, the eldest, had a keen, sometimes biting, sense of humor, but it was never mean spirited. Louise was married to Perry Joyce, an American, and they were very much in love. Louise was the least attractive of the three sisters, but her personality made her the best company. Andra, the youngest of the Derringers, was a lovely young woman of nearly seventeen.

"Here we are," Marshall said as they closed in on the family carriage. The driver opened the door as they approached. "Drop Miss Day at number three Bedford Square," Marshall ordered.

"Yes, sir."

They were assisted into the carriage, the trunks were loaded, and they started off. "I'll stop in briefly today," Marshall said. "Just long enough to coordinate the schedule for tonight. Or shall I just plan to pick you up?"

"I should see what my aunt and uncle are doing first."

"Tonight is the Fredrickson bash," he said as if vaguely insulted.

"Everyone will be there," Susan spoke up. "I'm wearing my new red Poiret. It is to die for."

"We must go," Marshall said to Ari.

The thought of a disagreement over it, especially in front of Susan, made her feel tired. "That's fine."

"I'll come around nine or so and spend a little time with your uncle."

"What will you wear?" Susan asked her.

Ari had a mad desire to scream. Draw breath, open her mouth, and scream. "I really don't know."

"Well, don't wear red."

"But it would match her rubies," Marshall teased.

"I've planned for this," Susan stringently objected.

"I will not wear red," Arianna stated.

Susan bobbed her head. "Good. And I'm wearing gold tomorrow. It has an almost oriental design in the bodice, swirls of orange and bronze. It's another Poiret."

Arianna looked out the window and enjoyed a momentary fantasy that involved opening the door and jumping from the moving carriage. The question was, could she move her legs fast enough not to fall on her face? Perhaps if she hiked up her skirt. "Is Andra in town?" she asked, hoping to steer the conversation to anything other than Susan and her attire.

"Of course," Marshall said.

When they pulled in front of her aunt and uncle's town house, Marshall climbed out, assisted Arianna, and then escorted her to the front door. It was opened by Mr. Fletcher, the butler.

"Miss Day, what a delight to see you! And Mr. Derringer. Welcome, sir."

Ari's spirits lifted at the sight of Fletcher. "Thank you," she replied as they stepped inside. "Are they at home?"

"Not at the moment."

"Then I'll be off," Marshall said. "I'll see you tonight."

She tensed as he leaned toward her, but he only delivered a peck on her cheek before leaving. The moment Fletcher closed the door behind him, she felt herself deflate a bit with relief.

Fletcher turned back with a warm smile. "How are you, Miss Arianna?"

"I am well. It's been an interesting summer, so far."

"So we heard. Africa! Did you enjoy it?"

She smiled. "It changed me forever."

"Did you see any lions?"

She nearly laughed at the awed expression on his face. "From a distance, yes. And antelopes and zebras and elephants. And many, many monkeys."

"Were you not afraid?"

"No. They didn't get close, and there were always men ready with a gun in case we needed them."

"Well, we're delighted that you're back safe and sound. You've been in our prayers."

The words touched her. "Thank you."

"Your aunt should be back in a few hours. She joined Lady Myers' for luncheon."

"They weren't expecting me."

"I know how delighted they will be. Your room is ready, as always, and I'll have your trunk sent up. Will you take lunch in the dining room, or would you prefer it sent to your room? Or the morning room?"

"The morning room, please." She started toward the wide marble staircase noticing the small changes here and there. She had spent no less than three months in this house every year since coming to England, but it was still a place she visited. It was grand, formal enough that she always felt somewhat out of her element upon arrival. Her aunt and uncle had always made her feel loved and welcome here and at their country home, but it was not her home.

Worse yet was the Derringer residence in Belgrave Square, which made her feel as if she were stuck in a stuffy, overcrowded museum. Practically every inch was taken up with elaborate rugs, wall coverings, busts, enormous paintings, and tables filled with pointless décor.

She walked into her bedroom at the far end of the second floor and experienced the same nostalgia that she always felt after an absence. She'd been allowed to choose her room when she was a girl, and she had chosen this one because of the window seat in the bay window. The windows cranked open, and she'd spent many happy hours there.

"Here you are, Miss Day," Joshua Weltz, the houseboy, said as he walked in with her trunk.

"Joshua! You've grown a foot taller!"

"I'm better than six feet now," the fifteen-year-old announced proudly. "Taller than my pa."

"Be off with you now, Joshua," a prim young maid ordered as she walked in.

"It's nice to see you again, Miss Arianna," Josh said with a shy smile.

"It's nice to see you, Josh," she returned.

"Miss Day, I'm Rachel," the young woman said, bobbing a curtsy. "I'll be your maid."

"Very pleased to meet you. When did you come to the house?"

"In March, miss. When April McCarthy left to get married."

"Oh, of course. Have we heard from her?"

"I didn't know her, miss, and I'm not one for gossip. Are there any special instructions before I unpack?"

"No."

As Rachel went about her task, Arianna walked over to the bookshelf and ran her fingertips over her old childhood favorites, *Black Beauty, The History of Sir Thomas Thumb* and *Little Women*. There were a dozen other beloved books she would still curl up with and reread from time to time.

"Which gown shall I prepare for tonight, Miss Day?"

"The pale yellow, I think," Ari replied with a shrug.

Rachel finished unpacking and walked out with her chin held high.

~~~

"You're here," Edith cried as she made her way across the drawing room toward Arianna. "How wonderful!"

Arianna beamed as she rose and embraced her aunt.

"I cannot wait to hear everything," Edith exclaimed. She pulled back but kept Arianna at arms' length and her smile instantly dimmed. "Are you well?"

"I am."

"Then why don't you look it?"

Ari had to laugh at her aunt's bluntness. "Oh my."

"Did you contract an illness in Africa?"

"No."

Impatience flared in Edith's eyes. "On the way there? On the way back?"

"No. I am not sick."

Edith released her. "Sit and tell me everything." They moved to the davenport and sat facing one another. "But before you begin, I should tell you I received a letter from your father."

Ari blanched. "Why? What did he say?"

Edith blinked in surprised at the strong reaction. "He asked that we encourage you to return to Charleston if a suitable marriage has not yet been arranged."

"Suitable marriage? Arranged? The nerve of him!"

"Apparently, there was some alliance formed when you were last there?"

Ari shook her head. An alliance? "There was not."

"A Mister Roger Barton?" Edith coaxed.

Roger! He was Jason's younger brother.

"Your father was not specific as to the nature of the alliance, but—"

"Any alliance involving Roger Barton was formed behind my back and without my knowledge. I will not go back to Charleston and be a part of his nefarious schemes," she stated angrily.

"Nefarious?" Edith repeated, somewhat amused. "My, my. That is a strong word." Ari did not recant, and Edith's amusement faded. "You were different when you came back from Charleston," she said suspiciously. "Withdrawn. Which is how you seem now. Not quite yourself."

Arianna turned away from her aunt's insightful gaze, which saw too much. "I am entirely myself."

"Ari, you know that I love you, as do both your uncles."

Ari looked at her and nodded. "Of course, I know that," she said quietly.

"We want what's best for you and keeping secrets that weigh heavily upon you is not good for you." She paused. "You have always been one of the most grounded, sometimes stubborn, and yet most delightful creatures I have ever known. You have your own mind, and you know what you want, but you seemed different when you came back from Charleston, and you seem different now. Rather lost."

Arianna thought about it and nodded slowly. "Removed from myself. That's how I feel."

"Why?"

"I'm … not sure where to begin."

"The beginning is usually a good place," Edith suggested lightly.

"Or maybe with the latest turn of events," Arianna said as she reached into her pocket and pulled out the engagement ring.

Edith gasped. "What is this?"

"Marshall Derringer put it on my hand yesterday."

"You're engaged?" Edith exclaimed. "Why in the world did you not say so? And why do you not seem pleased? Do you not wish to marry him?"

Arianna shook her head.

"But you said yes?"

"That's the thing. He didn't ask. He just assumed it would be a yes, that it *was* a yes, and he placed this upon my finger."

Edith took a moment. "Have you been wearing the ring since then or carrying it around with you?"

"I wore it until a short while ago."

"Darling, do you not realize that by wearing it, you've pledged your intention to marry him?"

"That's why I took it off. At first, I thought it was a good thing that he hadn't asked. It meant I didn't have to give an answer straightaway. But he is determined that we go to one party after another. They have a schedule all worked out."

"Let me see it on you."

Ari acquiesced and held out her hand.

"That diamond must be seven or eight carats."

"Six, he said."

"It's bigger than that," Edith mused, cocking her head to study the ring. "I can't say it looks like something you would have chosen, but it's breathtaking."

"It's *not* something I would have chosen," Ari stated flatly.

Edith peered into her niece's eyes. "Tell me about Mr. Derringer."

Ari leaned back with a sigh. "He is full of self-importance. He's the only son, you know, and has been raised like a prince by his mother. Doted on, spoiled. He doesn't believe he has a wrong thought."

"Most men don't," Edith rejoined. "And as to being doted on, Sullivan has done far too much of it for your own good. I know that you've had a marvelous time together on your adventures, and that you do what you want when you want when you're with him, but that's not real life, Arianna."

"That's also not my objection. I don't wish to always have my way, nor do I. You do Uncle Sully a disservice when you suggest I've had no rules and no guidance."

"I did not say that."

"I do not love Marshall."

"Oh, darling," Edith sighed with a shake of her head. "Do you realize how few wives actually love their husbands and vice versa? The fact is that marriage is expected, and this would be an excellent match. You say he's spoiled? He is wealthy! He is used to having his own way? Well darling, it's a man's world, especially when they have the clout of the Derringers."

"I appreciate your candor," Arianna said calmly, "as always. And you've made your opinion quite clear, but it is my decision."

"It is indeed, but I am your only close female relative, and I must offer my perspective and my strongly felt opinion that you should put that ring back on your finger and leave it there. You should accept the man." There was a light tap on the door, and they looked up to see Hettie, the parlor maid, at the door with a cart.

Ari was glad for the small reprieve. She didn't know what reaction she'd been expecting, but *that* hadn't been it and she needed a moment to adjust. She watched Hettie set out the service. Besides tea, there were scones made with Devonshire cream. It was amusing that Aunt Edith asserted she didn't lead a real life when this being waited on hand and foot was their norm. They did not get waited on hand and foot at Somersly Manor.

"Have you plans for tonight?" Edith asked, reaching for her tea.

"The Fredrickson affair," Ari replied. "Are you going?"

"No, I sent regrets. With the heat and my age, I have begun to send a good deal more regrets than acceptances."

"Your age? You're not even fifty."

Edith smiled. "I am fifty-two, dearest, and suffering the most dreadful attacks of over-heating." She shrugged. "It happens." She took a bite of scone and nodded her approval. "You are only nibbling. Are you not hungry?"

"Not really."

"What else do you have to tell me?"

"What do you mean?"

"Charleston? Africa?"

"There's nothing else," She sipped her tea. "May I invite Patience to spend some time here?"

"Of course. You know your friends are welcome."

"Thank you."

"How is she?"

"Fine."

"And the other girls?"

"Fine."

"Just fine? At your tender ages, there must be all sorts of intrigue and romance."

"I understand that Nan is in love, but I haven't seen her or Delia since returning home. They're here, of course."

"Invite them over, too! I cannot be young anymore, but I can still enjoy hearing about it. Preferably with some joy and excitement," she added wryly.

"I agree; that is how it should be."

"Oh, darling. Can you not choose to feel that way if you put your mind to it?"

"But if I don't truly feel it, how can I?"

Edith shrugged. "Pretend? Perhaps in the pretending, it will become real."

Ari considered. Her aunt generally gave the best advice. "I'll think about it."

Edith reached over and squeezed her hand lightly. "Why don't you go rest before dinner? You look peaked and it will be a late night."

"I think I will." She leaned over and kissed her aunt's cheek. "Thank you for your counsel."

"I wish only to see you happy."

"I know that."

~~~

Ari rose and left the room with an uncharacteristic solemnity, which made Edith question her own advice. Where was the vigor and effervescence Arianna always possessed in such abundance? She wondered if she should perhaps write to Mr. Day in hopes of discovering what exactly had transpired in Charleston three years ago. Perhaps Mr. Roger Barton was the key to understanding why Ari seemed so defensive and unhappy.

~~~

At the stroke of seven, Arianna entered the salon. She was not wearing the ring, a fact that Edith noticed immediately.

"Ari, my dear," her uncle exulted, holding out his hands.

Arianna walked into his embrace. "Uncle Wilbur."

"It feels like ages," he said, taking hold of her arms. "Now let me look at you. Pretty as a picture, as always."

"You do look better," Edith agreed. "Were you able to nap?"

"No, but I rested."

"Tell your uncle about Mr. Derringer."

"Should we not go into dinner first?" she hedged.

"No."

Wilbur looked at his wife, confused by her businesslike tone, and then back at Arianna. "Would you care for a glass of wine, my pet?"

"Please."

He walked over to get it. "How is my brother? I'm sure he loved stomping around the wilds of Africa."

Ari smiled. "He did."

"Nothing ever did scare him."

"The photographs will be wonderful. The wildlife and the scenery were beyond description. I cannot wait to see them."

He walked back and handed her a glass, then lifted his to her. "To having you home."

She touched her glass against his and then sipped. "*Mmm,*" she approved. It was delicious.

"Château Margaux," he said, his eyes twinkling.

"Mr. Derringer," Edith spoke up.

"Marshall Derringer gave me a ring," Arianna said hesitantly, addressing it to her uncle.

"He is under the impression they are engaged to be married," Edith stated, cutting right to the heart of the matter.

"Under the impression?" Wilbur repeated. "What does that mean? Did he not ask?"

"No," Ari exclaimed. "He assumed."

"Yesterday," Edith added.

"So, he assumes you want to marry him, puts a ring on your finger, and says … what exactly?"

"Well, first he asked if my wild adventures were at an end. To which I replied that I did not have any immediate plans for another trip. Then he pulled out the ring and put it on my finger. He said he'd already had it sized using one of my other rings."

"It's quite something," Edith said to her husband. "A diamond of at least six carats, I think maybe more, surrounded by rubies."

"Oh, my," Wilbur said.

"I don't remember exactly what he said next," Ari said, frowning with concentration. "He was babbling about all that we would do over the next month. Then he wanted to go show Uncle Sully the ring and—"

"What did he say to Sullivan?" Wilbur asked.

Ari bit her bottom lip and shrugged one shoulder. "Nothing. I explained he wasn't home."

Edith cocked her head sharply. "Was he at home?"

Ari hesitated. "Turns out that he was."

"Arianna!"

"Has Derringer asked for your hand?" Wilbur asked. "Has he spoken with my brother?"

"No, he has not asked for my hand. And as to speaking with Uncle Sully, this morning they exchanged pleasantries, and then Marshall asked what he thought of the ring, and Uncle Sully said it was quite something. Marshall asked his thoughts on the matter, and Uncle Sully replied that my happiness is all that matters to him. Of course, Uncle Sully said everything kindly, the way he does, and Marshall heard what he wanted to hear, which is what he does."

"I see."

There was a polite knock, and they looked over to see Fletcher standing in the doorway. "Dinner is served," he announced.

"Thank you, Fletcher," Wilbur replied.

Fletcher bowed before stepping out.

Wilbur looked at Arianna with a serious expression. "Do you want to marry the man?"

She shook her head. "I don't find him kind or interesting."

"Then why did you not politely refuse him?"

"He didn't ask."

Edith clucked her tongue and shook her head.

"You're right, Aunt Edith, I know I should have. I was stunned, really, and … there is a part of me, the practical part, I suppose, that wonders if I should marry him. I know most the world would think I should."

"That may be," Wilbur said, "but it's you who will see him across the breakfast table each morning and the dinner table each night. Everyone may think you should jump at this opportunity, but they will not be the ones spending every day and night for the rest of their lives with the man."

Edith blinked in surprise. "Good gracious," she remarked. "Haven't you become the old softie?"

He looked at her quizzically. "I don't know about that, but I cannot imagine spending my life with someone I do not love. Can you?"

"We were blessed in that regard," she replied. "But I have made my opinion on the matter clear." She paused and looked at Arianna. "And I stand by it."

"I see," he said quietly. He looked at Ari. "I believe I have, as well. That said, what matters, *all* that matters, is what you feel and wish to do. But decide quickly and let the man know. He is not the sort of man to accept rejection or embarrassment gracefully. This is not something that can wait."

"I know. I realize I've handled it badly."

"If you need more time," Edith spoke up. "Tell him so. Explain that you feel overwhelmed and would prefer to keep the engagement, or perhaps you should say proposal, to yourself for the time being."

Ari nodded.

"Let's go into dinner," Wilbur suggested. "You needn't decide anything at this minute or even tonight."

"Actually, she does," Edith said.

Arianna concurred grimly.

"Then, by all means, let's go have some sustenance and another glass of wine or two. Perhaps discuss some strategy."

Arianna smiled gratefully as she accepted his arm.

~~~

At nine-twenty, Marshall was shown into the withdrawing room where Arianna awaited him. "You look lovely," he said as he crossed to her. He kissed her cheek.

"We have to talk," she blurted.

He drew back. "What about?"

"Did you realize that you never asked me to marry you?"

"What are you talking about? The whole getting down on one knee nonsense?"

She shook her head. "No. I mean that you never asked. You asked about the traveling and, well, you put the ring on my finger."

He glanced down at her hand and frowned. "Where is it?"

She felt a tremor of nerves and straightened her shoulders. "I took it off because I do not wish to—"

"Marry me?" he said with disbelief. "You do not wish to marry me? You cannot be serious!"

"I do not wish to have anything announced yet," she said, fighting a ridiculous panic. "Because I am not absolutely certain."

He took a step back, clearly astonished.

Her neck ached from tension. "I'm sorry."

She noticed the muscle bulging in his jaw, betraying his agitation. "Sorry?" he practically spat. "What you are is *foolish*, Arianna. Your father is in trade and an American to boot. Your dowry is not even a fraction of what I could get."

She jerked as if slapped, which is what it felt like.

"I offer you *everything* and, you're not certain?" He took a few steps away and then turned back glowering. "I will go to the Frederickson affair by myself. You will retire early and think long and hard about your future. I will make your apologies and explain that you do not feel well. Tomorrow I will come for you in the afternoon, and we will take a ride through the park where I will ask you a certain question and you will provide an answer once and for all. Provided it is the right answer, we need never speak of this unpleasant discussion ever again. Do I make myself understood?"

Her throat was so tight she was unable to speak, even if she could have come up with something to say.

"For now, I will say goodnight." He hesitated a moment, as if he were contemplating saying something else, and then turned on his heel and left.

Arianna did not move for several seconds, and then she made her way to the closest chair and sank into it feeling stung and queasy. What was wrong with her, allowing him to speak to her like that? And yet, besides chastised, she felt guilty, as if she'd done something horribly wrong. Did that mean she *was* wrong? That she should marry him?

Moments later, she found herself shaking her head without even realizing she'd been doing it.

Chapter Fifteen

Marshall smoked as he waited for his mother and sisters to arrive at the gala because they had to be stopped from running their mouths until he had Arianna under control. He had gone in and made a quick round, grabbing a glass of champagne, but he needed another. In fact, he needed something stronger.

Damned chattering females.

They should have been there by now. When he saw the family carriage pull up, he took a final drag from his cigarette, stamped it out, and moved forward to meet them.

"What are you doing out here?" his mother asked when he reached her.

"I need to say something before you go in."

"What's that?" Susan asked, edging closer. Andra also crowded in.

"Do not say anything to anyone about the engagement," he said in a low voice.

"Why not?" his mother said sharply.

"I have my reasons."

"Are they your reasons or hers?" Susan asked with a smirk.

He gave her a look that made her curb her smugness.

"Did you have a disagreement?" Andra asked.

"I told you something was wrong with her," Susan said to her mother. "She was positively morose on the way here. You would have thought we were transporting her to her execution."

"Hush," Beatrix snapped.

"Yes, do stop talking," Marshall seconded.

"No one will say anything," Beatrix said to her son. "Girls."

"Of course, Mamma," Andra chirped.

"Susan," Beatrix said, peering intently at her.

"I was told to stop talking, remember?"

"And now I am telling you not to sulk." Beatrix turned her gaze on her son. "Is she here?"

"No. She has a dreadful headache. *That's* why she was quiet earlier," he said to Susan, who answered with a shrug. "Let's go in," he said irritably. "I need a drink." He offered his mother his arm and she accepted. "Are Louise and Perry coming?" he asked.

"I believe so."

"Well, tell them if you see them before I do."

"Is the engagement off?" his mother said under her breath.

"No. But going to Africa was hard on her and she's not recovered her strength yet. Now if you'll excuse me, I have people to see."

~~~

Edith knocked lightly on Arianna's door and then opened it. Ari was sitting up in bed, staring off in thought. There was an open book by her side. "I saw your light on. What happened?" Edith asked as she crossed the room.

"He got angry," Arianna replied dispassionately. "And insulted."

Edith sat on the side of her bed looking fretful. "Did you refuse him outright?"

Arianna shook her head. "I said I wasn't certain. I asked for more time."

Edith frowned. "What did he say?"

"Something to the effect that I was ungrateful. After all, I am an American and my father is in trade. Oh, and, uh, he could acquire significantly more of a dowry elsewhere."

Edith's jaw dropped. "Well, I never!"

"What dowry, Aunt Edith?"

"It's still the custom, darling. It's our gift to you."

"Why was I not told?"

"It's not a secret, but nor did we feel it needed to be announced. Frankly, I'm surprised that you're surprised."

"I don't want to buy a husband!"

"Don't be absurd. That's hardly what it is." Ari didn't reply. "So how did he leave it?"

"He will come for me tomorrow afternoon, at which time we will go for a drive in the park, and I will give him my decision."

"Tomorrow? That is all the time he gave you?"

"Yes."

Edith sighed. "I suppose you could plead for more time. I doubt he'll hurl a fresh batch of insults at you."

"I'm going to say no," Ari stated.

Edith didn't know what to say. An offer this good might never present itself again.

"I know that I've shocked you, and probably disappointed you. For that I'm sorry."

"Oh, Ari. We want what's best for you."

"I know you do, but you must trust that I know what that is and what it's not. When he left this evening, my knees were weak, and I felt sick to my stomach. He is a bully. His words and his tone and the expression on his face were hateful. Not at all how you speak to someone you love. And did I stand up for myself? No. I felt guilty and chastised like a child caught misbehaving."

"I'm so sorry."

"He said that he would go to the party and make my excuses, and I would go to my room and think long and hard about my future." She'd flushed angrily. "I am not a ten-year-old, nor is he my father."

"You're right."

"To think, it was an exchange of not even five minutes!" She shook her head. "If he can make me feel like that in so short a time, what would it be like to be bound to him for life?"

"Men can and do react strongly when their egos are injured."

"Can you imagine Uncle Wilbur talking to you in such a way?"

"No," Edith admitted. She shook her head. "No, I cannot. I am so sorry. I fear tomorrow will be a rather miserable experience."

"Yes," Ari agreed.

"But you will get through it."

"Yes, I will."

"And afterward I hope we'll begin to see some of your sparkle again." Ari began to cry, and Edith wrapped her arms around her and held her. "There, there. It's not the end of the world."

~~~

Marshall saw Louise and Perry and made his way to them. "Did you just arrive?" he asked when he reached them.

"We've been here nearly an hour," Louise replied. "And yes, we've been given our instructions and taken our solemn vows of silence."

"Good."

"If it shouldn't work out between yourself and Miss Day," Perry said. "Did I ever mention I had a cousin?"

Marshall nearly rolled his eyes. It was a joke because Perry had come to London to escort his cousin, Rebecca, for a season. Marshall had been enchanted with her up until the time that she opened her mouth and revealed a stutter. The rest of the family had liked her, they'd certainly liked the small fortune she represented, but he could not abide the thought of a wife with a stutter, much less children that stuttered.

"She is working on her impediment," Louise added. "And doing very well, we understand."

"How nice." Marshall glanced around the room. "Excuse me," he said before he left them.

"He is such a bore," Louise said. "Honestly, Rebecca is too good for him."

"And yet she fell for him," Perry replied. "She never fails to ask after him."

"I know," she replied sadly.

"If you'll forgive my saying so, I think Miss Day is too good for him."

"Oh, she won't marry him," Louise replied dismissively. "What I don't understand is why she simply didn't shoot him down

when he asked." She deliberated her choice of words and shook
her head. "I should not have said 'too good' though. I believe that
Miss Day will not marry him because she has too much
independence, which she knows he will not allow. Rebecca should
not marry him because she has a delicacy of heart that he will
crush with his indifference."

"Well said," Perry agreed. "Now can we stop talking about
your brother and dance?"

She smiled. "I thought you'd never ask."

~~~

"Doctor Thurman," Marshall said, clapping the older man on
the shoulder.

"Derringer," Leopold Thurman greeted. "Good to see you."

"And you, sir," Marshall returned. He'd had three or four
glasses of whiskey on top of the glasses of champagne, and he was
having to work at speaking clearly. "Say, you're with the Royal
Society, are you not?"

"I certainly am. Been a member for sixteen years."

"I know people who just returned from the Africa expedition."

"Oh? Who's that?"

"Sullivan Vinson."

"Ah! Brilliant photographer."

"Yes. He is good. I know his niece as well," Marshall added.

Dr. Thurman mouthed, "Oh," then clucked with his tongue. "I
have not had the good fortune of meeting the young lady, but I
hear she is remarkably spirited."

"Yes. One who has done quite enough traveling, I would say,"
Marshall said lightly.

"*Hmm.*" Dr. Thurman looked off, suddenly uncomfortable.

"I know about … what happened, of course."

Thurman looked at him with circumspection. "What do you
mean?"

"In Africa. I know that they got the man," he said in a low
voice.

Thurman drew back in surprise. "I see. Well, of course, that's not being announced at the present time. We're evaluating how best to handle it."

"Yes, I know. I was sworn to secrecy before I was told."

"I suppose so. Well, I mean of course you were. We all were. How is Miss Day? Are the two of you close friends?"

"You could say that. I believe we'll be married before long."

"Oh, my! Congratulations."

"It's not official yet, but I … do believe I'll ask. To answer your question, she's not quite recovered I think."

"She must have been terrified. I cannot quite imagine it."

Marshall looked straight ahead. His blood was suddenly running a few degrees cooler, and he suspected it would be noticed if he faced the good doctor at the moment. What had he just stumbled onto? "No," he said quietly. "Nor I." He cleared his throat. "What was your understanding of it, if I may ask?"

"That the man came into camp in the middle of the night and stole her away, right out of her tent."

Marshall swallowed.

"Thank God she was unhurt when they found them in the morning. Well … except for being shot."

His eyes widened. "Shot?"

"By the darts. The natives had poisoned blow darts."

"Oh, yes. That."

"The man took enough hits that he barely survived."

"But he did? Survive? For certain?"

The older man nodded. "It's my understanding he's returning here. Bluford is taking him under his wing."

"And John Emerson, of course."

"Yes. I meant that Bluford will be footing the bill. Provide for the poor chap and so forth."

Marshall shook his head. "Are they not concerned about his wild nature?"

"Emerson would not bring him back if he felt he posed a danger."

"Gentlemen," Ivan Helmsley said as he joined them.

Thurman smiled. "How are you, Helmsley?"

"Couldn't be better. Did you try the Bordeaux?"

"Yes," Thurman replied. "I thought it was very good."

"Excellent," Helmsley agreed with a knowing nod. "Either of you care for a game of billiards?"

"Why not?" Thurman accepted. "I've certainly seen enough waltzing to last a lifetime. Derringer?"

"Why not?" Marshall agreed, snapping back to attention. He'd used the last few moments to gather his wits. Arianna had lied to him, and he had every right to be furious with her, and yet he felt an odd sense of victory having discovered the truth that she obviously didn't want him to know. Not only did he have all the cards now, it felt as if he had just been handed the one that completed a royal flush. "I might even sample some of that Bordeaux."

Chapter Sixteen

E dith looked up from her desk in the drawing room the next afternoon. "It's a shame it will rain."

"It doesn't matter," Arianna replied as she stood peering out the window, her hands pressed to her stomach. She'd chosen to wear a crisply ironed shirtwaist of pale gray because it felt businesslike, and today she would attend the business of ending her short engagement to Marshall. What a fool she'd been not to shut it down as soon as he asked, or rather assumed.

She looked toward the door at the sound of Fletcher's distinct footsteps. A moment later he appeared and announced that Mr. Derringer had arrived. Ari picked up her hat and walked to the mirror. She put it on and adjusted it to the correct angle. She went for her gloves and began tugging them on.

"Are you ready?" Edith asked.

"I'm ready to have it over with."

"I'll be right here," Edith said.

Ari smiled at her and left, picking up her reticule on the way out. It contained the ring she would hand back to Marshall. *Thank you, but no thank you.*

Marshall was waiting by the front door chatting amiably with Fletcher. "Ready?" he asked cheerfully when he saw her.

It was an unexpectedly pleasant reaction, as if there had been no harsh words or hurt feelings between them only the night before. "I am," she said warily.

Fletcher opened the door for them, and they left and then the driver opened the carriage door for them, and they were assisted in. "What would we do if we ever had to open a door for ourselves?" she remarked when they were settled.

"There will always be someone to open doors for us. Why imagine otherwise?"

She barely held back a sigh of exasperation.

"I was going to drive the Phaeton today, but it clouded up."

Was he really going to act as though the harsh words of last night had not occurred? If so, it would be up to her to broach the subject. "Did you enjoy yourself at the party?"

"It was most interesting. I had an enlightening conversation with Doctor Thurman."

He wasn't going to make this easy. He was going to talk trivialities. "I don't know him," she said distractedly.

He turned to look at her. "No? He knows you."

She cocked her head, detecting a different tone. "I have never met the man that I recall."

"True, and yet he knows you by name."

"Meaning he knows someone in my family?"

"No. He knows *your* name."

There was definitely something strange in his tone. Something that was setting her teeth on edge.

"Would the comment have made more sense had I first mentioned that he is a member of the Royal Society?"

Ari felt her mouth go dry as her suspicion became full-fledged panic.

"So," Marshall said, shifting in his seat to better face her. "Why don't you tell me what happened in Africa again? This time, the *truth*?"

She looked away from his accusing gaze. "What did Dr. Thurman say? How did the subject even come up?"

"I brought it up. Told him I knew what had happened in Africa."

She closed her eyes, her shoulders rounded forward, and her face burned. She should *never* have told him anything. "You swore you would say nothing."

"But I wasn't told the truth of the matter, was I? He asked how you were after such a frightening experience, which of course you'd failed to mention, although I did not allow him to know that."

They had already reached Central Garden. Through her tear-blurred vision, it looked like a living Monet. As discreetly as possible, she placed her elbow on the armrest and reached up with a gloved hand to dab the corners of her eyes before a tear could escape. He might suspect he had wrought tears from her, but she would not provide him the satisfaction of the proof. "What is the point of this?"

"Oh, I may have a point or two to make, but first I asked you a question," he said sharply. "And you will do me the courtesy of facing me."

She took a deep breath and turned to face him.

"Tell me what happened. And you know what I mean."

What was there to tell when he already knew? Or was it simply to humiliate her? "I went to sleep, as usual, but woke when I was grabbed. I was taken."

"He dragged you behind him?"

"No. He lifted me and … tossed me over his shoulder," she said haltingly. "And he ran."

"Did you scream?"

"Of course, I screamed!"

"And the others didn't come out?"

"They came running, but it was dark. It was the middle of the night."

"How could fit men fail to catch him when he was running with you over his shoulder?"

"He's very strong," she stated as calmly as she could. "He had the benefit of surprise, and obviously he knew the jungle."

"Go on."

"He ran a long way, and then he climbed a tree with me still over his shoulder." She paused. "And then we slept."

"Slept," he repeated.

"Yes. On a sort of platform he'd fashioned."

"Let me get this straight. A wild man, who is very probably naked, sees you, steals you away, takes you to his … whatever it was, his lair, with you in your nightgown I presume, and then he simply lays down and goes to sleep. Is that correct? Is that what you're telling me?"

"He was not naked, and I was not in a nightgown. I wore what I felt was practical."

"Which in this case was what?"

She wouldn't tell him that. Even the thought of it had her face prickling with heat again. Damn him! She lifted her chin slightly. "A sort of shirt."

"Even so," he snapped.

"I have told you the truth. Yes, I was frightened out of my mind. I feared what he would do, but he set me down, inspected my head, which was bleeding from where I'd hit it on a tree limb, and then forced me to lie down on my side. He lay behind me, wrapped his arm around me, and tried to sleep. I spoke in hopes that I could somehow reach him, but he did not want to hear it, so he squeezed me. And that act of squeezing me so that I would be quiet was the most physical he got with me that night. Not counting carrying me off, of course. That I swear. On my life. On my mother's soul!"

He was silent a long moment. "Continue," he finally said in a less hostile tone.

"In the morning, the others found us. The men from camp had joined with villagers. They had crude weapons, blow-darts, and we were struck and made unconscious by the toxin in the darts."

"Why didn't you tell me this?"

"It was over and done with. I thought you would overreact, and I wanted to forget it."

"So you lied!"

"I did not lie. I simply did not reveal everything that occurred."

He gave her a look. "Arianna—"

"Nothing that I said was untrue. You asked if they'd found the man, and I said yes. You asked if I was part of the group that captured him, or something to that effect—"

"And you said no!"

"Which is true! I wasn't with the group that captured him." She paused. "I was with him."

"So you skirt around the truth and claim it is not lying! You know better."

"No harm was done. He meant no harm. He was nearly killed in the attempt, but I was not hurt."

"But he *took* you, Arianna. If nothing else, think of what it looks like! Don't you see? That is your problem. You do not think in practical terms."

She looked away from him wondering how much damage had been done because of what he'd learned. He could ruin her, especially now that she was ending their engagement. Would he?

"Fortunately for you," he continued, "I am practical."

She looked back at him. "What does that mean?"

"First of all, there will be no more traveling unless it is with me. And I can assure you that will only be to civilized places."

Oh, no. "Marshall—"

He held up his hand. "Because you are marrying me, you are safe. No matter what sordid speculation gets out about this half man, half beast, we will deny it. No one will dare challenge us."

Her gloved fists tightened from mounting tension.

"You and I will forget all about last evening's conversation. It never happened."

"But it did happen."

"I'm sorry if I hurt your feelings. I was angry."

"And I do not wish to hurt you," she said beseechingly. "But I do not think we should marry."

"Because of what I said?"

"No!"

"Because I didn't get down on one knee when I proposed?"

"You did not propose," she said tiredly.

"Fine then! I will. I'll get down on a knee if it means that much to you."

"It doesn't. You're not listening to me!"

"You're not saying anything," he exclaimed, raising his voice.

"I don't feel myself when I'm with you. You make every decision and expect me to go along with it."

He laughed without humor. "You must be joking. In case you haven't noticed, you haven't gone along with much of anything I've wanted."

"Marshall, you don't make me happy," she said pleadingly.

"I haven't been given a chance! If you would just be reasonable and give me the chance!"

"I might have been happy to give you a chance if you were capable of giving me room to breathe."

"I don't know what that means. What the bloody hell does that even mean?"

"I am my own person. I make my own decisions."

"Don't I know it? I didn't want you to go to Africa, remember?"

"It was the experience of a lifetime, and I am not sorry I went."

He shook his head and looked away from her, exasperated. "We will come to a meeting of the minds today, before we leave this vehicle."

His arrogance was exhausting. Did he ever hear one word she said?

He looked at her. "Put the ring back on and we will announce our engagement."

She shook her head. "I don't want to do that," she said quietly.

He pursed his lips and breathed deeply to regain some composure. "What if I give you a little time to adjust to the idea? Perhaps I have assumed too much."

More time wouldn't make a difference, but it would put off the inevitable for another day. He was not about to consent to ending the engagement yet. She would have to think of another approach.

"We will take a few days," he said.

"I need more than that."

"Fine! A week, then," he snapped. "Ten days. What is it you want?"

She looked out the window. Not this. She didn't want this.

"You will spend some time with my family in our home," he said in a calmer tone. "Which will soon be your home, and you will adjust to the idea."

She looked at him. "What if I choose to end the engagement?"

"You won't."

She struggled to contain her frustration. "What if I do? Will you be civil about it?"

"I don't know what I would be, nor do I want to contemplate it."

"But—"

"I'm giving you time, Arianna. That is all I can do for now."

Silence fell between them, and they each looked out their windows.

"Will you attend the … oh, hell, I don't remember what tonight is," he said. "But whatever it is, will you go with me, or would you rather stay home again?"

"I'll go," she replied quietly. "Can you at least tell me what color not to wear?"

Her humor took a moment to reach him, but it finally did. "She really can be too much, can't she?"

"No comment."

"Oh Ari." He grabbed hold of her hand. "I thought you'd be happy to marry me."

She felt a pluck of guilt at the unexpected vulnerability she saw in him. "I know."

"I still want you to be."

She didn't know what else to say. "I want you to be happy as well."

"Then it's decided. You'll marry me."

She smiled sadly.

He rapped on the roof, signaling the driver to turn around. "Do your aunt and uncle know about our disagreement last evening?"

"No," she lied and then flushed. She hated lying. It went against her nature and yet she'd done entirely too much of it lately. In fact, she'd lied or misled him three or four times in the last half hour.

"And of your wavering?"

"I mentioned that I had reservations to my aunt," she said slowly, trying not to fib any more than she had to.

"And what did she say?"

She hesitated. "It was a private conversation which I do not intend on repeating, but the impression she left me with was that I should accept your proposal."

The answer pleased him. "She's right, of course."

She withdrew her hand and looked away. What a pathetic picture she made. Hands folded demurely in her lap, posture very straight, profoundly aware of his posture and frame of mind, as if it was all that was important. That picture was everything she did not want to be. Everything she'd never believed she would become.

Marshall left her at the front door, and Ari walked into the house feeling the curious sensation of numbness again. *It was the lying. It was the deceit.* She'd first felt the numb spells when she was stranded in Charleston. Stranded and betrayed but, all the while, knowing she'd failed herself. And now she was experiencing the same thing because of Marshall.

No; because of herself. This was her weakness. Her inability to decide what to do. It was time to grow up and make an adult decision no matter how difficult it was.

Chapter Seventeen

L ord Dalton Bluford's heart swelled in accordance with the cheering of more than sixty thousand people as the parade of athletes of the Olympic Games began in the newly constructed White City Stadium. The procession was led by Cambridge and Oxford men in their blues, plus an Eton boy. "Our alma maters," his friend, Maurice Wallace, said proudly.

It was an odd sensation to be in such a large arena surrounded by so many spectators. The stadium was a marvel with a swimming pool and various platforms in the center of the track.

"It's my understanding the Swedes left in protest over their flag not being flown before the Games," Wallace said.

"Did they? Well, it seems incompetent on someone's part that we couldn't get the bloody flags right. The Swedes, the Americans, the Irish."

"Of course, they all think it was personal," Maurice scoffed.

Lord Bluford gave him a wry side glance. "Are you certain it wasn't?"

Wallace smirked. "Have you heard from North?"

"Yes. Several times. And Emerson. They should be here any day now."

"With or without the jungle man?" Wallace asked under his breath.

"With."

The cheering swelled as the Danish women gymnasts walked by waving happily. "Women in the Olympic Games," Wallace bemoaned.

"Why shouldn't they be?"

"I wonder if you'd had a grandson instead of your Vanessa, if you'd be quite so liberal in your views."

Lord Bluford grinned. "I like to think so."

"Are you not at all worried about the ... African refugee?"

"He's not African, he's English."

"You know what I mean."

"I'm not worried. If he's too unpalatable, I'll set him up in the country somewhere. I agreed to provide for him; I didn't say where it would be."

The American athletes began their walk on the track below, cheered on wildly by the American spectators.

"Good Lord," Wallace commented. "They are a brash bunch, are they not?" The American flag bearer passed the royal box, where every other flag had dipped in deference, but his flag remained defiantly high, and a clamor immediately ensued. "Did you see that?" Wallace cried. "He failed to dip the flag to the king."

Bluford looked around with mild amusement at the furious reaction of his countrymen. People were funny, and the older he got, the funnier they became.

~~~

After a trying afternoon of being measured and fitted for new gowns, Ari returned home ready for tea. She started down the hall to the drawing room but stopped short at the sound of her friends' voices. She rushed on and found Patience, Nan, and Delia with Edith. "You're all here!"

Patience jumped up to embrace her. "Nan was due back from visiting her Grandmama, so I collected her and then Delia and here we are."

Nan hugged her next. "Oh, Ari. We've missed you so much."

"I missed you," Ari returned.

"I won't stay terribly long," Nan said. "I'm staying at my brother's house."

"You must stay here," Edith rejoined. "At least for a few days. Unless you've promised otherwise."

Nan blinked. "It wouldn't be an imposition?"

"Of course not. We need more youthful energy around here. Four beautiful young women. We'll have such fun."

"So, where is the ring?" Delia asked, glancing down at Arianna's gloved hands.

Ari could have cringed. Apparently, Patience has shared the news. "In my room," she replied hesitantly.

"Why is it in your room? If it was me, I would nev—" Delia stopped abruptly. "Have you not consented?"

"We're taking a little time," Ari said cautiously.

"I'm sorry," Patience fretted. "I didn't know."

Ari reached over to take hold of her hand. "You couldn't have. Besides, I'm so glad you're here." She looked at Nan. "I want to hear all your news."

"Well, there's not really any *news*," Nan said, smiling and blushing.

They all sat. "I want to hear everything," Ari said. "When you first knew. What he said, what you said. I was so happy when I heard."

"I'm going to order tea to be served," Edith said, rising. "Don't say anything too exciting without me."

Nan blushed more profusely. "There's nothing, really."

Edith chuckled as she walked out.

Delia smirked. "Honestly, you're all acting as if Thad Mansfield is the catch of the season."

Arianna reached forward to touch Nan's hand because the best way to handle Delia's pettiness was to ignore her. "He's been in love with you for ages, but when did you know that you loved him?"

"Last year, I suppose, but I was—"

"Too shy," Patience spoke up. "I first saw the spark between them at the Stephenson's reception. I saw their eyes meet," she said dreamily. "It was so sweet; I thought my heart might burst."

"What did your mother say?" Arianna asked Nan.

"She already knew, because he'd asked my father for my hand."

"Of course, he did," Ari said. "He would do it right."

"We're going to marry either the nineteenth or the twenty-sixth of December. Which do you think?"

"If it's an official engagement," Delia said, "where's the ring?"

Nan lifted her chin slightly. "He is saving up for it."

Delia looked incredulous. "He asked you to marry him without a ring to offer?"

"The ring is so unimportant," Ari said.

"I agree," Patience said.

"Unimportant?" Delia exclaimed. "Are you mad?"

"I think the nineteenth," Ari said to Nan.

"I think so too," Patience agreed. "Everyone is so caught up in the joy of the season. Besides, December nineteenth has a pretty ring to it, don't you think?"

"Well then, there is one pretty ring," Delia quipped.

"Oh, do shut up, Delia," Patience snapped.

It was so uncharacteristic of Patience that all their jaws went lax for the moment, and then it was all Arianna could do not to burst out laughing.

"What about you, Ari?" Delia asked. "You actually do manage to land the catch of the season and … what?"

"We're thinking on it."

"What does that mean? Thinking on it? Did he put the ring on your finger? Did he ask you to marry him?"

"I would prefer not to discuss it, and I would appreciate it if you would not tell anyone else."

"I already did," Delia replied. "I told my mother. I'm sure we all did."

Nan bit her lower lip and looked sheepish, and Patience nodded regretfully.

Damnation. How fast was word already spreading then? "He did put the ring on my finger, which I shared with Patience. It just … took me so by surprise."

"May we see it?" Delia pushed.

"Perhaps later," Ari said, keeping her voice as light as possible.

"How big is it?" Delia asked.

"Are you going to the ball at the Hotel Russell tonight?" Patience asked Ari.

Delia let out a huff of disgust. "I am beginning to feel invisible over here."

Ari fixed her with a look. "I see you very clearly." She looked at Patience. "We are. Marshall was to come for me at nine, but I'll send a note telling him I'll go with you."

"Oh no," Patience replied quickly. "We don't have invitations. They were frightfully hard to come by, I heard. I mean, well, not that we would have been."

"I'm not altogether certain we're going either," Ari fibbed. "He may have mentioned another ball. Let me find out what the plan is. In fact, I'll send a note right now," she said, rising.

"I don't have a fine enough gown for the ball at the Hotel Russell anyway," Nan said.

"It's true," Delia agreed. "She hasn't had anything new in two years."

Nan colored with embarrassment. "It has not been two years," she stammered.

"She will be fine," Patience repeated, giving Delia a black look.

"Who will be fine?" Edith asked as she came back in. Behind her, one of the maids pushed the teacart in.

"Nan," Patience replied. "We were discussing the ball tonight at the Hotel Russell. We don't have invitations, but—"

"She hasn't anything appropriate to wear," Delia said sadly, "even if we could wrangle invitations."

Ari scowled at her, but Delia failed to notice. "I don't even know if we were going," Ari reminded them all. "And I'm not going without you."

"Oh, you're going," Edith said. "You're all going. I'll arrange it. And after tea, Nan and I will go to the dressmaker's shop. I'm sure there will be something readymade that will do very nicely."

"Oh, I couldn't," Nan burst.

"I insist," Edith said calmly. "It will be great fun and it will be my treat."

Ari smiled gratefully at her aunt and received a discreet wink in return.

Delia leaned forward to select a delicate sandwich from the tray. "I should take some of Wynonna's gowns for you. You're about the same size, and she looks so dreadful in everything she puts on, she usually ends up staying home."

"Oh, Delia," Nan objected.

"What?"

"She's your sister," Patience said sharply. "And a wonderfully sweet person."

Delia shrugged her shoulders. "Who looks like a horse."

Edith gasped. "Delia Bradford! That is a terrible thing to say!"

"But true," Delia said sweetly. "Why do you think she was named Wynnie?"

"It is not true," Ari retorted. "You just enjoy being cruel to her."

"Let us change the subject," Edith said stiffly. "Before the afternoon is spoilt."

"Have you been to the British-Franco exhibition?" Nan asked after a strained silence.

"Yes," Edith replied, relaxing slightly. "It's marvelous. You must experience it."

"I want to! There's so much to do this summer."

Chapter Eighteen

E merson watched Zan's fascination as they rode through the streets of London.

"There are so many people," Zan murmured. "Will I ever belong here?"

"This is where you came from. Besides, you told me yourself that you couldn't return to the jungle."

Zan looked at the older man. "Because I don't belong there anymore does not mean I belong here."

"I truly believe you will adjust."

"Is Arianna here?"

Emerson could have sighed. The subject of Arianna had not come up for days. He'd hoped Zan was beginning to forget her. "She spends time with an aunt and uncle who have a house here but, as I told you, her Uncle Sullivan is her primary guardian, and they do not live in London.

"Where do they live?"

"Northampton, sixty or so miles from here."

"When will you write to her?"

"I already have. It was sent as soon as we docked."

"So, we'll go see her now."

"I've asked if she will see you, but it will be up to her. If she will not see you, she will write, I'm sure."

Zan frowned darkly. "I don't want her to write."

"I know."

Zan looked forward and then out the window. "Will she want to see me?"

"I cannot say. I know that there was a man who was interested in marrying her."

Zan looked back at Emerson, alarmed.

"That was the case before she came to Africa. I don't believe she was confident that she wanted to marry the chap."

"Why did you not tell me?"

Emerson bobbed his head back and forth, considering how to reply. "I was hoping you might forget her."

"I will not forget her!"

"Zan, you need to understand that Arianna has her own life and her own mind. She's a modern young woman. Beyond asking to see her, there's really nothing else we can do."

"What does that mean? Modern?"

"It means she won't be ordered about. That's not to say she can't be swayed by loved ones, but she won't be told what to do and what to say. Honestly, I cannot see her settling with this man who wants to marry her. He's wealthy and from a good family, a fine looking enough fellow, and most young ladies would likely jump at the opportunity, but Arianna is not most young ladies. Not many of them would have come halfway around the world to see Africa."

Zan looked out the window again. "She is supposed to be with me."

"You do yourself a disservice if you focus only on Ari. After all, if it's meant to be, it will be. Don't you think?"

Zan was quiet for several seconds. "I don't know."

"One other thing, Zan—"

Zan looked at him. "Just one? Do you promise?"

Emerson grinned. "Your surname," he said carefully. "In our society, people primarily go by their surnames. Yours is Shaffer. Are you comfortable being called Mr. Shaffer?"

Zan hesitated and then nodded. "It's who I am."

"Yes, it is. And although your father had the same name, he is long gone, and that name is yours alone. It's fine to be called Zan, but your name by birth was Sebastian Shaffer."

"I like Zan."

"So do I. I'm not trying to change it. We just need to discover that ground where you and society can find a comfortable fit." The carriage stopped in front of Lord Bluford's Park Street home.

"We're here." Zan didn't reply, but Emerson saw the tension in him. "I'll be with you every step of the way," he said soothingly. "Remember, when in doubt, say nothing. That's easy, isn't it? When asked a question, try and answer, of course, but do not feel the need to expound too much and do not feel the need to make conversation if you do not feel like it. People who go on and on are very tedious." Zan gave him a pointed look and Emerson chuckled. "As you can attest to, I'm sure."

The driver opened the door for them.

"It will be fine," Emerson said quietly. "I promise you."

A pleasant looking butler in his fifties opened the door for them. "Mr. Emerson," the man greeted with a bow of his head. "Lord Bluford is expecting you."

"Thank you, Cline. May I present Mr. Shaffer," Emerson said as he stepped in.

Zan followed Emerson, although his gaze was drawn upwards to the high, paneled ceilings.

"Mr. Shaffer," the butler greeted. "How do you do, sir?"

"How do you do," Zan returned. He'd been instructed how to do this, and he had practiced, but the reality was more nerve-wracking than he'd imagined.

"If you'll come this way, gentlemen." Cline led them into a salon and excused himself to get Lord Bluford.

When he was gone, John gave Zan a reassuring nod. "You did perfectly, and you're among friends."

Zan stretched his neck. John was always telling him he did perfectly, but it didn't feel like it. It never felt like it.

"Do you want to sit?" John asked.

Zan shook his head and looked around the room at the furniture and the lavish décor. This did not seem like a place where someone lived. He heard footsteps and turned to the door as an older man appeared. He was a tall, lean gentleman with an energetic air about him.

"You're here," the man exulted.

"Lord Bluford, may I present my friend, Zan Shaffer?" Emerson said.

"It is a great pleasure," Lord Bluford replied as he came closer. He offered his hand.

"It is a pleasure to meet you," Zan returned uncertainly as he shook the man's hand.

"I'm so pleased that you've finally arrived." He turned to Emerson. "John. You look well." They shook hands.

"I am well, sir. Yourself?"

"Could not be better. I've been enjoying some of the Olympic Games. I'm sure you're glad to be back in time to see some of them."

"Yes, indeed."

"How was the voyage?"

"Smooth," Emerson replied. He glanced at Zan. "It was long of course, but we had much to do."

"I admit, I cannot wait to hear every last detail," Bluford said, directing it to Zan. "How everything unfolded, your perceptions and your memories. It's the most remarkable story I ever heard."

Ironically, it was John who had grown tense at Lord Bluford's zeal. Zan glanced his way and tried to send a silent message that he would be alright. "I hope it does not disappoint."

"Oh, that won't be possible. Shall we have wine in celebration, or tea, perhaps?"

"Tea would be welcome," Emerson spoke up. "And then perhaps, we could rest a while?"

"Of course. I'll have you shown to your rooms and have tea sent up. How would that be?"

"That would be excellent," Emerson replied.

"We can chat at dinner. Say at seven?"

"Perfect," Emerson said.

Zan realized that John was trying to buffer his shock. The odd thing was he suddenly no longer felt shocked. Lord Bluford may have been a bit eccentric, but Zan sensed great kindness in the man, as well. And while his home had an opulence Zan had never imagined, it was just a place where he was staying briefly.

"Zan, is there anything you don't care for, as far as food goes?" Bluford asked.

"I will try anything," Zan replied.

"That's the stuff! Excellent! Then if you'll follow me," he said, starting off.

"Shall I, sir?" Cline asked from the doorway.

Bluford turned back to them. "Cline will show you to your rooms, and I'll see you at dinner. We needn't dress if you don't want."

Zan looked at Emerson, confused by the statement.

"Thank you," Emerson replied. "We do need to acquire more of a wardrobe for Mr. Shaffer."

"Then it will be come as you are. And we'll set up something with my tailor tomorrow."

"Thank you, Lord Bluford," Emerson replied.

The old man nodded magnanimously. "Just so pleased you're here," he said to Zan. "Both of you," he added, directing it to Emerson with a smile.

"Thank you," Zan replied. For once, the response had come naturally.

"This way, if you please, gentlemen," Cline said, leading onward. He walked with a moderate pace and excellent posture, Zan noticed. "This is your room, Mr. Shaffer," he announced when he opened a door on the second floor.

Zan entered what seemed an enormous room.

"And your room is across the hall, sir," Cline said to Emerson as he walked over to open the door. "Shall I arrange for a valet for each of you?"

"I think not," Emerson said. "At least, not for the moment."

"Very good, sir. Is there anything else you need then?"

"I think we're fine. Thank you."

Cline started off, but after a few steps he turned back. "He knows how to call for someone?" he asked quietly.

Emerson nodded, and Cline walked on. John leaned against Zan's open door. "Is it large enough, do you think, or shall we request another?" Zan looked shocked and Emerson chuckled. "If you need something, you pull this," he said, pointing to the bell pull. "And someone will come. They've also offered a valet if you want one. A valet helps dress you."

"I dress myself."

Emerson nodded. "Why don't you rest a bit, and I'll see you at dinner. I'm just across the hall if you need me." Zan nodded, and John closed the door.

Zan made a slow circuit of the room, halting when he caught his image in the mirror. He went closer to it, observing how he looked and moved. It was uncanny to see himself as if from the outside. This was how others would see him. This is how Arianna would see him.

~~~

"There you are," Patience said when Ari came into her room that evening. Between visiting and dinner and getting ready for the ball, they hadn't had a moment alone. "Finally! I'm dying to know what has happened."

Ari leaned against the wall next to Patience who sat at a vanity table. "I told you how I feel."

"Yes, but ... your note," Patience said, turning to face Arianna. "I thought you'd reconsidered and accepted."

"The conversation went something like this. He said, 'I see you're in one piece.' I said, 'Yes, I am.' He asked, sarcastically I might add, if they'd found the wild man. To which I said yes, they had. He was shocked by that. I explained that they closed in on him and shot him with their blow darts, which were poisoned. He asked if I was with the party who found him, and I said I was not. Which is the truth." She paused. "I know this is boring, but I have to explain it all."

"It is *not* boring," Patience declared.

"He then asked if I was done with my wild traveling, and I said that I had no plans to go anywhere at present. 'Good,' he said, 'Then I wish you to have this.' And he reached into his pocket and pulled out a small box."

"The ring," Patience said breathlessly.

"Yes. The ring. Which he pulled out of the box and put on my finger explaining that he'd already had it sized. I really don't remember what the next thing he said was, but he was going on and on about us coming here, and the rest of the season, and he said he wanted to go show my uncle the ring." She paused. "Are you hearing what was not asked?"

"Will you marry me," Patience said slowly.

Ari nodded and then shrugged. "He did not ask. Will you be my wife? Will you marry me? Would you care to go by the name of Derringer? Nothing. None of it. He did not ask." Ari pushed off the wall and walked over to the bed and sat.

Patience followed.

"The first night here, we were supposed to go to a party, but I knew that I had to speak with him first. Before we went into public together. I had to tell him my feelings. My reservations. Aunt Edith had advised for me to ask for more time rather than reject him."

Patience nodded.

"Unfortunately, the conversation got heated. He was insulted that I wasn't certain I wanted to marry him. And that wasn't even the worst of what I felt."

"How were things left?"

"He felt insulted and so he insulted me back. I should be honored that he would marry me when he could get a much heftier dowry elsewhere. Oh, and there was the fact that I am an American and my father is in trade."

Patience huffed in objection. "How crass of him!"

"He declared he would go on to the party, and I would stay home and think about my future."

Patience frowned.

"He also arranged for us to meet the next afternoon, a carriage ride where we would iron things out."

"Did you go?"

Ari nodded. "I did. He's granted me a little more time to decide. We are not announcing anything just yet and I hope we never will."

"Then you're still thinking—" Patience said hesitantly.

"How to reject him without receiving a black eye in the process."

"Oh, Ari, he would never strike you."

"I don't mean that. I mean that he found out Sebastian took me."

Patience felt her breath catch. "No! How?"

"He approached a member of the Royal Society and asked questions. Claimed that he knew the facts. And I had given him just enough information to look as if he did, so the man blurted it all out."

"All of it?"

"That I'd been taken," Ari replied just above a whisper. "That's all they know."

"What did Marshall say?"

"He demanded to know why I hadn't told him the truth. Then he went on to say how terrible it looks and how much damage it could do to my reputation if people found out. He says I'm safe, of course, if I marry him."

Patience found herself at a loss for words. After all, this was Marshall Derringer they were discussing, and he'd resorted to virtual blackmail? Or had she misunderstood? "And if you don't?"

"That is the question," Ari replied darkly. "To be honest, I have spent every day of the last week avoiding a renewal of the conversation. You cannot imagine how taxing it's been."

Patience drew breath to speak, but a knock at the door distracted her. "Yes?" she called.

The door opened and Nan stepped in wearing a new gown of indigo blue.

"Oh, Nan," Ari said, popping up. "You look wonderful."

"You do," Patience agreed. "You look absolutely beautiful!"

"I've never had anything so nice," Nan exulted, her eyes shining. "And your aunt bought two others as well. I told her I couldn't accept such an extravagant gift, but she insisted."

"I'm so glad," Ari replied.

Nan came closer to join them. "I'm so excited about tonight. I can hardly believe we got invitations and we're really going."

"Speaking of excited," Patience said. "Is it very strange to realize you'll be married in a matter of months?"

Nan nodded, but she couldn't stop smiling. "It is."

"This may be an odd question," Ari said, with a curious expression, "But can you imagine not marrying him?"

Nan pondered a moment. "No. I know it's the right thing. We are meant to be together."

"I hear you talking," Delia called from down the hall. "Come into my room. I'm nearly ready."

"In other words," Ari said quietly. "Enough about you, let's talk about me."

The girls giggled as they left the room.

As expected, Delia was seated at her vanity, staring into her mirror as she applied lip color out of a small pot. Dressed in a gown of white and silver, she looked as breathtaking as she usually did, but when she rose, it was apparent how exquisite the gown really was.

"It's so beautiful," Nan admired.

"It is, isn't it?" Delia said, glancing down at herself.

"It really is," Patience and Arianna agreed.

"Girls?" Edith called. "Are you ready?"

Ari stepped back into the hall. "We're coming, Aunt Edith."

Chapter Nineteen

Marshall went to meet the occupants of the Vinson's carriage as they were assisted down, "Ladies," he said. "And gentleman," he added with a nod toward Lord Vinson. "Good evening."

"Good evening," Nan returned as she stepped from the carriage, her gaze on the imposing, eight-story Hotel Russell, which seemed to take up an entire block and was lit from every window.

"Mr. Derringer," Delia said as she followed.

Arianna was third to be helped down. Marshall smiled warmly and offered her his arm. She slipped a gloved hand through, and his other hand came down upon hers. "You look wonderful," he said.

"Thank you." She looked at the hotel with its terracotta façade and sculpted balconies. She'd seen it before, but lit up as it was, with a steady flow of beautiful people entering or waiting on the front portico, it was extraordinary.

"So, you've been catching up with your friends?"

"Yes. It's wonderful to see Nan so happy."

"Just as a recently betrothed young lady ought to look," he said lightly.

A surge of guilt hit hard. It hadn't occurred to her what an ungrateful wretch she probably seemed. She noticed Delia watching them.

"It's quite the glittering assemblage inside," Marshall said, speaking up to include the others. "The place was designed by Charles Fitzroy Doll. I understand he's replicating its dining room in the next White Star venture."

"What's a White Star venture?" Patience asked.

"White Star is a ship line. William Pirrie is forever going on about their ships."

"I know him," Wilbur spoke up. "And his partner, Ismay. They built the Olympic and are working on an even bigger one."

"Yes, the Titanic," Marshall said. "That's the one that will supposedly have an identical dining room. The plans are impressive. Whether they can pull it off or not remains to be seen, of course."

As they entered the lavish lobby, Ari's gaze was drawn to a massive chandelier and the long staircase. In the enormous, many-columned ballroom, the ball was well under way.

"I can't wait to dance with you," Marshall said under his breath. "It seems forever since I've held you closely enough."

Arianna took a moment to find her voice. "I'm looking forward to it as well." She couldn't recall a time she'd ever truly felt like a couple until that moment. It was a surprisingly pleasant feeling.

"Champagne for all?" Wilbur asked.

"Yes, please," Ari said.

As he signaled for a waiter, Patience gasped and grabbed Arianna's arm, having seen something amazing. "Ari, look!"

Ari followed her gaze to the other side of the ballroom where King Edward and Queen Alexandra stood surrounded by their entourage. It was a rare thing to be this close.

Patience blinked in astonishment. "I have attended a ball with the king and queen!"

"Yes, but it's not polite to be a namedropper," Ari teased. "What would your mother say?"

"She would say what I just said. My daughter attended a ball with the king and queen." Patience motioned to Nan, who was awestruck even before she'd realized they were in the presence of royalty.

Waiters were there with champagne, and Marshall accepted a glass and passed it to Arianna. He took another and looked around to make sure the others all had a glass. "To a wonderful night," he toasted, raising his glass.

A few hours and glasses of champagne later, Ari felt lighter and more settled than she had in a long while. Marshall had enjoyed her company and listened to her opinions as if they were valued. His parents and sisters had been gracious as well.

"Let's step outside for a bit," Ari suggested, eager to cool off.

"Of course."

They found an empty veranda and appreciated the night air before he spoke again. "I want you to know that whatever it takes to make you happy, I will endeavor to see it done."

She blinked, touched by the sentiment. "That's kind of you to say."

"I mean it. I want this marriage with all my heart." He paused. "Are you … less put off by the idea?"

"I am," she replied carefully. "But it occurs to me that we haven't talked certain practicalities."

"Such as?"

"My involvements such as the ragged school—"

"Oh, I know you enjoy your worthy causes, and it's laudable." He shrugged. "As long as the time spent on it is reasonable and the project is what I would consider safe and seemly, I do not object."

She was put off by the reply, especially when she hadn't finished her thought, but before she could speak again, Delia joined them.

"There you are," Delia said, directing it to Ari. "Am I intruding?"

"No," Arianna quickly replied. Actually, Delia had never been so welcome. Ari didn't want the evening ruined when it had been so pleasant. "I need to be excused for a bit, anyway."

"Patience and Nan just went that way as well," Delia said. "Which I have to admit was a relief. I adore them, of course, but you would think that they'd never been at a ball before. They're so awestruck."

"It's perfectly understandable," Arianna rejoined. She glanced at Marshall. "Perhaps the two of you could dance."

"I'm too warm at the moment," Marshall replied.

Delia shrugged. "I am overly warm myself. It's why I stepped out."

"If you'll excuse me," Ari said.

Marshall gave her a loving smile. "I'll be right here waiting."

~~~

"The two of you seem happy," Delia commented as she crossed to the railing.

"Yes. It's been a good night."

Delia snapped open her fan and began to cool herself. "Why the sudden change, I wonder?"

"What do you mean?"

"All her reticence about marrying you."

His pleasant expression vanished. "What did she say?"

"Nothing terrible. Only that she was taking some time to decide."

He shrugged. "I did spring it on her rather abruptly."

"Most women would have been thrilled."

"I don't want most women." He downed the last of his champagne.

The remark stung. He'd meant it to sting. "Only heiresses?"

"Only heiresses named Arianna who are clever and beautiful and have a pleasing nature."

"That does narrow it down considerably," Delia replied as lightly as she could manage.

"What about you, Miss Bradford? Why don't you choose one of the men drooling over you?"

She shrugged one shoulder seductively. "Perhaps I will."

"You shouldn't toy with them too long. They might lose interest."

She looked at him with an amused expression. "With me?"

He chuckled. "Are you sure you're giving them enough encouragement to keep them firmly on the hook?"

"It doesn't take that much," she said.

He glanced behind them to make sure they were alone. "Are you never worried that someone might talk? That a man might have too much to drink and forget he's a gentleman?"

She prickled with an uncomfortable heat. "I haven't the faintest notion what you're talking about."

He chuckled.

"Honestly, Marshall, just because you and I have shared … a moment or two."

"You're saying I'm special?"

She opened her mouth in strenuous objection and puffed indignation. "You didn't really think—"

"Sometimes I don't," he joked. "I do wish they'd bring a tray around. I could use another glass."

~~~

"Marshall is obviously in love with you," Nan said in the plush lounge area of the ladies room. A counter and chairs lined the wall and there were large bouquets of flower arrangements in the corners.

"He does seem completely smitten," Patience agreed. "I've never seen him so devoted."

"Nor have I," Ari admitted.

"Enjoy it," Patience urged. "You don't have to make a decision right now, but nor should you question every feeling you have and every word he says."

Ari nodded. That was what she had been doing.

"Let's go for refreshments, shall we?" Patience asked.

"Yes," Nan exclaimed.

"I'll go tell Marshall," Ari said, when they reached the corridor. She walked back into the ballroom. She smiled at her aunt and uncle who were chatting with friends, and she nodded across the room to Beatrix, who was watching her with a bemused expression. *Mother-in-law*, she thought. Perhaps she wouldn't be as insufferable as she'd feared.

She stepped onto the balcony interrupting Delia and Marshall in what appeared to be a strangely intimate looking conversation. They had their backs to her, but there was something so disturbingly sensual about their expressions in profile.

Marshall turned with a strained smile. "Darling."

Good Lord! His earlier devotion and adoration had been an act. She was surely the most foolish and gullible creature who ever walked the face of the earth. "I came to tell you we're going for refreshments," she said levelly.

"I think I'll go find the others," Delia said quickly. And guiltily. "Excuse me." She left avoiding Ari's questioning gaze.

"Arianna?" Marshall said, crossing to her. "You look bothered. What is it?"

"When were you intimate with Delia?"

He huffed with offense. "What? What are you talking about?"

"Was it when I was gone to Africa or before?"

"Arianna—" he objected.

She crossed to the railing and squeezed its wrought iron. "Is it your view that whatever can be kept discreet is acceptable?" Her eyes filled with tears, which made her furious with herself. She didn't even love him!

"Stop it."

She blinked and dabbed beneath her eyes, determined to get her emotions under control. She turned back to him. "I believe it's a fair question."

He took a moment to respond. "Discretion is extremely important, of course. I would never willingly hurt you. Some men do not care, but I do,"

She felt a core of cold inside her center. "And would that same rule apply to me, should we marry?"

He drew back, thrown by the question. "No! Absolutely not! It's different for a woman."

"Is it?"

"You know it is. This is an absurd conversation."

"When were you intimate with her?"

"I wasn't!"

She stared, unblinking.

"Not the way you're thinking," he added.

"You have no idea what I'm thinking."

"This has been a perfectly delightful night. Do not spoil it now."

"It's already spoiled, and I did not do it. It may seem foolish to you, but honesty is important to me. Honor is important." She paused and raked him over, head to toe and back again. "*You* possess neither."

He grabbed her arm with a brutal grip. "Stop it. You are overreacting. You got something in your head, and you are overreacting. There is nothing between Delia Bradford and myself, and quite frankly, I am through with this insipid conversation."

She jerked away from him.

He seemed to remember himself. He tugged at his collar. "I suppose I should be flattered that you're jealous."

She shook her head. "I am disgusted, not jealous."

His eyes narrowed. "We are through with this conversation."

"I also wish to be through with your company," she stated. She turned and walked away before he could respond. She felt foolish and conspicuous as she made her way back to her aunt and uncle. She was a fool to have believed him. It had been the same with her father. She'd put faith in him only to be used, and that betrayal had been devastating. What if she actually loved someone who then betrayed her? Would she even survive it?

"There you are," Edith said. "I think we're—" She broke off. "What's wrong?"

Ari shook her head. "I'm going with you."

"Why?"

"I have a headache." She suddenly felt too exhausted for explanations, but she didn't want to ruin the evening for Patience and Nan. Delia, of course, could jump off the balcony for all she cared. "Would you mind telling the others? I want them to stay and have a wonderful time."

"Yes," Edith agreed. "They should."

Wilbur looked from Arianna to his wife. "Ari and I will wait for you outside."

Edith nodded and walked off, glancing at the Derringers as she went. Marshall had rejoined them, and his face looked like a thundercloud. Obviously, he and Ari had quarreled again. It was a shame when things seemed to be going so well.

~~~

"Did you have another tiff?" Susan smirked.

Marshall glared at her. "Shut up."

"You did, didn't you? Was it about that Miss Bradford? I told you about her," Susan said, signaling for a waiter. "She's nothing but trouble."

"You don't have to tell me anything," Marshall retorted. "Do you really think I don't know when a female is in heat over me? But I should not be penalized for her infatuation."

Susan took a glass from the tray. "Do you want one?"

Marshall took one while sending her a hard look.

"If I may be perfectly honest," Susan said. "I don't think the two of you are a good match."

He gave her a withering look. "Delia and I?"

She returned the look. "You and Arianna, of course! She wears her heart on her sleeve. You'd be better served with someone with a cooler head."

"When I want your opinion—"

"I'm only trying to help," she interrupted. "For all our bickering, I do care. But the truth is, you have always wanted what you wanted until you got it. Remember those coins Grandpapa had that Louise wanted? Once she wanted them, *you* became adamant about having them, and you made such a stink that they gave them to you instead. Only then you didn't care anything about them."

"What in blazes do coins have to do with anything?"

"It's exactly the same thing. You've made up your mind that you want Arianna, but what if you're just being stubborn because she's resisting?"

"I'm not."

"Do you love her?"

"Of course, I love her. What a stupid question!"

"For your own sake, think about it," Susan suggested.

He seethed. "For your own sake, shut up."

~~~

"Do you think they had a disagreement?" Nan asked Patience.

Patience looked over at Marshall. He looked positively morose. "They must have."

Delia, too, looked at Marshall. Unfortunately, he happened to glance their way at the same instant and leveled a malevolent scowl at her. She turned her head, but her cheeks burned, and her stomach knotted.

Chapter Twenty

A ri lay curled up on her side the next morning trying to summon the will to rise and face the day. She wanted to tell Delia to leave and never come back, but if she did, she would have to explain why to the others, and that would spoil the few weeks left for Nan. That she would not do. Nan didn't have many opportunities like this.

Ari's breath caught at the thought of Nan's brother. They could go and visit Ben and Lara. It wouldn't take long to arrange. Nan would like it, Patience would be happy to go along, and Delia would want nothing to do with it which made it a perfect plan. The three of them would go and stay for a few days until she decided what to do next.

When she went down to breakfast, she was relieved to see only her aunt and uncle in attendance. She knew they were concerned about her because she hadn't explained anything on the way home, nor had they pushed. Aunt Edith had wanted to, but every time she'd begun, Uncle Wilbur had introduced a new subject.

"Good morning," Ari said.

"Good morning, dear," her aunt returned.

Ari went to the sideboard and helped herself to poached eggs and a crumpet.

Wilbur lowered his paper. "Care to hear what happened at the Olympic marathon?"

Ari sat, all ears. "Yes."

"It was held the day before yesterday, which was blisteringly hot, as you'll recall, and the race didn't begin until two thirty." He shook his head in puzzlement. "Wouldn't you think they'd start earlier when it was cooler?"

"A twenty-five-mile race in July? Definitely."

"Ah, but it wasn't the usual twenty-five miles," he said. "You see, the royal family insisted that it begin at Windsor, in front of the nursery, and end in front of the king's box in the stadium. That made the course longer by more than a mile."

"Are you teasing me?"

"I am not. The race ended up at twenty-six miles, three hundred and eighty-five yards. Have you ever heard anything so ludicrous? Think of it. Every other marathon in Olympic history will be twenty-five miles. Oh, except at the London 1908 games. That one was twenty-six-miles plus three hundred and eighty-five yards."

"You were telling her what happened," Edith said.

"Yes, yes. So one of the fellows racing, an Italian named Dorando Pietri, a small man, came from behind after twenty miles or so. It had been two of our athletes leading the way until then, but they'd faded. So Pietri takes the lead with an American chap named Johnny Hayes close behind."

Ari cringed. "Is this going to be another ugly American story?"

Wilbur waggled his eyebrows, refusing to answer straight out. "Pietri finally reaches the stadium where that final lap is taken—"

"Poor man," Edith said. "The paper said that he seemed bewildered with his hair sticking straight up and dust flecks all over him. He hardly knew where he was."

Ari leaned back, captivated by the story.

"But the crowd was with him," Wilbur said. "Cheering and chanting, willing him on. And then ... all went silent, which was followed by a collective gasp, because Pietri got turned around in his confusion and started going the wrong direction."

"No," Ari breathed.

"Yes. Then he collapsed. Officials went to his aid and lifted him up, but he fell again. Now here comes the American, closing fast. The crowd, other than the Americans, of course, is pulling for the Italian." Wilbur shrugged. "In the end, the officials took Pietri's arms and brought him across the finish line."

Ari looked from him to Edith and back again, puzzled. "But they can't do that."

"No. It was categorically against the rules, and the poor chap was disqualified. The queen still awarded him with a gilded silver cup though. Afraid he stole the glory, much to the Americans displeasure."

"It's a shame that these games have been so bad for our relations," Edith mused.

"Yes," Wilbur agreed. "As my lovely, half-American niece said, it has been ugly."

"And speaking of ugly," Edith said slowly. "Perhaps we should discuss—"

"Marshall?" Ari interjected.

Edith gasped and clapped her hand to her mouth to hide her smile. "I meant the situation, of course!"

"I know. I just thought a little humor couldn't hurt."

"No, indeed," Wilbur agreed.

"Can you tell us what happened?" Edith asked.

"There's not that much to tell, except that once again, I find myself desiring to put some distance between us."

"You quarreled last night, didn't you?"

"Not exactly," Ari replied as she toyed with her food. "Our values are just very different." She looked up at her aunt. "I'd like to go with Nan to see her brother and sister-in-law and spend a few days there. I'm sure Patience will go too."

"And Delia?"

"I don't believe she'll want to go."

Her aunt peered at her thoughtfully.

"She'll probably return to their townhouse."

"Is Derringer pressuring you for an answer?" Wilbur asked.

"He absolutely believes I'll marry him. But no, he's not pushing for us to announce it yet."

Edith gave her a bolstering smile. "You should try the sweet rolls. They're delicious."

Ari knew she'd been granted a reprieve from any further explanation. And from Aunt Edith, of all people, who desperately wanted to know every word that had been spoken. "I think I will," she said, rising.

~~~

At ten until eight in the morning, Zan walked out of his room at the same time John did.

"Good morning," Emerson greeted. "Sleep well?"

"Yes. And you?"

"No complaints."

They walked down the hall and started down the stairs. "Where did you send the letter for Arianna?"

"Northampton."

"When will we hear from her? How long does it take?"

At the base of the staircase, Emerson turned to face him. "I know how badly you want to see her but dwelling on it will not help. Try and focus on the hour and the task in front of you, whatever that is and may hold. You still have a great deal to learn and experience."

"Good morning, gentlemen," Dalton Bluford greeted.

Both men turned to him, and their collective gaze was drawn to the auburn-haired beauty walking at his side. She was perhaps twenty years of age with glowing porcelain skin, pale blue eyes, and great poise.

"May I introduce my granddaughter, Vanessa?"

Emerson bowed his head. "Lady Vanessa, it's a great pleasure."

"It's an honor to meet you, Mr. Emerson. I've been looking forward to it."

"This is Mr. Shaffer," Lord Bluford spoke up.

She smiled. "How do you do, Mr. Shaffer?"

"Very well, thank you," Zan replied with a slight bow. "I am pleased to meet you." From the corner of his eye, he saw Emerson's satisfaction and felt emboldened by it.

"I thought I would spend a few days with Grandfather. I hope you don't mind my company."

"We're delighted by it," Emerson replied.

"Shall we go into breakfast?" Bluford said, gesturing onward. "I, for one, am famished."

"When are you not?" she teased.

"Coffee or tea, my lady?" a maid asked her as she was seated.

"Coffee, this morning, I think."

"So, Emerson," Bluford said as he took some of the proffered eggs. "What is on the agenda today."

"Sightseeing."

A dish of sausages was offered to Zan, and he took some.

"What do you think of the city so far, Mr. Shaffer?" Vanessa asked.

"I find it fascinating," he replied.

"We have some lovely parks. Have you had a chance to visit any yet?"

"No. Not yet."

"Coffee or tea, sir?" a young, pretty maid asked Zan.

"Tea, please," he replied.

"Today might be an excellent day to visit a park," Emerson said, "Perhaps you'd care to join us?" he asked Vanessa.

"I would love to."

Zan kept his face impassive, although the idea made him uncomfortable.

"Will you attend any late season balls?" Vanessa asked, directing it to Emerson.

"I don't know. It's possible, I suppose. I may defer to your judgment on that."

"I would be so pleased to help." She glanced at Zan and then looked down at her plate, still smiling.

Chapter Twenty-One

Z an couldn't tear his eyes away from the crumbling tenements and hollow-eyed residents that congregated on broken steps and street corners. Filthy, half-naked children dodged here and there. There was a stench everywhere. They were in a comfortable carriage, so they could keep going, but these people were trapped. He saw it in their faces, and he felt it as unmistakably as when a predator had stalked him in the jungle.

They'd been guests of Lord Bluford for a week. Not long enough to get accustomed to the luxuries they'd been afforded, but this poverty was shocking. "Where are we?"

"It's called St. Giles. It's better than it used to be, but as you can see—"

"Why do they stand about?"

"Some are without work. Some of them *are* working, although not at what we might call above-board jobs. The belligerent ones, such as the women we saw fighting, probably started the day with gin."

"So many of them," Zan mused.

"Oh, yes. There are far more poor than well-off. Inordinately so. The majority of London is made up of working-class men and women and the poor. The way Lord Bluford lives is enjoyed by a very small percentage of the population."

"Would I have lived here?"

"I don't know."

"But I might have?"

"It's possible. We can still research and possibly discover where you came from. You may have family left here."

Zan had previously declined the offer, but he suddenly wanted to know. "How would we find out?"

"We'll hire an investigator. He'll pursue public records, birth records and so forth. Then he'll draw closer to the communities the records indicate and ask questions until he answers."

Zan was quiet for a few minutes. "May we stop and walk?" he asked.

"Absolutely." Emerson leaned forward to communicate with the driver. "Are we far from Kensal Green?"

"No, sir," the driver replied.

"We'd like to go there."

The driver tapped the brim of his hat.

"Ah, yes," Emerson said when he'd stepped down from the carriage. "It feels good to stretch the legs." They began walking. "I hope you don't find it too strange to walk in a cemetery, but it's safer than the streets around here and peaceful."

"I don't mind."

They walked in silence for a good distance. "You seem bothered," John commented.

"Why do some people have so much and others so little?"

"That is an excellent question, one that has been posed countless times before. By everyone … except the wealthy usually," John added with a wry smile. "In every civilized society, there has always been a ranking of classes, and that ranking revolves around the possession of money and land. With money and land comes title and respect and power. The wealthy tend to think of their status as a birthright, as their due. The middle class generally aspires to it. People of the working class are too busy just getting by to give it that much thought, and the poor too often feel there's no hope of rising above their stations. With hopelessness comes anger, despair, or resignation. That is why there is such an epidemic of drunkenness amongst the poor."

Zan stopped. "What will happen to me if Lord Bluford wants me to leave?"

"You will come live with me and my family. We do not live as Bluford lives, but we are more than comfortable." He paused. "I told you that before."

Zan nodded.

"Perhaps tomorrow, we'll travel to my home and spend a few days."

"I would like that," Zan said thickly.

"My wife would, as well."

"Jane. But I will call her Mrs. Emerson."

"Yes, that's the social norm. Of course, five minutes after she meets you, she'll ask you to call her Jane."

Zan smiled. "I would like to understand where I came from."

"Then we'll hire the investigator and get some answers."

Chapter Twenty-Two

Patience grabbed Ari's hand as the open-air carriage, driven by Ben Saint James, Nan's eldest brother, entered the Rotherhithe Tunnel. It had recently opened after four years of construction. Ben, one of the engineers of the project, had been involved from start to finish.

"Welcome to the largest subaqueous tunnel in the world," he said proudly.

"It does not seem very large," Patience fretted.

"Ah but think of the challenge it was to design and construct a tunnel beneath the river."

They took a sharp turn, nearly a right angle, and Patience's grip tightened.

"It's an adventure," Ari reminded her with a smile.

"You're more adventurous than I am," Patience fretted.

"We're now under the riverbed, ladies," Ben stated a few minutes later.

"That is amazing," Nan marveled.

"You should be so proud, Ben," Ari said. "It's a great accomplishment."

"I am. We all are."

Patience breathed easier when there was light ahead, meaning the end of the tunnel. "Thank you for showing us."

Ben chuckled. "When we get back home and you have a glass of wine or two, you may even be able to say that like you mean it."

When they walked back into the house on Elephant Lane, the scent of cooked beef and onions lingered in the air.

"We're back," Ben called.

They made their way into the kitchen where Lara, his wife, was snapping green beans at the table. A full decanter of wine and glasses sat awaiting them. "How was it?" she asked. Lara was a petite woman with dark, curly hair and luminous eyes.

"It was remarkable," Ari exclaimed.

"I'm so proud of my brother," Nan said as she sat and began helping with the beans.

Ben filled glasses and handed them around. "Don't ask Patience about it just yet," he said. "We're going to let her have a glass of wine ... and hopefully she'll unclench her fists."

"I wasn't that pathetic," Patience objected.

Ari waggled and massaged her hand and gave her a mournful look.

"Honestly, Ari! You're such a tease," Patience laughed.

"I recall how thrilling it was the first time I went through," Lara said. "Make that the first dozen or so times I went through."

"Oh, don't listen to her," Ben scoffed. "Next she'll be telling you I drag her down there every day."

Ari couldn't help but smile at the affection between them. She knew from Nan that Lara hadn't been able to sustain a pregnancy, but it hadn't made her bitter. In fact, she always seemed happy and gracious. She and Ben shared a love, like her aunt and uncle's, that would withstand the heartbreak of childlessness.

Lara pushed the bowl of beans back. "Let's go sit outside and play cards."

"Let's do," Nan said enthusiastically.

"If you don't mind, I'll just watch," Patience said as she rose.

"You mean until your trembling subsides?" Ben teased.

"Ben," Lara scolded. "If these girls didn't know you so well, I'd have to be apologizing for you."

"But we do," Patience assured her.

"Grab the bottle, Ari, will you?" Lara asked. "And Ben, the platter with cheese?"

"Yes, my queen," Ben called.

"Yes, his queen," Ari echoed.

"Which is the way it's supposed to be," Lara said, taking Nan's arm. "Don't you think?"

"Absolutely," Nan replied.

~~~

Zan strolled in Clapham Common watching people with rapt fascination. He and the Emerson family had picnicked earlier, and now Luke stood at a large pond with other children launching toy boats while his mother and grandparents watched from the shade of a giant oak.

Zan tried to imagine himself at twelve, spending this sort of lazy afternoon with a loving family, but he suspected it would not have been so. This would not have been his life. The better question was, could it be his life? One day could he be a husband and a father to children who would launch toy boats in a pond?

He stopped and watched three birds circling and dogging a considerably larger bird, who swooped and then soared in an attempt to be free of them. *Dogging*, he thought. That was not a word that Emerson had taught him; it was one inexplicably freed from his memory bank.

At the touch of a hand on his arm, he turned and looked at Jane. She was a woman of moderate build and height with fair, slightly graying hair and hazel eye flecked with amber.

Are you alright, she gestured.

He nodded. The others found it curious how easily he understood and communicated with her, but her gestures were easily understandable, and her face was expressive, her eyes eminently readable. She seemed to understand him as well. Sometimes she read his lips, but she also interpreted his gestures with no difficulty.

What are you thinking?

"I like this place. I would like to come here one day with a wife and a child."

"Why na?" she asked choppily.

Why not. Her words surprised him. He hadn't realized she ever spoke. "I wonder if I will have a wife."

She watched his lips and then looked into his eyes. "Ari?"

Her perception surprised him, but he nodded. John must have told her about Ari.

I hope, she gestured.

Me too, he gestured back.

"That is amazing," Ginny said to her father as she watched Zan with her mother. "You would think they've known one another for years."

"They're both amazing human beings," he said.

"He's so handsome," Ginny said. "You hadn't prepared us for that."

"I wish he were less so. He attracts so much attention because of it, and he believes all that attention is because he's so different."

"You have explained why people stare?"

"I've tried, but he thinks I'm being kind."

"The poor thing," she said. "The life he's had—"

"No, we cannot have that attitude. It was a miracle he survived as he did, and it was great good fortune that we found him. Now he's here and being offered a different life. He's healthy and strong, and ready for the next stage of his life."

"But I think of Luke being left alone in a vast jungle and it's heartbreaking."

"Yes, it is. But there are different kinds of loneliness, just as there are different ways of connecting in a meaningful sort of way. We think it must have been so terribly lonely because he had no one to talk to, but he had a different sort of family. They communicated. They interacted. They touched and showed affection and cared for one another. It's just that they didn't use words."

"You're pretty amazing yourself, you know," Ginny said.

"Thank you, my dear. That's kind of you to say."

"I'm not being kind. It's true."

He smiled. "I'm glad you think so."

~~~

Nan, Patience and Ari lay in the beds of their shared room.

"It was a good day," Patience said.

"Except for the tour of the tunnel?" Nan asked.

"No. That too. I did think it was interesting. Although dark in places and small, and it had sharp turns, and it was *under* the river."

"But except for that it was great fun," Ari said with a smile.

"Ari?" Patience said.

"*Hmm?*"

"What happened at the ball?"

Ari was quiet a moment, and then she sat up. "If you want to know, I'll tell you."

The girls nodded and Patience sat up.

"When I came back to the balcony, Marshall and Delia were engaged in what seemed an … inappropriately intimate conversation."

Nan sat up, alarmed.

"She immediately left, and I forced the issue with Marshall. He all but admitted that something happened between them."

"What do you mean?" Nan asked breathlessly.

"What did he say?" Patience asked.

"I asked when he was intimate with Delia."

There was a collective gasp from Patience and Nan.

"At first, he denied it. Then he said he would not discuss it. Finally, he said that he hadn't been intimate in the way I was thinking. I told him he had no idea what I was thinking."

"She wouldn't," Nan exclaimed. "Of course, I believe you, but there had to have been a misunderstanding."

"I don't know," Ari admitted. "I would like not to believe it of her, of both of them, but I do."

"Oh, Ari! May I speak with her?" Nan asked. "Find out the truth?"

Ari took a moment to reply. "Alright," she agreed. "Find out the truth if she's capable of it, but I think it's done for me."

"I think it's done for me too," Patience said sadly. "I rather feel like it was anyway. Her meanness is so unnecessary and draining. I find it frustrating and draining."

Ari nodded. "So do I."

"Let me try," Nan pleaded "I would hate for us all not to be friends anymore."

"That's because you're Sweetness," Patience said.

"Love," Nan retorted playfully.

"Uh, Spirit," Ari said, holding up her hand.

The girls laughed.

"You seem fine now," Patience commented.

"I am. I've enjoyed this. And I'm away from Marshall and Delia."

"Are you resigned to marrying him?" Patience asked.

"No. I don't want to marry him."

"I'm sorry, Ari," Nan said. "You deserve better."

"Yes, you do," Patience seconded.

Yes, I do. There had to be a way out.

Chapter Twenty-Three

Vanessa looked over her gowns, wondering which to wear for the day. Which might get Zan's attention? She pulled out a pale-blue day dress that brought out the color of her eyes. It was just right.

They would take a morning stroll, and they had a dance lesson in the afternoon. Perhaps she'd suggest a round of shooting in the archery range that had been set up. She would take an incorrect stance and ask what she was doing wrong. So far, that had been one of the few ways she'd managed to get his arms around her.

She hung the dress back and then walked over to her vanity. Sitting, she studied her freshly washed face, lifting her chin and turning her head from side to side, and then added the right amount of color for her cheeks and darkening on her lashes. She reached for a bottle of perfume but changed her mind. Zan seemed to prefer a fresh scent to an expensive French perfume. Come to think of it, so did she.

~~~

"Miss Arianna," Mr. Fletcher said when she walked back in the door after an early morning walk. "Good morning."

"Good morning," she returned.

"Your uncle is in the morning room."

She looked at him quizzically, wondering why he seemed so delighted. "Alright. Thank you."

"I should say *both* your uncles," he said meaningfully.

She squealed before dashing off. She barely managed to slow before rounding the corner into the morning room. Sully grinned as he rose. She threw her arms around him. "You're here!"

"Good gracious," Edith laughed. "You would think it had been ages since you saw him."

"It feels like it," Ari returned. "I am so glad to see you."

"And I, you. The house is not the same without you. It's quiet."

She slapped his chest playfully "Why are you here?"

"To visit, of course, if you don't mind."

"Oh, I mind terribly," she teased.

"I thought we might go for a ride this morning."

"I'd love to."

"You'll have breakfast first," Wilbur spoke up.

"Of course," Sullivan replied. He looked at Ari. "We were waiting for you." They all started toward the dining room. "I hear the girls are here."

"Yes. Did you just arrive this morning?"

"No, yesterday evening. You were already off to—"

"The Walters girl coming out," Edith supplied.

They entered the dining room. The sideboard was full of covered dishes. They each helped themselves to what they wanted.

"How was it, by the way?" Edith asked.

"Very nice. They had the most marvelous dessert. It was called *blanc de poire*. Have you had it?"

"White pears?" Wilbur mused. "I don't know that I have."

"Of course, you have, dear," Edith spoke up. "Pears are poached and then covered in a sauce of white chocolate."

"I don't recall that. Did I like it?"

Edith chuckled. "How did Miss Walters look?" Edith asked Ari.

"Happy … and very young."

"Well," Wilbur said. "When you get up in years, as we all are, the young just get younger and younger."

"Yes, indeed," Sully played along. "Can you remember back to when you were that age, Ari? I know it was so long ago."

"I try and think back on it sometimes," she replied sadly. "But you know how the memory goes."

~~~

Ari waited until she and Sully were in route to the park before she asked, "Why are you really here?"

"You think there is some clandestine purpose, do you?"

She folded her hands. "Is there?"

"Clandestine," he murmured thoughtfully, "*Hmm.* A few letters have come for you, and I wanted to personally deliver them. Is that clandestine?"

"It depends on the letters, I suppose?"

"Your father wrote," he said as he fished in his inside jacket pocket for the letter, which he then pulled out and handed to her.

"Chastising me for not going to Charleston, I'm sure."

He shrugged. "We might have guessed that would follow."

"And the other letter?"

"Read your father's first."

She wrinkled her nose. "Must I?'

"You should."

She tore open the envelope, pulled out the one page, and read. As she progressed, her expression changed to one of shock and alarm.

"What is it?" Sullivan asked. "Has something happened?"

She looked at him a long moment without speaking. "I didn't want you to know," she admitted. "I never wanted you to know."

"Know what?"

She sighed as she looked down at the letter, too ashamed to look him in the eye. "When I went home three years ago, my father was very charming at first. It felt as if I didn't know him, had never known him, but he was just what I wanted him to be." She made herself look Sully in the eye. "We had a talk one day, and he confided that he had amassed a significant amount of debt."

"Oh? I'm sorry to hear that."

"He said it was due to things beyond his control, lost cargo, the price of cotton, I don't remember what all. He just kept stressing that none of it was his fault. I didn't understand why he was telling me until he said that he had a way out of the mess, only it involved a very great favor from me."

"Why do I have a bad feeling about this?" Sully asked with a look of anxiety.

She loathed what she had to tell him, but it wasn't going to get any easier. "He asked me to marry a man by the name of Jason Barton."

"What!"

"He said that Jason desperately wanted to make me his wife. The Bartons, who are wealthy, if it's not obvious, had agreed to satisfy all my father's debts if I would marry him."

"Obviously you declined!"

"At first, yes."

He closed his eyes and exhaled loudly. "Oh, Arianna."

She had to finish it now. "He pleaded. He said otherwise he'd be ruined. He also said we'd be a family again, that we'd be able to see one another all the time. I didn't love Jason, I didn't even know him, but I'd met him, and he wasn't a bad sort. It was foolish beyond words of course. I know it now." She grimaced. "No, I knew it then. But after I'd made the commitment—"

"Are you saying you got married?"

Tears filled her eyes and spilled over. She nodded. "When I think back on it, it seems like a bad dream. As if it didn't truly happen. But it did."

"Where is this he, this Mr. Barton?" he asked as he fumbled to retrieve a handkerchief from his jacket pocket, which he handed her.

She dabbed at her face. "He contracted a fever a matter of weeks after we were married, and he … died. Many did."

Sully took a moment to digest this. "How tragic." He looked out the window and thought about everything before looking back at her. "Had you developed feelings for him?"

She hesitated and then shook her head. "No. Never."

"And what you said about your father confiscating your ticket home. Was that true?"

"Yes. But after Jason died, I confronted him and demanded it back. By then, I didn't care what he thought or said or did. In those miserable weeks of married life, my father had not been there for me. We hadn't suddenly become a family. He hadn't meant what he said. He does not love me, and he never has."

"Oh, Ari. He made a terrible, almost unforgivable request of you, but I don't believe for a moment that he doesn't love you. It's simply that he loves himself more. But why didn't you want me to know?"

"Because I used such poor judgment," she said brokenly. "No, more than that. I went against my own judgment. I knew how much that would disappoint you."

"Oh, dear girl. We make foolish choices when we're young. Do you think I never made irresponsible decisions that I later bitterly regretted? At least, yours was for a good reason. For the love of a father. I would have been disappointed in *him*. Not you. I would have only hated that you had to go through such a wrong and distasteful thing."

She took hold of his hand. "I don't deserve you."

"Ari, you deserve love and care and everything else that your heart desires. You have brought more joy to me and to your Aunt Edith and Uncle Wilbur than we ever imagined. Don't you know how much richer you've made our lives?"

She dried her eyes again, knowing the truth. She didn't deserve him. She didn't deserve any of them.

"But why did you look so stricken earlier? What did your father have to say in his letter?"

She passed the letter for him to read. "He says that I should return to Charleston and marry Jason's brother."

"You are not serious!"

"I wish I wasn't."

He adjusted the letter to better read it.

"Something about levirate marriage," she murmured, shaking her head. "I've never even heard of levirate marriage."

"This is absurd! No one in civilized society practices levirate marriage. In obscure African villages, yes, but not here and not in America either."

"What is it?"

"In a closed society when outside marriages are not allowed, a widow can be forced to marry her deceased husband's brother or another member of his family. I'm not absolutely certain how it works. But—" He held up the letter. "—this is absurd."

"He also wrote to Aunt Edith."

His jaw gaped. "And proposed this?"

"No. He suggested she help convince me to come home if a suitable marriage not already been arranged."

"Unbelievable! I will write to him and—"

"No. I will write him," she stated calmly. "There are things I need to say once and for all."

He sighed. "What you've been through, it should never have happened."

"I let it happen, Uncle Sully. And I thought I'd learned my lesson. I thought, after that, I'd be strong enough and wise enough to always listen to my own instincts."

"You are," he stated firmly.

The carriage came to a stop.

"You are," he restated.

"You are the most wonderful man in the entire world, but if that were true, I would have told Marshall no. When he first suggested marriage, I would have said no." The carriage door was opened, and Arianna was assisted down. When Sully was beside her, she took hold of his arm, and they began strolling. It felt like more needed to be said about Charleston, but she didn't know what. He had excused her, but she was so ashamed of herself.

They passed a couple who nodded in passing. "Morning," Sullivan said.

"Good morning," they returned.

"What was the other letter you mentioned?" she asked.

"The other letter is from Emerson."

She stopped abruptly and turned to him, suddenly breathless. "Do you have it?"

"I do. It's the real reason I'm here. To be honest, I didn't think your father's would hold any matter of import." He reached into his pocket for the letter. "I also received word from Emerson, so I have some idea of the content of yours."

"Oh?" He handed the letter over, and she tore it open, and began to read.

Dearest Arianna,

As my new friend, Sebastian, and I near the end of our journey home, only a few weeks behind you, I write this in fulfillment of two requests, yours and his. As to how he fares. In health, he is well. He's been able to adapt to our diet and routines. As to the progress of his education, his transformation is nothing short of astounding.

He must have been an exceptionally bright lad, but he bottled that knowledge inside his mind and eventually forgot it. Once the cork was popped and he began to trust himself, it poured out. He works hard all day, every day, to perfect his language skills and to learn the ways and manners expected in society. He is <u>driven</u> to do well.

It took time before he trusted me enough to share what he remembered of his childhood. His father frequently drank to excess and was sometimes quite a brute. He brought his family with him to Africa despite the objections of his wife and her family.

Ladies who have been frequently brutalized are sometimes not emotionally or physically capable of standing up to their tormentor. It seems that Catherine Shaffer was such a woman. Sebastian remembers his father beating him in the presence of his mother, and her doing nothing to stop it other than crying and pleading.

Even though he understands what happened to his parents, he still has profound issues of abandonment. He had an immediate resistance to being called Sebastian. I believe the reason why is that, firstly, metaphorically, he had to let Sebastian die in order to become a creature who could survive in the jungle. Secondly, he resents anything that has to do with his parents, most especially his father. I asked if he would like to

be called by another name, and he affirmed it.
He chose Zan. That is what he is called now.

"Zan," Arianna said, glancing up from the letter. "He's called Zan."

"Yes," Sully replied.

She went back to reading.

Onto his time in the jungle. When the hostiles
came for the group, he hid. He does not
remember how long he remained hidden. Nor
does he recall the time following. What I've been
able to piece together is that a group of apes,
who are generally gentle and social animals,
discovered him and recognized him as helpless
and in need.

One female took to caring for him. This band,
which he thought of as his family, was comprised
of one silverback, the senior male, and four
females, plus their young. With great apes, when
the young grow up, they go off on their own and
join another band or they start one. Zan
recognized that it was time to go when he found
his mate.

More on that subject later.

Ari's heart pumped hard as she thought back on the gestures Sebastian used that first morning indicating she was his. That's what he'd thought. Her face grew warm as she continued reading.

As an anthropologist, this has been an
enlightening adventure. I did not know how
much or how well apes communicated, but Zan
does amazing impressions. Apes use scores of
vocalizations to communicate, including grunts,

growls, and roars, but they also whine, chuckle, bark and hoot. We know all about the chest-beating, but depending on the situation, they also might throw objects or stick out the tongue or slap. His stories are so amusing. He has an excellent sense of humor and of irony. Because there is an innocence about him, he can pull my leg for quite a while before I realize what he's doing.

I mentioned that Zan is driven, and so he is. He is driven to learn and to do whatever he needs to do in order to see you again. He desperately wants this. More than that, and please forgive my bluntness, he wants you. He is single-minded in that regard. Perhaps when we get to the city and he gets his bearings, he will see other ladies and become less fixated, but I am not at all certain of it.

You see, when he saw you in camp, he became convinced you were the mate he had longed for. He believed then, and he still believes, that the fates brought you there for him. This is not a conviction that is easily discarded.

He and I have so much ground still to cover. After beginning instruction on the expectations of society, morals, ethics, etc., he has become noticeably withdrawn. Perhaps it is simply that we're getting closer to home, and he feels overwhelmed and uncertain as to how or if he will be able to fit into this 'new' society. I like him immensely, but by no means is he easy to understand. He is complex, and there may be damage that cannot be undone. Wounds that cannot be fully healed.

You, my dear, must decide whether you will see him again or not. If you will, we will happily come to you. If not, I make no judgment. I do not know where things stand between you and Mr.

Derringer. I ask only this, if you choose not to see Zan, will you please write to him explaining your position? If you could let me know, as well, I would greatly appreciate it.

You are a remarkable young woman. I wish you every happiness. I meant what I said to you in Africa. If not for you, I do not believe we would have made contact with Zan, and I'm so glad that we did. He has enriched my life. I believe his life will be better here, and I hope you will take comfort in that.

Our plan is to go to Lord Bluford's town residence on Park Street in Grosvenor Square and stay for the next month or so. Please write to us there.

Fondly and sincerely yours,

John Emerson

Arianna looked up at her uncle. "He's here!"

He nodded. "That is why I am here."

"I want to see him!"

"I thought you might, which is why I went there first."

"You did?"

"Yes."

"You saw him?"

"No. He was out with Emerson, but I saw Lord Bluford. I would have passed on your letter from Emerson no matter what, of course, but I wanted to assure myself that you would be in no danger should you wish to see him."

"What did Lord Bluford say?"

"What a remarkable man Zan is. Gentle and quiet and polite." He grinned. "They've hired a dance instructor to teach Zan the basics."

"He's learning to dance?"

Sully nodded. "Not only that, but Lord Bluford's granddaughter, Vanessa, is assisting … and very much smitten with him."

The heat that bloomed in Ari's face was embarrassing, but it couldn't be helped. "May we go this afternoon?"

"I am at your beck and call, my dear. How is four o'clock?"

"It's perfect!" They started to walk again. It was difficult for Ari to quell the butterflies in her stomach. She would see Sebastian. Today. This very afternoon. He was there and doing well and learning to dance. She couldn't quite grasp it.

"What about Derringer? Where exactly does that stand?"

The reminder of Marshall dampened her spirits. "Did Aunt Edith fill you in?"

"I know about everything up until last night."

"Last night, I am happy to say, I did not see him." Two children dashed by them laughing, a girl chasing after a slightly younger boy.

"Are you still deciding?" he asked.

"No. I have decided. I just have to find the right time and the right words to tell him."

"You should know that word of the engagement is out at home," he said grimly.

She nodded. "And you should know that he found out what happened in the jungle," she said reluctantly.

Sully stopped and looked at her, clearly startled.

"That's why I have to be so careful."

The words sunk in, and he looked away. "Oh, dear. That is not ideal."

Chapter Twenty-Four

Sullivan and Arianna were shown into Lord Bluford's drawing room where he quickly joined them. "Hello, Sullivan!"

"Good afternoon," Sully returned. "Lord Bluford, may I introduce you to my niece, Miss Arianna Day?"

"Miss Day," Bluford said extending his hand.

"It is a great pleasure," she uttered as she took hold.

He did not shake her hand but merely held it. "The pleasure is all mine. I have heard such excellent things about you." He released her hand. "My granddaughter is staying with us as well, and she is most anxious to meet you."

Ari smiled. "And I, her."

"Sit and be comfortable, please."

"Thank you." Arianna followed her uncle to the settee, and Lord Bluford sat on a chair across from them.

"Will the others be joining us?" Sullivan asked.

"John returned home for a visit. If he can convince his wife to return with him, she'll be staying with us for a while. She's deaf, you know," Bluford added worriedly. "I'm not quite sure how one conducts a conversation with a deaf person, but I suppose we shall find out."

"She is charming," Sullivan replied. "She reads people well, their lips and their expressions. It is remarkable how much she understands. As well, she and John communicate fluently which he then relays."

Bluford nodded thoughtfully. "*Hmm.*"

"And what of Zan?" Sully asked.

"He went home with John but returned yesterday. At the moment, he and Nessa are working with Mr. James, the dance instructor."

Ari stiffened. She had to work to keep breathing evenly.

"Would it be possible to see them?" Sullivan asked.

"Not to interrupt though," Arianna added quickly, stammering slightly. "We would not wish to interrupt." She knew she was blushing and would have liked to fan herself.

"Of course, we can see them," the older man replied cheerfully. "We'll go up to a balcony and look down at them. That should not interrupt a thing."

"We haven't seen him since Africa," Sully said. "So it will be nice to catch a glimpse, and then perhaps we can leave a note." He looked at Ari who nodded. "Perhaps asking him to visit at his convenience."

Lord Bluford slapped his legs. "Let's go. We'll have tea when we return." He rose and led the way from the room.

As she followed, Ari pressed a hand to her stomach where butterflies had whipped themselves into a frenzied flutter. She was about to see him again. It didn't feel quite real.

"I find it nearly inconceivable that he came from the depths of the wild," Bluford said as they walked. "One would not believe it to see him today."

Ari heard strains of music, and her anxiousness increased.

"It's not difficult to find Nessa and Zan in the afternoon. One only needs to follow the sound of the victrola." There was a sudden burst of laughter from ahead. "And mirth." He chuckled. "Our Zan is not taking to the steps without some difficulty, but he is able to laugh about it." Lord Bluford did a quick double-step to open a door. "This way."

Arianna went through the doorway first and started up a flight of stairs feeling strange, almost disoriented.

"I think that's what most impresses me," Lord Bluford continued from behind her, his voice resonant in the stairwell. "It's not so much that he could be taught to speak again but that he has a sense of humor and wonder. One would think he'd be resentful knowing what he's been robbed of, but he's quite the opposite. I thoroughly enjoy his company. I feel more alive in it."

Ari reached the balcony and stepped just far enough in to see over the railing. She realized she was holding her breath and released it. Below, a fussy-looking man was standing with his hands steepled together while a couple danced a basic waltz. She focused on the man, the breathtakingly handsome man, and experienced a head rush that set her face aflame. It was Sebastian, but he looked so different. Tears sprang to her eyes, so she canted her head away from her uncle and Lord Bluford so they would not notice. Pressing the backs of her fingers to her lips, she put her full concentration into controlling her emotions.

"Will you look at that?" Sully marveled quietly. "I would not have known him."

Vanessa was beautiful and lithe with auburn hair that had been styled in an elaborate arrangement. Ari's gaze dropped to Zan's hand on her back and felt a sharp pang of jealousy.

Zan missed a step and they stopped again, breaking apart and laughing.

Mr. James scowled. "You must concentrate, Mr. Shaffer Shall I go back to counting aloud again?"

"You do count very well," Zan replied.

His voice, Ari thought. All she'd heard in the jungle were one-syllable responses.

Vanessa laughed, but Mr. James was not amused.

Ari turned away. "Let's not interrupt," she said softly. She walked on and, a moment later, she heard the men following. Thank goodness. She was not prepared to see Zan now. In fact, she was suddenly feeling a bit ill. "Lord Bluford, might we take tea another day?" she asked when they'd reached the corridor again.

"Of course," Bluford said.

"Are you unwell?" Sully asked worriedly.

"No. I just remembered another engagement I made for today. For which I'm so sorry."

"It happens," Bluford assured her. "Don't give it another thought."

The front door was in sight, the butler waiting to open it for them. She wanted nothing more than to make a mad dash for it, but she made herself walk at a moderate pace and then stop in the foyer and turn back to Lord Bluford. "It was a great pleasure to meet you, Lord Bluford."

He smiled. "You are everything I heard and imagined, my dear, and that is a compliment."

She managed a weak smile. "Thank you."

"When will we be able to see some of the African photographs?" Bluford asked Sullivan.

"Soon."

"I'll arrange a dinner party for the unveiling. Only those in the know, of course."

Sully nodded. "That would be nice."

"Good day to you both," the older man said.

Sully took hold of Arianna's arm as they walked to the carriage. "Are you ill?"

"No."

"You're flushed and you're trembling."

She watched the carriage with a sort of tunnel vision, as she'd had in the Rotherhithe Tunnel. They reached it, and the driver opened the door for them, having scrambled from his seat. Ari managed to keep herself together until the carriage started in motion and then the tears started. They rolled down her face and she couldn't stop it.

"What is it?" Sullivan asked tenderly.

She shook her head, unable to speak.

"Tell me what is wrong."

"N-nothing," she stammered. "I don't know!" She fell into his arms and sobbed.

~~~

Inside the ballroom, Zan took his position again, but he felt himself being watched. He glanced up at the balcony box and saw Lord Bluford leaving with another man.

"Are we ready?" Mr. James asked impatiently.

"Yes," Zan replied, despite a sudden, gnawing restlessness.

"And one-two-three," Mr. James called out. "One-two-three."

Zan botched the step again. He stepped back from Vanessa. "Will you excuse me for a moment?"

Vanessa blinked in surprise. "Yes."

"But—" Mr. James started to object.

"I am sorry, but I have to see to something," Zan said. He left quickly. He went through the main corridor but didn't see anyone. He started toward the drawing room, and nearly collided with the butler. "I saw Lord Bluford," Zan began.

"He's just gone to his study," Cline replied.

"He's with someone?"

"No, they left."

What was this odd feeling in his stomach? "Who was it?"

"Sullivan Vinson, the photographer, and his niece."

Zan couldn't breathe. Ari had been there. "Why did they leave?"

"She said she had another engagement." He paused. "But she didn't look well," Cline confided. "She seemed fine when they arrived, but when they left—"

Zan headed for the front door. He stepped outside and looked around, but they were gone. He looked out at the carriages on the street but there was no way to know which was theirs. Claws of frustration ripped at his insides. She had just been there. She'd come to see him. In fact, she *had* seen him, and then she had left looking as if she felt ill. Because she so hated and feared him after what he'd done to her?

He'd never meant to hurt her, but how would he make her understand that, especially if she could not stand the sight of him? He went to the carriage house where he spotted Carlton, one of the drivers.

"Hallo," Carlton called cheerfully when he saw him approaching. "Lookin' for me?"

"Yes. Do you know where—" Zan broke off because he didn't know Arianna's aunt and uncle's name. John had spoken of Sullivan Vinson frequently. His only hope was that Ari's other uncle was Sullivan's brother, and they were well enough known to be found. "Do you know the home of a man named Vinson?"

"There's a Lord Vinson has a home in Bedford Square. Is that who you mean?"

"Is his brother Sullivan Vinson?"

Carlton frowned. "The photographer? I couldn't swear it."

He had to try. He had to hope. "Can you take me there?"

"Sure, I can. Know him, do you?"

"I know his niece. Will you take me?"

"Yeah, yeah. I'll take you. It's not far at all."

~~~

"I'm sorry," Ari sobbed.

"*Shhh*, it's alright."

Ari pulled away from him, shaking her head. "It's not." She wiped her face.

"What do you mean?" he asked calmly, reaching into his pocket for his handkerchief. He handed it to her.

"Nothing," she said. She dried her face. "I don't know. I don't know when I became such a mess. It was just so … overwhelming to see him. Don't you think it was overwhelming to see him?"

"Yes, I do. I could scarcely believe my eyes. But is that all?" She nodded as she looked out the window. She was still breathing in gulps and with difficulty. He didn't push her while she collected herself. "What are your plans for this evening?" he finally asked when she'd calmed.

"I am staying in and going to bed early. The others are going to … something or the other. I find it more exhausting than they do. It positively exhilarates Delia."

"You are a very different young woman than she is."

Ari nodded in agreement but didn't comment further.

"Does that Derringer fellow know you're staying in?"

She sighed. "I'll send him a note when we get back."

"One of us should write to Emerson mentioning that we stopped by. And pass on an invitation for them to call at their convenience when he returns. Or one of us could write to Zan directly."

She instantly perked up. "I promised to let John know my decision about seeing Zan. Not that it won't be obvious."

"You are anything but obvious, my love. I know you well and even I don't understand what's going on in that pretty head of yours."

"Be grateful for that," she said wryly.

He smiled wickedly. "Do you think it would be easier to have Delia's mind for a day?"

"Well, let's see. If I did, I would be thinking—" Ari frowned heavily and stuck one finger up in the air "—about what I will wear tonight and how I will look in it." A second finger went up. "How I look at the moment." A third finger shot up. "How all the men in the room looked at me the evening before. A fourth finger. "What I will wear tonight and how I will look in it."

Sully laughed gustily.

"That's really not fair of me," Ari relented. "What noble thing am I thinking or doing at the moment?"

"I do not worry about your mind or your heart for a moment. After all, who was it that recently raised a decent sum of money for the suffragist movement?"

They stopped in front of the house, but Ari didn't move. "I didn't realize you knew," she admitted.

"Of course, I knew."

"I didn't want to be secretive—"

"Oh, yes you did," he rejoined.

"I went about it as anonymously as I could because I didn't want you to receive any backlash,"

"I know."

The door was opened for them, and a footman his hand. "One moment, please," she said to him.

"Of course," he said, taking a step to the side of the carriage to afford them some privacy.

Arianna looked at her uncle. "I believe in the cause, but I know how heated and unreasonable it makes some people. Men and women."

He nodded. "I believe in the cause too."

She smiled gratefully.

"But even if I didn't, you should always act on your convictions. We do not share a mind, although we have many similar opinions. We will not always agree, but that doesn't mean we each don't follow our own hearts."

"I never want my position to be damaging to you."

"I'm proud of that mind of yours. I'm proud of your strength and your compassion."

She loved him so much; there weren't words to express it. "Thank you for everything," she said, taking hold of his hand. "For coming with the letters and for listening and helping and not judging."

"That's what an uncle is for."

"You are more father than uncle to me, and I am a better person for having grown up under your care."

He ducked his head, touched to the point of getting emotional, but then looked up and smiled at her.

"And now I have notes to write," she said with a smile.

Chapter Twenty-Five

A ri repeatedly splashed water on her face. Looking in the mirror as she patted her face dry, she wondered what it said about her that the thought of staying home and going to bed early gave her such a feeling of relief. It wasn't normal.

After writing her notes, she left her room to find Fletcher, but she had no sooner stepped into the hallway than she saw him approaching. "I was just coming to find you," she said. "I have some messages I need sent out."

"I'll take them. Someone is here to see you."

She could have groaned. The last hour had been trying, and she wasn't up to a visitor today. "Who is it?"

"His name is Zan," he said questioningly.

She drew in a sharp breath.

He drew back because of the expression on her face. "Shall I send him away?"

"No," she exclaimed with enough passion that heat flared in her face. "No, I'll see him. He's a … an acquaintance. May I have—" she touched the top envelope, "—that one back?"

He handed it back.

Damn the heat in her face. How guilty did she look anyway? "Is the drawing room occupied?"

"I'm afraid so. The young ladies are entertaining the Dehart sisters."

She thought of the morning room, which was sure to be unoccupied, but they would have to pass the drawing room to get there, and she didn't want to be seen. "What about the library?"

"Your uncle may have gone there. I can check."

"The salon?"

"Not in use."

"Will you show him there, please?"

"Of course. Right away."

As he walked off, she rushed back to her mirror again and saw that her color was high, and her hair could be neater. Her eyes were red-rimmed and there was evidence of her crying, but it was no matter. He was here. He'd found her. Her heart was soaring as she left the room and ran into Delia in the hall.

"Good gracious," Delia exclaimed. "Where's the fire?"

"I beg your pardon. I didn't see you," Ari replied coolly, continuing on.

"I didn't realize you'd returned," Delia said, turning to watch her. "Where are you off to in such a hurry?"

Ari turned back, trying to look impassive. "Nowhere. Downstairs."

"I'm getting my sampler to show the Deharts. They're here, you know."

"Yes. Fletcher mentioned it."

"Are you joining us?"

"Not at the moment."

Delia looked at her curiously. "What are you up to?"

"Delia," Ari objected.

"Arianna," repeated in the same tone.

Ari felt the first pricks of anger. "If you will excuse me," she said testily before walking on.

"Ari!"

Arianna turned back to face her.

"Did Nan speak with you?" Delia asked, taking a step toward her.

"She did. She said you claimed nothing untoward ever happened between yourself and Marshall."

"Because it didn't! I swear it!"

Ari nodded curtly. "I'm glad."

"I only wish I understood what he did or said to give you such a notion. You don't think he meant to make you jealous, do you?"

"If he did, he should have known better. Jealousy was not what it made me feel."

"Oh, Ari. How long have we been friends?"

Ari relented to a degree. Perhaps she had been unfair, not even giving Delia a chance to explain or defend herself. "What *were* you talking about that night on the balcony?"

"You mostly."

"What about me?"

"I'm not proud of it. I know that I flirt."

"So do I. Just tell me."

"I teasingly asked him what I could do … I don't remember precisely how I phrased it, to have as much good fortune in landing a fiancé as you've had."

That *was* something Delia would have asked. "What did he say?"

Delia averted her eyes. "I don't recall exactly."

She was lying. "Delia, what did he say?"

"Swear that you won't tell him I told you."

"Fine. I swear."

"He said I hadn't a chance because I wasn't an heiress."

Ari felt as if she'd been slapped. "An heiress?"

Delia nodded.

"But I'm not." Was she? Was she to inherit all of this? She'd never thought about it. And that's why Marshall wanted to marry her? It was a sickening thought. And it was absurd given the wealth of the Derringers.

"I'm sorry," Delia said.

For once, Delia seemed sincere. "Thank you for telling me. If you'll excuse me." She walked on.

~~~

"You're welcome," Delia said under her breath. She cocked her head, waited for Ari to start down the stairs, and then followed at a discreet distance.

~~~

The knowledge of what Marshall thought was a shock and a low blow, and yet Ari felt stronger with each step down the staircase. What she'd learned only bolstered her resolve. Besides, Zan was waiting for her. Zan, whom she desperately wanted to see.

She reached the first floor and picked up speed as she went. She neared the door to the salon and stopped to glance both ways before she stepped inside. Zan stood in the center of the room.

"Ari," he said.

She was too breathless to speak, and so she closed the door behind her. Turning back, she clutched her hands together to conceal their trembling as best she could. As she came further into the room, tears blurred her vision, but she willed them away. She stopped an arm's length from him. "Hello," she managed.

"Hello."

"You look well. Different. I can see it's you, but—"

"You came to see me. Today."

She looked down at her hands. "We did. Yes." She looked back up and into his searching gaze. Those eyes. She'd forgotten how beautiful and blue they were. How devastatingly handsome he was. "I just learned you were in London this morning."

He frowned. "But John wrote—"

"Yes, but I was here, and the letter went home. To Northampton. My uncle brought it last night, but—" She was chattering like a magpie and trembling life a leaf. She needed to get a hold of herself. "Won't you sit?"

He went and sat, looking uncertain. She followed and sat catty-corner from him. If she shifted just a bit, their knees would touch. A part of her was tempted. She longed to touch him. To simply reach out and touch him.

"Why did you leave?" he asked reluctantly.

She blinked. "Do you mean today?"

He nodded.

"I didn't wish to interrupt your lesson."

"I don't care about dancing."

The intensity of his reply made it hard to think clearly. "You will when you attend a ball," she said lightly. "My goodness, it's simply incredible that we're sitting here like this. You look like you belong here."

"I don't belong anywhere yet."

The words wrenched her heart. "Do you miss the life you had?"

"It was what I knew. This is harder to know."

"I am very impressed with what you've accomplished in so short a time," she said earnestly.

"It seems a long time to me."

"I'm certain that's true. With all that's changed."

He leaned forward slightly, his expression searching. "Ari—"

"Yes?" she said breathlessly.

"I did not mean to hurt you."

The statement took her off guard. Tingling with embarrassment, she looked down at her hands. "I know that."

"You do?"

She made herself look up and meet his eyes, despite her too-warm face. "I never thought you did."

"When you left today, I thought you could not bear to see me."

Her hands flew toward him; the words were so alarming. "No! Oh, no." She placed her hands back into her lap and tried to calm herself. "I wanted only not to interrupt. In fact, when I got back here, I wrote a note asking to see you. And John, of course."

He sighed with relief. "You are why I came here."

"I'm so glad you knew where to go."

"I do not mean today. You are why I came back to England."

She was too overwhelmed to form a reply.

His expression turned fierce with frustration and desire. "How do I be with you?"

"Oh, Zan," she said, shaking her head. "No, you can't … I mean, th-there are rules for how people meet and conduct themselves socially. You cannot say that."

"There are too many rules," he complained.

She felt a mad compulsion to laugh. Her heart was pounding mercilessly. "That may be, but we cannot get around them. We have to meet in public or with supervision. As friends. Do you understand?"

For a long moment, he was silent. "You're not going to marry that man."

Ari drew back in surprise, but before she could frame her reply, the door opened, and Delia stood there affecting innocence.

"I beg your pardon," Delia said. "I didn't realize you were in here."

Ari inwardly seethed. Delia was a conniving nuisance. As Zan stood, Arianna struggled to remain composed. "We're waiting on my uncle," she said calmly. "This is Mr. Shaffer. He is a friend of … my uncle's." Ari looked at Zan and found his gaze both calm and curious. She stood to be by his side. "Mr. Shaffer, may I introduce Miss Delia Bradford from Northampton?"

Zan inclined his head. "Miss Bradford."

Delia came forward, all smoldering eyes and avid interest. "How do you do, Mr. Shaffer?"

"Very well, thank you."

Ari was proud of Zan's composure, and resentful of Delia's intrusion. "Unfortunately, he doesn't have long today," she said pointedly enough that Delia would get the message.

"Well, I won't stay and interrupt your … visit," Delia replied. "Mr. Shaffer," she said with a long-perfected fluttering of her eyes and the slightest of curtsies.

"Miss Bradford."

Ari waited for Delia to leave before speaking again. "You were perfect," she said quietly. "You ought to be so proud of yourself, of what you've accomplished."

"When can I see you again?"

His directness stole her breath.

"Tomorrow?" he pushed.

She glanced at the door wondering if Delia stood there trying to overhear. That would be like her "Let me go and get my uncle for propriety's sake. I know he wants to see you. Can you wait a few minutes?"

He didn't smile, but almost. "Yes."

She'd intended to go at once, but his presence was so commanding. She could not help but experience a flash of memory of being tossed over his shoulder and carried away. If only he could do it again. "It is so good to see you," she admitted.

"It is good to see you. I did not know what I would do if you would not see me."

Tears sprang to her eyes. She looked away from him and then forced herself into motion. Delia was not in the hall, which was a relief. Ari hurried to the library, but Sully was not there. She went and found Mr. Fletcher in his small office. "Do you know where Uncle Sully is?"

"No, but I can look, if you wish." He started to rise.

"No, thank you. It wasn't important." She went back to the salon and was glad Delia was not there. It would have been like her to come back in with a flimsy excuse. She really was the biggest flirt in all the world.

Zan was still standing. She closed the door again. "My uncle is resting."

"I could come back tomorrow," he said hopefully.

She barely restrained a joyful smile. "Yes. Let's plan on that."

"I should go now?"

"It's probably best," she said hesitantly. "With Delia having seen you."

"She is your friend?"

She took a moment to reply. "She is a long-time acquaintance."

He walked to her and glanced down at her hand before reaching for it. He brought it to his lips, his gaze locked on hers, and pressed a kiss to it. He lowered her hand but continued to hold it. She knew she should pull it away, but she did not. She ought to have taken a step away from him, but she did not.

"Is that alright that I kiss your hand?"

Her throat was too tight to speak for a moment. "Yes. We're friends."

"Friends," he repeated thoughtfully. "You will call me Mr. Shaffer."

"Unless we're alone. And you will call me Miss Day."

"Miss Day," he repeated. "And we are friends."

There seemed to be a glint of humor in his eyes. "Yes. We met through mutual friends. John Emerson and Charles North." She paused, frowning thoughtfully. "What are you telling others about where you came from?"

"I have heard Lord Bluford say that I've been abroad for many years. Overseeing a plantation in Africa."

She nearly giggled. "Ah. What sort of plantation?"

"As my friend, should you not know that?"

She laughed, delighted to be teased by him. "I can be so forgetful."

"Coffee."

"Ah, yes. I do seem to recall that now."

"Do you like coffee?"

"I do."

"Do you drink it in the morning?" he asked with an entirely different sort of sparkle to his eyes.

She felt herself trembling again. "Sometimes."

"Perhaps I will, too."

She withdrew her hand, aware of the extent of her blushing.

"Maybe we will drink coffee together sometime," he said. "In the morning."

"It's possible," she said.

"How do you take your coffee?"

"I like cream and sugar." Had she just stammered again?

"I like cream and sugar," he said.

Was her imagination running wild? He seemed to be suggesting more than he was saying. His nearness had her heart pounding.

"Ari."

She jerked slightly. "Yes?"

"Does your uncle hate me?"

"No! He was wary in Africa. Concerned for me. That's why we left when we did."

"Wary," he repeated.

She nodded. "That's all. He was afraid you would—"

"Take you," he supplied when her sentence broke off. "He was afraid I would take you again."

She couldn't speak for a moment. "Yes," she said just above a whisper.

He nodded slowly. "I would have."

She gasped, but not with offence. She was glad he'd said it. Glad he thought it. "Zan, what happened between us—"

He inclined his head toward her subtly.

"No one can know. Do you understand?"

He nodded. "I understand."

"I told one person," she admitted. "Patience, my closest friend, but I trust her completely. I'd trust her with my life. She would never betray my confidence."

"I told no one. I will tell no one."

She nodded.

"You will not marry that other man."

She blinked. No, she wouldn't, but she couldn't say that. Not yet.

"You will marry me."

She was stunned and then she attempted to appear disapproving, but joy was exploding throughout her body. It was everything she could do not to burst into delighted laughter and throw herself into his arms. Oh, to have that sort of freedom! "You cannot say that," she chastised lightly. "It's simply not done. There are … there are rules."

"Too many rules."

She was continually blushing and breathless, and her nipples had grown noticeably erect. It was time to assert some control. She reached behind her and opened the door. "I'm looking forward to seeing John again," she said as she started out.

"I do not know when he'll return with his wife," he said, falling into step with her.

"I've not met her yet. I know that she's deaf and that she communicates through gestures and through John, of course." Ari noticed a smile tugging at the corner of Zan's lips. "What is it?" she asked. "What are you smiling at?"

"I like the thought that I could talk through gestures and through you. It would have been easier."

She couldn't help laughing at the unexpected levity. It occurred to her how free and happy she felt with him. She wanted more of it. She wanted so much more of it. They neared the front door, and Mr. Fletcher was not in sight. Had he sensed her desire for privacy? "Shall we say tomorrow at four?"

He nodded. "Four."

"If John is back and able to join us, that would be wonderful."

"I will tell him if he returns before then."

"I am so glad you came," she said quietly.

His gaze caressed her face, and she felt her body respond again. Too much. She made herself open the door.

"Tomorrow," he said.

She smiled and nodded and then watched him stride to the waiting carriage, but she closed the door before he could turn back and catch her staring. She leaned back against it, her hand to her throat, overwhelmed by emotions. She felt like the bubbles in a glass of pink champagne. Zan. Her Zan. He had come here for her. He wanted to marry her. The exhilaration she felt was dizzying.

~~~

Ari started back to her room but segued to her uncle's room and knocked lightly so as not to disturb him if he was sleeping.

"Come in," he called.

She opened the door. He was sitting in bed reading in his sock feet. "Zan was just here. I was going to get you, but Mr. Fletcher thought you were resting."

"Zan? Was here? Just now?"

"Yes,"

He huffed a small laugh. "It must have been a nice visit. You're positively glowing."

She stepped in, shut the door and walked closer. "It was a wonderful visit. He feared I hated him for … scaring me in the jungle."

"Which you clearly do not."

"No, of course not. I think he's—" she broke off, searching for the right word. She couldn't blurt *wonderful* again. "Remarkable."

"I agree."

"He's coming back tomorrow at four."

"Oh?"

"To see you. I said if John could join us that would be lovely."

"I look forward to it."

She beamed another smile.

"Where have you been anyway?" he asked with a teasing smile.

"What do you mean? I've spent the day with you."

"In body perhaps, but I haven't seen this vitality in some time."

"I was thinking the same thing myself." She started to the door.

"I suppose you've decided to go out tonight?"

She turned back, shaking her head. "No. I'm staying in," she replied no less cheerfully than before.

"Ah."

Ari left and closed the door behind her.

"Oh, dear," Sullivan said under his breath.

~~~

Arianna encountered her friends in the corridor.

"There you are," Patience said. "You missed the Deharts."

"Was it a nice visit?" Ari asked.

"Yes," Patience replied.

"More importantly," Delia said, "how was *your* visit?"

"Fine, thank you." Ari went to her room and the others filed in behind her.

"You must have had a nice time with your uncle." Patience said. "You seem so much happier now."

Ari went to the window seat and perched in it, and Patience came and sat beside her.

"I don't think visiting with her uncle made her look like that," Delia stated smugly.

"What do you mean?" Patience asked. When she didn't receive a reply, she looked at Ari. "Did you call on someone who was interesting?"

"Rather, one called on her," Delia said. "And I must say, I have never seen a more beautiful man in my life."

"Beautiful?" Nan laughed. "How can a man be beautiful?"

"Oh, I've seen beautiful men," Patience agreed. "You know, if they're pleasing to look at with masculine features, we call them handsome. If their features are more … perfect, I guess, they can be beautiful."

"Oh, he was masculine," Delia declared. "Very."

"Who was it?" Nan asked Ari. "I want to see him."

"It was a Mr. Shaffer," Delia said. "And I want to know more."

The girls all looked at Arianna expectantly.

"His name is Zan Shaffer," Ari stated. "He's a friend of—"

"Of your uncle," Delia supplied when her voice trailed off.

Ari silently cursed the heat in her face. She was trying to appear calm and detached, but she looked anything but. "Actually, I should have said he was a friend of a friend of my uncle's."

"What friend?" Delia pushed.

"John Emerson," Arianna replied shortly.

"Is he really beautiful?" Nan asked curiously.

"He's so handsome, you can scarcely breathe when you see him," Delia exclaimed. "Tell us about him. Who is his family? Why have we not heard of him?"

"Are you under the impression you know everyone in London?" Ari asked lightly, wishing she could change the subject.

"The extremely handsome, rich, eligible men from the ages of eighteen to thirty-five? Yes."

"Is he all those things?" Nan marveled.

"No, he's not," Ari replied. "Delia is making too much out of it."

"I am not."

Patience watched Arianna, sensing some significant change in her.

"So, about tonight—" Ari said.

"No, not yet," Delia said. "Zan Shaffer first. What sort of name is Zan anyway?"

"His Christian name is Sebastian," Ari replied. Out of the corner of her eye, she saw the shock on Patience's face. "But here I must disappoint you, Delia. He is not an heir to a fortune nor is he wealthy."

"He's certainly a gentleman though," Delia said. "He was dressed very well. He's not even moderately wealthy?"

"I don't believe so. No."

"I wonder if he'll be at the gala tonight," Nan said.

"I'm not going," Ari spoke up, seizing the opportunity.

"Why not?" the girls all asked at once.

Ari laughed at the chorus. "Because I'm tired."

"You don't look tired," Delia commented.

"Well, I am. I need a night off."

"Did you let Marshall know?" Delia asked.

Nan suddenly looked uncomfortable.

"I did," Ari replied. "I sent him a note."

"I'll stay home with you, if you'd like," Nan offered.

"Don't be silly. I want you to go and have a wonderful time. You haven't worn your new green gown yet."

"I thought I might save it for the Harvest Ball. Do you think your aunt would mind?"

"Of course not."

"Who is Mr. Shaffer's family?" Delia asked. "Are they in trade?"

"She already told you he's not wealthy," Patience said. "I would think that answers that for you."

Delia folded her arms. "She doesn't know for certain, does she? How could she?" She shrugged a shoulder. "I'm curious."

"He was orphaned as a young boy," Ari informed her. "He has no family."

"What will you wear tonight, Delia?" Patience asked.

"I'm wearing green so don't wear yours," she said dismissively to Nan. "Was he a ward of someone then?"

"No, not really," Ari replied impatiently.

"What does that mean, 'not really?'"

"Patience, what will you wear tonight?" Nan asked.

Delia huffed. "If I didn't know better, I would swear you were all trying to change the subject."

"Perhaps because that one is exhausted," Patience said sweetly.

"I don't think it's exhausted at all but go ahead and be secretive."

"No one is being secretive," Ari replied quickly. "There's simply nothing else to tell."

"On a different subject," Nan spoke up looking at Delia. "Do you not favor someone by now? I would say you have at least two men in love with you."

Delia scoffed. "More than two, I would hope."

Patience rolled her eyes. "Really, Delia. You ought to try a measure of modesty sometime."

"I believe modesty to be supremely overrated, although I'm sure I could manage to appear it if it was called for."

"You must favor one over the others," Nan prodded. "Mr. Printess, maybe? He's so dashing."

Delia turned and started from the room. "Just because you have one and only one suitor does not mean I have to decide on one for myself."

"I swear," Patience snapped. "You continually get meaner as you get older!"

Delia whirled back around. "I am not mean," she retorted. "I am honest! Nan, did you think that was mean?"

Nan gave Patience an appeasing smile and a shrug. "I do only have one suitor, but that's perfectly fine with me."

"Well, of course, it is," Ari declared. "All any of us need is one if he's someone you care for. Someone who makes you happy."

"And he does," Nan said with a serene smile.

"I am not mean in the least," Delia fumed. "And you saying that makes me think that you don't know me at all, which hurts since you're supposed to be my closest friends."

"Let's not be angry with one another," Nan cajoled.

Delia sniffed. "I need to lie down for a while. If you'll excuse me," she added acidly.

"Always the dramatic exit," Ari said just above a whisper once she'd gone.

"If only being an actress was a more respectable profession," Patience joined in. "Think how good she'd be."

"Plus, there are all those mirrors in one's dressing room," Ari added.

They heard a door slam. "Oh, we'll pay now," Patience said, shaking her head.

"Actually, you'll pay. I'm staying home tonight."

Nan rose. "I'll get the door on my way out and leave you two to talk."

"You don't have to leave," Ari objected.

"I know." Nan left with a bounce in her step.

"Honestly, I think Delia is jealous of her," Patience said when the door was closed. "Delia has always acted so superior, but it's Nan who's in love and has someone in love with her."

Ari nodded.

"Now," Patience said. "About your visitor."

Ari sighed happily.

Patience gaped in astonishment. "You're in love with him!"

Ari blinked.

"How can you be? He was wild."

"He's not anymore. I want you to meet him because you'll see. He's coming again tomorrow."

"What if Marshall finds out?"

"Zan is a friend of my uncle's. There is nothing wrong with receiving him. It will be fine. Don't worry."

"Was it not terribly awkward to see him? Did you think about—"

"It was not awkward. Somehow, it's as if we completely understand one another."

Patience pouted. "Are you really not going tonight?"

Ari shook her head. "I just want to climb into bed early and sleep."

"And dream?"

Ari grinned. "There's nothing wrong with that, is there?"

"No, but Marshall is not someone to be trifled with. He's got his pride."

"Of course, he does. It's as big as the Derringer houses. All put together."

Chapter Twenty-Six

Patience made a point of staying close to Delia just in case Marshall showed up. There was more than one event happening, so he might not, especially since learning that Ari was not attending. Patience fervently hoped that was the case, until the moment she spied him across the room, which meant there was no more time for discretion or coyness. "Let's not say anything about Ari," she said, glancing first at Nan, who nodded in agreement and then Delia.

"To whom?" Delia asked as if insulted.

"To Marshall, of course."

"Is he here?" Delia asked, looking around.

"Please give me your word," Patience said firmly.

"Fine, I won't say anything about Ari. What would I say?"

"Anything about her visitor today," Nan spoke up. "Although it was perfectly innocent, you know that Marshall might get prickly about it, especially since she didn't come this evening."

"You mean especially in that she doesn't seem to want to marry him," Delia said. "Why she doesn't put that ring on her finger and declare her engagement to the world is utterly beyond me. Why is she so reluctant? Has she ever said?"

Patience looked away, and Nan looked uncomfortable.

"Well? Has she?"

"Not to me," Nan replied.

"She may very well marry him," Patience said. "She simply doesn't want to be pressured."

"It's that headstrong streak in her," Delia declared. "An American trait."

"You really dislike Americans, don't you?" Nan asked quizzically.

"I find them crude and lacking in both taste and manners."

"Ari is none of those things," Nan objected.

"She certainly is not," Patience seconded.

Delia rolled her eyes. "Because she's lived here. We influenced her."

"Ladies," Marshall said.

They'd been so engrossed in conversation, he'd all but startled them. "Good evening," Patience said, blushing and wondering what he might have overheard.

"You all look lovely," he commented politely.

"Thank you," Delia said with a lift of her chin, determined to remain calm. Something had been started in motion, and it was something that needed careful control. Things had very nearly spiraled out of her control at the Hotel Russell, but Marshall seemed civil enough now.

"I would like to introduce my third cousin, Reginald Hailey." Marshall said, opening his arm to welcome another gentleman into their midst.

Patience looked at Mr. Hailey, who was looking at her with beautiful pale green eyes, and her breath caught. He was a redhead, carrot red to boot, and he was handsome.

"May I present, Miss Bradford, Miss Saint James, and Miss Caldwell," Marshall said, indicating each with an upturned hand.

"Ladies," Reginald said with a slight bow.

"How do you do, Mr. Hailey?" Delia said.

Patience tried to speak but found herself breathless.

"So, Ari wasn't feeling well yet again," Marshall said, looking at Patience.

"She was a bit tired." Her voice sounded ridiculously strained to her ears. "After spending the day with her uncle who came to town," she added. She wasn't looking at Mr. Hailey, but she was aware of him. Aware also that he was watching her.

"I am so looking forward to meeting her," Mr. Hailey said. "She sounds remarkably adventurous."

"She is," Patience replied with a smile. How funny, when she looked right at him, she was less nervous. He seemed nice.

Nothing at all like Marshall. "She has a wonderful mind, and she's amusing and clever." She glanced at the other girls. "Isn't she?"

"Oh, yes," Nan agreed. "Ari is easy to love. In fact, I rather think it's impossible not to. She has that sort of … generosity of heart. Does that make sense?"

"Yes," Patience replied. "It was excellently put."

"She does not much care for this sort of event, however," Delia said. "Perhaps she's too adventurous for the likes of it."

"Where is your home, Mr. Hailey?" Nan asked.

"Here. Bedford Square."

"Oh?" Delia asked, suddenly interested.

"My family has owned the same house for a hundred years. It's all I've ever known."

"Except for the time you spent in Turkey," Marshall said.

"Turkey?" Delia exclaimed.

Reginald smiled. "An exotically beautiful place, in case you were wondering."

"Why there?" Delia persisted.

"A wild hair, I suppose. I also spent time in Vienna, Hungary, and Bulgaria. I wanted to experience cultures that were different from ours."

"Ari will be fascinated," Nan said. "Not that we're not," she added quickly. "It's only that she's quite well-traveled."

"One of the reasons I'm looking forward to meeting her."

"Why have we not met you before?" Delia mused.

"Probably because he was in Turkey last year," Marshall stated.

"I have seen you," Reginald said, glancing from one to the other and ending on Patience. "But I wasn't able to arrange an introduction until now."

Patience blushed.

"Would you care to dance, Miss Caldwell?" he asked.

"I would like that," Patience replied breathily. "Mr. Hailey." He offered his arm, she accepted it, and they walked toward the dance floor.

Nan's smiled having seen a definite spark between them.

"Why do you look like that?" Delia asked. "It's a dance, not an engagement."

Nan ignored her. "Did you start somewhere else this evening, Mr. Derringer?"

"I did. Yes. At one of my clubs actually."

"I see. I was told there are other balls tonight, which is why I was asking. How do people even choose which ones to attend, I wonder?"

"Well first you have to be invited," Delia said.

"If you receive more than one invitation, I meant to say."

"Has that ever happened to you?" Delia asked.

Nan's pleasant façade faded.

"Excuse me," a male voice said.

Nan turned and found a young man addressing her.

"Would you care to dance?" he asked. "It's the quadrille next."

"You should," Delia encouraged.

Nan's hesitation was because of leaving Delia with Marshall, but the young man seemed nervous and vulnerable. Besides, Delia had promised. "Yes, thank you," Nan replied.

"I never much cared for this dance," Marshall said after they'd walked away.

"I enjoy almost every dance," Delia replied. "You couldn't have kept me away tonight."

He took a glass of wine from a tray being offered. "Another?" he asked Delia.

"Please."

He handed her one. "I say 'another.' I don't even know if you had one."

"Life is for living, Mr. Derringer. Of course, I had one. And I shall have more. And I will laugh and dance and have a wonderful time."

He lifted his glass to her.

They sipped and looked to the dance floor. "I'm pleased to see you're speaking with me," she said without looking at him. "You seemed put out with me the last time I saw you."

"No," he said dismissively. "I was irritated with Arianna."

189

Delia experienced a rush of exhilaration, tempered only by Patience sending a worried glance her way. "I don't know what they are so concerned over," she murmured confidentially.

"What do you mean?"

"Patience and Nan. They seem to be afraid I'll say something."

Marshall noticed Nan glance their way. "Something about what?"

"No idea, really."

He looked at Delia. "Something about Arianna?"

She shook her head. "Honestly, I have no idea. I saw her today, of course. Before she went out with her uncle and again later when someone called on her."

"Did she seem alright?"

"I haven't seen her so lively in quite a while."

"She seems to get worn down more easily since returning from Africa," he commented.

She bit on the inside of her mouth, agitated that she could not steer the conversation better. The dance would end soon, and she might not have another opportunity. "As I said, she seemed perfectly well when I saw her. It was by accident of course because we had callers."

"What was by accident?"

"Seeing her with her visitor. You see, we had the Miss Deharts visiting. Do you know them?"

He cocked his head slightly. "What visitor? Who called on Arianna?"

She frowned thoughtfully. "*Hmm.* What was his name?"

He frowned. "His?"

"A friend of her uncle's, I believe she said."

"Is that so?"

"That's what she said, and I don't know why she would be untruthful. Although, he was—"

"What?"

She rounded one shoulder forward slowly. "Magnificent to behold, if that's not too silly a description."

"I don't know who or what you consider magnificent to behold," he said stiffly. "So I am not altogether sure how *silly* it is."

"And I don't know how to explain it, nor do I know who he is. Ari said he was not really a member of society."

"Then why was he calling?" he asked testily.

She shrugged. "I couldn't say. Their visit seemed rather intense."

"What do you mean by that? Was she alone with him?"

"Yes." She gasped softly. "I remember now. It was Zan Shaffer."

"Never heard of him."

"Nor had I. Although I would not mind learning more. I don't suppose you could find out? Confidentially? For me?"

"Who was the friend of her uncle?"

"John Emerson."

His eyes widened as the music stopped. "Emerson!"

"Marshall, please. You'll get me into trouble."

"What are you talking about?" he asked angrily.

"I shouldn't have told you. The others … they didn't want you to know. Please don't say anything."

He turned his back to the dance floor, his expression stern. "What did this man look like?"

"He was one of the most handsome men I've ever seen," she said quickly, watching the others as they came back toward them. "Perhaps thirty years of age. Brown hair, blue eyes. He was tall, well over six feet, and quite fit."

"He didn't appear unkempt or—"

"No," she whispered. "He seemed a perfect gentleman."

"That was fun," Nan said as she rejoined them.

Patience and Reginald returned, rounding out their group. Patience eyed Delia warily. "What are you two talking about?"

"Nothing of significance," Marshall replied with a tight smile. "Will you excuse me?"

"Of course," Delia replied calmly.

He inclined his head and then walked away, discarding his glass at the closest opportunity.

Patience looked at Delia no longer attempting to look pleasant. "Was it my imagination or did he seem bothered about something?"

"Oh, he's always been moody," Reginald said. "You mustn't take it to heart."

"I thought he seemed fine," Delia said.

Patience and Nan exchanged a look.

Marshall walked outside and lit a cigarette wondering if it was possible. A man of about thirty, not in society and a friend of Emerson's. Meeting with Arianna. Alone. Surely it had not been the jungle refugee. "No," he murmured. It was an absurd notion. Still, why had she been alone with him?

He'd allowed her too much freedom. Tomorrow, he would see her, and they would make plans to announce their engagement. Furthermore, she would have no more male callers, nor would she break any plans that they'd made. He took a drag of the cigarette and felt more resolved. He was sick and tired of being surprised by mysteries and half-truths. In fact, tomorrow he would call on Lord Bluford and learn the specific whereabouts and condition of the savage.

The more he thought on it, the less likely it seemed that the caller could have been him. After all, a savage, more beast than man, could not possibly have been civilized in so short a time. To pass himself off as a gentleman? No. Impossible. In fact, the entire encounter might have been nothing more than a friend passing on a message to Sullivan Vinson through Ari, who may have intercepted it because he was out at the time.

It was Delia muddying the waters. She was a manipulative troublemaker if ever he had seen one. If she were his to deal with, he would have taken a razor strop to her backside until she couldn't sit for a week. Then she might have thought twice about stirring up trouble for the mere satisfaction of it.

He dropped his cigarette and stomped it out, his decision made. He would enjoy himself tonight, call on Lord Bluford tomorrow, and then go straight to Arianna. By this time tomorrow, their plans would be set.

~~~

At a ball a mile away, Lord Dalton Bluford stood with his son and daughter-in-law, watching Vanessa sweep around the dance floor in the arms of Jonathon Gilbert Douglas. One day, before long, Douglas would be the earl of a sizable estate. He was in love with Vanessa and had been for ages.

"Why can't she have feelings for *him*," the still lovely Priscilla Bluford sighed. Jonanthan was striking with fair hair and a mustache. He was kind and intelligent and tall and of an excellent pedigree. He was perfect for Vanessa.

Gregory looked at his wife. "I know, but it's her turn. She must make her own choices."

"But not this Mr. Shaffer," she rejoined.

"You should meet him," Dalton spoke up. "I dare say you might be impressed. I find myself liking him more each day. It's not as if they would ever be poor. She inherits."

"Have you considered what people will say?" Priscilla asked her father-in-law. "I'll tell you what they'll say. That he is part animal. That he has to be."

"I don't believe that's true," Dalton rejoined with good humor. "Meet him, Prissy, and you'll see."

She sighed in frustration. "He will never be fully accepted. He will always be regarded as—"

"We can control what people learn," Dalton interrupted.

She gave him a sideways look. "I'm surprised it's been kept under wraps for this long."

"As I said, I can control that. Really, I'd made up my mind to do it anyway."

"Oh?" his son spoke up. "I thought it was to be made public, a triumph for the Royal Society and the Museum."

"That was the initial thought," Dalton conceded. "However, I have funded this venture and I have sufficient sway to get my way in this. The Society, as you know, is a small association of like-minded gentlemen who have a profound interest in the furthering of science but also in humanity. We must think of Zan. Consider his interests above our own. If the true nature of the expedition did get out, it would be a sensation."

"Yes, it would," Gregory agreed.

"And he would never be able to enjoy any sort of a normal life," Dalton continued. "He would always be a … curiosity."

"That's putting it mildly," Priscilla interjected. "And it was precisely my point."

"There's to be a meeting of the Society next week," Dalton said. "I'm going to address the subject then. This is something I can do for Zan, and I intend on doing it."

"Good for you, Father," Gregory regaled. "The man's had a horrific life. This seems the least we can do for him."

The music transitioned, and Vanessa changed dance partners. "I do feel it's time Vanessa came home though," Priscilla said. "I know this Mr. Shaffer has turned her head, but it is not a suitable match."

"Father and I will leave that to you to discuss with her," Gregory stated with an amused expression. "And I don't want to be anywhere in the vicinity when you do."

"Don't exaggerate," she rejoined. "She may feel an infatuation, but she is a reasonable, intelligent young woman."

Both men smirked and turned away.

"Men," Priscilla huffed. "You don't believe we *can* possess beauty and intelligence at the same time, do you?"

"In great abundance, my love," her husband replied. "As well as sweetness." He paused. "And stubbornness."

Priscilla shook her head, but grinned.

Jonathan watched Vanessa from the sidelines. She was exquisite. There was not another word for it. He'd loved her since they were fourteen, and he'd been so certain she would be his wife, but it felt as though she was slipping away from him. Why?

"How are you, Douglas?" Sir Alistair Harrison asked as he joined him.

"Well, thank you. And you, sir?"

"Can't complain, other than my hip has been giving me a devil of a time. But only when I move."

"Well, if that's all," Jonathan jested.

Harrison shrugged. "What's one to do? Either you age and take on an ailment or two or you die young and leave a good-looking corpse."

"Indeed."

"So where are you off to for the season?"

"The usual. Our house near Lancing," Jonathan said distractedly, still watching Vanessa.

Harrison grunted. "Cooler weather, good hunting. I am looking forward to it."

Jonathan gave him a half-hearted smile. "I am, as well." The music ended and Vanessa and her partner went their separate ways. Vanessa rejoined her friends who spoke with animation, as women often did. He always wondered what it was they talked about. Across the way, her parents and grandfather stood chatting amiably. He caught Priscella Bluford's eye, and she gave him a sad smile that made him feel a pang of anxiety. Had Vanessa written him off? He could stand it no longer. "Excuse me, will you? There's someone I must speak with."

The man waved him off, and Jonathan went to Vanessa's group. "Ladies," he said amiably before looking at Vanessa. "May I have a moment of your time?"

"Of course," she said lightly.

"Perhaps out of doors?"

"Alright."

They didn't speak again until they were outside and alone on a veranda. "Have I lost you?" he blurted.

She blinked. "I beg your pardon?"

"You heard me," he said gently. "This is me, Nessa. I've known you for most of your life, been in love with you for most of mine. Tell me, please. What have I done or not done?"

"It's not that," she admitted sheepishly.

"Then what is it? Someone else?" Her expression instantly confirmed it. She didn't want to hurt him, but there it was. He turned away to collect himself. How had he not seen it coming? Who was it? Would she tell him if he asked? "Does he love you as I do?"

"Jon—"

He turned back to her having made up his mind to take the high road. He would not ask who it was. It would be evident in time anyway. "I hope he does. I love you enough to sincerely hope that." She looked guilt-ridden, and he battled a wave of emotion. "Will you excuse me?" he asked just above a whisper since he did not trust the strength of his voice. His heart felt like a boulder as he walked away.

Chapter Twenty-Seven

The next morning, Zan stared at John in surprise. "It's from the private agent of inquiry?"

"Yes," John replied. He and Jane had returned with the report from the man hired to discover all he could about Zan's background. "He worked quickly."

"Do I have family here?"

Emerson smiled. "You do." He handed the report over. "Would you like to read it, or shall I give you the quick gist of it?"

"Tell me. Please."

"There is no family left on your father's side, but your mother's sister, Mrs. Aileen Murphy, is alive and well. She's married and has a family."

"So I have cousins?"

"You do. Five first cousins and some of them have children."

Zan took a moment to absorb the news. "Where are they?"

"On the east side of the city. Pelham Street in Spitalfields."

"Do they know about me?"

"Yes. The agent told them in order to get the information he needed."

"What did they say?"

"They were shocked. Naturally. But they are highly anxious to see you."

Zan ran his hand through his hair and then nodded. "I'll go now."

"Perhaps we should write first," Emerson suggested.

"I won't stay if they don't wish it, but I will go." In fact, the anticipation building in his chest made it difficult to breathe. If he didn't go soon, it would turn into a dark anxiety. Wondering what they'd be like. Wondering if they'd accept him or if they would see him as an animal.

"Shall I go with you?"

Zan shook his head. "Thank you, but I have to start relying on myself."

"It doesn't have to be today," Emerson replied with a worried expression.

"I'll be fine. Even if it doesn't go well, I see Ari this afternoon."

Emerson smiled and nodded. "I am so pleased about that."

Zan lifted the report. "Pelham Street."

"Number sixteen," Emerson said. "But why don't you change back into the clothes you first wore here?"

"Why?"

Emerson hesitated a moment. "They're not wealthy," he said carefully.

Ah. His clothes were too fine. "I will change."

Zan raised his hand to knock on the door of number sixteen Pelham Street and then lowered it again. He looked around at other homes that looked similar to this one. The buildings were old, but the porches and walks were well swept, and no garbage was in sight. Pots of flowers graced steps and porches. This is where he had come from. Either this place or someplace very like it.

He took a deep breath and knocked. The door was quickly opened by a very pregnant woman of about twenty-five years of age. For an instant she stood as if frozen with shock, and he understood the reaction well since they resembled one another. It was a peculiar moment and his skin rippled up in gooseflesh.

"Sebastian?" she uttered.

He nodded. "Zan. I'm called Zan."

"Oh my." Tears sprang to her eyes, and she stepped back smiling. "Come in! Please, come in."

He stepped in, and she shut the door behind him.

"Mother, come quickly," she called. "Sebastian has come. Zan," she corrected herself, although she was only speaking to him. "I'm Mary Sue. I'm your cousin."

"How do you do?"

She laughed lightly. "I'm quite well."

"Sebastian?" a woman said from behind him.

He turned and felt a jolt of recognition that weakened his knees.

"Oh," the woman whispered. She came forward slowly, holding her hands in front of her as if to receive something.

"This is my mother," Mary Sue said. "Your Aunt Aileen."

He nodded, knowing somehow.

Aileen embraced him wholeheartedly, rocking him slightly in her sturdy arms. She pulled back to study him, clearly overcome.

"He's got the Hewitt look," Mary Sue commented, still smiling. "That was our mothers' name," she explained. "And most of us born to the Hewitts have the look. Like peas in a pod people have been known to say."

The thought was pleasing and intriguing. He'd been warmly welcomed by Lord Bluford. He was also welcome at the Emerson's home, but this was different. He felt like one of Luke's puzzle pieces that had found its correct placement. It was not just the physical resemblance, the similar blue eyes, it was something that ran deeper.

Blood deep.

"Are you well?" Aileen asked searchingly. "You look well."

He nodded. "I am."

"Let's go sit. I want to hear everything!"

A little girl of eight years of age or so appeared and was staring at him with unabashed interest.

"Ivy, this is our cousin, Zan," Mary Sue said. She looked at Zan. "She's Norma's. My elder sister's."

"How do you do?" Ivy said with a curtsy.

"Very well, thank you. And how are you?"

She giggled. "Fine, thank you."

"Come," Aileen said to Zan with a proud maternal smile. She led the way through a narrow hallway and into a sitting room in back.

"Run and get your mother," Mary Sue said to Ivy, who then dashed up the stairs.

"Sit here, dear," Aileen said, offering him the best chair.

He wasn't sure of the proper etiquette, so he accepted. The floral fabric of the chair was worn, the arms covered with doilies, and he could feel a loose spring beneath him. "Your family all lives here?"

Aileen sat across from him. She nodded. "Except for you. Yes." Her expression was part bewildered, part awestruck.

"Shall I get Papa?" Mary Sue asked.

Aileen sighed. "If he feels up to it," she replied softly. She looked back at Zan. "This won't be your only visit, will it?" she asked hopefully.

He shook his head. "Not if you'll have me."

She nearly winced at the words. "Oh, Sebastian."

As Mary Sue walked away with a quiet step, he wondered if he'd said something wrong. Maybe he should have allowed John to come with him.

"There was an accident at the mill," Aileen confided. "Joe's hand was … mangled. He lost it in the end. I tell you to prepare you." She looked down at her own hands clutched in her lap, then back up at him. "He's having trouble accepting it. There's the pain, of course, but it's more than that. He's never been one to complain about pain. Or to complain about anything."

Zan tried to imagine living without use of a hand and couldn't. "When was the accident?"

"Three months now."

"I'm sorry."

"We all are. He's the backbone of the family, and this is quite a family."

"There are five children?" Zan had scanned the report on the way here, but his thoughts were in a muddle.

Aileen nodded. "Joe and I had three, Norma, Mary Sue, and Fredrick, and we took in my brother's children when he got into trouble. He's passed now, God rest his soul. He was always in one mess or another. Ended up in Newgate before he died. That's a prison."

It struck a note of familiarity. Many things were. Their faces. The smell of this house. An iron doorstop in the shape of a dog.

"I only hope Thom doesn't follow in his footsteps, but he enjoys his ale, and he's quick to resort to a brawl. I think it's only a love of us that's kept him out of prison or worse."

"How old is he?"

"He'll be twenty-five this year. A few years older than Freddy." She smiled tenderly. "You are the senior of the cousins. Then Norma is three years younger that you. She used to follow you around everywhere. She's the one who called you Zan. She couldn't pronounce Sebastian, so she tagged on to the end of it and it got turned into Zan."

He felt a painful chill up his spine. It was like grasping at shadows, but he felt the truth of it.

"Then Mary Sue, Thom, Fred, and then Ellie. She's seventeen and pretty as the day is long. She's recently found work as a front parlor maid for a family named Westcott," she said proudly.

"How old were Thom and Ellie when they came to live with you?"

"The last time, Thom was ten, and Ellie wasn't but three. Bless her heart, she doesn't remember her mum and da at all."

"Then their mother died too?"

Aileen shrugged. "She was another troubled soul. It was her that dropped them off on our doorstep. We never saw her again." Aileen sighed softly. "I can still recall so clearly, Maggie drunk and beyond caring, and young Thom so stoic. He was angry, but he thought if he kept it all inside him, he was in control. He still thinks that. Of course, he's anything but in control when he drinks too much and gets annoyed about something."

"And Ellie?"

"Poor little waif. At only three years old, with eyes like saucers, she just wanted someone to cleave onto. And you," Aileen said with a sad smile. "You might have been right here too."

"Did we live here?"

"For a while. This was my parents' home, where Cat and Timmy and I grew up, but Joe didn't get along with your father, so your parents left. Took rooms down the street. Cat and I never let it come between us though. We were thick as thieves, we were."

"Cat," he said quietly. "My mother."

She nodded.

Mary Sue stepped back through the doorway and behind her was another woman and Ivy. "Zan, this is my sister, Norma."

Zan stood as Norma came forward. She reached for his hands, and he took hold. Her hands were rougher than Ari's or Vanessa's but warm and firm. She was not as attractive as her younger sister, but she had a pleasing face and the look of the Hewitt's. Tears shone in her eyes.

"You could have knocked us over with a feather when that man came to tell us you were alive," she said. "But here you are."

A man in his mid-fifties stepped into the doorway looking disheveled. He'd obviously been napping. He braced his bandaged stump in his good hand, and Zan felt a strong sense of pity.

Norma moved to Zan's side. "This is my father, Joe."

Norma continued saying something, but Zan couldn't follow because of the rush of memory he was experiencing. Of his uncle and his father. Yelling. There had been blood. His blood. It tasted metallic in his mouth. It was his uncle, the man standing before him, that had stepped in to shield him from a blow. Later, it was his uncle's strong arms that held him and made sure his arm wasn't broken again. Zan's eyes filled. "I remember," he whispered.

The room had grown silent.

Norma wrapped an arm around him. "Are you alright, Zan?"

Zan swallowed. "I remember," he said to Joe. "You protected me."

Joe came forward and stopped in front of him. He reached out to cup his nephew's face with his good hand. "You look good, Sebastian."

"It's Zan, Papa," Mary Sue said tenderly.

"Zan," Joe repeated with a nod of his head. "Norma used to call you that." He stepped back as if uncomfortable with the affection he'd shown. "Is it true you were in the jungle? Alone?"

"I wasn't alone, but there were no other people."

Joe looked at his wife. "She tried to convince them to let you stay with us."

"Joe," Aileen said quietly. "Don't."

Joe looked back at Zan. "And your mother wanted it too, but your father wouldn't hear of it."

Zan nodded, vaguely recalling it.

"Taking a babe to the wild African jungle," Joe muttered angrily.

"I was eight," Zan said with a wan smile.

"No, dear," Aileen rejoined. "You were six. About to be seven."

He looked at her, confused.

"Your father kept saying you were old enough. 'About to be eight, about to be eight,' he said. Cat corrected him once." She took a deep breath, and her mouth tightened.

"Your birthday is the twenty-eighth of July," Norma said up.

"Happy belated birthday," Mary Sue said with a ghost of a smile.

Aileen reached over and took hold of his hand. "Not a day goes by that I don't think of you and your mother, and not a July twenty-eighth goes by that we don't remember the day of your birth."

He struggled to maintain his composure. He hadn't fathomed how heart wrenching this was going to be. He looked back at Joe, feeling a strong connection to him. "I'm sorry for your accident."

"Me too," Joe replied wryly. "A man with one hand. Don't rightly know what I'm supposed to do now."

"Let's sit," Mary Sue urged.

"Yes," Norma agreed.

A slam of a door and the shrieking of young voices filled the air.

"Boys," Joe hollered.

Two young boys, both about five or six years of age, peeked into the room looking wary. "Sorry, Gramps," one muttered.

"Come meet your cousin, Zan," Norma said. They came close, and she placed her hands on the shoulders of one. "This is my youngest, Rob, and this is Mary Sue's Freddy," she said as she smoothed back his tousled hair with an affectionate grin. "They've been digging for worms. Can you tell?"

Freddy frowned up at her with confusion. "He's not our cousin. He's too old."

The women chuckled, and Zan with them, his heart warmed by the familial bond so evident in the room. There was something else, as well. A sense of pride that this was his family.

"Zan is my first cousin, so he's your second cousin," Norma explained to the boy. "That's the way it works."

"Will he live here now?" Rob asked leaning his head back against his mother's skirt.

"He can if he wants," Joe spoke up.

Zan flushed with gratitude. "I have somewhere to live, but I would like to visit."

"Just don't ask me to let you go yet," Aileen said as she reached over to pat his arm. "You don't even seem real. You seem like a dream that's floated in the door."

"He knocked, Mama," Mary Sue teased, winking at Zan.

Chapter Twenty-Eight

Z an returned to Lord Bluford's home with little time to spare before he needed to leave to see Arianna. He quickly washed and changed his clothes. When he was ready, he found John in the garden with Jane.

"How did it go?" John asked.

Jane's gaze was curious as well.

Zan smiled. "It was good. They know me. They look like me."

John smiled with relief. "I'm so glad to hear it."

"I remembered things. I'll tell you, but I have to go to Ari now."

"I'm sure it feels good to say that. Shall we come with you or give you a few minutes alone?"

"I would like a little time alone with her," he admitted.

"Go," John urged. "We'll be there soon."

~~~

Marshall was led to the study of Lord Bluford's town residence, but the sight of a man approaching from the far end of the corridor stopped him in his tracks. The man was so arresting in both his appearance and bearing, that the description Delia had used, *magnificent to behold,* leapt to mind. But he could not possibly be the wild man. He possessed far too much confidence and charisma to have lived his life in an African jungle until recently. Still, he was here in the home of the man who had supposedly pledged to support him.

"Sir?" the butler asked, having turned back.

"Yes, coming."

"Mr. Derringer," Lord Bluford greeted when Marshall was shown in. "Good afternoon."

"Good afternoon, Lord Bluford. Thank you for seeing me."

"My pleasure, I'm sure. Sit, please."

Marshall moved to one of the chairs across from where Bluford sat in the middle of a settee, not having bothered to rise.

"To what do I owe the honor?"

"I'm a friend of Miss Arianna Day," Marshall began, watching for a reaction in the older man. He received none.

"Afraid I don't know the lady."

"She's the niece of Sullivan Vinson."

"Ah. Well, I do know him." He frowned pensively. "As a matter of fact, I have met your Miss Day then. Lovely girl, about my granddaughter's age. You were saying?"

"I believe you're aware of the recent expedition to Africa," Marshall said.

"I am. A group of intrepid explorers went in search of a new breed of great ape. They did not find them, but the African jungle is a massive area. Massive. Perhaps they'll try again at a later date. I don't know."

"I was hoping you might tell me about the man," Marshall said, getting to the point.

"What man is that?"

"The man who was found in the jungle."

Bluford blinked and cocked his head. "I beg your pardon?"

"Living amongst the apes?"

Bluford grinned. "It sounds to me as if someone has pulled your leg, Mr. Derringer. I mean no offense, of course, but that is … well, preposterous."

Marshall resisted the urge to loosen his collar. "I thought so at first too, but it was confirmed."

"Confirmed? By whom?"

"Doctor Thurman."

"Ah, Leopold. A good man, but—" he paused and leaned forward slightly "—was he drinking at the time?"

Marshall forced himself to take a moment before replying. He wasn't an idiot. He recognized when he was being stonewalled. "May I inquire about the man staying in your home?"

"Which home?"

Marshall chewed on the end of his tongue as agitation bubbled inside him like molten lava. "This home. I saw him just a few minutes ago. A striking man, about thirty years of age—"

"That would be my friend, Mr. Shaffer."

Marshall barely resisted the urge to cry *Aha!* "Would this Mr. Shaffer happen to be from Africa?"

Lord Bluford stuck a finger in the air as if having made a discovery. "Perhaps that is where the root of the story came from. Shaffer is from England, of course, but he spent many years in Africa overseeing one of his family's plantations."

"Is that so?"

"Indeed. But that tale of living amongst apes? What a lark! He'll get a laugh out of that."

Marshall craned his neck, his collar suddenly too tight. "Has John Emerson been working with him?"

"Working with him?" Bluford asked with a puzzled expression. "They're good friends. Emerson's work takes him all over the world, as you may know. I believe they met when Emerson traveled to Africa on some project."

So many convenient answers and not one of them truthful.

"How is your family?" Bluford asked pleasantly. "Are they all in town?"

"They are. And they're well, thank you."

"I hope you'll pass on my regards."

"I shall," Marshall replied. He rose knowing that he was being excused. Not that it mattered since he wasn't going to get any honest answers from the man. "Thank you for your time, Lord Bluford." The old man nodded graciously, but his shrewd eyes glittered with amusement. *Amusement at my expense*, Marshall thought bitterly as he left.

Chapter Twenty-Nine

A ri paced between the library and the foyer waiting for Zan to arrive. She had arranged for Sully to join them at quarter past the hour and Uncle Wilbur and Aunt Edith at half past. If Zan arrived on time, she would have fifteen minutes alone with him. Which might not be perfectly correct, but nor was it scandalous.

When she heard Zan arrive at the appointed time, excitement coursed through her, and she had to take a moment to rein it in before she stepped out to meet him. "Thank you, Mr. Fletcher," she said. "I'll show Mr. Shaffer to the salon."

"Very good, Miss Day," Fletcher replied.

"My uncles and my aunt will be joining us," Ari said to Zan, but mostly for the butler's sake. She gestured and then took the lead.

"The Emerson's will be coming, as well," he said.

"Wonderful. I am so looking forward to meeting her and to seeing John again."

They walked into the salon and gravitated toward chairs positioned close together. "How are your dance lessons progressing?" she asked as she sat.

"I am not good."

"We all get better with practice."

His blue eyes gleamed. "Perhaps you could practice with me."

His intensity made it difficult to reply. "Do you plan to attend any balls?"

"I go where they take me."

"What's been your favorite thing, so far?"

"This."

She looked down at her lap to buy a moment.

"I embarrassed you?" he asked,

She looked up and met his eyes. "I'm fine," she assured him. She wanted meaningful conversation between them, but she also needed him to understand the need for restraint and prudence. "The truth is, I am encumbered at the moment. I need to decide how to go about doing what I have to do," she said haltingly.

"With the man who wants to marry you."

She blinked in surprise, but it was a relief he understood. "Yes."

"Do you love him?"

Her eyes widened and then she looked away from his questioning gaze, aware that her face was blazing. "You should not ask such a thing. It's too personal and too blunt."

"Do you?" he persisted.

She looked back at him, ready to shut down the inquiry, but his vulnerability made it impossible not to be honest. "No."

"Could you love me?"

She bolted out of her seat.

He stood as quickly. "I should not have asked."

"No! You sh—c-cannot!" She turned away needing a moment. Soon her family would arrive, and they would look like guilty lovers. Which is exactly how it felt.

"Shall I leave?"

She turned back to him. "No," she replied emphatically. "But you cannot say things like that. Especially now as I'm—"

"Encumbered?" he supplied when her voice faltered.

"Yes." She sat again.

"I did not have these troubles in the jungle," he murmured as he took his seat.

She nearly laughed. A forbidden, romantic *tête-à-tête* was precisely what this felt like. "I suppose not." Their gaze connected and held. She knew she shouldn't but, "What do you understand of marriage?" she asked quietly.

"When a man and woman love each other, they marry," he stated.

In a perfect world, yes. "Unfortunately, many marry for less noble reasons than that."

"What reasons?"

"Expectations. Money. Family connections. Improving one's position in society."

He frowned. "It should be that when they love each other, they marry."

"Yes. It should be that way."

"Then he protects her and provides for her. They come together in body and then sometimes there are children."

She was taken aback until she imagined the son they might have together. A beautiful child, so like his father. The picture was so clear, it left her shaken.

"Ari?"

"We should converse on more trivial subjects," she said haltingly. "The weather or—" She broke off when she heard her name. *Oh, no.* That hadn't been Marshall, had it?

"—believe Miss Day may be in the drawing room," Mr. Fletcher was saying, speaking louder than usual. *To warn her.* She stood with a gasp, and Zan rose with her, cognizant of her alarm.

"Really, sir," Fletcher said. "Allow me to go find her and—"

"It's fine, Fletcher, really," Marshall snapped.

Arianna grabbed Zan's hand, and they dashed toward the dining room barely clearing the salon when Marshall walked by, followed closely by Fletcher. She pressed herself flat against the wall filled with panic.

"Who is that?" Zan asked quietly.

"Him," she whispered.

"Ah. He will be angry to find me here."

She nodded.

"I would be angry," Zan said. "If I were him."

I wouldn't want to hide from you.

"I should go?"

"No. I'll get rid of him." She nearly recoiled at the words as they tumbled out of her mouth, but she meant them. "Give me a few moments and then go back into the salon. I'll be back soon." He nodded, and she left through the dining room door, stepping into the hall just in time to see Mr. Fletcher and Marshall look into the drawing room at the end of the hall. They saw she was not there and turned to come back. She started toward them hoping to pass the salon door before they reached it. It had been a foolish move on her part. She should have exited through the salon door.

"There you are," Marshall said in an annoyed tone as he closed in. "I need to speak with you."

"Arianna? Is everything alright?" Sully asked from behind her.

She turned to him desperately trying to remain calm and praying that Zan still lingered in the dining room. "Could you go into the salon and keep Zan company?" she asked quietly, so Marshall would not hear.

His eyes widened, and he glanced worriedly at Marshall, who was nearly to them.

Ari hurried forward to reach Marshall before he reached the door to the salon, but she was a fraction of a second too late. He reached her, drew breath to speak, but glanced in the salon having seen Zan from the corner of his eye. His jaw dropped, and then he clamped it shut and scowled accusingly at Arianna.

"Mr. Derringer," Sully said, stepping up beside Ari. "I hope you're well."

"Well enough," Marshall replied coldly without taking his eyes from Arianna. "We need to talk."

"Why don't we go into the library?" she asked hoping to get him to the other end of the house.

"The drawing room will do fine," he stated.

She acquiesced and started forward, walking stiffly. In the drawing room, she turned to face him, clutching her hands together.

"I know who that man is," Marshall ranted. "I also know you saw him yesterday, *alone*, and here he is again today." He blew a breath through his nostrils like an enraged bull. "You will explain this outrageous behavior!"

She drew a breath determined to speak calmly. "I do not feel it is outrageous to meet with a friend."

"Friend?" he scoffed. "Is he or is he not the wild man who abducted you in the jungle?"

Her throat closed and she couldn't speak.

"How does that sort of experience qualify as grounds for friendship? But even if he was a *friend*. Really, Arianna! Alone with a man like that? Even Americans have better sense, and you've been here since you were a child. You most definitely know better!"

She lifted her chin. "I am glad you're here, because we do need to talk."

"Yes, we do. Because there are new rules starting this moment."

"Rules?" she repeated incredulously.

"Or call it an understanding; I don't care, but you will not, I repeat, *will not*, entertain any men without proper supervision *and* my permission. Is that clear?"

She didn't trust herself to speak.

"Furthermore, you will not break any plans that we have made unless it is a true emergency. No more sending me a note because you are tired. You will put the ring I gave you back on your finger, and you will leave it there. We will announce our engagement tomorrow evening, and we will marry the first Saturday in December."

"No."

He cocked his head as if uncertain he had heard correctly.

"I will return your grandmother's ring to you. I care about you, and I wish you well, but I do not want to marry you."

"Oh, but you will, Arianna."

She drew back. "I beg your pardon?"

"You should beg my pardon!"

"Marshall—"

"By now everyone in Northampton knows of our engagement. We only need to announce it here. And we will tomorrow evening."

She shook her head. "I don't know how to say this any more clearly, but I am not going to marry you."

"If you refuse to do as I say," he began and then paused dramatically. "Are you listening?"

She refused to respond.

"I will hire the best barrister in London, and we will bring suit against you for breach of promise to marry. I certainly do not need your family's money, but I will take it."

It felt as if the breath had been knocked from her. "You wouldn't!"

"Oh, I would, Arianna. I will. Furthermore, I will bring suit against Mr. Shaffer," he said, enunciating the name sharply. "For alienation of affection. Lord Bluford may have taken him under his wing, but he won't be stuck paying a hefty award when we win. Which we will."

She felt sick to her stomach. "Do you actually expect me—"

"I am not finished! Should the lawsuit go public, go to trial, everything will come out. There are always journalists in the courtroom, and I'll make damned sure of it this time. Do you think they won't jump all over a story about a dangerous wild man living here, who until a very short time ago lived amongst apes in Africa? The story of how he abducted you and kept you will be splashed across every newspaper. You will be ruined, and he will be reviled as the freak of nature that he is."

Arianna took a step back, reeling at his viciousness.

"If that is not what you want," he finished quietly, "You will do exactly as I say."

She couldn't speak or move. How had she ever, *ever*, considered a life with him? He was horrible. He was heartless. But if she refused him, he would do what he'd threatened. He would utterly destroy Zan's chances at a decent life. He would humiliate Aunt Edith and Uncle Wilbur and Uncle Sully. How clearly she could see it. Not only that, he would enjoy doing it. He would claim she'd brought it on herself.

"Now go upstairs to your room and put the ring back on your finger."

He'd won. She knew it and she wanted to leave, wanted not to see his hateful, spiteful face for one more instant, but her legs felt like planks of wood.

Impatient, he grabbed her arm and propelled her to the door, where he gave her a shove. "Go! And return quickly! Before I change my mind."

She moved forward almost too dizzy to see straight. Aunt Edith and Uncle Wilbur had stopped in the corridor ahead, and they were looking at her so queerly.

"What's wrong?" Edith asked worriedly as Ari reached them. Ari shook her head unable to utter a word. She tried to keep moving, but her aunt had taken hold of her arms. "You're white as a sheet!"

"Ari?" Zan called.

She pulled away from her aunt and kept moving. What choice was there? Marshall would ruin him. He'd ruin them both. Zan deserved a decent life. He'd been denied one for too long.

"Ari!" Zan called as he came after her. He was following her because he didn't know better. He didn't understand the rules of propriety. *Too many rules.* He was right; there were too many.

Zan grabbed her and turned her around to face him. "What's wrong?" he demanded.

She shook her head.

"Get your hands off my fiancée," Marshall demanded as he strode toward them.

Zan ignored him and studied her, and she wanted to explain, to say something, but she couldn't. Her eyes filled, and she couldn't stop them from spilling over. She loved him, wanted to marry him, and she would never be able to see him again.

"I said," Marshall started again, grabbing Zan's arm, "get your—"

Zan shoved Marshall and sent him flying backwards into the wall. He slid down it, gasping for air. Sully, Wilbur, and Edith looked on helplessly, and from the other end of the foyer, John and Jane Emerson and Mr. Fletcher looked the same, having just appeared.

It was a terrible, surreal moment. Ari wanted to burst into tears, run away and hide like a child, but she wasn't a child. She was a woman who had made a mess of her life. Worse, it was conceivable she'd made a mess of Zan's life. Zan turned back to her with an expression of ferocity. She knew he would kill to protect her, but she had to protect him. "I have to marry him," she said quietly. "I'm so sorry."

His face filled with such hurt, and he shook his head. "No!"

Her throat and chest hurt terribly, and a flood of tears were coming, so she walked away. She bypassed the main staircase because she wasn't confident of the strength in her legs, and she would not collapse in front of everyone. She'd made enough of a scene for one day.

~~~

Wilbur walked over to Marshall Derringer and offered a hand up, but the younger man ignored it. He struggled to get back to his feet while glowering at Zan.

"I don't understand what's happened here," Wilbur said quietly. "But I think it best if you leave now."

Marshall straightened his jacket. "Arianna is my fiancée. He will leave first."

Emerson reached Zan. "It's best if we go," he urged.

Zan glared at Marshall. "What did you do to her?"

"That is none of your business! She's going to be my wife. *My* wife. I will do and say whatever I wish! You, however, will never see her again."

Emerson squeezed Zan's arm to get through to him or to at least stop him from charging Derringer, which looked probable. "He is a jackass," Emerson said under his breath as he stepped in front of Zan, breaking Zan's eye contact with Derringer. "We'll have to resolve this another time. For now, we should go."

The words finally filtered through Zan's beleaguered mind. He looked down the hall Arianna had disappeared into and then nodded.

"Another time," Emerson said to Sully.

"Yes," Sully returned.

The Emersons followed Fletcher to the door with Zan braced protectively between them. When they were gone, and after an awkward silence, Marshall cleared his throat. "None of that should have occurred. Arianna has used exceedingly poor judgment. But as of today, we put this nonsense behind us once and for all. Arianna and I will marry the first Saturday in December. It won't be a long engagement but long enough. We will announce it tomorrow evening."

Wilbur pursed his lips. "Is that what she wants?"

"Yes," Marshall declared. "And now I will see myself out. If you would let Arianna know that I'll call for her at seven tomorrow evening. We'll dine with my family. In fact, why don't you all join us?"

It was Edith who responded. "Unfortunately, we have a prior engagement," she said coolly.

"Another time then," Marshall said, beginning to look supremely uncomfortable. "Good day."

"I'll go see to Ari," Edith murmured when he'd gone, and then she walked on.

Sullivan and Wilbur faced one another. "What in bloody hell was that?" Wilbur asked quietly.

"I do not know," Sullivan replied grimly. "But I will have the answer."

Edith went down the main level corridor, glancing in each room she passed on the way to the back staircase. She climbed the steps and made her way toward Arianna's room. Outside, thunder cracked, and Edith came to an abrupt halt, beset by a memory of another afternoon many years ago that had quickly grown dark with the approach of a storm. Ari had only recently arrived in England. Edith had found the girl huddled in the window seat of her room crying. "What's wrong?" Edith had asked gently as she gathered Ari into her arms.

"I miss my mother."

"Well, of course you do," Edith crooned. "That's only natural."

"I wish she'd been happier. I wish she'd stayed here."

Edith smiled tenderly. "If she'd stayed here, we wouldn't have you." She handed over a lacy handkerchief and Ari wiped her face. "Grief is a terrible thing, my love, but the pain lessens in time. Love remains. The good memories. But the pain of missing her will ease. You'll see."

"Do you think anyone will ever love me the way Uncle Wilbur loves you?"

"Of course, I do. I know it."

"My father didn't love my mother that way."

Edith smoothed Arianna's hair back. "What makes you say that?"

"She told me."

Edith drew back in surprise. "What did she tell you?"

"To hold out for true love. She said she didn't want me stuck in a loveless marriage. That it was better to be alone."

"That doesn't mean she wasn't loved."

Ari shook her head. "My father didn't really love her. I think that's why she died."

"No, Ari. She contracted a fever. An illness. It couldn't be helped." Edith kissed the top of Ari's head and held her tighter. "But whatever the truth is about your father and your mother, *you* will find a wonderful, caring man, and you will be happy. You're so special to us, we would refuse to see you married to anyone that doesn't deserve you."

Now, standing in the middle of the corridor, Edith clapped a hand to her mouth. She said that but then, when it was time to live up to the words, she'd tried to convince her to marry that odious Mr. Derringer. She cringed with shame. Not five minutes ago, Ari had stood white as a sheet and shaking from head to toe telling the man she loved she was marrying another. It had been agonizing to witness. And it was what *she* had advised.

"Lady Vinson?" Patience said as she approached. "Is something wrong?"

Edith lowered her hand and shook her head. "Help me find Ari?"

"Of course. Is something wrong?"

Edith merely nodded and then watched as Patience turned and went to Ari's room, knocking as she opened it and stepped in.

At first glance, Patience thought Ari was not there. She started to leave but then heard a soft sob. Stepping further in, she saw Arianna crouched on the floor in the corner, her legs drawn up, her arms wrapped around them, her head buried in the void. "Ari!" She rushed over, dropped to her side, and reached for her. "What's happened?"

Edith stepped inside the room and closed the door. She walked to the edge of the bed near the girls and sat. "Arianna, listen to me. You do not have to marry that man."

"I d-do," Ari stammered.

"No, you do not! I was utterly wrong in advising it. We will show him that—"

"He'll bring s-suit against us," Ari cried, lifting her red, tear-streaked face. "For breach of p-promise to marry. And he'll ruin Zan. He'll ruin him! I c-can't do that to him!"

"*Shhh* now," Patience cooed. "You'll make yourself sick."

"I don't care. I deserve it!"

"Stop it," Edith snapped. "I will not hear such foolishness. There will be a way out of this mess."

Ari shook her head stubbornly.

"Your aunt is right," Patience said. "There has to be a way."

"There's not, there's not, there's not," Ari said, shaking her head.

"Get another handkerchief, will you, dear?" Edith said to Patience.

Patience got up and fetched several handkerchiefs. She brought them back, and then turned and went to the bowl and ewer.

"Dry your face," Edith ordered. "And breathe deeply. Making yourself ill will not help matters."

Patience poured water into the bowl, wetted a cloth and brought it back. She sat close to Ari and touched the damp cloth to Ari's cheek and forehead. "Close your eyes."

Arianna obeyed, exhausted from her cry and the raw, searing emotions that had ravaged her. She felt the cloth on her eyes and leaned over onto Patience's shoulder crying softly again. Patience and Edith exchanged a look, and then Edith got up and left to go speak with her husband and Sullivan. Together they would find a way to extricate Arianna from Mr. Derringer's clutches.

~~~

"What did he say to her?" Zan asked as they rode back to Park Street.

"I don't know," Emerson admitted. "But whatever it was, it had quite an impact."

"I have to see her."

"Let's find out what we can first."

"She was happy until he got there," Zan seethed.

"I'll send a note to Sullivan. We need the facts."

"No. What I need is her, and she needs me."

"I understand your feelings, Zan, but this is not only your decision."

Zan looked out the window but looked back when he saw Jane communicating something. Emerson looked at him. "She thinks I should return immediately after dropping you both off."

Zan nodded. "I'll go with you."

"I don't think that's a good idea. Let me find out what I can first. Arianna is in no frame of mind to see you or anyone else. You saw her."

Jane reached forward and took hold of Zan's hand and gave it a squeeze. Their gazes locked, and he knew that she understood his anguish.

~~~

As Marshall was driven to his club, he felt a choking fury at the gall of that ruffian. That monkey boy. Laying a hand on him? Perhaps he didn't understand how things worked in the civilized world yet, but he would.

What this situation called for was exposure. Not too much, because Arianna's name could never enter into the picture, but enough so that people learned exactly what Zan Shaffer was despite his handsome face. Magnificent to behold? Those words made him want to spit.

A lawsuit was not the way to go, no matter what he'd had to threaten, because he would look like a cuckolded fool, but an exposé in *The Times* would accomplish the deed brilliantly. He would find the perfect journalist to run with the story. And what a story. It was both sensational and true. Best of all, he would never have to accept any blame, because he would pass on information anonymously.

He would be blameless, Ari would be secured, and Shaffer would be exposed. Marshall rotated his shoulder, which was sore from where he'd hit the wall. "We'll see who ends up battered," he muttered.

~~~

Arianna made her way downstairs an hour later, having repaired her appearance as much as it could be. She found her aunt and uncles sitting with John Emerson in the drawing room.

"Arianna," Emerson said as he rose.

"I'm glad to see you again, John," she said in a quiet, measured voiced that clearly revealed how much of a toll the afternoon had taken. "Although, I wish the circumstances were different."

"As do I," Emerson said as he noticed the ring on her left hand. "So. It would appear you're to be married."

"Yes."

"Ari," Edith spoke up sharply.

Ari looked at her. "It's done, Aunt Edith, and I would prefer not to discuss it anymore." She looked at each of her uncles. "It is my decision." No one replied and so she looked back at John. "Do you think I should explain it to Zan, or would it be better coming from you?"

"I don't think he'll accept it from anyone but you."

She nodded.

"What will you tell him?" Sully asked as he crossed the room to reach her.

"That I am to be married and I—" Her voice broke, and she had to take a moment. "I cannot see him again."

"I could send him directly back," Emerson said. "He wanted to come with me, but why don't we wait a day or so? Give you a bit of time to be certain."

She shuddered. "It won't make a difference."

"Arianna," Sully said. "You are wrong in this decision." He tipped her face up with his finger beneath her chin. "Do you know how I know?"

She didn't dare speak for fear of losing the frail grip of self-control she'd managed.

"Because the light has gone out of your eyes. I know you think you have no choice, but we should discuss this."

She turned away from him, dangerously close to losing all control.

Sully looked at John. "Walk with me?"

Emerson nodded and followed him from the room as Edith crossed the room to Ari. "We can fight Mr. Derringer and win," Edith declared. "You should not let him get away with strong-arming you into marriage."

"I can't discuss it anymore," she said in a choked whisper. "I love you but I … just can't." She left and returned to her room to write to Zan. She could not leave things hanging and she could not allow him to languish under false hope. And, truthfully, she could not risk seeing him again. Not and maintain her resolve. He would want to take her away. Or he would toss her over his shoulder and run again.

If only!

But that was pure fantasy. It would pain her to do it, but she would be firm and unmistakably cool. She would make herself appear shallow, concerned only with a good name and a hefty allowance. It was sickening, but she would do it.

A half hour and a dozen failed attempts later found the hateful deed done, although she lacked the energy even to shove the letter into an envelope.

"Ari?" Patience said from the door.

Ari looked at her.

"You're so pale. Did something else happen?" Patience shut the door behind her and came closer. Ari handed her the letter wordlessly, and Patience took it and read. After only a few lines, her eyes widened, and her lips parted in surprise. She glanced up at Arianna and then went back to reading.

"Ari," she said softly when she'd finished it. "This is not you. You do not want to send this."

"Don't you understand? I have to or Marshall will ruin him."

"But if you send it, can you live with yourself?"

"I cannot see him hurt because of me. I have to do this. He'll hate me, but it's better that way. In the long run, it will be easier for him. Don't you think it will be easier for him?"

"I don't know, but it does not feel right. At least sleep on it."

Ari shook her head slowly. "If I don't send it right away, I will weaken," she said brokenly.

Patience sighed. "Then hand me an envelope. I'll take it down."

Ari hesitated a moment and then handed one over.

"I hate this," Patience declared.

Ari nodded but made no reply. After all, what was there to say?

~~~

It was utterly improper etiquette, but Patience took the letter to Lord Bluford's home and asked the butler to see Mr. Shaffer. He showed her to the drawing room, and quickly fetched Zan Shaffer. When Zan appeared in the drawing room where she waited, she understood Delia's description and Arianna's torment.

"Yes?" he asked uncertainly. "You asked to see me?"

"My name is Patience Caldwell. I'm Ari's friend."

He nodded. "She told me." He came further into the room. "Would you care to sit down?"

"No, thank you. I cannot stay. I was supposed to see that this got to you," she said, glancing down at the letter she held.

He looked at it. "It's from Ari?"

"It is ... and it isn't," she replied hesitantly.

"I do not understand."

"Mr. Shaffer, she cares about you very much, but she is engaged to another man, and she is going through with that engagement. She will marry Mr. Derringer. The purpose of this letter is to let you know that she can never see you again, not alone. He's forbidden it."

Zan shook his head. "She cannot marry him."

"She is. I'm sorry, but she is."

"Why? Why would she? She doesn't love him."

"She'd promised, you see," she said haltingly. "At least, that is what he understood. So, it's expected that she'll go through with it." She paused. "She has decided to go through with it."

"I love her," he said.

Patience fought the emotion welling inside her. If only she could blurt out the truth. If there was any man alive that could take on Marshall Derringer and somehow win, she was surely looking at him. But it wasn't her decision or her place. "Then you must honor what she asks. You must let her go."

He looked at the letter she held. "What did she say?"

"All sorts of things she does not mean and that she hates herself for."

He looked into her eyes, baffled by the statement.

"She feels she has to do whatever she can to ... make you understand she cannot see you again." *To push you away.*

He looked away, breathing deeply to quell the pain.

"I am so sorry."

He nodded but kept his face away from her.

"I should go."

He reached for the letter.

She looked at his hand and then placed her own in it. She dared not look at him for fear of bursting into tears. "Each of us is the friend of a friend," she said quietly. "Which makes us friends, in a way." She withdrew her hand. "Will you please trust me on all that I've said and on not leaving this letter with you?"

He considered. "She wrote things she didn't mean?"

She took a shaky breath and nodded. "So that you would hate her and be able to ... to be free of her."

"I could never hate her."

Patience nodded. "I know. I feel that," she said softly. "More than anything, she wishes you to be free and happy."

"I can only be happy if I'm with her," he said beseechingly.

"Try. For her sake. Please, try."

"You are a good friend to her."

"I love her so dearly. I wish I had the power to change things, but I don't." She glanced down at the letter. "Will you trust me on this? On not leaving it with you?"

He peered into her eyes. "Ari trusts you; I trust you."

"I am so sorry to have met like this." She left, holding her head high, despite the tears that threatened. In the foyer, the butler opened the door for her and then shut it behind her.

Chapter Thirty

A ri felt a nudge.

"Ari," Patience said.

It was morning. Mid-morning from the look of it. Ari felt dull and heavy, and her head ached, which was puzzling until she recalled the events of the previous day, and then she wanted to curl back up and sleep and never wake up.

"I'm sorry to wake you, but we're leaving." When Ari didn't move, Patience lay down beside her, facing her, fully dressed, her feet hanging off the side of the bed.

"I wish you weren't," Arianna said miserably.

"I am so sorry for how things turned out."

Ari managed a weak smile. "I'm glad for you though. I cannot wait to meet your Mr. Hailey."

"He's hardly *my* Mister Hailey. I just met him. Although I hope … one day, perhaps. He is rather wonderful." Patience's smile dimmed. "I am so disappointed in Marshall."

Ari pulled herself up and leaned against the headboard. She felt as if she weighed five hundred pounds. This is what it was to exist without a hope of happiness.

Patience got up and smoothed her skirt. "When will you come home?"

"I wish I could go with you right now."

Patience gave her a pained smile. "Do you know one good thing though?"

"No," Ari stated so flatly that Patience had to laugh, although it was a sad, short laugh.

"It's possible we'll be family one day. You'll marry Marshall, and I'll marry Reggie—"

"I couldn't love you more if you were my Siamese twin," Ari said. "But there can be nothing good about marrying Marshall."

The clock began chiming. "I have to go," Patience said fretfully.

Ari rose up on her knees and embraced Patience.

"Come see me as soon as you get home," Patience said, stepping back.

"I will."

~~~

The only comment Marshall made to Ari as they rode to his family's town residence for dinner was, "I hope you're not going to be petulant this evening."

It didn't require a response, so she did not give one. She had entered into a state of emotional paralysis, a velvety haze of disconnectedness, and it was a relief. It was far better than heartache and self-loathing.

She gave a proper, if restrained, greeting to his mother, sisters, and Mr. Joyce when they arrived. As usual, his father was elsewhere. Sometimes she got the feeling that the man did not care much for his son. She understood that feeling well enough.

She sat where directed and rose when expected. Had she answered all the questions asked of her? She must have, although she could not have repeated what those questions were. As dinner ended and everyone rose to go into the salon, she could not recall anything that had been discussed. Or anything that had been consumed, for that matter.

"Would you care for a stroll in the garden?" Louise asked her. "The roses are all still in bloom."

"I believe we've all smelled the roses quite enough," Marshall rejoined. "Personally, I'm sick of them."

"Arianna?" Louise said, ignoring her brother.

Beatrix Derringer kept walking. She was torn between being incensed by Arianna's lack of vitality, and satisfaction that Marshall had won whatever conflict had been waged between them. Perry urged Andra onward, recognizing what his wife was trying to do. Susan lingered, entertained by the scene, but Marshall was growing agitated.

"We'll have brandy," Marshall stated, taking hold of Ari's arm with a bruising grip.

"A breath of fresh air might do her some good," Louise snapped, stepping up as if prepared to do battle.

"I think not," he replied, leading Arianna on.

"What has he got on her?" Louise murmured when they'd gone.

"I have no idea, but something," Susan replied with a smirk, her eyes glittering. "I wonder how we can find out?"

Louise gave her a look of pure disgust and walked on.

Susan huffed in objection. "What?"

"How dare you," Marshall fumed on the way home. "How dare you act like a wounded thing? Like the walking dead? How dare you!"

Ari watched the streetlights. How strange it was that he'd won, and she'd lost, but he didn't feel like he'd won, and she didn't feel at all.

"You do not want to play this game with me," he warned.

That was true enough; only it wasn't a game. It was something else, something she didn't know the name for.

"I know what you're doing, and it won't work," he blustered. "You'll only make things harder for yourself."

How could things be harder, she wondered.

It was disorienting to find herself in bed later because she could not recall walking inside or undressing, but it was a good thing. All she wanted to do was sleep.

Chapter Thirty-One

E merson climbed from the carriage, having reached his destination, Swinson & Sons Fine Jewelers. He entered the shop and found it far more impressive inside than out. The exterior was plain with only a modest sign to mark the place, but inside there were thick Persian rugs on the floor, couches of dark red velvet, and glass cases filled with gleaming jewels and trinkets of every sort and color.

"Mr. Swinson, please," Emerson asked a young clerk. "I have an appointment."

"Your name, sir?"

"John Emerson."

"He's expecting you. This way, if you please."

Jacob Swinson met him at the door to his office. He was a small man with stooped shoulders and thick spectacles, and there was a slight quivering to his extremities. "Mr. Emerson," he greeted with a deferential dip of his head.

"Mr. Swinson. Thank you for seeing me."

"Of course. I've been looking forward to it. Do you have the gem with you?"

"I don't know that it *is* a gem," Emerson admitted as he pulled Zan's rock from his pocket. "As I mentioned, it belongs to my friend." He held it out for inspection.

Swinson's jaw dropped as he reached for it and brought it close to his face, examining it closely. He swallowed, looked at Emerson with astonishment, and then walked to his desk where he pulled out a magnifying glass. He sat and continued studying it. "Please, sit," he said distractedly, not looking away from the rock.

Emerson sat and watched the man with growing excitement. "Do you know what it is?"

Swinson looked up and blinked. "It is a diamond."

"A diamond? But it's yellow."

The man nodded. "Canary yellow, which is the most valuable of the yellow diamonds. These are found only in Africa that I know of. Where did your friend get it?"

"Africa," John replied. He exhaled strongly and shook his head in astonishment. "A yellow diamond. How remarkable! I had no idea there was such a thing."

"Have you never heard of The Star of South Africa? It's a diamond of yellow-brown color, which is not as valuable, but it's large. Uncut it was twenty-five carats, I believe. Cut, it was over ten. Or the Tiffany Yellow? It was nearly three hundred carats in its uncut state. Or the Red Cross Diamond? That one is over two hundred carats and worth a king's fortune."

"And it's yellow as well?"

"Yes. It's a marvelous thing. When you look at it, you can clearly see a small Maltese cross in its topmost facet." Swinson looked down at the rock in his hand with an awed expression. "This should be handled by only the finest gem cutter." He looked up and met Emerson's eye. "I can recommend someone and oversee the process. I can also arrange for a sale if your friend wishes. For a small commission."

"I'll speak to him and recommend it. How much might it be worth?"

Swinson rolled it slightly in one hand and then the other. "I would say in this rough state it is between twenty-five and thirty carats. Once cut, best guess, it will end up at, say, fifteen carats. As to the value, much depends on its characteristics once it's cut, but perhaps five thousand pounds. Perhaps more."

Emerson's jaw had gone lax. "And there's no doubt in your mind that it's a diamond?"

"No. There is no doubt." He held up the diamond and slowly twisted his wrist. "In this sort of artificial light, it's even more magnificent than a white diamond. Also, a yellow diamond will absorb bright light, which it then emits, becoming luminous in the dark."

John felt shaken, he was so surprised. "I'm delighted. My friend has recently had bad news."

"I would venture to say that this should turn things around for him," Swinson replied.

"I hope so."

~~~

Zan sat in his aunt's kitchen peeling apples and listening to the ladies of his family chatting. He didn't feel well, because he hadn't been able to sleep or eat much for days. Arianna had chosen Marshall Derringer. Whatever it was that Derringer had said or done that afternoon, she was resolute in the decision to become his wife. John had reluctantly confirmed it when he'd returned from the Vinson's home. Patience had reconfirmed it. All that was left for him to do was learn to accept it.

But how?

Being with his family was the only thing that provided solace. He liked this kitchen with its stone sink and worn wooden table. Pots of all sizes hung on racks, as did bunches of herbs. A cupboard had dishes and crockery enough for everyone. There were baskets and small barrels of foodstuff. Onions, potatoes, cabbages, carrots, oats.

Mary Sue sat across from him mending holes in socks. Norma sat next to him, helping with the apples. She was still red-faced from doing laundry. She and her mother and sister took in other people's laundry for income. In this house, everyone worked except the children.

And Joe since the accident.

"What smells so good?" Joe asked, lumbering into the kitchen after a nap. "Hello, Zan."

"It's a lovely side of beef," Aileen replied cheerfully as she leaned over the roaster to check it. "Zan brought it."

"He brought wine as well," Norma said. "We were waiting for you to open it."

"I'm here. Open it!"

Mary Sue chuckled as she got up and went to fetch a bottle. Zan had brought three large bottles from Lord Bluford's vast cellar at the older man's insistence. He'd personally selected them.

Joe peered at Zan critically. "You alright?"

Zan nodded but didn't look up from his apple.

"You don't look alright."

"Leave him alone, Joe," his wife chided. "He has some worries, is all."

"Don't we all," Joe said as he sat at the table. "Anything we can help with?"

Zan saw Joe was addressing him. He gave him a wan smile and a shake of the head. "No."

"Who are we waiting for?" Joe asked his wife.

"Rodney just got home. He's washing up," Mary Sue said.

Rodney was Mary Sue's husband, Zan recalled.

"And Fred should be down directly," she continued.

"Wilson may be working late," Norma interjected. She looked at Zan. "A shipment's going out in the morning. He's foreman, so he has to make sure it's ready."

"What kind of factory?" Zan asked.

"They package food," she replied as she rose, taking the pot with her. "Mostly in tin coated cans, but also in cardboard."

"Here, Mama," Mary Sue said, handing her a cup of wine.

"Thank you, love. And thank you, Zan," she added, lifting her glass to him. "And please be sure and thank Lord Bluford. It was so kind of him."

He nodded. "I will."

"What's he like?" Joe asked.

"A very good man," Zan replied. "He listens. He likes to laugh. He is generous."

"I'm sorry we don't have proper wine glasses," Mary Sue said to Zan as she handed him a glass.

He smiled. "It doesn't matter."

"Papa." Mary Sue handed him a glass.

He took it and sipped and nodded. "That's good. Better than good."

Zan looked at his aunt who was leaning against the counter, enjoying her wine for a moment. She, too, was red-faced from the heat. "I remember an older man with a…mustache," Zan said.

Aileen gave a wistful smile. "That was my papa. Your gramps."

Gramps.

The front door slammed, and Mary Sue looked curious and then left the kitchen.

"What do you remember of him?" Joe asked Zan.

Zan shook his head slowly. "His face. His mustache. He had big hands."

Joe chuckled. "And a big heart."

Aileen sighed. "I remember you sitting on his lap as he taught you to whittle."

Zan felt a chill. *A bird!* They'd whittled a bird.

"Nicked your thumb good once," Joe said. "But it didn't stop you from trying again."

"How he loved you," Aileen sighed. "His firstborn grandson."

Norma brushed the apple peelings from the table into a bin but then looked up sharply as Mary Sue led a young woman in whose eyes were swollen from crying. "Ellie," Norma cried. "What's wrong?"

Zan stood. Joe and Aileen turned to look at the girl, but Ellie's gaze was on Zan.

"This is Zan," Norma said.

"Zan," Ellie said softly.

She was remarkably pretty, even having been crying. "Hello, Ellie."

"Oh, my," the young woman marveled. "You do look like us. Especially Thom."

"What's wrong?" Joe asked Ellie gruffly. "Is it Junior?"

Ellie colored with embarrassment. "I don't want to talk about it."

"Did he say something again?" Joe pushed.

"It's not so much what he said," she replied miserably.

"What *did* he say?" Joe demanded.

She looked miserable. "He asked when I was moving in. I said that I wasn't. At least not for now. That my family wanted that I stay home for another year. Then he said, but you're not a baby to be told what to do, are you?"

Joe's expression hardened. "Anything else?"

She shook her head. "No. I told you, It's not what he said. It's how he … watches me. I get such a sick feeling sometimes."

"That's your instinct," Mary Sue said soothingly. "And you must listen to it."

Norma nodded. "I think you should leave that place."

"Leave? But it's a good situation! What if I can't get another as good?"

"Sweetheart, you have to be safe," Aileen stated firmly. "And if you feel you're not, if that's what your gut says, then you're not. So, you leave before there's trouble."

She gave a small whimper. "What would I say?"

"We'll think of something," Mary Sue assured her. "Sit down."

Ellie sat.

Zan did as well.

Aileen went for a glass and poured some wine in it, then carried it to her. "Here. It'll help calm your nerves."

Ellie's brows lifted. "Wine?"

"Good wine," Mary Sue said with a smile for Zan.

Ellie looked at Zan regretfully. "What a terrible way for me to meet you. You must think I'm a weak little ninny."

"No," he said with a shake of his head. "I do not."

Norma started for the door. "I'll see to the children."

Ellie fidgeted. "I'll give it a bit more time," she said to Joe. "Maybe he'll stop."

Mary Sue cocked her head. "Now listen to me, little sister."

A pained expression crossed Ellie's face and she looked at Zan. "She always calls me that right before she lectures me."

"And I won't disappoint this time. Gabriel Westcott sounds like a man-boy who always gets his way and has never been made to answer for anything. If he forces himself on you—"

Ellie gasped and blushed scarlet.

"Well, that is the fear, isn't it?" Mary Sue continued. "And if it happens, you will be ruined. Plain and simple. He will pretend that nothing happened. Or that you were to blame. You, my girl, will be ruined."

"And so will I be," Joe declared, his eyes gleaming. "Because I'll kill him. One handed or not."

"There are three hands between us," Zan said grimly.

Joe nodded in satisfaction.

"Stop that, both of you," Aileen said hotly, looking from Joe to Zan. Finally, she looked at Ellie. "Your safety is not something that should ever be thought of as a luxury. That much should be your right. We're strong people and we work hard, but no one should be allowed to mistreat you or make you afraid."

Ellie nodded.

"If you feel you're not safe then you're not. You are not one to exaggerate or imagine things that are not true. And Zan," she said looking at him. "We just got you back, and I will *not* lose you to sheer foolishness! As God as my witness, I will not."

Zan glanced at Joe, who gave him a wink. He'd never been so happy to be scolded. It made him one of them. "You will not lose me."

"I'm home," was shouted by a man, making Ellie jump. "Don't say anything to him about it," she pleaded.

"No, we won't," Mary Sue agreed. She looked at Zan. "Thom," she said in explanation. "That's the last thing we need."

Aileen nodded in agreement. "Wash up," she called. "Supper's ready."

Within minutes, there was a convergence of family, their eyes gleaming with anticipation. They moved around the table and sat close together.

"You must be Zan," a young man said as he offered his hand. "I'm Freddy. I hate that I missed you the other day. You are staying a few days, aren't you?"

"Yes, he is," Aileen said. "Bunking in your room."

"Good," Freddy said. "I want to hear every single thing about you." He sat and reached for a biscuit.

"Blessing, first," his mother admonished.

He smirked as he withdrew his hand. "You're going to feel really badly if I starve to death one day while waiting for the blessing."

She grinned as she placed a bowl of vegetables on the table.

"The prodigal nephew," a male voice said from the doorway. He could have easily been mistaken for Zan's younger brother.

"Thom," Ellie said apologetically.

Zan didn't know the word prodigal, but he noticed the looks of disapproval from his aunt and uncle, so it must have been unkind. "Nice to meet you, cousin," Zan returned.

"Your hands clean?" Aileen asked Thom sharply.

Thom moved in and sat. "Yes, my hands are clean," he replied. "Just because we can't all dress like gentlemen and smell like flowers—"

"Either keep a civil tongue in your head, or you can eat your supper outside," Joe warned.

"Who wants to say the blessing?" Aileen asked. "Thom?"

Thom bowed his head. "Thank you for this food we're about to receive. Amen," he said in a single breath.

The children giggled, and Norma gave Thom a stern look, but Aileen shrugged and said, "Let's eat."

~~~

"You asleep?" Thom asked that night.

Zan, Fred, and Thom lay in a small bedroom. Fred had insisted on taking a makeshift pallet in between beds, claiming he could sleep anywhere, and his soft, rhythmic snoring was proof it was true. Zan had taken Fred's narrow bed for the night, and Thom was in his bed not even four feet away.

"No," Zan replied.

"Why are you here when you've got a big fancy house to stay in?"

"Because my family is here."

Silence.

"I've never even seen a house like that," Thom murmured. "Not on the inside."

"You could come see it. Stay with me."

Thom scoffed. "I wouldn't know how to behave, and they wouldn't know what to make of the likes of me. They'd probably be afraid I'd steal something."

"I think you know how to behave."

Thom raised up on an elbow and glared daggers at him, visible even in the dim moonlight. "What would you know about it? You've got no worries. Got rich people vying to take care of you." He paused, seeking more ammunition. "You know you would have been just like us if you'd stayed. You'd be busting your arse on the dock like me or somewhere else barely getting by, making the rich man richer."

Zan watched the shifting shadows on the ceiling, one hand propped behind his head. "Yes."

Frustrated that he couldn't get a rise, Thom lay back down. "I'd go off to Africa if I could come back like you. Buy me a ticket. I'll go."

Freddy stirred, rolled over on his side, and passed wind, then continued snoring.

"I think about smothering him with a pillow sometimes," Thom grumbled.

"What is it you want to do?" Zan asked, turning his head to better see his cousin.

"What? Is this a game? We pretend that I have a choice of what I do with my life? Like I'm some grand gentleman? Like you?"

Zan waited.

"How the hell would I know? I don't have a choice. I never had a choice. It's up at six, at work by seven, a bite at noon, and home again at six, too tired most days to do anything but sit around like an old man until I crawl into bed. You want my life? You want to trade?"

Zan looked back at the ceiling. "I had no choice about going to Africa. I was not much older than Rob and Freddy when my parents and everyone else we were with were slaughtered. I was alone." He paused, thinking back on it. "I had given up when an animal, an ape, found me and cared for me, as strange as that is."

Thom didn't reply.

"Sometimes I saw villagers from a distance, but I did not understand their words. They feared me. I understood that. Be sure, if you want to trade lives that you can cope with having no one to speak to. No one to share your life with."

Thom's expression had not changed greatly, but it might have been less angry.

"Then a woman came for me," Zan continued. "She found me, and I found her. I love her, but I cannot have her. She's marrying another. A proper, rich gentleman." Zan considered leaving it there, but something still remained unsaid. "If there is not something you want to do, why are you so angry?"

"Leave me alone."

"Do you want me not to come here anymore?"

Silence. "What do I care what you do?" Thom finally muttered and there was a ring of resignation, maybe even regret in his voice.

Chapter Thirty-Two

L ord Bluford looked around the room at his fellow Royal Society members, some of whom sat on the museum's board of directors. "It would seem then that we are in agreement." He saw nothing but nodding heads and murmurings of concurrence.

He'd given a stirring speech about their responsibilities toward a fellow human traveler whom fortune had not favored. He had also plied them with excellent libations and the finest cigars that money could buy. It certainly helped that no glory hounds had headed up the expedition. In fact, he'd made it a significant part of his case, saying that if Charles North and John Emerson were amenable to keeping the fruit of their labor secret, who were they to argue?

"Therefore, the primary accomplishment of the African expedition will remain undisclosed, held in trust by this brotherhood. We, each and every one of us, pledge to deny that any man was discovered on the African continent and transported back here to be reintroduced into society. All in favor?"

"Aye," rang out.

"Any opposed?"

The silence that followed was sweet to hear, and Emerson, in back of the room, breathed easier. He caught Charles North's eye and nodded. North nodded back.

"I am both appreciative," Bluford concluded, "and honored to be part of this great society."

~~~

"Mr. Derringer?"

Marshall looked up from his paper to the dark-haired young man standing before him. He wasn't an impressive looking man, but he had an air of intelligence. "I am," Marshall said. "Nicolas Manning?"

"Guilty as charged," Manning said, extending his hand.

Marshall hesitated a moment, and then shook it. "Sit, please. Care for a drink?"

"Yes. Scotch, if they have it."

"Oh, they have it." Derringer looked up and caught the eye of an attendant. "Scotch for my guest."

"So, this is how the other half lives," Manning said as he glanced around the room. "Expensive tweeds, dark wood, and smoky elegance. The muted sounds of male conversation accented by the occasional breaking of billiard balls."

Marshall smiled appreciatively. "You're the writer."

"I am. Though hardly the only one. How did you happen to ask for me?"

"Your piece on the Eulenberg scandal. That sordid mix of political intrigue and homosexuality. It was well done."

"Thank you."

"I have an equally fascinating story for you, although the Kaiser is not involved of course."

"I think we've heard quite enough about him anyway."

"Here's the thing," Marshall said. "I cannot have my name associated with the story at all. That must be a condition of my revelation."

Manning shrugged. "You wish to pass on some facts anonymously. That's not unusual, nor is it a problem."

"I'll have it in writing."

The attendant returned with the scotch and quickly walked away. Nicolas picked up the lead crystal glass and took a sip, both for the pleasure of it and to buy a moment. It was an excellent scotch, smooth and undoubtedly expensive. "Do you want it in writing before you tell me what it's all about?"

"I do. I've already had an agreement drafted." He reached for a leather-bound folder from which he produced a one-page document and a fountain pen.

Manning glanced over the document and signed it without hesitation.

"Bring another round," Derringer called to a passing waiter.

Nicolas shoved the signed form across the table and leaned back.

"You won't believe it at first," Marshall stated. "It sounds so fantastic, but if you dig deep enough, you'll find proof."

Nicolas took another drink. He wasn't in a position to frequent clubs like this, so he might as well enjoy it, no matter what rubbish the pompous Derringer served up. The ambiance and scotch were worth the cab fare it had cost him. "Alright."

"What would you say if I told you a white man, an Englishman, had been discovered living amongst apes in Africa after spending most of his life there?"

"I would say you are still in the fantastic stage."

Derringer grinned. "Indeed. But it is the truth. He was abandoned in the wild when his parents were murdered. They were missionaries or something, part of Bishop Hannington's unfortunate party."

The writer's curiosity was peaked.

"The discovery of the man was accidental," Marshall continued. "The British Museum and the Royal Society had authorized and funded an expedition to central Africa after learning there is or was some new breed of ape. This was based on skulls recently found. They went in search of the new breed and … instead discovered the man."

"When was this?"

"Recently. The man has just been returned to London. I've met him."

"Met him?"

"Yes. He's staying with Lord Dalton Bluford."

Nicolas felt his jaw grow lax. "You're saying they found a wild man living amongst apes, and civilized him that quickly?"

Marshall's lip curled. "As much as someone like that can be. And to make the story even more interesting, he is handsome. Thirty years of age or so. John Emerson has been working with him."

Derringer was handing out names and facts that could be easily checked. The tale sounded like a hoax of some sort, but the scotch was good, and he would play along for now. "Will they announce it soon?"

"I would think so. It could be you who breaks the story."

And makes a colossal ass of myself. "Do you know the man's name?"

"I do. It's Shaffer. Zan Shaffer."

"This is all very specific and verifiable."

"It ought to be but I'm quite certain you'll run into a stone wall or two. They won't want the word out before they are ready for it to be out."

"Do you mind if I make some notes?"

"As long as my name stays out of it, I don't mind at all."

"The agreement I signed mentioned a Miss Day as well. Who is she?"

"She is part of the story that I will not have told."

"So, she is part of the story?"

Marshall grinned coldly. "Always remember this, Manning. I can make your career or break it. It's your choice."

It all sounded like claptrap, but if there were facts to back up the wild tale, even if it was some elaborately constructed hoax, it was still a story worth writing. "I understand, but I should know the facts."

"And so you will. All the important ones."

"I am listening, sir. With rapt fascination."

~~~

"It was a good night," Lord Bluford said to Emerson as they rode home.

"Yes," Emerson agreed. "I'm greatly relieved and grateful to you for seeing it done."

"I like Zan. I can even see him becoming part of my family."

Emerson glanced at Bluford wondering at the man's tone.

"My granddaughter is quite taken with him, you know."

Obviously, he knew this, but how to react?

"Although," Bluford continued, "her mother is not … well, let's just say that she's not well pleased. However, I would do anything in my power to make Nessa happy. As I said, I like Zan. I greatly admire his capacity for learning and his zest for life."

John nodded.

"Vanessa will eventually inherit my estate. It passes first to her father, of course, although I plan on granting her the London house as a wedding gift. It will be passed on after the marriage, so that she retains full possession no matter what occurs in the future, but I see no reason why Zan could not become lord of the manor after my son passes. What do you think?"

John blinked. "Have you discussed this with your granddaughter?"

"Yes, but not with my son and daughter-in-law. We'll have a family dinner tomorrow and discuss it. I was hoping you might take Zan out to my club and have the same discussion with him."

"Discuss the possibilities, you mean to say?"

"Exactly. In a few days I'll sit down with him myself and make an official proposal as to what's to be, but he ought to be prepared for it."

"I see."

Bluford grinned happily. "I'll send word to my club to expect you. Or shall we go there now and have a drink? I do feel like celebrating."

Chapter Thirty-Three

Zan strolled the grounds at first light, pondering everything he'd learned in the last few days. He was suddenly wealthy, and an heiress wanted to marry him. "Wealthy," he said under his breath testing out the word to see how it felt.

It didn't.

"Married," he murmured.

No, he didn't feel much of anything. He loved Ari. He would always love her, but she didn't want to marry him.

He'd be able to help his family financially, and that thought alone gave him pleasure. He didn't know how he would tell them, but it would make a difference in their lives. They could buy a bigger home, and Joe could get the best medical care. His aunt and cousins wouldn't have to take in laundry anymore. Ellie wouldn't have to worry.

What was his work going to be? A man needed something to clutch onto and feel part of. Something to do, to accomplish, but what job would be right for him? He had missed too much growing up here. There was too much he did not know.

~~~

From her second-floor bedroom window, standing in a silk wrap with her hair loose, Vanessa watched Zan. He was glorious, both so strong and gentle. He was mysterious. He made her feel protected, but he also he made her feel a wild longing.

Before long, he would be her husband, and they would lay together and make love whenever they wanted. She pressed on the tight spot of her stomach and sighed.

~~~

From their third-floor window, Jane saw Zan as well. She turned to her husband who was buttoning his shirt.

He seems unhappy, she gestured.

John nodded. "He's had his heart broken." He went for his cufflinks and walked to her for assistance. "The sad thing is that Arianna's heart is broken as well," he said as he passed the jewelry into her hands and held out his arm. "But I can't let him know that or he'll never be able to let her go."

Jane fixed his cuffs, and then signed, *You owe him the truth.*

"I don't know the truth, my love. And what we owe Zan, in my opinion, is the best opportunity for a good life."

She straightened his collar.

"Think of it," John continued. "He'll have everything he could ever need or want as the husband of Vanessa."

"Na Ari."

"No. Not Ari. But I'm afraid that ship has sailed. Derringer has got her just where he wants her, pinned in a corner."

She's not married yet.

He smiled. "You, my love, are an optimist and a dreamer." He leaned in and kissed her cheek. When he pulled away, she gave him a look, pulled him close, and kissed him properly.

~~~

"Hello," Emerson called as he walked to meet Zan on the back lawn. "What a fine morning."

Zan turned to him. "Why does Vanessa want to marry me?" he asked when Emerson reached him.

"Uh—" The question had thrown him.

"She is in love with me?"

"Well, I … yes, I think she believes she's in love with you."

Zan pondered John's wording. "What about Ari?"

"What about her?"

"Should I tell Vanessa?"

"Tell her your feelings for Ari?"

245

Zan nodded.

"In my opinion, no. It would serve no purpose."

They began walking. "The money from the rock," Zan began uncertainly.

"Yes?"

"I want to help my family. I want to give them enough to buy a good house."

John nodded. Zan had said so first thing.

"I don't know how much that is."

Emerson shrugged. "It depends on where the home is. I know there's a house near us for sale, slightly larger than ours, seven or eight bedrooms I believe, and they want eighteen hundred for it, which seems exorbitant. But location is the thing. Your family will need to decide where they want to go. There are commutes to think of amongst other things."

"I want to give you money too."

Emerson was touched. "Thank you, truly, but we have more than enough. I lectured steadily at Cambridge for more than twenty years, you know, plus I was commissioned to conduct studies and reports throughout the years, some of which paid obscenely well. I do appreciate the thought, though. I really do,"

"I want to find work."

Emerson shrugged. "Most gentlemen don't work. There's no shame in that."

"I am no gentleman," Zan stated.

Emerson grunted "Let's go have breakfast. I'm hungry. Are you hungry?"

Zan gave a halfhearted nod, and they started to the house.

"Have you thought about how you'll tell your family?"

"I thought I'd tell my uncle first."

"*Hmm.*"

"Or my aunt and uncle together. What do you think?"

"Is he the sensitive sort? Might this hurt his pride?"

Zan frowned, flustered. "I don't know."

John stopped and turned to Zan. "It's a wonderful thing that you'll be able to make the lives of your family easier," he said soothingly. "I have absolute faith that you'll handle it the right way. Tell you what, after breakfast we can play with some figures.

I don't know how much your family earns on a weekly basis. Four working men, and the ladies contributing," he murmured, doing a quick calculation in his head. "Maybe thirty shillings, all told? There are twenty shillings in a pound. Does that help?"

"I think so."

"I can give you an idea of what a hundred pounds will buy. What a thousand pounds will buy."

"Do you think I should marry Vanessa?"

John took a moment to reply. "I cannot answer that for you. It's too personal a decision. She is lovely and kind and beautiful, and I believe she'll make an excellent wife. Of course, if you don't care for her—"

"I do care for her. She's kind, as you said."

Zan's heartache was so palpable, it made Emerson hurt. "Let me ask you this. Could you be as happy with Vanessa as with anyone … other than Arianna, of course?"

Zan sighed quietly. "I suppose."

"That's worth considering. After all, you don't want to live your life alone." They started walking again, Zan looking like a condemned man.

~~~

A fast-moving front had brought rain and cooler air, a fact that Ari appreciated as she sat on the side terrace with Sully having tea and listening to the musical calls of birds. "What time is your train?" she asked.

"Noon. I'll leave right after this."

She wished she could go home too.

"Ari, there is something I must tell you."

She looked at him, tensed for bad news given the concern she saw in his face. "What?"

"I saw Emerson last night."

She stiffened. "Oh?"

"It's possible Zan may marry Vanessa Bluford."

It was a struggle just to keep breathing.

"It would, of course, put him in good stead for the rest of his life," he added.

"I see," she said just above a whisper. "Did … you're saying he agreed to it?"

"I was led to believe he is leaning that way."

She looked away fighting for composure. She felt tears threaten and so she rose and walked to the edge of the terrace, careful to keep her face turned away from Sully. All that mattered at this point was protecting Zan. She'd thought it and said it to herself a thousand times. This was no time to weaken. Not when he had such an opportunity for security. "I'm glad it cooled off," she said in a thick voice that betrayed her turmoil.

Sully's chair squeaked against the brick floor as he scooted back. She heard his footsteps, and a moment later she felt his hands on her shoulders.

"There is to be a dinner party in a few weeks," he said, squeezing her shoulders lightly. "A celebration of Zan's rescue. I've agreed to return for it, with the photographs, and you can expect an invitation. At that time, they'll likely announce the engagement."

She nodded.

"Are you alright?" he fretted,

She nodded again.

"I could stay."

She grabbed a breath and turned to face him. "No. You have things to attend to. I will be fine."

He considered her for a moment and then accepted with a sigh. He leaned in and kissed her cheek and then left.

The moment he was gone, tears began to stream down her face. She walked to a corner spot where she wasn't likely to be seen and cupped her mouth to contain the sounds of her agony.

Chapter Thirty-Four

A ri walked through the congested train station watching warily for anyone that might want to stop her. It was childish to be fleeing, but she had to change something. Even a day or two of walking on the seashore sounded like salvation. The very ground beneath her felt like quicksand, a mire of misery. If something didn't change quickly, it would swallow her whole.

She passed a pale lady about her age who looked as wretched as she felt. Ari stopped short and turned back, surprised by the belated recognition. "Wynonna?"

Wynonna turned to face her. "Arianna," she said as if just noticing her.

Ari walked to her, alarmed by how despondent she looked. "What are you doing here?" she asked lightly.

Wynonna shook her head as if the answer was beyond her.

Something was most definitely wrong. "Are you here to see someone?"

"To *not* see someone."

"I don't understand."

Wynonna shook her head and took a step back. "Please don't let me keep you. You are catching a train or perhaps meeting someone."

"No," Ari replied. "Rather I was thinking about it. Thinking about running away for a few days, if you must know."

"Then we have that in common."

The truth dawned on Ari. "You needed to get away from Delia?"

"And my mother. They're equally horrible. Or nearly."

"I understand," Ari commiserated. "Honestly, I don't know how you've stood it this long."

Wynonna grimaced as if in great pain and then she burst out laughing.

It was so bewildering a reaction that Ari drew back.

Wynonna clapped a hand to her mouth to stifle the laughter. "I'm sorry," she exclaimed a moment later. "It's just … I didn't think anyone would understand."

Ari shook her head slowly. "Only everyone that knows your family."

Wynonna released a long sigh. "You cannot know what a relief it is to hear that. Earlier today, I knew I could not take another minute of being there. I packed a few things, and I had Crawley drive me to the station. I don't even remember buying the ticket. I suppose I said Euston Station."

"And you arrive to find me here waiting for you. I have to believe that's fate lending a hand."

"So do I," Wynonna replied earnestly. "Thank you, Arianna. You have helped more than I can say. To know that I'm not completely mad."

Ari took hold of her arm and turned her around. "Come with me."

"Where to?"

"Home. To my aunt and uncle's."

Wynonna resisted. "But you were leaving."

"And now I'm staying."

Wynonna stopped. "I don't want to keep you from—"

"I think fate put me here for myself as much as for you."

Wynonna studied her as if almost afraid to hope it was true.

"I am also trapped by a hateful bully," Ari confided.

Wynonna's eyes widened.

"So, we'll be good for one another. Besides, running away for a few days wouldn't be worth the consequences I'd face."

"But you're Delia's friend."

"I do not believe Delia is capable of being a friend. I think I always knew it on some level, but it was driven home recently."

"What do you mean? What happened?"

Ari started them both moving forward. "I'll tell you on the way home."

~~~

Zan knocked on the door and then waited until it was opened by Ivy, who lit up at the sight of him. "Hello," she said.

"Hello, Ivy."

She opened the door wider and stepped back, and he saw Mary Sue coming toward him. "Family doesn't knock, Zan. And you don't need to send a note ahead either."

He stepped inside. "I was hoping to speak with my aunt and uncle."

She grinned. "I know. Your note said," she teased. "Mama, Zan's here," she called toward the kitchen. "Papa's upstairs," she said. "I'll get him."

"Papa's right here," Joe said as he came downstairs, his stump held in front of him for balance. "Hello, Zan."

Aileen emerged from the hall at the same time. "Come have some cider, dear."

"I was hoping we could go for a ride," Zan said, looking from Aileen to Joe, who seemed nonplussed at the suggestion.

"A ride?" he repeated.

"In the carriage. Lord Bluford's carriage."

"It's so pretty," Ivy exclaimed. "It's got two huge, brown horses in front!"

"Why?" Joe asked bluntly.

"Joe," Aileen scolded lightly. "I think a ride would be very nice if that's what Zan wants." She untied her apron and handed it to Mary Sue. "We'll not go inside any place, will we? I'd have to change."

"No," Zan assured her.

Joe shrugged. "Alright," he agreed in a resigned voice.

"Oh, wait," Mary Sue said. She hurried away and promptly returned with a teakwood box about the size of a cigar box, which she handed to Zan. "Thom made this for you."

"For me?" he asked as he took it.

She nodded and smiled. "For your cufflinks and such."

The box was simple, but smooth and elegant with ZS carved into the surface. "It's beautiful," Zan said quietly. He opened the box to find a note.

> *Zan,*
> *I don't want you to stay away. I might even take you up on that visit sometime if you can put up with me.*
> *-Thom*

Zan shut the box, moved by the gift.

"He's good with his hands," Mary Sue said. "He doesn't have the tools for fancy woodworking, but he borrows them and usually makes something for the man he borrows them from. You should have seen the small round table he made last month. Sold for a pretty penny too."

"He didn't say," Zan replied.

She nodded. "He's slow to let people in."

"If you see him before I do, will you tell him I said yes?"

She cocked her head. "Yes?"

He grinned. "I can put up with him."

She laughed. "I'll tell him."

Aileen seemed daunted to climb into the grand carriage. Joe remained expressionless, even as he found it somewhat awkward to maneuver. Zan came third having held his hands out to assist his uncle if needed, which it wasn't. Besides, Mary Sue grabbed Zan's wrist and shook her head to stop him from helping. When they were all in, she stepped back with a wave.

Zan sat facing his bewildered aunt and uncle with his back to the driver.

"What's this about, then?" Joe asked when they started in motion.

Zan felt overwhelming doubt. What if he offended them? "Do you ever wonder what I would have been like if I'd stayed here?"

"I think you would have turned out much like you are," Aileen replied. "You were a thoughtful, gentle boy. Smart as a whip and kind. So patient with Norma who followed you everywhere."

"You'd have ended up working on the docks," Joe added. "Or in a mill. Who knows? She's right. You were smart and such a good lad. You mighta' been running a place by now, but you can't go back, Zan."

"I know. I also know I would have been safe with you."

"You'd have been safe at home," Joe corrected. "But life isn't safe." He held up his stump. "Not at work and not on the streets, especially here on the east end."

"You're the only family I have."

Aileen reached forward and took Zan's hand. "Are you wanting to come live with us?"

"It would be nice to know I had a place if I ever needed it."

"You do," she replied without hesitation.

"You do," Joe echoed. "We'll make room and gladly."

"I may be getting married."

Joe and Aileen exchanged a look. "To who?" Aileen asked.

"To Lord Bluford's granddaughter."

"Oh, my," Aileen breathed. "Well, that is something."

"Do you love her?" Joe asked.

"I care for her."

Joe pursed his lips and nodded. "Marriage can be a cold place without love, Zan."

"I do love someone," Zan admitted.

"Arianna?" Aileen guessed. "I knew it," she said a moment later when she saw confirmation written on his face. "I knew by the way you talked about her."

"So why don't you marry her?" Joe asked.

"She's marrying another man."

"Oh," Aileen breathed. "Is that why you're so sad?"

Zan blinked. "I—"

"Let him be," Joe chided. "You don't always have to know everything about everything."

"I want to tell you both something," Zan said anxiously. "About something I had in the jungle. Something that was given to me before my parents were taken."

Joe nodded. "Take your time," he said. "We're in this fancy rig now, and it's not so bad. I don't remember the last time I was taken about town in a fancy carriage with leather seats and velvet sides."

"I remember when," Aileen said with a smirk. "Never."

"There was a rock," Zan said, needing to get it over with.

"A rock," Aileen repeated.

He nodded. "A yellow rock. My mother gave it to me and then she had me hide."

Aileen released a shaky breath.

"There was shouting, and she was taken. They were all taken. But I survived and I kept it, the rock. I brought it here, and it is valuable."

"Was it gold?" Joe asked.

"No. A diamond."

"A diamond that's yellow?" he asked. "I never heard of the like."

The carriage pulled over and all of them glanced out the window at a grand looking building beyond.

"We found out a few days ago," Zan said. His aunt and uncle looked baffled and somewhat alarmed. "This is my bank. It's also your bank."

"What are you talking about?" Aileen asked.

Zan reached into his pocket and pulled out a paper, which he handed to his uncle.

Joe glanced at the paper, which had a series of numbers. "What is this?"

"I have an account in that bank, and I made one for you, too. For the family."

"A bank account," Aileen repeated. "You opened a bank account for us."

Zan nodded. "It's in your name and that number," he said, lifting his chin toward the paper. "It holds three thousand pounds."

Aileen gasped.

Joe's jaw dropped. "We…we can't accept that," he uttered when he recovered from the initial shock.

Aileen looked at her husband too stunned to know what to think or say.

"It's for a house," Zan said. "A bigger house."

Joe scoffed. "Three thousand pounds? We could get a new house, or maybe two, a couple of these fancy rigs," he said gesturing about. "Some horses to pull it and—"

"Joe," his wife rejoined.

"Three thousand pounds is a fortune, my boy!"

Aileen's eyes filled. She took hold of her husband's arm. "Sebastian is no longer a boy, he's a man who's lived a life we can't even imagine. Who's come into a sum of money and wants to share it with us. You are being ungrateful."

"Ungrateful? I don't even believe it!"

"The bank is there," Zan said calmly. "You can go in and get it if you want."

"I'm not calling you a liar, Zan. I just don't understand. This much money. I wouldn't know—"

"It's alright," Aileen said leaning into him. "We don't have to decide what to do right now." She looked at Zan. "It was lovely to think of us. And we thank you for the thought. For the gift. Even if we cannot accept it."

Zan took a moment. "You just agreed to accept me in your house knowing I'd be a burden."

"You wouldn't be a burden," Joe retorted. "You'd pull your own weight. Like we all do. Or did," he muttered as an afterthought.

"That's what I'm doing," Zan stated.

"You don't have to buy your way into this family, Zan," he returned. His dark eyes shone from unshed tears. "You are part of this family."

"Then accept my gift."

Joe leaned back and looked at Aileen who was watching him warily, and then looked back to Zan. "It isn't all your money, is it? You didn't give it all away, did you?"

Zan shook his head. "No."

"You swear?"

Zan grinned. "I will not lie to you."

Joe looked at his wife again.

"You don't have to decide right now," she said. "But it's a grand gift he's making us. And it's from his heart."

Joe cleared his throat and pursed his lips, fighting emotion. "Alright, then," he whispered.

"I'm not sorry," Zan said wistfully.

"For what?" Aileen asked.

"For everything that happened." The realization was sudden, but so blindingly clear, that tears sprung to his eyes. "It was my life and Arianna came for me. Now my life is here, and I have you. I have my family."

Aileen began to cry, and the men had to take a moment to collect themselves.

"Do you want to go in?" Zan asked.

Joe looked at the bank and then back at him.

"It's your money," Zan said. "They just hold it."

Joe looked hesitant. "I don't know how."

"I'll show you. They're nice to you when you have an account."

Joe barked a laugh. "I bet they are." He looked at his wife. "Do you want to go in?"

"No," she replied fervently. "I'm not dressed for it."

Joe grinned at Zan. "Women."

~~~

Nicolas Manning nursed his second glass of ale and glanced around the dim tavern. He'd spent much of the last three days here hoping to encounter one of the men from the African expedition who supposedly frequented the establishment. Tracking the names of the men who'd taken part had been easy enough; locating the men was an entirely different matter. And getting them to talk had proved fruitless so far. "Sorry mate, confidential information," had been a constant refrain.

He had spoken to four men so far that would neither confirm nor deny that a white man had been found and/or rescued and/or captured. They'd confirmed that Sullivan Vinson had been part of the group and that his niece, Arianna Day, had traveled there with him, so that was something.

He knew the name of the alleged wild man, and he knew where he was supposedly staying, but one did not simply waltz into the home of Lord Bluford demanding an interview. He'd watched the home and he'd even followed the man he suspected was Shaffer, but he was always with someone. Derringer had been right about the man being handsome, which would help the story sell, if there was any truth to it.

The innkeeper cleared his throat and Nicolas glanced up to see him look pointedly toward the door. *Finally!* Nicolas rose and stretched his legs as the newest arrival made his way to the bar, greeting others as he went.

Manning walked over to him. "Mr. Reece?"

The man looked at him. "Last time I checked. And who would you be?"

"My name is Nicolas Manning. May I buy you a pint?"

Reece fixed him with a look. "How do you know my name?"

"I'm a writer with the *Times*."

"And?"

Nicolas grinned and held up a finger to buy a minute, then leaned into the bar to order the man a pint. He paid for it, passed it over, and then suggested a corner table, which Reece agreed to. When they were seated, Reece drank half the glass down before looking at him expectantly.

"I'm doing a story on the African expedition you just returned from."

"Why? We didn't find the apes they was looking for."

Reece was a cool customer. "I heard you found something else."

"Yeah? What's that? Deliverance from evil?" Reece grinned and bobbed his head back and forth. "Not me. I'd rather be a sinner than a saint any ole day."

"I heard you discovered a white man who had been abandoned as a boy."

"How long you been sitting here drinking, Mister … what was it?"

"Manning. Nicolas Manning. How much are you getting paid not to talk? It's possible I can pay more."

"I get paid for a job and then I do the job. I do it well and then I get offered another job. See how it works?"

"Of course. I'm the same."

Reece snorted. "I doubt that." He downed the rest of his ale and wiped his mouth with the back of his hand.

"Granted, your work is more physical," Nicolas said. "Hunting, tracking, and so forth, while I work at more of a mental level, researching, writing, breathing life into stories."

"You don't think hunting and tracking requires a mental level?"

"No, I do. Of course, I do. My point was that we both work for a living. We take on an assignment and we do it to the best of our ability. I'm simply hoping you'll agree to provide a little information." He paused. "As I said, I can pay."

"Taking your money wouldn't be right when I ain't got jack shite to tell you." Reece rose. "But good luck to you."

"I already know the story. I just need confirmation. It would be a very easy thing to get paid for."

"In that case, good luck with your confirmation."

The words had a definite ring of finality, and Reece's expression had gone stony. When he stalked away, Nicolas silently cursed three wasted days of sitting on his arse.

~~~

Edith sat at her vanity brushing her hair, very much lost in thought. Wilbur had set his book aside and watched her. "What are you thinking about?" he finally asked.

Her gaze focused on him in the mirror. "I was wondering why people are often cruel when it's so unnecessary?"

"Wynonna's family? Or your own?"

She shrugged.

"The similarities are rather glaring," he said. "It was courageous of you to share some of it with her."

"I didn't think of it as courageous, and I didn't mean to upset Arianna," she replied regretfully.

"Ari is fragile these days, and she loves you. She hates to hear of you being mistreated."

She rose and walked over to sit facing him. "I am the luckiest woman alive."

He smiled. "I'm glad you think so, my love."

"I know so. If only all gawky, ugly ducklings could have a knight in shining armor come to the rescue."

His smile vanished. "Don't ever say that. You are none of those things."

"I know I'm not," she relinquished. "But I learned to grasp my beauty, if you will, through your love. What if Wynonna isn't so fortunate?"

"There's no reason to suppose that." He lifted her hand to his lips and kissed it. "I thank God for you, Edie. Every, single day."

She smiled. "And I, you. We really are so blessed."

At the same moment, Wynonna smiled to herself as she finished the story of *Sara Crewe.* It was a story for girls that Ari had shared, and now she knew why. She closed the book, hugged it a moment, and then set it on her bedside table. She would not turn into a bitter Miss Minchin, even if no one had ever treated her as a princess.

The way she'd been welcomed here was extraordinary. She'd never experienced more kindness and generosity. And then to learn Lady Vinson had endured a similar upbringing as her own was astonishing. And empowering.

Lady Vinson was attractive but no great beauty, although one could have never convinced her husband of that. Why couldn't it be the same for her? She ran her hands over the faintly raised scars on her arms. If Lady Vinson had ever performed such self-mutilation, would Lord Vinson still love and adore her? *Yes*. So why couldn't it be the same for her?

There was a light tap on her door. "Come in," she called.

The door opened and Ari stepped in. She shut the door and crossed the room. Her eyes and face were still puffy from crying. "Hello."

"Hello. I just finished reading the book your loaned me and I loved it." Wynonna threw back the sheet and covers on the other side of the bed. "Care to join?"

Ari got in and tugged the covers back up. "I always thought I was so strong. My whole life. Most of it, anyway."

"You are, but you have a soft heart. I shouldn't have shown you the scars."

"I hate that you were in that sort of pain," Ari said brokenly.

"I know. And I know it's nearly impossible to understand."

Ari took hold of her hand and squeezed it.

"I feel like being here has saved me," Wynonna said with an amazed smile. "When I stepped off that train, I didn't feel as if hope really existed. The possibility that I one day might be loved seemed nothing more than a fairytale. But I see your aunt and uncle, and I know love exists. Hope exists."

Ari nodded. "Before I saw you at the station, I couldn't stop dwelling on my own misery. You helped put things into perspective. From now on, when I begin to feel sorry for myself, I'm going to hold my blessings right in front of my face."

"I never told you this," Wynonna said, "But when you first came to live with your uncle, I thought you and I would be best friends. But I made the mistake of telling Delia, who then claimed all of you as her own special dominion."

Ari shook her head. "She said you didn't care for our company."

"And I used to hear stories of the ugly things that had been said about me. Mostly by you."

Ari huffed. "I never!"

"I know that," Wynonna replied earnestly. "I've known it for a long time but, by then, you and Delia really were friends."

"Well, now you and I are the friends we always should have been. I only wish that I would have been there for you when you needed it."

"The past is the past. It may be that everything will work out in the end. Perhaps Marshall Derringer will conveniently fall into an old well shaft and break his neck."

Ari gasped and then laughed. "I cannot believe you said that!"

Wynonna shrugged. "And then Mr. Shaffer can come back into the picture."

Ari's smile dimmed. "No. That could never be. It's too late. He has a beautiful heiress who loves him. They will marry."

Wynonna wished she could give Ari a fraction of the hope and optimism she suddenly felt.

"You know the most sickening part of everything?" Ari asked.

"Marshall's face with his big lips?"

Ari chortled. "Oh, Wynnie. You are awful!"

"Do you know I even like being called Wynnie by you? Delia made such an issue of it being a horse sound and me having a face like—"

Ari scowled. "No! No more talk of Delia's meanness. I cannot stand it."

"Agreed," Wynonna said. "What were you going to say before I made a joke about Marshall's fat lips?"

"I was going to say that the mess I'm in is entirely of my own doing."

"No," Wynonna objected.

"It's true," Ari stated. "When Marshall first brought out the ring, I could have thanked him for the honor, but refused him. I could have explained I had no wish to hurt him, but believed we were not suited to a life together. I would have been free of him. He would have been miffed, of course, but he wouldn't have known anything about Zan. He would have had nothing to use against him. Or me."

"Keeping you a virtual prisoner," Wynonna said.

Ari sighed. "Honesty could have prevented it."

"Perhaps you weren't certain of what you wanted when he first asked. That's nothing to be ashamed of. You could never have imagined what would happen."

"I should let you get to sleep." She got up. "I'll see you in the morning."

"Goodnight."

Ari started to the door,

"Ari?"

Ari turned back from the door. "Yes?"

"If I've learned one thing, one hard lesson, it's this. Hating yourself, punishing yourself, it doesn't help anything get better."

Ari thought about it and nodded. She smiled sadly. "Goodnight."

Chapter Thirty-Five

Wynonna assessed her appearance in the full-length mirror. Her shirtwaist was white with narrow yellow and orange stripes, worn over a light brown skirt. She looked good. One of Lady Vinson's bits of wry wisdom occurred to her. *Dear one, if you don't love yourself, why would you expect someone else to?*

She left the room and headed downstairs for breakfast. She, Arianna, the Vinsons and the Emersons were going to the Franco-British Exhibition today.

"Morning," Ari called from behind her. "You have quite a spring in your step."

"I'm so looking forward to the exhibition. And it's what I said last night; I feel my life right in front of me, and I know I just have to reach out and grab it."

"I don't suppose you could bottle that and give me some?"

"As a matter of fact, I'm on the lookout for just the right bottle. I want it to be pretty enough for you."

They chuckled as they walked on. They took the stairs at a quick clip then started toward the dining room, appreciating the savory scents. Edith was alone in the room, perusing the paper. "Morning," both girls said at once, making them laugh.

"A choir," Edith delighted. "How marvelous. Good morning to you both. Ari, a letter came for you."

Wynonna went to the sideboard while Ari went to her place and picked up the waiting envelope. "It's from Patience," she said with a smile. She sat and a maid poured her a cup of tea. "Thank you. Where's Uncle Wilbur?" she asked her aunt.

"He's seeing to one item of business before we go. *One.* He promised."

"Will the Emersons meet us there?" Wynonna asked.

"Yes."

Ari was intently reading her letter.

"Not bad news, I hope," Edith said.

"No," Ari murmured without looking up. She finished and looked up with a smile. "Not at all." She rose and went to the sideboard, shoving the letter in her pocket. She took her time filling her plate to regain some emotional footing. Patience had admitted to not passing on the letter to Zan. It didn't change anything, but Ari was glad he hadn't read it. She hadn't meant what she'd written.

Ari had already seen the exhibition, but it was just as captivating on this occasion. Beyond the Uxbridge Road Arch was a breathtaking city of ornate white buildings, palaces, pavilions, walkways, and foot bridges, all with an oriental flare, all built from a new wonder material called fibrous plaster, and all spread out in breathtaking glory around a manmade lake. The grounds encompassed one hundred and forty acres and were filled with exhibitions from every major country in the world.

As they stood taking it all in, a passenger boat went past in the lagoon. Everywhere people strolled, women with parasols, men in herringbone suits and hats.

"You must come again at night," Edith said to Jane.

At night, John signed.

"There are lights in front of Congress Hall," Edith continued. "All the colors of the rainbow. The entire court is lit with electric lamps."

"Some sixteen thousand of them," Wilbur said. "Or so the literature says."

"What a time we live in," Wynonna marveled.

"Wait until you see Machinery Hall," Wilbur said. "In fact, let's go!"

Three hours later, after a meal at the Popular Café, Ari proposed livelier amusement.

"The rides?" Wynonna asked with an excited smile.

Ari nodded.

"Not I," Edith replied.

"Not any of us, I imagine," John agreed.

"But you two go on," Edith said. "Have fun."

"Take a cab home when you're ready," Wilbur suggested.

Ari nodded, and she and Wynonna hurried off.

Edith gave Jane a look. "Even if my feet weren't feeling the punishment of however many miles we've walked, I don't think I could walk that fast."

Jane chuckled and nodded in agreement.

"I want to see the Senegalese Village," John said.

What is it? Jane signed.

The African village, John signed.

She mouthed *oh* and nodded.

Wilbur flipped through the booklet he'd purchased and read a description of the Senegalese Village. "'Here, in a cluster of mud huts, one hundred and fifty African negroes brought over by Messrs A. Bouvier and Fleury Tarnier work as they would back home.'"

"I do believe the exhibit is designed to demonstrate how *beneficial* the European influence is," John said wryly. "Truth be damned."

Jane swatted at him.

"What?" he asked with a grin and shrug.

"I can't," Wynonna declared breathlessly, looking up at the Flip-Flap, the ride that had caused the most sensation. Two long, counter-balanced iron arms, each with a car at one end that held fifty or so people, lifted two hundred feet in the air passing the opposite car. "It's too high."

"It's safe," Ari wheedled, just before the air was split with screams and peals of laughter as the cars reached the apex.

Wynonna shook her head fervently.

Ari pouted. "You'll be sorry later if you miss it."

"At least, I'll be alive and in one piece to be sorry."

"I could go with you," Zan said from behind her. "If you want."

Ari whirled about to face him, her heart thundering. She was so overwhelmed that, for a moment, she couldn't speak.

"I hope you don't mind that I came," he said.

She shook her head aware that her face was on fire. "No," she said breathlessly. "No, I'm ... I'm very pleased," she returned stammering in her nervousness. "This is my friend, Wynonna Bradford."

"A pleasure, Mr. Shaffer," Wynonna said even before Ari could announce him.

"The pleasure is mine," he returned.

"I would be ever so grateful if you would accompany Arianna on that thing," she said glancing at the ride. "That way I don't have to feel guilty that she's going alone."

"Don't be silly," Ari said. "You don't need to feel bad if you don't want to go. I just think you'll regret it."

Wynonna waved them off. "I will be right here praying for your safe return."

Ari and Zan both smiled. After an awkward moment they started off together.

Wynonna watched them go. Ari and Zan seemed perfect together and it was apparent they were in love. It was appalling that Marshall Derringer would claim Arianna's hand by such devious means. Why did evil people always prevail?

Marshall.

Delia.

People who bullied or charmed or bought their way through life and got away with everything. They took what they wanted and discarded or destroyed anyone or anything that got in the way.

She was suddenly determined to turn some of that around. It was high time.

"You once said we were friends," Zan said when they stood at the back of the line. "I hope that's still true."

Ari couldn't bring herself to look at him. "Of course, it is. I care about you and wish you well, and I believe you wish the same for me."

"I do."

An eager group of people behind them talking excitedly amongst themselves. Zan and Ari drew a bit closer together.

"May I ask you a question?" he asked quietly.

"Yes."

"The reason you chose him, is it because he's wealthy?"

She fought back tears as she shook her head. "No."

He looked at her longingly. "That is the truth?"

She forced herself to look at him. "I swear it."

"So, it would not matter if I had wealth?"

Her throat ached terribly. "No."

"I had to ask," he said quietly. They moved up as the line shortened. "Invitations went out today for a dinner in my honor," he said. "Will you come?"

She opened her mouth to reply and then shut it again. The thought of being present when his engagement to the beautiful Vanessa Bluford was announced was agonizing.

"I would not be here except for you," he added.

She looked further off, trying to maintain her composure. "Are you glad you're here?" she asked when she could get her throat relaxed enough to force air through.

"Yes." They moved up again, close to getting on the ride. "Will you come?" he asked. "For me?"

"If it's important to you," she replied reluctantly.

"It is."

She nodded. "Alright."

"Ready?" one of the attendants called. "Climb aboard if you dare."

Zan and Ari moved forward, paying one attendant and moving past the other who was counting. They found a spot in front and faced forward.

"No hanging over the side," an attendant called.

"I might need you to hold my hand," Zan said attempting to sound more lighthearted than she knew he felt. "Isn't that what friends are for? Offering comfort if they can?"

She grinned. "Among other things. I certainly don't want to be thought of as mean-hearted."

He stuck out his hand.

She laughed, feeling happier than she had since the last time she'd seen him alone. Before Marshall had arrived and ruined everything. "The ride hasn't even begun yet!"

His eyes glittered. "Hasn't it?"

She took hold of his hand, and immediately knew it was a mistake. His nearness and the touch of his skin made her weak with longing. They felt a jolt and a sense of movement as they lifted upwards. Smiling passengers began to laugh nervously and hold on to one another as the ground grew more distant.

As observers below watched, pointing, and shielding their eyes from the sun, cries and squeals and laughter commenced. It was frightening but thrilling. Zan released her hand and put his arm around her, and she turned into his protective embrace knowing it would be the last time she'd ever be this close to him.

The other car passed theirs, its riders squealing and hollering every bit as much as this one. Ari squeezed her eyes shut wishing the ride could go on and on. Or get stuck. Even at the top. She opened her eyes and breathed slowly trying to preserve the moment in memory. When they neared the ground again, Zan pulled away, and she felt the physical separation like a rip in her soul. They didn't speak as they reluctantly exited.

"Had you been on the ride before, Mr. Shaffer?" Wynonna asked when they rejoined her.

"No," he replied smiling politely.

"Tell me truthfully, was it wonderful or frightening?"

He smiled. "I liked it."

"Do you think I would faint, Ari?" Wynonna asked looking up at the top again.

"I don't," Ari replied. "I really don't."

"If I was willing, would you go again?"

"Yes! I'd go again and again!"

"Mr. Shaffer?" Wynonna asked.

He looked at Ari as if to gauge her reaction.

"Please," Arianna said, her heart swelling again.

"Let's go," he said.

"Then what's after this?" Wynonna asked excitedly as they moved toward the back of the line. "The Spider's Web or the Canadian Toboggan?"

Zan and Ari exchanged a smile. She wondered if he was as happy as she was.

Chapter Thirty-Six

A ri entered her room carrying the invitation from Lord
Bluford that had arrived that afternoon. She felt lonelier
and more hollow than she'd ever felt, almost more than
she could bear. She and Zan had stolen a few precious hours
yesterday, but they wouldn't be able to do it again, and the thought
of going to the party and seeing him with Vanessa tormented her.

She'd told him that she would go, but she *couldn't*. She wasn't
strong enough. What if she lost control and began to cry? Wail?
Blubber like an idiot? That's what she felt like doing. Then
everyone would know. No, she couldn't go. It wouldn't be fair to
anyone. Not her, Zan or Vanessa Bluford.

She sat at her desk and wrote a carefully worded regret. It took
four attempts since she kept crying onto the parchment and
blurring the ink. When she'd completed the task, she dried her face
and blew her nose, determined that there would be no more crying.
Regret, yes. She would have profound, possibly crippling regret for
the rest of her life, but there would be no more crying over
circumstances that could not be changed.

She went downstairs to find Fletcher before she could change
her mind and rip up the regret. Unfortunately, she found him with
Marshall, who had just been admitted into the house. Her heart
plummeted.

"Hello," Marshall said.

"I wasn't expecting you," she said as civilly as she could
manage.

"I came for tea and to arrange our schedules for the next few
weeks."

"I suppose we'll take tea in the drawing room," she said
directing the last of it to Fletcher. Ari handed the sealed envelope
to him. "Will you see that this goes out?"

"What's that?" Marshall asked before Fletcher could respond.

"A regret," Ari said.

"To what?"

She balled her fists at his insultingly condescending tone. "A dinner party, which I'm not attending."

"A dinner party where?"

She hesitated. "Lord Bluford's."

"You don't say? When?"

"Does it matter? I'm not going."

"I thought we were going to make these decisions together. Remember?"

Ari glanced at Mr. Fletcher, but he was studiously avoiding looking at either of them. "We'll be in the drawing room," she said and turned to go.

"Don't send that yet," Marshall said to Fletcher. "We may go."

Ari turned back to face him, livid, but he took hold of her arm and propelled her forward. "What's the dinner party for? Any special reason?"

She yanked her arm from his grasp. "It's my understanding that Mr. Shaffer is getting engaged to Lord Bluford's granddaughter, if you must know."

"Bluford is allowing his granddaughter to marry *that*? What is the world coming to?"

Ari bit her tongue and said nothing. He was trying to bait her, and she would not rise to it. They turned into the drawing room.

"I'd like to go," Marshall announced as he sat.

"Were you invited?"

He smiled coldly. "You were invited along with a guest, were you not?"

"I cannot bring you!"

"Of course, you can. It will be amusing."

"It will not be amusing, and I do not wish to go. After the altercation between you and Mr. Shaffer—"

"That won't be repeated. It's possible that I overreacted that day. I think he and I both did. It's behind us. Forgotten."

"My, but you do forget easily," she said acidly.

"You had best guard your tone," he warned. "Sit down."

She moved to a chair and sat, hating him profoundly. If only there was a nice, deep well shaft nearby that was just out of earshot.

"I have composed the list of functions we'll attend over the next few weeks," he said pulling a folded piece of paper from his inside jacket pocket. "There are dates and times."

"What happened to us deciding together?"

"When you begin to behave as a loving fiancée, we shall. Continue to act childishly, and I have no choice but to be the sole decision maker."

"Don't you mean tyrant?"

He smiled coldly as he set the list on the table next to him. "Must you always be overdramatic, my sweet? Really, it's tiresome."

She worked at not responding.

"What day is Bluford's dinner party?"

She considered not answering, but he'd find out anyway and probably embarrass her even more in the process. "Next Saturday."

"A week from tomorrow at seven?"

"Cordials are at seven."

"Good. We'll go. Now ring for tea, won't you, darling? I have an appetite."

She rose and walked to the bell, hating him with every fiber of her being.

~~~

Marshall walked through the busy office of *The Times* as men bustled about.

"Help you, sir?" a man asked, noticing him.

"I'm looking for Nicolas Manning."

He pointed down one of the aisles of desks. "That way, almost to the end."

Marshall continued, passing a group of men who were passionately discussing the validity of charges of bias by the judges of the Olympic Games.

Manning looked over and saw him coming. "Mr. Derringer."

"Hello, Manning. Any luck on your story?"

"I'm afraid not. I managed to track down some of the men from the expedition, but no one will talk."

"Did you offer them money?"

"I did. It didn't tempt any of them."

"What about Shaffer himself? Can you not get to him?"

"I was hoping to have solid facts first."

"My advice is to get to Shaffer. Get him talking and trip him up. He's not very intelligent. Too long spent with monkeys."

"I'll try."

"There's to be a dinner at Lord Bluford's home next Saturday evening. I'm going and I can't help but think that if we can get you in there, you can find all the proof you need."

"Get me in? How?"

"I'll give some thought as to how we proceed but hold the evening open."

"I shall!"

Chapter Thirty-Seven

They had reached Lord Bluford's home. Arianna could barely stand to look at Marshall, but for Zan's sake, she would have to pull off a convincing performance. It would have been so much easier not to be present this evening. Why had Marshall insisted? To punish her or to make a show of having won? Although that was absurd when Zan had ended up engaged to Vanessa.

Her heart was in her throat as they made their way into the salon for drinks. She was trying to repress the dread she felt, but she was rigid with it. Lord Bluford greeted them cordially and introduced them to his son and daughter-in-law. Arianna said the correct things in a controlled tone and moved on as quickly as possible.

She saw Vanessa speaking with an older woman, and then she noticed Zan in a small group in the center of the room. Even turned sideways as he was, she knew that he'd become aware of her. He turned his head slightly toward her, as if working up the courage to look at her fully. She looked away as Marshall handed her a glass of wine. She took it with a trembling hand.

"Are you alright, darling?" he asked with a warning edge to his tone and expression.

She gave a slight nod but couldn't speak. His face was tight; he knew better, but they moved on, speaking to other guests. With every step, she knew where Zan was and that he discreetly watched her.

When Sully showed up, she could have wept with relief. Surprisingly, Marshall also looked pleased. The moment Sully joined them, Marshall excused himself, and left the room.

"How are you?" Sully asked her.

"Better now that you're here. You look very nice."

He grinned. "I am very nice."

~~~

Marshall walked outside and looked around until he heard his name called. Manning was coming toward him, walking briskly, and dressed in presentable enough evening wear.

"I'm here," Manning said.

"Good. Work your way around the house. I'll go through and find a back door to let you in."

"Is there not an invitation for me?" he asked worriedly.

"Not exactly, but it doesn't matter."

"Aren't they going to notice an extra guest at dinner?"

Marshall gave him a look. "You're not dining with us. You're doing whatever it is you do. Observing. Talking to people whenever possible. Watch who gets drunk and then pump them for information. That sort of thing."

"So you are sneaking me in. And then where am I to be?"

"We'll find a place where you won't be seen. At least, until enough people are circulating freely that you can go unnoticed. For now, the important thing is to get you inside."

"And if I'm caught?"

"Say that you're a friend of mine. That you're looking for me to pass on a message."

Manning obviously didn't like it.

"You won't die," Marshall sneered. "Just remember why you're here. This might well be the story of your career. Work for it. It'll be worth it."

~~~

Arianna had seen Vanessa from a distance, but she was even more impressive up close. She was gracious and well-mannered. She wanted to hear all about the African excursion and listened with keen interest.

While Sullivan was talking, Ari made the mistake of glancing at Zan, and their gazes locked. As usual, his expression was intense, but she couldn't be certain of what he was feeling or thinking. She looked away from him and only then realized she was holding her breath.

~~~

Marshall found a back door down an empty corridor and snuck Manning in. "I found a place for you to wait," he said as he led the way toward the center of the home. "Keep the door cracked, and you'll be able to watch the coming and going of people."

"Door to where?" Manning asked worriedly.

"Just come on."

When they reached it, Marshall stopped and looked around to make sure the coast was clear before he opened the door to a good-sized walk-in pantry. It contained tablecloths, silver, and odds and ends. He motioned Manning inside and then quickly shut the door despite the panicked look on the writer's face.

He found a carafe of port and a glass and carried them back to Nicolas. "Don't get drunk," he warned as he handed them over. "I need you sharp."

~~~

Ari was seated midway down the dining table and on the same side as Zan, so she could not see him. It was one small blessing. She just needed to get through another few hours and they could leave.

After an elaborate meal, Lord Bluford stood. "Thank you all for joining us this evening," he said. "It is an evening of celebration, although I am purposely not mentioning any specifics just yet. For now, gentlemen, if you'd care to join me for a smoke and a brandy."

There was a murmuring of excitement and a scuffing of chairs as the men rose and began a genial, talkative exodus. Marshall gave Ari a smile as phony as he was and left with them. John Emerson stayed seated. He would remain by Jane's side all evening and be happy about it. Ari envied them.

She noticed Sully filing out with the men. He was speaking with one man and then turned to say something to Zan. She wondered what he said.

~~~

"I have a gift for you," Sullivan said to Zan.

"Oh?"

"I have to dash to my carriage and get it. I'd rather give it to you in private, if you don't mind waiting a bit."

"I don't mind."

Sully headed one way and Zan waited, appreciating a few moments of quiet when he didn't have to strain to listen, comprehend, and respond appropriately. There was a burst of deep laughter from the smoking room and then a tinkling of polite laughter from the dining room. The sounds made him feel excluded, and yet he did not feel like joining in the merriment.

A life path had been forged for him, and he would go down it, but it did not fill him with joy or a sense of belonging.

He'd invited his family this evening, but they'd politely refused. "It's not the kind of place we belong, dear," Aileen had explained apologetically. "We wouldn't be comfortable. And we'd make them uncomfortable, too. You understand, don't you?"

He did, but he didn't like it. He didn't belong here anymore than they did, but an allowance had been made for him.

A lady stepped from the dining room closely followed by another and another. He retreated into an alcove so as not to be seen as more of the ladies made their way to the salon at the front of the home.

Sullivan Vinson returned with leather folders and handed one to Zan.

"What is it?" Zan asked as he opened it, although a reply wasn't necessary. It was photographs. The first one was of a majestic silverback, and the picture was so clear that Zan knew what the ape was thinking by the shrewdness of his expression. He glanced up at Sullivan, impressed and awed, and then flipped to the next picture, which was of a landscape that was so familiar he felt his breath catch. "I know this place. There is a waterfall here," he pointed to the far right of the picture.

Sully smiled. "Yes."

"I did not understand what you did until now," Zan murmured as he flipped to a photograph of zebras. "You catch a moment, a place—"

"Yes, I try."

"They make me remember."

The next was a candid shot of Arianna, and Zan froze as he studied it. She hadn't been aware that it was being taken. Clutching a pair of binoculars to her chest, she had a reflective expression. What had she been thinking?

He felt Sullivan watching him, so he moved on to the next photograph, which was of him as he'd been discovered. Zan's breath caught. He couldn't stop staring at it. He hadn't seen himself as he was then. He hadn't seen himself in a mirror until he was shaved, his hair was cut, and he was wearing clothing. How odd that he'd gotten used to his current appearance in so short a time.

"You remember that fellow?" Sully asked gently.

Zan nodded. "I was without language so … the memory is deep and wordless. But I remember."

"I understand."

Zan couldn't shake the shock of it. This is what he'd looked like when he'd taken Arianna. It was no wonder she'd been frightened of him. He flipped to the next shot of him seated next to Ari. The expressions on both their faces made his chest ache. He shut the folder, not able to guard his expression well enough. "Thank you."

Sully nodded. "I'm off to give Ari copies, as well. It feels important to do that before anyone else sees them. Will you excuse me?"

"Yes."

Sullivan hesitated. "Zan, when you were first brought to camp unconscious, we didn't know if you would live or die. I wondered then if we had done you a favor in finding you. Taking you from that life, bringing you into this one. Was it the right decision? Are you glad of it?"

"I am glad of it," Zan replied thoughtfully. "Although I feel more sadness now. More confusion."

Sully took a moment to respond. "This modern life is not always an easy one. There are inequities and injustices and they do make us sad. I believe the key is to keep going, keep searching for what is meaningful. Through that we find happiness."

"What you do, photography, do you think I could learn to do it?"

"Of course, you could! I'll teach you if you like."

"I would like that. Very much."

"You'll come to my home for a stay, and I'll teach you what I know."

"Thank you."

"I'll enjoy it. Now if you'll excuse me, I'll go find my niece."

When he'd walked away, the corridor was empty for the moment, so Zan went to a chest a few feet away and slid the folder behind it where it wouldn't be seen or bothered until he retrieved it.

He went toward the salon warily, wanting to position himself to where he could see Ari, but not be seen. Fortunately, Sullivan had led her to a secluded spot where it was possible. He watched as she began flipping through the pictures, smiling with both pride and pleasure. Then she came to one and her smile vanished. An expression of pain and longing replaced it, and he felt his heart beat faster. He knew at that moment that she felt what he did.

He was so absorbed in watching her that he did not notice Vanessa observing him. When he did, he saw the hurt on her face and clarity in her eyes. He turned and walked away, loathing himself for hurting her when she had been nothing but kind to him.

~~~

From his hiding place, Nicolas watched Zan walk into the smoking room, looking bereft. As silently as he could, being somewhat unsteady after consuming most of the port, he crept from the pantry and retrieved the folder.

He'd felt sure the night had been a total waste of time, but the interaction between Sullivan Vinson and Zan Shaffer had changed his mind. Marshall Derringer was a smug ass, but he'd been right about Shaffer and the expedition. Nicolas returned to the pantry, leaving it ajar for the light. He withdrew and shuffled through the photographs until he came to the picture of the wild man. Zan Shaffer. He broke into a jubilant smile and had to restrain himself from crying out in sheer excitement. It was proof. He *would* have the story of the decade.

As he thumbed through the other photographs, he could have cried with joy for what this meant to him. Recognition, acclaim, a raise in his salary. Ladies would admire him. He'd have his pick of them after the story broke.

The door swung open startling him and two men stood there.

"Told you," one of them exclaimed.

"What are you doing in there?" asked the other.

"Wha—"

They hauled him out.

"*There's* the carafe from the drawing room," the first man said.

"I can explain," Nicolas cried.

"You can explain to Lord Bluford after the party," one said as they hustled him along the back hall.

"What kind of a thief gets drunk in the middle of his thieving? You must be the stupidest one in the world."

"I am not a thief! I was invited. You're making a mistake."

"Oh, were you invited … into the silver pantry?"

"No, I … one of the guests tonight—"

"Shut up!"

They reached a door and opened it, revealing stairs to a cellar. They forced him down. Between the steep, narrow stairs, only wide enough for two of them, and his equilibrium being off, they were terrifying seconds. At the bottom, one of them snatched the folder from his hands. "What's this?"

"It's mine! Give it back!" Nicolas made a grab for it and was rewarded with a blow to his midsection that knocked the air from him.

They forced him into a small dark room, slammed the door and locked it.

"You can't do this," Nicolas yelled hitting the door. He tried the knob, but it would not turn. "Let me out! Let me out of here!" It was inky dark and silent until he heard a soft scuffle behind him. *Rats*. He quivered with disgust, then hollered and beat on the door again, hoping someone would hear.

~~~

Arianna realized Vanessa had joined them and quickly shut the folder.

"I am a great admirer of your work, Mr. Vinson," Vanessa said. "I would very much like to see your photographs, if you've no objection."

"These few are a gift to Ari," he replied reluctantly. "I have more and different ones that will be shown later, but—"

"Of course, you may see them," Arianna said not wanting to appear secretive. She handed them over. "Mr. Shaffer looked quite different. Naturally."

"Naturally," Vanessa said with a smile. "Would you care to step out on the veranda with me?" Vanessa asked, looking from one to the other.

"Actually," Sully said. "If you'll both excuse me, I'd like to speak with the Emersons."

Vanessa nodded graciously.

"A breath of fresh air would be most welcome," Ari replied.

"Good. May I call you Ari?" Vanessa asked as they walked on.

"Yes, of course."

"Zan calls you Ari. He's talked about you quite a lot. And you must call me Vanessa. I believe we share some things in common."

They stepped out onto a covered veranda appreciative of the cooler, rain-sweetened air. It was still sprinkling. "Yes," Ari replied. "I understand you're to announce your engagement this evening."

Standing by a flickering gaslight lamp, Vanessa opened the folder and flipped through, lingering the longest on the one of Ari and Zan. Finally, she shut the folder and handed it back. "Thank you for letting me look at them."

"Of course."

"May I ask you a personal question?"

Ari blinked. "Yes."

"Why are you marrying Mr. Derringer?"

Ari couldn't respond for a moment.

Vanessa smiled sadly. "I apologize for being so blunt, but I think the answer may be important."

Ari was puzzled by the question and Vanessa's tone. "I don't understand."

Vanessa stepped closer to the edge of the veranda looking out at the night. Raindrops glistened on the wrought iron railing. "I am discovering things tonight. Things about Zan. Things about myself." She turned to face Ari. "My mother has been strongly opposed to the idea of my marrying Zan, so naturally, it made me want to do it all the more." She shrugged and smiled wryly. "Mothers and daughters." Her expression suddenly changed to one of regret. "Oh, I am sorry! That was a thoughtless thing to say."

Ari shook her head. "No. It wasn't. Not at all."

Vanessa studied her a moment. "You really are so lovely. I see why Zan loves you."

Ari froze. Her eyes filled.

"Ari! I should not have—"

Ari was horrified to feel the tears stream down her face, but she couldn't stop them. She shook her head and held out a finger to beg for a moment, all the while knowing that her resistance was shot. The dam had broken. It was what she had been afraid of. She should never have come here tonight. She should have refused.

"I'll be back in a few moments," Vanessa said tenderly. "Just wait. Please? Trust me?"

Before Ari could respond, Vanessa stepped back inside. A moment later, the curtains were drawn shut. Ari felt a rush of gratitude for privacy, and a strong urge to jump the railing and make her way back home.

~~~

"What are you doing?" Priscilla asked Vanessa when her daughter reached her. "We need the air."

"Mamma—"

Priscilla blinked, having detected a change in her daughter. "What is it?"

"I'm not going to marry Zan."

Priscilla sighed deeply and then beamed a joyous smile. "Thank God you've come to your senses!"

"I need your help getting the ladies occupied elsewhere."

"Why?"

"I'll explain it all later. I promise."

Priscilla turned to face the room. "Ladies and gentlemen, if you would please follow me, we've a game or two in store for anyone who wishes to join in. The others will enjoy watching." With a self-assured smile, she led the way from the room.

Sullivan looked at the curtain-drawn door to the veranda and then at Vanessa. Vanessa gave him a nod as if to reassure him. He got the message, although he was still puzzled and concerned as he filed out with the Emersons.

Vanessa followed the group part of the way down the corridor but then broke off to go for some handkerchiefs. She hurried back worried that Arianna might have left, but she was still there. She'd stopped crying, but she would not be able to erase the evidence of it from her face. Her eyes were swollen, and the tip of her nose was pink. Vanessa handed her a handkerchief and gave her a moment to repair her face as best she could. "Are your gloves wet?"

Ari glanced up at her, perplexed by the question.

"From gripping the railing as you thought about bounding over it and running away?"

Despite Arianna's misery, she smiled. "They may be a little damp."

"That is why you and I shall be good friends. We think alike. Here," she said as she stepped forward. "Let me." She used a hanky to gently wipe a smudge from below Ari's eye. "There. Good as new."

"You're very kind, but I know better."

Vanessa smiled. "The others left for a different part of the house—"

"How did you manage it?"

"I gave my mother what she wanted. I do believe she would have sent them to the moon if I'd asked."

Ari experienced a throbbing panic. "What do you mean, you gave her what she wanted?"

"I told her that I'm not going to marry Zan."

Ari shook her head. "No! Why not?" she asked breathlessly.

Vanessa studied her, intrigued and touched by the response. "You needn't be upset for him. I would never see him hurt. I think he is wonderful."

"Why are you not going to marry him, then?"

"Because I need something he cannot give me."

"What?"

Vanessa hesitated a moment. "His heart."

Ari turned away battling another wave of searing emotion.

"One evening not long ago," Vanessa continued calmly, "I was at a ball dancing with a man who … well, who loves me. And I have very strong feelings for him as well. I always have. We might well have become engaged, but it was just so expected. Maybe I'm eccentric or spoiled or I don't know what, but do you ever want to resist something just because everyone expects you to do it? You begin to feel as if you have no choice in the matter and you resent it."

Ari turned to face Vanessa again.

"Anyway, this man asked if my … new interest, meaning Zan, loved me as he did." She paused. "The simple truth is that he does not. And I deserve to be loved like that. As you do. As we all do. So please, tell me why you are marrying Mr. Derringer."

Ari shook her head. "It's arranged," she said weakly.

"Ari," Vanessa said gently.

"Zan deserves a good life. Please! I don't want to destroy that for him."

"But he loves you. I saw him watching you earlier, and I knew it beyond the shadow of a doubt. I agree that he deserves a good life. He deserves to be with the woman he loves, especially when she also loves him."

Ari pressed her hand to her mouth, unable to speak for a moment. "He would not have asked to marry you if—"

"He didn't ask, He consented to it after you accepted Mr. Derringer. Arianna, why don't you and I band together and make certain the right things happen here? Two bright young women shaping the world around them. Taking charge of our lives."

"I cannot be with him," Ari said beseechingly.

"Why not?"

Ari was torn. She sighed deeply. "I will tell you if you promise not to tell anyone else."

Vanessa nodded. "I promise."

Ari took a deep breath and exhaled. "I cannot be with him because if I do, Marshall will hurt him."

"What do you mean?"

"He'll bring a lawsuit."

"That's absurd. What lawsuit?"

"Two actually. He'll bring suit against me for breach of promise to marry and against Zan for alienation of affection."

Vanessa drew back. "He wouldn't! It would make him look jilted and foolish. He has too much pride."

"He swears he would, and I have to believe it."

Vanessa shook her head as she thought about it. "Well, you needn't be concerned about Zan on that score," she finally said. "He has nothing of his own. What could Mr. Derringer possibly win from him?"

"It's not what he can win. It's the vengeance he can exact. Because of the lawsuit, Zan would be … exposed."

The truth dawned on Vanessa. "Oh! Oh, I see. Isn't he clever?"

"Yes, he is," Arianna agreed dispassionately.

"And of course, you're also damaged in the revelation."

"Yes."

Vanessa studied her for a moment. "But that's not what you care about."

Ari hesitated. "No," she admitted.

Vanessa nodded. "It's all clear to me now."

"As I said, it's done," Arianna said tiredly.

"Yes, he's so very clever. I see."

Ari leaned against the railing, exhausted. "May I ask a favor?"

"Yes. Anything."

"Will you get my uncle? I wish to leave without being seen by anyone else."

"Of course. Will you forgive me for upsetting you?"

"There's nothing to forgive. It's the situation that's upsetting."

"Thank you for being honest with me."

"You do deserve to be loved fully and completely," Ari said. "But I believe with every fiber of my being that Zan is capable of that. I know it! Please don't make any sudden decisions that you may regret. Give yourself time to be absolutely certain of what you want."

Vanessa nodded and then walked back inside.

Ari closed her eyes. She felt a terrible pressure in her chest. Why, oh why, did she make a mess of everything she touched?

~~~

Sullivan lingered outside the smoking room. He saw Vanessa coming toward him, the very picture of grace.

When she reached him, she asked, "Would you be so good as to ask Mr. Shaffer if I might have a word?"

"Certainly." Yet he hesitated. "Arianna is—"

"A lovely and remarkable person," she interjected. "I look forward to getting to know her better."

"I can see the two of you being good friends. You strike me as being alike in many ways."

"I take that as a great compliment."

Sullivan bowed his head and then went into the crowded smoking room where he made his way to Zan. "Lady Vanessa wishes to have a word," he said discreetly. "She is in the corridor."

Zan thanked him and extricated himself, passing Marshall. Neither man acknowledged the other.

~~~

"What was that about?" Marshall asked Sullivan, having reached him.

"Lady Vanessa asked to see him," he replied coolly.

Marshall grunted. "I imagine they'll be making the announcement soon."

He could not bear the man's company. "If you'll excuse me, I need a drink."

~~~

As Sullivan walked away, Marshall glanced around wondering where the intrepid journalist had gotten himself off to. He wasn't in the pantry any longer. Hopefully he'd pinned someone down and was getting something juicy for the exposé. Once the story broke, he would never again have to look across a room and see Zan Shaffer where he didn't belong. Perhaps the man would return to the monkeys.

~~~

When Vanessa saw Zan coming, she started in search of a private place to speak. Zan followed her into the morning room where she shut the door. "I care about you very much," she began in a low voice.

"I care about you, as well."

"I know you do, and I hope that we will always, *always,* be good friends … but I cannot marry you."

"I understand."

"Yes, I think you do. I know that you love another."

"I did not mean to hurt you."

"In all honesty, I don't feel hurt," she replied softly. "I feel … awakened. I've also just learned that Arianna consented to marry Mr. Derringer when he threatened to expose you if she did not."

Zan drew back.

"Do you understand the implications?" she asked gently.

"You're saying … she was trying to protect me?"

She nodded. "Yes." She could see he was shocked by the knowledge. "She loves you," Vanessa said. "I'm certain of it."

He drew in a sharp breath.

"She is on the side veranda of the salon. You should go to her. And when you do, please tell her two things for me. First, that I apologize for breaking her confidence, although I think she will understand. Also tell her not to worry about Mr. Derringer's threats. We shall band together and find a way to crush him if he tries to hurt you or her."

"He threatened her?" he asked darkly.

The change in him was minute, more sensed than seen, but she felt it profoundly. He'd always been gentle and polite, but suddenly he was the protector – angry, but controlled, menacing because of his physical strength and prowess, fully capable of wounding or even killing anyone who threatened that which he loved. "He wants to marry her, you see, and he was prepared to make that happen using any means he had to. She can explain."

He took a step backward, anxious to leave but unsure of protocol.

"It's alright. Go. I need to speak to my grandfather anyway."

"Shall I get him for you?"

"No. I'll find him. Go," she urged.

Zan hesitated and then left.

Chapter Thirty-Eight

Arianna heard the curtain pushed aside and instantly felt his presence. So, Vanessa had gone to Zan instead. She lowered her head dreading what was to come. Did he realize she'd probably ruined his chance at a life with Vanessa?

He stepped closer to her, stopping directly behind her. "You were protecting me?"

His presence was so tangible; she could feel him even though he was not touching her. "She should not have told you."

"She asked that I pass on her apology but thought you would understand."

He didn't sound angry. Perhaps he didn't yet understand the damage she'd done. It was only right that she be the one to admit it.

"You will not marry him," Zan stated.

She sighed and shook her head. "I have to."

"I will not let you."

She turned to him. "You don't understand what's at stake."

"I do understand. I don't care. You will marry me, and we will be happy. We won't care what he says or what he does. We'll be too busy living."

Hope unexpectedly flared so glaringly she couldn't think clearly. She could see herself with him. Lying with him, making love to him, sharing meals, and having conversations and taking long walks and caring for him. The pictures were so sweet and clear that, now that she'd allowed them to creep into her consciousness, she could not imagine not marrying him. *That* was what Sully had meant. "Oh, Zan," she breathed.

"I could only ever be happy with you," he said.

"But you must understand how difficult it—"

"I understand that I love you," he interrupted. "You do love me," he said, although it sounded more like a question.

The vulnerability in his face was too much. She would have rather ended her own life than hurt him. "Yes. I love you." Her voice broke.

He drew her close. "Marry me."

The words were precious, and she melted into his embrace. Her trembling subsided because she felt secure and so perfectly content in his arms. "I want to, more than anything," she admitted. But could she? Was she being fair? She pulled back. "I will … if my family agrees to it."

He touched his forehead to hers. "I will not let him hurt you."

She wanted to believe it. Her heart ached from the wanting. He studied her face in the flickering light, and then kissed her. His lips were finally on hers. His body close to hers. She felt delirious with desire and need. She clung with the same breathless intensity that gripped him. Her hands stroked his back and she pulled, wanting him closer, wanting more. Wanting everything.

When they parted reluctantly, breathing hard, she knew he would not let any other man near her. She would be safe with him and happy, and she would make him happy. She didn't want to leave him, but they were here, and things had spiraled out of control. "I'll leave here with my uncle tonight, and I'll send a message to Marshall in the morning. I'll speak to him as soon as possible."

"Or I will tell him," Zan said darkly.

She smiled tremulously but shook her head. "I need to do it."

"What will you tell him?"

"That I will not marry him, no matter what he does."

"Good."

"You do understand that we might be exposed. You might be exposed."

"I don't care."

She put her hands alongside his face. "I don't care either," she pledged.

"I have things to tell you," he said, reluctant to let her go.

"I know. And I have things to tell you. We'll have time now. All the time in the world. But we mustn't disrupt this evening more than it already has been."

He considered and nodded.

"Will you get my uncle for me and ask him to meet me at the carriage?"

"When can I see you tomorrow?"

"I'll send a message when it's all done."

"When can we be married?"

A tear spilled over and tickled her cheek. He wiped it away and watched her lovingly. Her relief and joy and gratitude were beyond description. "Soon. We'll decide tomorrow. I promise."

He kissed her, and went to do as she'd asked, leaving her staring after him in wonder.

~~~

Close to midnight, Lord Dalton Bluford dinged his spoon against his glass. "If I could have your attention," he called to the guests.

Marshall looked around the ballroom but didn't see Arianna. Where had she gotten off to? He turned his gaze to Shaffer, standing so composed. Marshall imagined him finding out he'd been exposed for who and what he really was. He could not wait!

"I have a rather exciting announcement," Bluford said. "My friend Zan Shaffer and I enjoyed the Olympic Games very much."

Marshall wondered what that had to do with anything. Vanessa stood by Shaffer's side looking as regal as usual. What was wrong with these people, marrying such a glorious creature to a savage who'd come from nothing? Who *was* nothing?

"I have pulled together some worthy advisors, and we have come up with a plan to open a training facility for future Olympic Games!"

An excited murmuring went up.

Marshall was stymied by the announcement. No one else seemed thrown in the least, only impressed and interested. Had Arianna been mistaken regarding what this evening was to

291

celebrate, or had she misled him? He looked at Shaffer and found the man's gaze trained on him, his expression piercing, almost threatening. Marshall suddenly had the feeling he'd been set up somehow. He narrowed his eyes allowing his raw hatred of the man to show.

"What a marvelous idea," someone remarked.

"What will it be called?"

"It will be called The Bluford Olympic Training Facility, and we will train the world's next champions!"

"Here! Here!"

"How exciting!"

"To you, sir!"

Glasses went up and conversation splintered. Marshall made his way out of the ballroom and down the hall looking into various rooms for Arianna. The butler was standing post near the front door and so he made a beeline to him. "Have you seen Miss Day?"

"Yes, sir. She left with her uncle."

Marshall saw red as he clenched his fists. He took a step toward the door, and a footman moved quickly to open it for him.

Chapter Thirty-Nine

I agree with Lady Vanessa," Sully said as they rode home. "I don't believe for a moment that Marshall Derringer will bring a lawsuit. It is an empty threat meant to force your hand."

"What if it's not?"

"I thought that was already decided. You accept the consequences."

"I do and Zan does. Willingly, wholeheartedly. I meant from the family's perspective. What if he goes after you or Uncle Wilbur and Aunt Edith?"

The carriage stopped in front of the house. "If he insists on trying, so be it. We aren't without friends in high places, you know. Worst-case scenario, he wins. We won't end up in the poorhouse. Truth be told, it's your future inheritance that's at risk. Are you willing to risk it?"

"Yes!"

He grinned and shrugged. "So, it's decided."

She beamed a smile. "I can hardly believe it. I went from despondent to deliriously happy in a matter of hours."

"You deserve it," he said tenderly.

Sully walked into the drawing room where Wilbur and Edith were engaged in a backgammon game. "Good, you're still up," he said.

"Even better," Edith returned, "you're here. You can play in my place."

"Can't abide losing anymore?" Wilbur teased.

"There is such a thing as winning gracefully, you know," she retorted.

He chuckled. "Where's the fun in that?"

Sully poured himself a brandy.

"How did it go tonight?" Edith asked, rising. "How's Ari?"

"Edie," Wilbur objected. "You're not even going to finish this game?"

"You win," she stated flatly.

He made a face, shook his head, and began to reset the pieces.

"The evening was very interesting," Sully replied as he pulled up another chair to the game table. "I have quite a story for you."

"Oh?" Wilbur asked.

"It begins in Africa."

Edith sat back down, all ears.

~~~

Ari had written the note, dressed for bed, and climbed in, but excitement would not allow her to relax. She could still scarcely believe what had transpired. Tomorrow she would see Marshall and end things with him once and for all. More importantly, she and Zan could begin planning their future.

Thank you, God!

Thinking a sherry might help settle her nerves, she threw on her robe and started downstairs, but before she made it there, she heard Marshall's raised voice from the drawing room. She hurried toward it because this was her battle to wage and to win, and no one else's.

"You'll have to speak to her tomorrow," Wilbur stated firmly from the drawing room.

"It's alright," Ari said. "I'm here," she said as she turned into the room. *Not properly dressed, but here.*

"Good," Marshall said starting toward her. "We need to speak!"

"She is not dressed," Edith huffed, coming closer. She took off her shawl and put it around Ari.

"I want to get it over with," Ari pleaded in a whisper.

Edith sighed. "We'll step out." She gave Marshall a withering look. "We'll be in the salon."

Ari watched her aunt walk out followed by her uncles.

"Have you been trying to make a fool out of me?" he demanded.

"No, I have not," she replied evenly. "But I will not marry you."

He took a step toward her. "I thought I made it clear what would happen."

"You did. You made it very clear."

"So! You'll see monkeyboy destroyed?"

"I will not marry you," she repeated emphatically. "What you choose to do about that is not something I can control. We will fight you, of course."

"And lose!"

"I'm willing to take that risk. So is my family." He'd drawn too near, and he was livid. "Please be reasonable, Marshall," she said as she edged back. "Why would you want to marry someone who does not love you?"

"You will learn to love me."

"No, I will not. I love someone else."

"That savage? I'm going to destroy him. You watch! He'll be humiliated and run out of town on a rail."

"No, you will not! We will not let you!"

He grabbed her arm and the back of her neck brutally, yanking her close. "Go put on some clothes," he hissed in her face. "We are going home."

"I will not!"

He dug his fingers in and began dragging her from the room. "Then I'll take you like that." She dragged her feet and flailed at him, but she couldn't make him stop.

And then Zan was there. Marshall halted, but Zan hands had closed around his neck. Ari jerked away and saw that Marshall's face was already red, his eyes bulging. "Stop," she cried. "Zan, stop it!" She shouldered in and pulled at his arms, but they might as well have been beams of iron.

Sully, Wilbur, and Edith had come running. Her uncles were pulling at Zan, but he had not relinquished the chokehold. Zan would kill Marshall before their eyes, and they would be unable to stop him. In desperation, Ari gripped his face in both her hands. "Do you want a life with me?" she cried.

Zan released his hold, and Marshall dropped to the floor gasping for air.

"That is all I want," Zan said.

"He tried to kill me," Marshall rasped.

Zan glowered at him. "Put your hands on her again and I will kill you," he swore.

Ari had a grip on Zan's arm, but she wouldn't be able to stop him if he charged again. Marshall must have realized it too. He scooted away until he reached the wall and got back to his feet.

"I'll have you arrested," Marshall ranted still gripping his neck and struggling to breathe.

"For coming to Arianna's defense?" Edith demanded. "After you attacked her?"

"That's ridiculous! I did not attack her."

"You will leave this house at once," Wilbur demanded.

"You're making a mistake," Marshall declared. "You don't even know how big a mistake."

"Get out," Wilbur insisted. "Now!"

"This way," Sullivan said coldly, gesturing onward. "I'll show you."

"I know the way," Marshall spat as he stalked off.

"I'll make sure of it," Sully said to the others before following.

Edith turned to Arianna. "Are you alright?"

Ari nodded, but she was shaking.

Edith looked at Zan. "Mr. Shaffer. Please listen to me. If you hurt, or God forbid, kill that man, whatever the provocation, you will go to prison or you will be hung. That is not best for anyone. Cool heads must prevail."

Wilbur held out his hand to her. "Come," he said to her. "Let's make certain the man is gone."

As Edith followed him, Zan wrapped his arms around Arianna and lifted her off the ground. The force of his hold nearly cut off her air supply, but she endured until he began to relax with the acceptance that she was safe.

He set her down. "I love you," he said, peering into her eyes.

She realized how shaken he was. Tears had pooled in his sapphire eyes. "I love you," she uttered shakily. "I love you so much."

~~~

Nicolas Manning was led down into an elegant, wood-paneled study where Lord Bluford and a formidable looking constable waited. His eyes had barely adjusted after the darkness of the cellar, and now he experienced panic. All the other guests had gone, including Derringer apparently.

The cad.

"You break into my home," Bluford began quite calmly, even conversationally.

"No! No, sir, I was let in." Manning swallowed hard and shifted nervously on his feet. He was more sober now but still not enunciating as clearly as he ought. He cleared his throat determined he would conduct himself with dignity, or as much as he could possibly salvage from this debacle.

"By whom?"

"A guest of yours. Marshall Derringer. I did nothing wrong."

"To come into a home without invitation, no matter who sneaks you in is, indeed, wrong."

"What's your name?" the constable asked.

"Nicolas Manning. I am a writer with *The Times*. I was only after information. A story."

The constable cocked his head sharply. "A story?"

"Yes. On Mr. Shaffer."

"Who?"

"He's a guest in my home," Bluford interjected.

"And this Derringer?" the constable asked him.

"He was here for the evening," Bluford replied. "A guest at a party I held. He is a most unpleasant fellow."

"This Derringer comes for a dinner party and sneaks you in?" the constable asked Manning.

"Yes," Manning admitted. "It was on his behest that I write the story, although I signed an agreement to keep his name out of it."

"If you were only here to slink about and sniff out some story, why were you found in the silver closet drunk as a skunk?"

"It was a hiding place, nothing more. I swear! I took nothing. I am not a thief!"

Bluford and the constable exchanged a look, and then Bluford reached for the leather folder that had been taken from him. "I believe this was taken from you once you were hauled out of my silver?"

Nicolas licked his lips.

"Does that belong to you?" the constable asked Manning sharply.

Nicolas hesitated. He wanted it desperately, but he couldn't very well say yes.

"Before you answer that," Bluford spoke up. "You should know that we know who it really belongs to. We know who took the photographs and whom that individual gave them to. They do not belong to you. You stole them."

"I was borrowing them because they're proof!"

"Proof?" Bluford repeated. He opened the folder and began to look through the photographs. "Of what? The African excursion? That's not exactly a secret. You stole something that might have easily been given to you had you asked."

Nicolas drew himself up. "Do you admit then that a man was found living in the jungle amongst great apes? One Mister Zan Shaffer?"

Bluford grinned. "Oh, my. Derringer once spouted the same nonsense to me."

"It's not nonsense," Manning declared, directing it to the constable. "Look at those pictures and you'll see."

"I have looked through them," the constable replied. "And I don't know what the blazes you're going on about. What I do know is that if Lord Bluford here wants me to haul you in, I'll do it. Gladly. Charges of trespassing and theft."

Manning felt his knees go weak.

"Constable Booke," Bluford said, turning toward him. "Could you do me the service of writing up a report but hanging onto it?"

"What do you mean, sir?"

"I mean that I do not wish to press charges at this time. This man is drunk and he was foolish, but I would not like to see him clapped in jail … unless he reoffends."

The constable looked at Manning darkly. "They always reoffend."

"I am a journalist," Nicolas cried. "Not a thief!"

"That's what you say," the constable muttered.

"Perhaps you did not mean to be," Bluford said in a reasonable, paternal tone. "Perhaps this was nothing more than a series of bad choices and foolish mistakes. I don't know. But you have been branded a thief now by myself and by this man of the law. Now, the constable will make a report, but he will keep it confidential unless I choose to do differently. I will not do that if you and I come to an understanding. I am not an unreasonable sort, Mr. Manning, nor am I without a heart."

"I meant no harm."

Bluford nodded sagely. "Thank you, Constable Booke," he said excusing him. "I think you have all you need?'

"If you're sure," Booke replied.

"I am."

"Then I'll be on my way. Goodnight, Lord Bluford."

"Goodnight."

The constable sent one last scowl Manning's way and left.

"Have a seat, Mr. Manning," Lord Bluford said.

Manning made his way to a chair and sat, feeling sick to his stomach from the excess of port and the stress of the last few hours.

"There is no story," Lord Bluford stated. "Do you understand?"

"That's the condition?"

"Yes. That is the condition for you to go free and to remain free. You will not write a story on Mr. Shaffer nor will anyone else at *The Times*. If they do, the constable's report goes forward. You will be discredited and possibly jailed."

Manning huffed his objection. "I cannot stop Derringer from—"

Lord Bluford held up his hand. "Derringer has been jilted and he is looking to injure Mr. Shaffer out of jealousy. We can deal with him. Let us focus on you. You will not write the story. If someone else does, you will be our primary source of discrediting them. You will explain how Derringer came to you, told you the tale, and how you investigated and found no credence to it whatsoever. Are we agreed?"

"You ask as if I had any real choice," Manning replied bitterly.

Bluford shrugged. "Because it's polite."

Manning shook his head. He couldn't even hate the old codger; he was so bloody charming. "Do you always get your way, Lord Bluford?"

Bluford pursed his lips and thought a moment. "So far."

Chapter Forty

The butler walked to Harold Derringer at the breakfast table and leaned in to convey that a constable was at the door. The master of the home glanced at the butler in surprise, and the butler handed him the man's calling card.

"A constable," Harold exclaimed, squinting at the card of C. Philip Booke, Metropolitan Police Service. "Whatever for?" he muttered.

"What is it?" His wife, Beatrix, said from the opposite end of the table.

Andra, Susan, Louise, and Perry all looked at him expectantly.

The butler cleared his throat. "He asked for young Mr. Derringer, my lord," he said quietly. "But you said—"

"Yes, yes, I know what I said," Harold replied while glaring at his wife who had done nothing but spoil and excuse Marshall's drinking and gambling and overspending and nonsense for the whole of his life. "Is he in his room?"

"Yes, my lord."

"Escort the constable to the morning room, and then go get him. I'll be there presently."

The butler bowed his head and walked off.

"I hardly think all the scowling is necessary," Beatrix said dismissively. "It's probably nothing. Everyone overreacts these days."

Harold rose and tossed his napkin on the table. "Oh, yes. The fault lies with anyone and everyone except your precious boy."

"I find sarcasm to be rude and pointless," Beatrix returned.

Harold fixed her with a look of steely determination. "And I find myself ready for a change."

There was a beat of silence in which Beatrix visibly twitched. "All I said was … try not to overreact," she added meekly.

He turned on his heel and left the room with a scowl.

"Oh, dear," Susan said under her breath and with the slightest of smirks. "He is aggravated, isn't he?"

Andra bit on her bottom lip and looked at her mother. Perry and Louise exchanged a look, and Beatrix Derringer exhaled through pinched nostrils as she looked toward the ceiling with an anguished expression.

"Good morning, sir," Harold said to the police officer as he turned into the room.

The constable stood erect, his hands behind his back. "Good morning, Mr. Derringer."

"So, what's this about then?"

"Is your son at home?"

"He is. He'll be here shortly. In the meantime, I would like to know what this is about."

"Very well, sir. He attended a dinner last night at the home of Lord Bluford."

Harold nodded patiently.

"It seems that he wanted some sort of investigation done on one of Lord Bluford's guests."

Harold cocked his head. "My son wanted some sort of an *investigation*?"

"Yes, sir."

"That makes no sense to me but sit, Constable Booke." Harold came further into the room and sat. "Do go on."

Booke sat. "Well, sir, your son snuck someone in to conduct this investigation."

Harold drew back. "I beg your pardon?"

"He snuck someone in a back door. A writer with *The Times*. It seems that Mr. Derringer found an unmanned back door, snuck the man in, and then hid him."

"This is ridiculous!"

"That may be, sir, but the writer was discovered."

Harold heaved a heavy sigh. "My son frequently drinks too much, gambles too much, runs his mouth entirely too much, and does far too little of any value, but this, quite frankly, seems ... absurd."

"Sir, the journalist, a Mr. Nicolas Manning, could be charged with trespassing and theft, which would make your son an accessory to the crime."

"So, this Manning was a thief?"

"He claims he is not, but he was discovered with a packet of photographs that were not his. And he was loitering in a hall pantry of sorts. He claims he is nothing other than a writer who was after a story, one your son put him onto."

"It sounds to me like the man is looking for someone to blame for his crime."

"But how did he know your son's name or that he was there last night? Besides that, Lord Bluford said your son came to him asking for information about this man he wanted investigated."

Harold shook his head in bafflement. "What man? Who are we talking about?"

"His name is Shaffer. He's a Londoner that spent years in Africa running a plantation."

Harold drew breath to speak, but then Marshall appeared in the doorway looking like death warmed over. "Where were you last night?" he asked Marshall sharply.

"What is this?" Marshall asked sluggishly.

"I asked you a question."

Marshall sighed heavily as he leaned against the doorjamb. "I attended a dinner party at Lord Dalton Bluford's home. Why?"

"Come in here where we can see you better," his father commanded.

"I'm comfortable here," Marshall returned churlishly.

"May we offer you some coffee or tea, sir?" Harold asked the constable. "I've a feeling this may take a while."

Marshall moved into the room huffing with indignation. "What, for God's sake?"

"Was Mr. Manning one of the guests last evening?" Harold asked.

Marshall's eyes filled with alarm, but only for a moment before he composed himself. "Who?"

"Don't bother," his father snapped coldly. "We know you let the man in. He was discovered."

Marshall crossed his arms. "What makes you think I let him in?"

"He says so," the constable spoke up.

"Well, he would, wouldn't he? If he was caught there, he wants to place part of the blame on someone else. He probably heard my name mentioned or something."

"Stop," his father exploded. "Just stop. You are embarrassing yourself. And me!" He looked at the constable. "Are charges being leveled toward my son?"

"No, sir. Not at this time. A report has been made—"

"With no proof," Marshall objected. "For God's sake, he's a journalist. Anyone could have snuck him in to find … whatever they wanted to find out."

Harold glowered at him. "How do you know he's a journalist?"

Marshall licked his lips. "I recognize the name. He wrote a piece I read not long ago."

Harold turned back to the constable. "A report, you say?"

"Yes, sir. If Mr. Manning and Mr. Derringer do not reoffend, what happened will remain private knowledge. That is Lord Bluford's wish."

"I see."

"I, for one, find your presence offending," Marshall declared glaring at the constable. "I find the presumption of my guilt offending."

"Stop speaking," Lord Derringer ordered his son as he got to his feet. "Constable, thank you for coming."

"You're welcome." He stood and gave a curt bow of the head. "I'll take my leave now."

"Did you see how smug he looked?" Marshall seethed when the constable had gone.

Harold straightened his jacket and left the room.

"Father, wait," Marshall called.

Harold kept walking.

"It's a misunderstanding," Marshall called.

Harold made his way back to the dining room and sat heavily.

"Well?" Lady Beatrix asked.

"Marshall smells like a brewery, looks like hell, and he smuggled someone into Lord Bluford's home last night to do a bit of snooping."

"What? What poppycock! Why would he?"

Harold looked at his son-in-law. "Perry, my boy, what would you think about going home for a visit?"

"I'd be amenable," Perry said looking at Louise, who shrugged and then nodded.

"I wouldn't mind," she said to him. "We could go to New York first and then travel to Chicago to stay with your family."

"Why are you asking that?" Beatrix asked her husband sharply.

"Because I wish for them to go for a nice long visit, and I want Marshall to accompany them. Or more accurately stated, I wish for Marshall to go, and Perry and Louise to accompany him."

Beatrix scoffed. "Ship our son off? Is that your solution?"

"It's a start! And before he goes, I will fill him with the fear of God. Tell him that I'm thinking of cutting him off entirely if he does not straighten up and begin making his family proud, rather than ashamed." He looked at Perry. "You're a good man. Influence him all you can."

"Thank you, sir. I shall."

"And you're a good woman and a wonderful daughter," Harold said to Louise.

She smiled affectionately at him.

"So, please," Harold continued, "work on your brother."

"We'll do all we can," she assured him.

Harold looked over at Susan. "And while I'm attempting to set my family on the right course, I think you should accept Mr. Neville's proposal, for whatever my opinion counts."

"Of course, it counts," she declared. "Your opinion means—"

He held up a hand. "I loathe empty flattery. Save it for your mother."

Beatrix huffed.

"And me, Pappa?" Andra asked. "What shall I do?"

He looked thoughtful. "What do you think, Louise? What could our Andra do to improve herself?"

"I cannot think of a single thing," Louise replied with a warm smile for her youngest sister.

"Nor can I," he said to Andra. "I wouldn't change a hair on your head."

She smiled with delight. "May I go with them too? I've never been to America."

"If you wish. But do not fall in love over there, my pet. I will not consent to any arrangement that takes you so far away."

"Oh, I couldn't bear to live away from my family. I just want to see it."

"Speaking of marriages," Beatrix said acidly, directing it to her husband. "Have you forgotten that Marshall is engaged to be married? What of that? What is he to tell his fiancée?"

Harold shrugged. "She can wait, or she can go along, but *he* goes."

Beatrix rose. "If you will excuse me, I shall go speak to our son. Perhaps get *his* side of the story."

"I will *not* excuse you," Harold stated. "Not for that. You will not intervene, nor will you continue enabling his slack morals."

Her eyes widened. "How can you speak to me so?"

"I find the words flowing out of me, long overdue as they are."

"You wound me," she declared. "You really do."

"I doubt that, my dear. Now sit back down or go attend other matters, but you will not run to our sniveling son so he can fill your ears with tales of how he has been injured."

She sat stiffly, her lips pressed tightly together.

Harold looked at Perry. "How soon can you be ready to go?"

"You are paying for this," Louise spoke up. "Aren't you?"

Harold grinned. "Ever the practical one. Yes, my dear, I will gladly pay for the trip and even buy a trinket for you at that store you like."

"Tiffany and Company?"

"Yes, Tiffany's."

"That's not fair," Susan pouted. "Can they get something for me, too?"

Harold looked at her. "Shall you go along, as well?" he asked in a decidedly cool tone. "Then you can pick out your own."

Susan looked confused, wondering if she'd just been insulted. She glanced at her mother, but it was obvious Beatrix didn't know what to make of it either.

Chapter Forty- One

elia restrained herself until the maid left the room before she ripped open the correspondence from Jack Printess. She read eagerly.

> *Dear Miss Bradford,*
>
> *I am in receipt of your note, but, alas, must convey my regret at being unable to escort you to the Harvest Ball, as I have already made arrangements to escort a lady. It should be a fine event, as usual. I feel certain I shall see you there.*
> *Cordially,*
>
> *Jack Printess, Esquire*

Delia released a shuddering breath. She felt dizzy and chilled. She was ruined. Somehow, she was ruined. She thought about the wording of his note. Had that bit about escorting a lady been a veiled insult? Had he been implying that she wasn't a lady or was she reading too much into it?

Was she losing her mind?

When no one had asked her to the ball by the first of September, an unheard-of predicament for her, she'd sent a few notes of coy inquiry, leaving little doubt that she was available to escort. One by one, regrets and refusals had come back to her.

Why?

Except she knew why. This was Arianna's doing. It was because of whatever Marshall had said to her the night of the Hotel Russell ball. Delia had thought they'd gotten beyond it, but that had to be it. What she didn't understand was how everyone else knew about it, but she'd been receiving decidedly cool receptions from men and women alike for a few weeks now.

She had initially assumed it was end of the summer sulkiness and jealousy, but it was more than that. But what? Marshall would not have said anything. Nor would Arianna, now that she thought about it. It was not her way. Patience and Nan had certainly not said anything. They had rather ignored her since their time in the city, but they were not gossips. They were not even competitive.

She suddenly thought of Wynonna who, inexplicably, was staying with Lord and Lady Vinson. She felt a wave of nausea.

"Mamma," she screamed. She crumpled the note furiously, unable to breathe. She was probably dying this instant, and it was all Wynonna's fault. That cow! That despicable horse-faced cow!

"What in the world are you bellowing about?" her mother asked from the doorway.

"Wynonna has ruined me!"

Mrs. Bradford sighed dramatically. "And how has she managed to do that?"

"Rumors! Spreading horrible rumors."

Mrs. Bradford noticed the crumpled letter in Delia's hand. "What do you have there?"

"No one wants to take me to the Harvest Ball," she cried. "Me!"

Mrs. Bradford came into the room. "Who says so?"

Delia shook her head and dabbed at her eyes.

"I am in no mood to play games, Delia. What rumors are you talking about?"

"How do I know? All I know is that suddenly I am reviled. In a different way than before. By men!"

"What men?"

"All of them. All that count."

"Either speak sensibly or what is the use of me standing here?"

Delia rose and began to pace, her mind racing. "We must find out if it was her," she muttered.

"Are you going to tell me what the rumor is?"

"I don't know," Delia cried whirling around to face her mother. "Stop asking me!"

Her mother's look turned icy. "May I see the letter you've crumpled?"

"It's not a letter, it's a note. A regret. From Jack Printess who is not available to escort me to the ball."

Mrs. Bradford's jaw went lax. "You didn't *ask* him? Tell me you did not!"

"I hinted that I would be interested in arriving on his arm."

"Delia!"

Delia threw the wadded letter across the room. "I will find out who has done this to me and destroy them!"

Mrs. Bradford shook her head and held out her hands as if balancing herself. "Calm yourself." She walked to a chair and sat. "Writing to Mr. Printess was a poor choice, indeed, but not exactly beyond the pale. We can survive that."

"It was not just Mr. Printess," Delia admitted.

"Oh, dear God."

Delia wrapped her arms tightly around herself. "I am ruined," she whimpered.

"What is the rumor?"

"I don't know! How would I know?"

"What do you suspect it may be?"

Delia hesitated. "It … may be that I …behaved inappropriately with a gentleman."

Mrs. Bradford was silent for a long moment. "Which gentleman?" she asked in a hushed voice.

"Does it matter?"

"Of course, it matters! What a stupid question!"

"Marshall Derringer."

Mrs. Bradford looked toward the ceiling with a cluck of her tongue.

"I'm assuming," Delia added weakly.

Mrs. Bradford leveled her gaze at her. "Was this inappropriate behavior of an intimate nature?"

Delia shrugged.

"Have you heard this rumor? Are you certain it's being circulated?"

"No."

Mrs. Bradford sagged with relief. "Then is it not likely that circumstances and perhaps a guilty conscience are conspiring to make you believe it?"

Delia refused to answer.

"Honestly, Delia, the constant overreaction will be the end of me!"

"I am not overreacting! Something has changed. Someone has conspired to ruin me. I *feel* it!"

"Have any young ladies of your acquaintance acted differently toward you?"

"Yes!"

"Is there one you could press to find out why?"

"Besides Nan and Patience?"

"Yes, besides your closest friends."

Delia harrumphed. "I don't know that I have any friends."

"Well, if you don't, there must be a reason for it," Mrs. Bradford stated coldly. "Why don't you stop feeling sorry for yourself and get to determining what rumors, if any, are circulating, and who started them."

Delia turned away from her mother. Her life was in shambles, and *this* was the support she got?

Her mother rose. "Once we know the facts, we can best decide how to proceed to minimize whatever damage there may have been to your reputation."

Delia heard her mother walk to the door with a heavier than usual step.

"I will say one last thing," Mrs. Bradford added. "You were given great beauty and every advantage that could be given to a girl. I only hope you have not taken these gifts and tossed them to the wind. I had thought our only quandary would be which offer to accept."

Delia turned to face her. "It's not *our* quandary; it's *my* quandary, Mamma. It's my life."

Mrs. Bradford lifted a brow and her chin. "So, it is." She turned and walked away, her heels clicking sharply.

"If Wynonna did this, I want her committed to an asylum," Delia cried. "She is insane!"

Mrs. Bradford speedily returned to the doorway. "Do not scream," she uttered in a low voice. "Do you think the servants don't have enough to gossip about?"

"She will have to be committed," Delia asserted. "It is the only thing that will save me."

"Find out where the rumors came from, and we will deal with it accordingly. I do not believe Wynonna would do such a thing, even given your poor relationship."

"Then you are naïve. She hates me."

"Because you torment her," Mrs. Bradford stated matter-of-factly. "You always have."

"She hates you too, you know."

"Don't be ridiculous. No child hates their mother."

Delia looked smug as she folded her arms.

"Spiteful," her mother said with a shake of her head. "I am deeply disappointed by how spiteful you are."

"Well, you made me."

"Then shame on me," her mother said levelly before walking away.

~~~

Delia walked into the parlor on the following Monday, having been summoned. George, her second cousin, was visiting with her mother. He'd been an awkward thing as a youngster, and he had never grown out of it. She usually avoided him. "Hello," she greeted.

He stood with a weak smile. "Good afternoon, cousin."

They kissed and sat, and the most awkward moment in all of history ensued, at least to her thinking.

"So," Mrs. Bradford broke the silence. "Were you able to make the inquiries we spoke of?"

George contemplated his hands resting on his legs and cleared his throat. He looked wretched. "Yes. It seems you may have unwittingly switched some letters you sent," he said apologetically.

"What?" Delia breathed. She felt a wave of confusion and alarm. "No. What letters?"

"It appears you wrote to Mr. Printess but accidentally sent it to Mr. Morehead? And vice versa."

She shook her head. "No, I did not!"

"It was recently. Three and a half weeks ago, I believe."

"I did no such thing," she cried. "What did these letters supposedly say?"

"Um, rather p-personal things," he bit out blushing wildly.

Delia looked at her mother, nearly wild with panic. "It's a lie! It's a trick!"

"They had some, um, references, that rang true to the gentlemen."

"What references? What are you talking about?"

George looked miserable. "I think you may have called Mr. Printess a … lion charmer?"

Delia bolted out of her chair. That had been a private joke. No one could have known about it. Except for—

Mrs. Bradford looked at her, her face white with shock. "Delia?"

Delia shook her head. "It was Wynonna," she said breathlessly. "She has done this!"

"Be quiet," her mother snapped. "George, dear, is there anything else we should know?"

"I don't know," George admitted, looking at his aunt. "I started with Printess since Delia had mentioned him, and he told me about the switch. It seems he and Morehead exchanged the letters and—"

Delia's knees went weak, and she collapsed in the chair. This wasn't happening. It was a nightmare. "Oh, my God."

"I'm sorry to have brought bad news," George stammered. "I should go."

Mrs. Bradford nodded. "Thank you, Georgie."

Looking as if he might be ill, he escaped as quickly as his legs would carry him. For long moments, there was no sound but the deep-pitched ticking of the grandfather clock.

"How damaging were these letters?" Mrs. Bradford finally asked.

Delia glared daggers at her. "I don't know since I didn't write them," she screamed. "Don't you listen? Don't you ever listen? It was Wynonna! She did this! I told you! I told you she did it!"

Mrs. Bradford stood, incensed, and startled. "Stop it! You stop it this instant, or I will slap you into next week, so help me God!"

"She has ruined me," Delia cried bursting into tears. "I am ruined!" She sobbed and hit her fists into her legs. "Ruined! Ruined!"

Mrs. Bradford shook her head rapidly but uttered no words. She sat again, dizzy with distress.

Chapter Forty-Two

January 1909
Chicago, Illinois

A sturdily built man stepped through the front doors of *The Chicago Daily News,* removing his hat as he approached the front desk.

"May I help you?" a balding clerk with spectacles asked him in a disinterested tone.

"Please. I'd like to make an appointment to see whoever is in charge of office supplies."

"What sort of supplies?"

"Pencil sharpeners. I am a wholesaler for pencil sharpeners, but I also sell directly to newspapers, such as—"

His pitch was interrupted by a man entering the building in a highly inebriated state.

"What have we here?" the clerk complained under his breath. "Help you, sir?" he said, speaking sharply to the drunken man.

Judging by the man's fine clothing, he was a gentleman of means.

"Yes. I've got a story," the man, a Brit, slurred. "Who is your best writer?"

"Why don't you tell me what it's about, and I'll get the right man for you?"

The gentleman considered and sniffed. "I'll tell you this much. There was a man recently found in the African jungle after having been raised by apes."

The clerk and the pencil sharpener salesman glanced at one another, each trying to maintain their composure.

"It's true and I can prove it," the drunk insisted. "The savage may be protected by a great lord protector, but it's all true."

"Why don't we start with your name, sir?"

"My name is Marshall Derringer," the man said enunciating as clearly as he was capable. He sniffed. "So, who's the right man?"

"Unfortunately, he's out on a story at the moment. Why don't I have him contact you when he gets back? Where can he reach you, sir?"

Marshall's eyes narrowed. "What's his name?"

"Gulliver, sir. John Jacob Gulliver. Maybe you've heard of him?"

"No. But I don't know you Americans."

"Your address, sir?"

Marshall fished in his pocket and came out with a card, which he handed over. "That's the address. Family of my brother-in-law," he said struggling to get the words out.

"I'll see that he gets it, sir."

"Tell him it's important. The story must be told. The savage is in London right this minute acting the part of a gentleman. And getting away with it."

"After being raised by apes?"

"Well, he was a child when he was abandoned, you see. To be fair, his parents couldn't help it. They were murdered. Savagely. Everything that happens in the jungle is savage. Most of it anyway. But these apes found him and cared for him. Did I say he was a white man?"

"No, sir."

"He is. From London. A fine-looking white man. Trying to pass himself off as a *gentleman* and getting away with it. Protected by a great lord."

"Fascinating. And how do you know this, if I may ask?"

"Because of a *lady*," the gentlemen practically spat the last word. "Who went to Africa with her uncle. Which is preposterous, but there you have it. They were looking for *him,* but he found her. Understand?"

"*Hmm.* I think so."

"They were all looking for the wild man, and all the while he is watching them. And he takes her right from under their noses. Took her off to the jungle. God only knows what really happened then. I won't even try to protect her anymore."

The clerk nodded and murmured.

"Did I tell you *love* bloomed between them?" Marshall Derringer laughed bitterly.

The clerk shook his head. "No." He seemed to be thoroughly enjoying himself now.

A driver walked in looking uncomfortable. "The carriage is right out front, Mr. Derringer. We should go."

Derringer brushed him off. "You will send him to me, this Mr. Tolliver?"

"I will, The very moment he walks in the door."

Derringer murmured something unintelligible and stepped back. "Do you know I went to a party for him before I left? A party. For him. At the grand house of the great lord. We toasted him. Raised our glasses, and the great lord said, 'To our Zan.'" Derringer began to laugh and then tripped. Fortunately for his backside, the driver caught him.

"What an unusual name," the salesman murmured. "Tuharzan?"

"Come on, sir," the driver said to Derringer. "Let's get you home."

As the driver assisted the drunken man out of the building and into the carriage, the pencil sharpener salesman turned back to the clerk, "There is no Mr. Gulliver, is there?"

"Of course not. But that man won't even remember being here when he wakes. Speaking of names, did you want to leave your card?"

"Yes, please, and some information." The man opened his case and pulled out a brochure with pencil sharpener models and prices and handed it over. "And my card," he said reaching into his pocket and producing it.

The man looked at it. "Edgar Rice Burroughs," he read.

"At your service, sir."

"I'll pass it on."

"To Mr. Gulliver?"

The clerk grinned. "Hardly, sir."

Epilogue

September 18, 1914
Muirhead Hall, Oxford, England

Sullivan tapped lightly on the nursery door so that Edith would not be startled.

She turned with a smile, beckoned him in, and then rose from the rocking chair. "Welcome," she said softly. "I've been watching over the sleeping angels."

He quietly stepped to the crib where four-month-old Andrew slept and smiled down at the rosy-cheeked babe. Another crib was stationed catty-corner, and he walked closer to peer into that one as well. "Nan's?" he asked softly.

She nodded. "Baby Euless."

He smiled. "Sturdy looking fellow."

She nodded again, and they left the room together. "Is Drew not the most beautiful baby ever?" she marveled as they made their way to the staircase.

"How could he not be with Ari and Zan as his parents? But I believe you said the very same of Theo and Victoria, as well."

She laughed. "Because they were!"

"Not that we're biased," he teased.

"You do know that you're spoiled, don't you?" she declared. "You get to see the children all the time. When you're not romping off on some adventure, that is."

"I do know that," he admitted. "And when I am off romping, I miss them dreadfully. We never had Ari at those tender ages. It is so remarkable to watch them grow and change."

"Yes, it is."

"It's daily. I see daily changes."

A maid came toward them. "Listen for the babies?" Edith asked.

"Yes, m'lady."

Edith and Sully started down the staircase. "Where is everyone?" Sully asked. "The butler said they were all out except for you."

"Out of doors, he meant. Down at the lake for the most part. Zan took Theo fishing, and then the Emersons followed, and then the rest of the men trailed off. The ladies are on the grounds going over the final details of the wedding."

"How are preparations going?"

"It's well in hand. It will be casual, you know, which is how they want it."

"Suiting of their personalities," Sully commented.

"Yes. And of course, it's how Ari and Zan did it."

Sully looked at her. "You think Wynonna chose an outdoor ceremony because it's what Ari chose?"

Edith shrugged. "She adores Ari. And it *was* the most perfect wedding."

"What about Wynonna's family?"

Edith stopped and turned back to him with a shake of her head. "We've become her family these last five years. She wrote her parents telling them of the betrothal, but she did not invite them. She didn't want them here. She felt it would spoil the day."

"So, no Delia?"

"Oh, good Lord, no. I don't even know what's become of her."

"She married some distant cousin a few years ago. I saw them once. He's a homely fellow, bless his heart, and she looked anything but happy."

Edith sighed. "I could almost feel sorry for her, but she damned herself."

He nodded.

"All so unnecessary," Edith sighed. "If she'd just been nicer, if she hadn't been unkind, think of how glorious her life might have been. I wonder if she'll ever understand that."

"I don't know," he murmured. They walked on and he opened the back door for her and then followed her through.

Some thirty yards away was a large white tent. In the distance the lake sparkled, and he could make out several people standing in front of it. He didn't have to see Zan to know he would be watching over Theo far more than he was fishing.

"Unca Sawy," three-year-old Victoria cried from just outside the tent. She broke into a mad dash for him, her golden-brown hair gleaming in the sun.

"We must work on those Ls," Edith said.

Sully chuckled. "All in good time." The little girl reached him, and he swept her up into his arms. Here was the most beautiful child in all the world. Well, here and at the lake and upstairs sleeping, all of them, a perfect mix of Ari and Zan. "Hello, darling."

Ari stepped from a tent, her hand shielding her eyes from the sun, and waved.

"We're coming down," Edith called to save her a trip.

"I found a piwocatta," Victoria told Sully as they walked.

"A caterpillar," Edith corrected.

"Did you?" Sully asked. "And what did you name the fellow?"

She thought about it. "Sawy."

He laughed. "I think that's marvelous. Do you know what your caterpillar will turn into one day?"

She looked at Edith, who nodded. "A buhdafy."

"That is right. A beautiful butterfly."

"Hello," Ari called, meeting them halfway. She leaned up to kiss his cheek. "How was your trip?"

"The roads are dreadful," he complained with a smile. "But I enjoyed the drive."

"You should have come on the train with us," she said cheerfully. "The rails were smooth."

"How were the little ones?"

"Perfect. Drew slept the entire way."

"Hello, Mr. Vinson," Patience called. Behind her were Nan and Wynonna.

He waved. "Hello, girls," he called back. "So, the wedding is to be right here," he said.

"She won't hear of anything else," Edith said with a shrug. "Daniel is our gardener, and she met him here, so—"

"It makes perfect sense," Ari said. "And I know he's the right one for her," she said to Sully. "Do you know why?"

"Because she can't imagine not marrying him?"

She smiled and nodded.

"You two have such odd banter," Edith remarked.

~~~

At the head of the table, Wilbur stood, following the wedding dinner.

Sullivan, sitting to his left, dinged his knife to his glass until there was silence.

"Thank you, brother," Wilbur said. "On this joyful occasion, we do not forget that the Great War has begun. God willing, may it come to a swift and just end. While our thought and prayers remain with our soldiers and with the victims of war, we should never refrain from celebrating life, love, and new beginnings."

There were nods and murmurs of concurrence all around. Wynonna looked to Daniel, her new husband, with a blissful smile, and he took hold of her hand, still not quite believing his good fortune.

"So, my dear friends and family, join with me in raising a glass to the bride and groom, Mr. and Mrs. Rivers. Long life and sublime happiness to you both!"

Sullivan reached for his glass of wine and raised it, then sipped as he looked around the table, seeing not just the people he cared about most in the world, but images that would be indelibly etched in his mind. One day, when he died, if they cut open his mind, or heart for that matter, that is what would come floating out, hundreds upon hundreds of precious images. Moments caught and tightly held.

His beloved brother, enjoying the role of surrogate father at the moment. It was Wilbur who had walked Wynonna down the aisle.

Wynonna, who'd never been so happy, and Daniel Rivers, who lived to see it so.

Patience and Reginald Hailey, who were devoted to one another. Their little ones, Greta and Merilee, were upstairs in the nursery with Victoria and the babies, but his mental picture included the fair, curly-haired pixies.

Nan and Thad Mansfield, who had had their first child, and were over the moon about it.

Dalton Bluford who had made a surprise appearance and was as spry as ever. He was seated next to five-year-old Theo, Zan and Ari's firstborn, and the two of them had been having an animated conversation over dinner.

Edith, seated at the far end, wore a high-necked gown of lavender. She presided so gracefully and naturally. Next to her was Jane Emerson and then John, of course.

Sullivan caught a tender glance between Arianna and Zan that warmed him through and through. They were so very much in love. So perfectly meant to be. They and their children, Theo, Victoria, and now baby Drew, utterly filled his heart.

Later, perhaps tomorrow, he would tell them he was headed off to photograph what he could of the war. Exactly where he was going, he did not know. Perhaps it would be Paris or the western front of Belgium or Luxembourg or even Africa again, wherever the next campaign started up. He needed to see it and to capture what he could. People needed to know.

"And now," Wilbur said. "My brother has something for us."

"Yes," Sully said. He rose. "It's not my wedding gift to you," he said to the newlyweds. "That was done properly, I believe. It received Arianna's approval."

Ari laughed and nodded at the happy couple.

"It is something else," Sully continued, "Something rather interesting to share with you all." He looked back and gave a nod to the boot boy who was waiting with a box. The lad came closer.

"No hints?" Lord Bluford asked playfully.

"I would wager it is photographs from your adventure last year with that Bingham fellow," Wilbur guessed. "The lost city of the Incas."

"Good guess," Sully said. "But not right."

"By the way," Lord Bluford said, "I was greatly relieved you didn't go on that tragic South Pole venture with Scott."

"Weren't we all," Wilbur said. "And he was asked to join, you know."

"Why didn't you, if I may ask?" Reginald Hailey inquired. "Did you have a bad feeling about it?"

"No! Honestly, I knew I would have had a bad feeling if I went. In my feet, my nose, my fingers. I am not fond of freezing weather."

"What is this unexpected gift?" Edith asked eagerly.

"It is a book of fiction," Sullivan replied. He nodded again to the boot boy who began handing them out. "The story tells the tale of a British couple who travel to Africa and have a child. A boy. Unfortunately, the couple dies, and the child is left on his own. Quite abandoned."

Everyone looked at Zan, aghast. He, too, looked stunned.

"He's found and taken in by great apes," Sullivan continued.

"Who wrote it?" Ari cried.

"An American by the name of Edgar Rice Burroughs. He penned the story for a magazine a few years ago, and apparently it was a success, so now there's this," he said accepting his copy and holding it up.

"But how?" Patience asked. "How could they know?"

"That is the question, isn't it?" Sully asked.

"Tarzan," Nan read. "Where did the 'Tar' come from, I wonder?"

Everyone was looking at the novel they'd been handed, *TARZAN Of The Apes*, and flipping through pages. It had been copyrighted in 1912.

"What happens to Tarzan in the story?" Edith asked Sullivan.

"He's found by English explorers, a man and his beautiful daughter, Jane."

Emerson looked at his wife who smiled and gestured something.

Zan nodded and chuckled. "She says she's flattered," he spoke up.

Everyone laughed.

"But that Arianna has no competition," Emerson added.

Ari smiled at the jest, but she was disturbed by the book.

"Eventually Tarzan comes back to England," Sully continued. "You see, he has a wealthy grandfather that's still alive."

"Named Bluford, I hope?" Lord Bluford spoke up to more laughter.

"No, they made Clayton the name. Lord Clayton."

"So many similarities," Wilbur exclaimed.

"Too many," Edith mused as she skimmed the first page.

"But it is fiction," Sully reminded them. "Supposedly all made up. No one is pointing a finger at anyone that we all know and love."

"But listen to how it begins," Edith said. "'I had this story from one who had no business to tell it to me or to any other. I may credit the seductive influence of an old vintage upon the narrator for the beginning of it and my own skeptical incredulity during the days that followed for the balance of the strange tale.'" She glanced up and saw all eyes riveted upon her.

She looked back to the book and read further. "'I do not say the story is true, for I did not witness the happenings which it portrays, but the fact that in the telling of it to you I have taken fictitious names for the principal characters quite sufficiently evidences the sincerity of my own belief that it *may* be true.'"

"Marshall?" Patience suggested. "He went to America for those few months."

"It wouldn't surprise me," Ari agreed.

"What do you think, Theo," Lord Bluford said, leaning over to show the book to the child. He tapped the picture of a musclebound, half naked man with his hand lifted to his mouth as if to yell. "Is that your pappa?"

Theo looked at the cover and then up at Bluford, baffled. "No," he exclaimed wrinkling his nose. "That's my pappa," he said pointing to Zan.

Zan gave him a nod and a wink.

"Tarzan," Ari said to Zan, shaking her head in astonishment.

"Jane," he said to her. They smiled and then laughed and everyone else joined in.

Jane Shoup is an award-winning author who lives in North Carolina with her husband, Scott, an over-attached dog, Gabby, and near her three adult daughters (her most avid readers) and their families, including six amazing grandchildren.

Please visit her website at janeshoup.com

www.ingramcontent.com/pod-product-compliance
Lightning Source LLC
Chambersburg PA
CBHW070914260626
47162CB00007B/2667